C.M. O'NEILL

Blood of the Covenant

To those who lived, loved and fought in the shadows of history, from whose lives I've drawn the threads to weave this tale. May these stories breathe life into your forgotten existence and honor the legacy you've left behind.

Contents

Blood of the Covenant

BY

C.M. O'NEILL

"No man ever steps in the same river twice,
for it's not the same river and he's not the same man."
— Heraclitus

Prologue

Late October 1653, Cape of Good Hope settlement, Africa

For eons, the craggy mountain stood guard over the southern tip of Africa, the last sentinel of land before the vast ocean spread as far as the eye could see. At its foot, a lush forest grew in unabashed abandon, fed by moisture trickling down the rocky façade. Beyond, a wide inlet gathered the waters of the Atlantic into a capricious bay that could serve as safety or doom for the presumptuous explorers in their fragile wooden ships, who brazenly imagined they could tame the seas and conquer the lands.

The morning sun lit the sky with fierce joy, making the ocean sparkle so brightly that only fools or the curious dared stare directly at it, and escape the experience with naught but tears in their eyes.

Sebastiaan De Vries marched across the deck of his ship, reached the railing, and with a smooth swing of his long legs, stepped onto the rope ladder dangling down the hull. He disappeared over the bulwark. Moments later he dropped with a dull resonance onto the Cape of Good Hope's surprisingly sturdy wooden pier.

The small pier could only accommodate one ship of average size at a time, but the workmanship was a study in perfection and longevity. He could see Mattheys' hand in every blunt feature. He wondered if the old carpenter, who had served so many years on his uncle's ship and who was a constant presence in Sebastiaan's upbringing, still lived. And why should he not? It was only a little over eighteen months ago that Sebastiaan had last seen him, the same day he'd kissed Danielle for the last time and left for Batavia to tend to his dying father, with the promise to return as soon as he could. A promise he'd kept, but neither of them had anticipated the lifetimes they'd both lived in those months and all that would come to pass during their separation.

His three ships, the *Danielle*, *Annabella*, and *Abigaille*, had entered Table Bay well past sunset the previous evening. The winds were calm, and the water of the traitorous bay was unusually smooth, so they had pushed on with a silver moon and the flickering of the settlement's cooking fires to guide them to their destination. By the new day's first high tide, the *Danielle* had dropped anchor in the mouth of the narrow but deep Fresh River, adorned now with its neat, sturdy little pier. The *Annabella* and *Abigaille* would remain behind the breakwater, awaiting their turn to be unloaded. All three ships were brimming with supplies essential for the new settlement, from fine dinnerware to the most robust and state-of-the-art building equipment known to the industry.

This morning, as dawn broke over the settlement, the three captains – Sebastiaan, his uncle Captain Davit De Coninck, and Captain Hooghsaet – stood agape, staring at the transformed landscape before them.

Beyond the glittering white beach, where once a muddy and untamed wilderness loomed, stood a large fort complete with curtain walls studded with culverins. Next to it sprawled a small but thriving village with buildings for industry and wattle-and-daub residential dwellings, all neatly spaced and separated by wide dirt lanes. Even the lush forest surrounding the natural clearing seemed to have pulled back in the face of such bold expansion. It was safe to assume the small settlement extended beyond what the eye could currently see, as the previous night, small fires had glimmered surprisingly far both inland and along the coastline.

With his feet once more firmly planted on dry land, Sebastiaan turned his back on the brilliant water and paused for a moment to cast a calculating glance over the unfolding scene. Governor Jan Van Riebeeck, accompanied by a handful of soldiers, was making his way through the gates of the fort's hornworks toward the new arrivals. His uncle and Captain Hooghsaet had disembarked ahead of him and were advancing on the fort with ground-eating strides. He shook his head at their evenly matched gaits. The two always seemed to be locked in some sort of race. Nothing was ever done in half measures, not even a leisurely stroll.

Even from a distance of nearly thirty feet, Sebastiaan could see the disbelief on the young governor's face as he recognized the two captains. His lip curled and his gut soured at the sight of the dark-haired man. For now, he would bank his hostility and focus on gathering as much information as possible about Danielle's disappearance, leaving the announcement of his generous contribution to the settlement to his uncle. People were suffering, and his wealth was vast enough to ease some of that. It was a simple statement of fact, not an act of benevolence to garner accolades.

The impending meeting with Governor Van Riebeeck would test him in ways he was hesitant to explore just yet. This was the fool who'd decided Danielle's fate, the man who had failed to keep her safe and, when she vanished, the one who had abandoned the search after a mere two weeks before declaring her dead. It was only his uncle's stern words and persistent counseling over the last three months that now kept him from walking over to Van Riebeeck, tearing off his right arm, and beating him to death with it.

Sebastiaan refused to accept that she had perished. The resolute belief that she was still alive burned deep in his core. He would find her, and if it took the rest of his life, then it would be a life well spent.

With restrained but determined strides, he strode toward the gathering. The pier vibrated softly, heralding his approach, De Coninck's shoulders shifted with tension and Hooghsaet's eyes stole a quick glance over his shoulder.

Governor Van Riebeeck turned toward the shadow that fell over him. He was explaining his ties to the newly arrived captains to the man at his side when he froze, his eyes fixed on the young man now standing before him. The blood drained from the governor's face, as though a spigot had been opened at his feet – a reaction all too common in those who believe they face a ghost.

Sebastiaan's eyes turned cold, and his lips pressed into a thin, hard line. He neither offered his hand nor uttered a word of greeting.

Governor Van Riebeeck stared at Sebastiaan, feeling as though he'd just swallowed a large spoonful of fine bone dust. He could not pry his tongue from the roof of his mouth as it grew drier with every breath he took. *He's alive!* Blinking hard several times, he tried to corral his scattered faculties. Eighteen months had passed since he last saw Captain De Coninck's young nephew, but it might have been a lifetime, for the changes he noted in the redoubtable figure standing before him.

The muscles no longer wrapped around his tall and broad frame in the way young men's often do; instead, they were now knitted close to the bone, their consistency hard and formidable. Van Riebeeck's eyes rose past the broad neck to the strong and stubborn jaw that seemed to be carved from stone. Only the rhythmic ticking of a muscle belied its flesh-and-bone composition. Finally, after exploring the harsh and unforgiving landscape of the once soft and welcoming face, his eyes connected with Sebastiaan's, and his skin turned damp and numb. The once-jovial young sailor had been replaced by an almost unrecognizable, hardened version of himself. The transformation was stunning and disturbing in equal measure. What force could have carved a boy into a man in such a short time with such brutal efficiency?

"We thought you'd died," Governor Van Riebeeck breathed and belatedly offered a hand in greeting. It required an unusual amount of focus to keep it steady.

"You thought wrong," Sebastiaan's graveled voice scraped past his lips. Then he looked down at the proffered hand, raised his own, but not to shake. Instead, he pointed to the fort behind the governor. "Let's talk inside."

And with that, he moved forward, vaguely registering the surprise in the governor's eyes and how his body twisted to avoid being shouldered out of the way. He saw the man with the unnaturally light blue eyes and white hair standing by the governor's side reach for his rapier, and he wished for him to draw the blade, but the man's hand stilled on top of the weapon where it remained – pity.

Walking on the same ground she had walked, breathing the same air, hearing the same sounds, and looking at the same buildings, he could see her dart across the open space, dark hair flying like a banner behind her, her phosphorus-green eyes sparkling and alive with laughter. Or was she trapped within these walls? Was she scared and nervous, looking for a way out, searching the ocean for a sign that he had come for her? The hostility inside him rose and finally knotted in the back of his throat, forcing him to swallow and blink rapidly to dispel the signs of his heightened state.

It was only when two firm hands gripped his forearms that he noticed his uncle and Hooghsaet were flanking him. They had reached the steps leading to the fort's main entrance.

Governor Van Riebeeck rushed up the steps, opened the doors, and showed them inside. His man followed at a discreet distance. Once inside, they waited in a large, open, square space. Two hallways extended from either side, and at the back, a set of stairs led to another level, most likely the governor's living quarters. Moments later, Van Riebeeck ushered them into his chambers.

"Breathe," Hooghsaet spoke in a voice meant for Sebastiaan's ears only, while his uncle cast him a stern look as they filed through the door. The air inside the room shifted from cool indifference to a thick amalgamation of Sebastiaan's pent-up emotions and the governor's unspoken but palpable unease.

Moving to stand behind his desk, the governor pointed to the chairs in front of it and seated himself once his guests were comfortable. He was pleasantly surprised to see Captains De Coninck and Hooghsaet again. Having made the initial journey from Holland to the Cape with them, he had experienced firsthand their worth, integrity, and bravery. Seeing De Coninck's nephew, however, was a shock, pleasant at first until the full meaning of it had dawned, and with that, the dread for what must now be done.

Danielle's loss was a festering wound inside Van Riebeeck that he would not allow to heal. He still felt her presence everywhere. Sometimes he could almost hear her light and fast footsteps on the stone floors of the hallways or the muted sounds as she settled in her small room for the night. He saw her in his wife's eyes as she often stared sightlessly out over the ocean, and he had wished for her when his son was born. She was his responsibility, his ward, and more often than not, his conscience, speaking to him like no other had dared, humbling him, and then offering a hand to pull him from his knees.

In this moment, staring into De Vries' unyielding eyes, he understood why people yearn for confession – the chance to lay bare their souls, declare their sins, faults, and failures before another, and beg for absolution. Van Riebeeck took a deep breath, understanding the truths he must reveal.

"Mister De– "

"We must compliment you on all you've achieved in such a short time, Governor Van Riebeeck," Captain De Coninck spoke. "It is truly remarkable. To imagine, when we'd left the Cape a year and a half ago, there was nothing but washed-out foundations and a few tents." He was leaning back in his chair, the ankle of one leg resting on the knee of the other, relaxed and at ease.

"Aye, it is a pleasant surprise to find such a fine fort and village to greet us," Hooghsaet's voice rumbled with his approval.

The praise the men offered warmed Van Riebeeck, and he felt himself bask in it like a boy receiving recognition from his tutors.

Before he could reply, a soft knock fell on the door, and Mrs. Boom's solid form appeared as she used her hip to push it open. All the men rose as she entered with a heavy tea tray. Hooghsaet, being the closest to the door, immediately reached to unburden the woman. His timing could not have been more fortuitous. Her stare froze on Sebastiaan, and with a sharp gasp, she let go of the tray. Her large, round eyes instantly filled with tears.

"Oh, sweet Jesus!" she cried, raising her hands to her round cheeks. "Mattheys said he thought he saw you, but I could not believe it. How could such a thing be true? I had to see for myself. And here you are in the flesh. All this time, we thought you were dead. We've mourned your loss and nursed that poor girl through her misery and heartbreak, only to have you return and lose her." Mrs. Boom spoke without pause, and then she flung herself at Sebastiaan and wrapped her soft arms around him, weeping as if her heart was breaking.

Sebastiaan was stunned by the outpouring, and for a moment, he could not remember the woman's name. He patted her gently on the back, absorbing the shaking of her shoulders. Then it came to him – Anke Boom, the gardener's wife. She'd been something of a mother figure to them all during their voyage and the first few weeks after setting foot on land. The woman was impossible to dislike, for she was as quick to give a tongue-lashing as she was to provide a warm meal and a kind smile.

Embarrassed at her outburst, she pushed away from him, noting the dark patches her tears had left on his white linen shirt.

"Oh dear, I've made a mess of you." She sniffled loudly and clumsily tried to wipe the moisture from his clothing. "Are you hungry?" she asked, ignoring everybody else in the room.

"No, thank you, Mistress Boom," Sebastiaan replied with an affectionate smile, "but I will stop by the kitchen later to beg a slice of fresh bread, if there is any to be had."

A sunny smile lit her blotchy face, and she nodded fiercely, causing a few gray curls to escape the mobcap on her head.

Mrs. Boom's arrival had eased some of the tension in the room, but with her departure, Van Riebeeck knew his reprieve was over.

"Your praise is much appreciated, but our success, if it can be called that, came at a high price," Van Riebeeck said as he settled with a steaming cup of tea in front of him. He sighed deeply, and then the words seemed to flow from him like water from a brook that had been blocked for too long.

"At first, all went well. The wave of dysentery many had contracted on the voyage was under control, and all seemed motivated to get out and about after the constant rains; therefore, progress on the fort was steady. Soon after, and this was perhaps my first of many mistakes, I replaced Miss Van Aard with a newly arrived surgeon. The number of dysentery patients soon increased, and at some point, we had only thirty healthy men doing everything from building to fishing. Trading with the native tribes for fresh meat proved more difficult than anticipated. It became apparent only much later that Harry, in whom I had placed considerable trust, had poisoned every well with the Saldanhars almost from the start. We would have starved had it not been for Miss Van Aard's willingness to tend to the tribe's ailments and illnesses, for which they had rewarded us most generously."

The governor spoke for nearly an hour without interruption from his audience. He relayed all that had transpired; the successes, failures, and miscalculations.

"I appointed Elias Coopman as my second-in-command." Looking more directly at Captain De Coninck, he paused to give him time to place the name. "You'll remember he was aboard the *Drommedaris* with us from Holland," Van Riebeeck supplied, and after De Coninck's slow nod, he continued to describe the role Coopman had played.

The telling was meticulous. He openly revealed his actions and decisions without justifications or explanations. It wasn't until the end, when he came to the part that heavily involved Danielle – her rushed wedding and her subsequent disappearance – that his speech slowed and his words became more measured.

"I made a mistake in trusting Elias Coopman," Van Riebeeck admitted. He opened a drawer, extracted the packet of letters he had found in Coopman's house the morning of Danielle's disappearance, and handed it to De Coninck. He waited for the letters to be read by each of the men while he absently sipped his tea.

There was a moment during his telling, when he'd relayed the events around Danielle's wedding, that De Vries' body had gone as taut as a bowstring. The muscles in his neck tightened until every vein stood like ivy vines against a tree trunk, pulsing with his suppressed anger. To his credit, he remained seated and did not reach across the desk to clamp his hand around Van Riebeeck's throat.

As Captain Hooghsaet reached to lay the neatly grouped letters on the desk, Sebastiaan's head slowly rose, and his eyes locked with the governor's.

"And this is the man you forced Danielle to wed?" he asked quietly. Leaning forward, he rested his forearms on his thighs, moved his feet apart, and laced his fingers.

The governor noted each movement, and though the actions were harmless, they failed to soothe his already frayed nerves, and his heart bucked uncomfortably against his breastbone.

"I only found those letters the morning after– " Van Riebeeck swallowed the rest of his words and slammed his mouth shut, as he belatedly realized how much he was about to reveal. It was best to keep the events surrounding that morning shrouded by the past.

"The morning after what?" Sebastiaan's eyes narrowed, and he moved closer to the edge of his seat, tilting his head slightly to the side.

Van Riebeeck swallowed to ease his sticky throat. It felt as if he'd run miles without a drop to drink. Raising the cup to his lips, he noted it was empty. Sebastiaan's eyes bored into his, and the room fell deathly silent, all waiting for his response.

"The morning … after her … um," he exhaled a shaky breath. "The morning after her wedding," he finished, then reached for the teapot but never lifted it.

"You mean the morning after her wedding night!" Sebastiaan roared, as the delicate cord that held his composure in place snapped. "The morning of the day she disappeared!" The walls shook with the volume of Sebastiaan's voice. He leaped to his feet and planted his fists on the surface of the desk, his face inches from the governor's. "Stop measuring your words, Governor, and tell me exactly what else you'd discovered that morning. And this time, be very careful not to leave anything out."

Van Riebeeck nodded. He fought the instinct to push his chair back, and when he spoke, the memories caused his voice to tremble.

"I was called to the house." Van Riebeeck paused. Despite the fresh warning, he contemplated his next words. "There were signs to suggest she was ill-treated the night before."

Van Riebeeck's words made Sebastiaan's vision blacken around the edges. Images from his nightmares – of Danielle crying, calling his name, her body covered in blood – flashed through his mind. He felt himself swaying on his feet. Searching for an anchor, his fingers closed around the nearest solid object on the desk. The compact weight in his hand became the focal point of his anger. The turmoil inside him reached its zenith, and every muscle in his body responded.

A small scraping sound, which left a faint echo in its wake, sounded a split second before the heavy crystal inkwell met the wall behind the governor missing the window by a hand's breadth. The glass shattered in a clap not too dissimilar from the discharge of a musket, leaving a large black stain to bloom on the wall and the wooden floor.

Governor Van Riebeeck felt the rush of air as the object sailed past his head an inch above his shoulder and belatedly closed his eyes.

"Show me." Sebastiaan forced the words past his tight lips.

"Show you what?" Van Riebeeck whispered, his voice failing him in the face of the tempest.

"The house, you imbecile!" Sebastiaan thundered before turning on his heel and leaving the room. The slam of the door seemed to shake the building on its foundations.

Breathing heavily and with shaking hands, Van Riebeeck rose and made to follow, but Captain Hooghsaet's hulking form blocked his path.

"Give the lad a moment to gather himself," he soothed. Steering the governor back to his chair, he continued, "There is much we still need to discuss. Let's start with the three ships, not flying Dutch colors or the VOC banner, currently lying at anchor in the harbor."

Governor Van Riebeeck was badly shaken, but instead of sitting, he went to the wine cupboard. The uneven clinking of the brandy carafe against the rim of the glass was the only sound following Hooghsaet's calming words. Taking a therapeutic swallow and letting the liquid burn its way down the back of his throat, he realized that amidst all that had happened, Captain De Coninck had remained silently seated in his chair, maintaining the same relaxed posture as before.

Slowly and deliberately, Van Riebeeck turned to him. He had done the best he could under the circumstances. De Coninck had always supported him, and he knew that now, as before, the level-headed captain would understand. But instead of the reassurance and cognizance of a friend, he found himself staring into a face almost unrecognizable for its lack of emotion and warmth. A cold, sharp shiver charged down his spine.

Sebastiaan walked blindly into the open courtyard. Had he not left the room, he feared he might have killed the governor. Shattering the inkwell – if indeed that is what it was – had done little to cool his blood.

Struggling to banish Van Riebeeck's words from his mind, he focused on the surrounding sounds. Shouts came from the training field where he presumed the soldiers were being put through their paces, mingled with the clanging and banging of construction. Mrs. Boom's voice floated to him as she called to somebody to stop dawdling and mind the oven. His ears caught the fort's bustle as his feet carried him away from the main building.

A stone archway separated the inner courtyard from the outer, and he headed for it, but movement caught his eye, and he glanced aside. The image of Mattheys hobbling toward him while making heavy use of a walking stick drew him to a stop. The sight of his old friend brought a crooked smile to his face, and he watched as small dust clouds puffed around his shuffling feet as they moved with all possible haste.

"Mattheys," Sebastiaan greeted and gathered the weathered, spindly old body in a hug, smothering Mattheys' laughter. That in itself was a momentous occasion. He couldn't recall, in all his years, having ever known the old man to laugh out loud; cuss and curse, yes, and perhaps, on an uncommonly good day, a faint, knowing smile, but all-out laughter – never before.

"You're a sight for these old eyes, my lad!" Mattheys exclaimed as he pushed away from Sebastiaan to look him up and down. "And here I was, aggrieved at the news of your demise, but how happy you've made me today." Pointing his walking stick toward the ocean, he said, "Let's walk for a spell, aye?"

Sebastiaan walked beside Mattheys, listening as the old carpenter told him about the strife they had faced with the construction of the fort and houses and the poor quality of the workforce.

"Aye, and aren't they shite, the lot of them? Whatever had to be done, had to be taught first. How most of them have gotten to where they are in this life remained a never-revealed mystery to me. From thatching to fishing, from setting traps to laying a level foundation. *Jesus*, what a trial it was, but they are getting better now, at least since I got this walking stick." He smiled, displaying his many missing teeth. "I wallop the younger ones firmly, and after the second rap on the noggin, their hearing and understanding are much improved. A fine tool for motivation and education." He lifted the cane and made a show of studying it as if seeing it for the first time.

They walked until Mattheys pointed to a large log on the beach. Sebastiaan waited for Mattheys to settle himself before sitting down beside him. Leaning forward, he rested his arms on his knees once more. A long, companionable silence stretched between them, which Sebastiaan was in no hurry to disturb. The log was close to the tree under which he had kissed Danielle for the last time. The sight deepened his grief, her memory sharp in his chest.

"I sat on this very log with your girl, watching the *Leeuwerik* sail into the bay, thinking you were on it." And just like that, the wound was ripped open and left to bleed freely. A knot formed in Sebastiaan's throat, and this time, he could not hold back the tears, knowing there would be no judgment from his friend.

After a while, he wiped his face, inhaled deeply, and said, "Tell me everything."

Mattheys didn't need time to collect or measure his words. Once he started, he held nothing back. He spoke from his heart, and Sebastiaan heard raw verity in his words like a hammer striking true.

"After they'd told her you had died, she was bitter for a long time. Raged against the world, against the governor. Locked herself away from everyone and everything. Became quite reckless. In the end, it was that recklessness that had seen her trapped in a marriage not of her making." Sebastiaan hung his head between his shoulders, listening to the recount of events, letting the words rip him to shreds.

"That bastard Coopman did her a nasty one. I never went to the house, never saw the chaos, but heard plenty from Anke Boom. She, her daughter

Elsje, and Mistress Maria went there afterward to clean up. They came back quiet and pale and remained like that for days." Mattheys fell silent and stared at the ocean.

"Do you believe she is dead?" Sebastiaan asked. He knew she wasn't – how else would his heart still be beating? – but he wanted to hear Mattheys' opinion.

Mattheys turned to him with a pained expression and a small shake of his head.

"I don't rightly know. My innards don't want to believe it, even though my mind cannot find an alternative. But it matters little what I or anybody else believe, 'cause judging by that look in your eye, you've already made your mind up, haven't you?" It was not a rhetorical question, and he stared at Sebastiaan, waiting for his answer, seeing things Sebastiaan was praying he would not ask about.

"Yes," Sebastiaan replied, "I have."

"Then, lad, this will be farewell for us."

Before Sebastiaan could question the odd statement, Mattheys continued.

"Don't look like I've just asked you to marry me. I'm old, and my time here is done. There is this pain," Mattheys placed his hand below his stomach, "it's been torturing me for years, but of late, it's letting me know that it will not go away unless it takes me with it."

"Mattheys," Sebastiaan said as sadness constricted his throat yet again.

"No, lad, it is as it should be. I've had me a good life, but I must say I long to see my wife and my three girls again."

Sebastiaan stared at him, unable to put words to his thoughts.

"They died when I was at sea," Mattheys continued. "Some illness took them all within the span of two weeks. When I got back, all I had to come home to were four cold graves and a house taken by the landlord."

Isn't it strange how a child saw only what there was to see? Growing up on his uncle's ship, Mattheys was a part of Sebastiaan's world, and not once had he stopped to think that he might have had a life before joining the crew. It was odd to imagine this cantankerous old man as once the father of three little girls.

"They'd be missing you as well."

"Aye, they had their peace and quiet for long enough. So, this is it, lad. I'll see you on the other side, hopefully many years from now." Mattheys and Sebastiaan rose together, and he pulled the old man in for a long hug that ended with a few sharp back slaps. Then Mattheys started his solo trek back to the fort, leaving Sebastiaan to stare after him.

After a few strides, Mattheys stopped, as if he'd forgotten something, turned around, and pointed toward the east.

"Follow the trail leading through the fruit orchard. It will end in a clearing in the forest. That's where the house is."

Sebastiaan watched until Mattheys climbed the high dune that separated the beach from the land around the fort and then headed for Danielle's house.

The forest had already reclaimed much of the open space around the house. Sebastiaan didn't waste time studying the outside of the dwelling. He noted the location upon arrival: remote and quiet. Then he made his way up the two wide steps leading to the green double front door. Testing the handle, he found it locked. Ramming his shoulder into the place where the two doors met, he obliterated the locking mechanism meant to keep out unwanted visitors, and stepped inside.

Even though the day was bright and the sun almost at its zenith, a dull gray light shrouded the inside of the house. Stepping over the threshold, he made a quick study of the interior. A utilitarian table and chairs stood in the center of the large room. On the left was an empty area that ended with a wide fireplace, clearly intended as a sitting room. To his right, a spacious kitchen with a generous hearth and empty shelves. All the surfaces were dull and covered with a thin layer of dust. Being less than a year old, the house still held that newly built smell. No food had ever been cooked here; no laughter had rung between these walls. The depressing thought drove him deeper into the dusky house.

His booted steps marked his progress down the hall, which ended in a utility room with a door leading to the backyard. The back of the house mirrored the front, though the space was interrupted with several rooms. An empty chamber next to the washroom offered little interest. He turned left and discovered the only other furnished space in the house – the bedroom.

Standing in the doorway, he felt a fist close around his heart. A large, beautifully carved four-poster bed stood against the east wall, stripped bare of all coverings and mattress. There was a dark stain on the wooden floor near one of the end posts. A chest stood at the foot. In the corner, against the opposite wall, a washstand with a bowl and pitcher waited to be used.

Something about the bowl and pitcher drew him closer. The set was not new; perhaps they were given to her as a gift. Their graceful beauty stirred a wave of melancholy that washed over him. He could picture Danielle filling the bowl with water before dipping her hands and gently bringing it to her face. He trailed his finger along the thick, rounded rim and the small blue flowers painted on the cream porcelain.

"Where are you?" his lone voice echoed off the bare walls. The sounds of insects and birds drifting in from the forest outside were his only reply. He went to open the shutters; she would have hated the darkness of this room. The light immediately dispelled some of the gloom, and Sebastiaan turned toward the chest at the foot of the bed.

He assumed it would be empty, the contents removed with the bedding, but lifted the lid nonetheless. What he found drove him to his knees.

The chest was filled with Danielle's meager possessions. Why had nobody laid claim to these? Instead, the clothes lay folded as if patiently waiting for her return. He lifted a white linen shirt and let it unfold. Holding the garment up, he took in every detail before crushing his face into it and inhaling deeply. It held no trace of her scent, only the cedar tang of the wooden box in which it had lain undisturbed for months. He reached for the next item, her beloved breeches. Unfolding the small pair of pants, he smiled as the image of her darting across the beach fluttered through his mind. She looked at him over her shoulder, her green eyes dancing and alive with stubborn determination, hell-bent on whatever she was about. Blindly, he reached for the next piece of clothing, unfolding it, pressing it to his face, rubbing his stubbled cheek against it before he reverently put it aside to lift the next. There was not much. She had only what she needed and perhaps a few indulgences. He reached the bottom of the chest sooner than he wished, but what he found there made the tears already streaking his face fall harder, causing his shoulders to fold and shake with sorrow.

Staring back at him was a charcoal drawing of a face captured in bliss: Danielle's vibrant smile revealing even white teeth, eyes glowing with maternal tenderness, and a softened face. Maria Van Riebeeck must have drawn the moment while they were still aboard the *Drommedaris*, sailing from Holland to the Cape, for it also showed a small child giving her a cheeky wet smile in return – Antoonie Van Riebeeck, Maria's little boy who'd perished on the journey.

Slowly, he lifted the charcoal drawing, turned it over, and read the brief note on the back.

> *I meant to give this to you months ago.*
> *Please forgive my tardiness.*
> *Happy birthday, my dearest friend.*
> *Maria*

Clutching the portrait to his chest, Sebastiaan sank back on his heels and let desolation engulf him.

I will find you, he vowed. *If it takes the rest of my life, I swear, I will find you.*

He did not know how long he sat on the floor, holding her image to his heart, but it must have been some time because his face had dried, and his legs felt stiff. He was tired to his marrow as he reached for the small pile of garments next to him, folding them as well as he was able and laying them back in the chest.

Voices from somewhere near the front of the house pulled him to his feet. He closed the lid, folded the charcoal drawing in half, tucked it carefully inside his shirt, and headed for the door.

His uncle and Governor Van Riebeeck were standing in the front room as he came down the hall. Something must have shown on his face, for the governor's pallor turned a sickly color, as seemed to be his habit of late.

"I – we have tried to find her." Van Riebeeck's voice rang higher than usual with the sudden admission.

Sebastiaan had had enough. He needed to be away from this house and the settlement. He needed silence and distance and wished the governor had stayed in his fort where he was safe. Just seeing him standing in her house made his blood roil with renewed aggression.

"You've tried," Sebastiaan sneered with menace. "I know what it looks like when somebody tries, Governor Van Riebeeck." He spat the man's name. "You didn't try. You put on a spectacle, searched for a couple of weeks, and for what? To appease your conscience, your wife, or those looking on?"

Van Riebeeck inhaled to speak, undoubtedly to defend or explain himself, but Sebastiaan cut him short.

"If you had tried as you so boldly claim, you would have found her, dead or alive. And if not, you'd still be at it. Don't tell me you've tried." Sebastiaan pushed past him into the bright afternoon sunlight flooding the front yard. He briefly noted the ocean glittering in the distance from between the trees. It was indeed a beautiful place to build a house.

It was well past dark when his uncle sauntered into the *Danielle's* stateroom. Sebastiaan tipped his chair back onto all four legs and snapped his feet off his desk.

"Drink?" he asked and pointed to the chair reserved for visitors.

De Coninck nodded absentmindedly. "Yes. Bring the bottle."

Sebastiaan carried two heavy crystal glasses in one hand and a bottle of exquisite Scottish whisky in the other.

"No more brandy?" De Coninck lifted the glass, peering at the amber liquid.

"Not tonight," Sebastiaan's eyes were turbulent when he handed his uncle a glass.

They sat back in their chairs, sipping and savoring the smoky richness as it rose in the back of their throats.

"Today was not a day I wish to repeat soon," De Coninck exhaled, closed his eyes and leaned his head back against the chair.

"No," Sebastiaan replied, staring into his glass.

"What do you want to do?"

His uncle knew full well what he planned to do. They'd been discussing it for months. He believed in his heart and soul that Danielle was alive. He would find her, even if it meant disturbing every rock on this godforsaken continent, and he would have to do it alone. His uncle needed to take care of De Vries Enterprises. He couldn't lose that as well, for it would have to fund his search and secure a future for everybody depending on him.

"My plans have not changed. In fact, I'm leaving at daybreak."

"I suspected as much." Sadness cast deep shadows over De Coninck's face. "I only wish you'd take Arent with you."

"You know I can't. He will not deny me if I ask, but he has problems of his own that he needs to see to, and he will need you." Sebastiaan had promised Arent the use of the *Danielle* to rescue a woman currently enslaved in a harem off the African coast.

"Women," De Coninck growled, "they only complicate matters."

Sebastiaan knew his uncle spoke in general, but the statement rankled nonetheless.

"This was not Danielle's fault. It all started with that weasel of a governor. If he had not shown up on the morning of our departure, begging her to stay, none of this would have come to pass." He drained the glass, slammed it down on the desk, and shoved it aside.

"If she'd known Maria was sick, she would have stayed of her own accord. You know that girl did not take well to being ordered about. God knows she is yet to meet a kindly meant suggestion she's willing to obey." Sebastiaan appreciated his uncle's attempt at levity. "The governor is a good man, Sebastiaan. A man facing extraordinary hardships, and he is young, don't forget that. For one so young, he has not done badly altogether."

"I can't forgive him."

"You don't need to, but don't condemn him either. For your sake, not his." De Coninck's eyes shone with a paternal light as he looked at his nephew.

"Uncle, I have to right this wrong. How can I continue to live my life knowing I gave up on her?"

Neither spoke for some time. Everything said here tonight had been said before.

"Allow me a small word of caution," De Coninck did not speak again until he had Sebastiaan's full attention.

"I know things are gnawing at your insides right now. I was in your shoes only a few months ago. When you went missing, I lost all sense of myself. I had only the one goal, and that was to find you. Be careful that this does not consume you. I can't lose you again."

"What is your meaning?" Sebastiaan asked. He loved the man like a father, and he needed his support, not his doubts or his fears.

De Coninck shook his head and stared the dancing candlelight glowing against the cabin wall.

"I know how you get when your back's against the wall. You lash out, see a wrong, and feel the need to right it, believing your strength is limitless. It's admirable. But if you follow this path, and I am not saying you shouldn't, understand that a life of violence awaits, with little chance of settling down. Everything inside you is at a fever pitch right now, and it'll take time to find peace. Just don't leave this world with nothing but blood on your hands."

"What I need is Danielle back where she belongs. And where she belongs is with me." Sebastiaan had not meant to raise his voice, but his words left him on a near shout.

"I know," De Coninck's voice held a gentle rasp as he pushed from his chair. "Get some rest. I'll see you in the morning."

***

"Godspeed, my boy," De Coninck had spoken against Sebastiaan's ear as he'd held him tight.

Sebastiaan had said his goodbyes early this morning before the breaking of the dawn, leaving his friends and the only family he'd ever known behind. His uncle's words had settled deep in his heart, muddling his thoughts now as he tried to make sense of the buckles and straps dangling from the saddle. The large black horse staring at him with undiluted judgment in its brown eyes did not help matters either.

All his life, he'd walked or sailed to wherever he needed to be, but for what lay ahead, he needed a horse. Well, three, to be exact, and he had chosen three of the biggest and most robust-looking animals. Now he must figure out how to attach the saddle to the creature's back in a way that would prevent it from coming off unexpectedly.

"Are you trying to saddle the governor's horse, sir?" an uncertain voice sounded from behind him. Sebastiaan spun around to meet the face behind the words.

"It's my horse now, and yes, I am trying to do just that. And you are?"

The man was tall, with the open and honest face of a farmer. Deep lines bracketed his mouth, and faint creases etched his forehead. His dark hair, graying at the temples, suggested he was about ten years Sebastiaan's senior.

"John Van Leyen, sir," the man replied and bowed his head. "Stable master."

"Well, John, if you can show me how to saddle a horse, I would be much obliged." Sebastiaan reached over to shake the man's hand.

"Do you know how to ride, sir?"

"Just Sebastiaan, and no, but I assume the skill will come to me, if not out of generosity, then by necessity."

Van Leyen shook his head at the statement but let the point rest. The man was hopefully not riding into battle soon, as this was not a skill bestowed upon a person like a blessing from above simply because he needed it.

"Only the one horse you're planning to commandeer, then?" Van Leyen asked as he looked about the stable.

Sebastiaan pointed to two more horses. Van Leyen nodded in understanding. Sebastiaan had chosen the two biggest horses, considering no other traits but brute strength.

"But you prefer the black?" he asked again as he moved to saddle the slightly smaller dapple-gray to its left.

"Yes, I do," Sebastiaan nodded as he watched the man place a different saddle on the wrong horse.

"I thought you meant to assist me in saddling this horse. Or did you misunderstand?" Sebastiaan's annoyance was steadily growing. The man was not generous with his words, and it seemed his hearing was in short supply as well.

"I heard you. I was hoping to ride this one," Van Leyen replied in even, smooth tones, as if answering Sebastiaan's questions and soothing the horse simultaneously.

Sebastiaan narrowed his eyes at the man's back. "I mean to leave the settlement and not return for some time. This is not a recreational trot on a Sunday morning."

Van Leyen's hands stilled in their task, and he looked over his shoulder to where Sebastiaan loomed in the entrance to the stall, not missing the sarcasm in his words.

"I know what you're about, sir." Van Leyen turned to Sebastiaan, words catching in his throat. "I wanted to ask permission to come along, but asking doesn't sit well with me." He shrugged self-consciously.

"And how did you come by this knowledge?" Instantly suspicious, Sebastiaan took a step toward the stable master.

Van Leyen saw the fire light in the younger man's eyes but held his ground.

"I share a house with Mattheys, and I'm perhaps the only man he trusts because I know how to keep my mouth shut and my opinions to myself."

Mattheys – the bastard. Sebastiaan had no doubt the old carpenter was trying to interfere in some way.

"Did he put you up to this?" Sebastiaan demanded.

"I did not need to be put up to anything. This is something I wanted to do. I owe her that much for all she's done for me and others." Van Leyen's chin set at a stubborn angle as the skeins of an emotion Sebastiaan could not identify flitted across his face. There was a story behind the man's carefully guarded features, but for now, the obvious stared him in the face. This man could be very useful to him. He would need somebody who knew something about horses to accompany him.

"What do you owe her?" he asked, not entirely trusting the man or his motives just yet.

"I was a sailor on the *Goeie Hoop*, coming here from Holland." The *Goeie Hoop* and the *Drommedaris* were two of the first three ships to bring settlers and supplies to the Cape. When dysentery broke out among the sailors of the *Goeie Hoop*, many died, and many more would have, had it not been for Danielle's dogged determination to save them. "I watched her treat my shipmates, as I was one of the lucky ones who'd not succumbed to it. Then, earlier this year, she saved the life of a man who was as close as a brother to me, and she showed me kindness when nobody else did."

Van Leyen swallowed thickly and then continued after a moment in which he seemed to battle with a decision whether to do so or not.

"I was the first to arrive at her house that morning. I found my friend dead on the step by the front door. Coopman had cut his throat. By then, she was already gone, meaning she was not in the house any longer," he added as he saw the groove form between Sebastiaan's brows.

"Everybody searched, but you must know that people are just that – people. Many saw the search as a break from their daily toil, and I cannot say that all searched with the diligence and thoroughness required. So, when the governor called an end to it, saying that we must all make peace with the fact that she might be dead, I continued. It takes up most of my time still. Every day, I go out there, hoping to find something." Van Leyen stared toward the forest, invisible from where they stood in the enclosure of the stables.

"Two days after she disappeared, I found Coopman's body at the bottom of a ravine. It had taken me a good few hours to climb down to him. He was lying on his back with a spear deep in his chest," Van Leyen spoke, but it was clear from the distance in his eyes that his mind had returned to that day.

Confusion creased Sebastiaan's face. "A spear?" he asked.

"Yes," Van Leyen answered, perplexed. "Had nobody told you?"

"No, all they told me was that he was found dead at the bottom of a cliff. I presumed he had fallen."

"That he did, but I am of the opinion that he met his end on the ledge above." Seeing how Sebastiaan was trying to picture the scene, Van Leyen continued.

"I searched the body and found another wound, just below the breastbone, in this soft bit." He pressed a finger to the spot on his own chest. "It was this wide," holding his pointer finger and thumb a distance apart. "A wound made by a blade, no doubt. Put me in the mind of that dagger she wore on her hip. She carried it every day without fail, went nowhere without it." At the mention of the dagger, Sebastiaan closed his eyes. It must have been the one he'd given her right before he'd left.

"So, I climbed back up to the ledge, meaning to have a look around. There wasn't much to see; it was just an open space. Then I followed the tracks that led up the mountain, made by whoever was on that ledge. We know it was Coopman and, most likely, Miss Danielle. I followed the tracks all the way back to the house. I searched the house, thinking of finding the dagger, but it was not there. Then I went to the fort, searched her room there – nothing." Van Leyen let the statements hang between them as he turned to continue his task of saddling the horses.

"What are you saying?" Sebastiaan's voice held a raspy edge.

"I don't think she's dead. Like I said, I searched and am still searching every day. If some wild animal had gotten to her, I would have found a scrap of clothing and perhaps that dagger. No, sir." He shook his head. "I think she fled, quickly and quietly, and I think she had help." Van Leyen finished the last part of his telling in hushed tones, as if afraid of being overheard.

"Help from whom?" Sebastiaan wondered.

"From whomever threw that spear," Van Leyen replied.

"Have you told this to anyone?"

"No. I know from personal experience how harsh the governor can be when somebody breaks the law."

"So, you think she is out there somewhere? Doing what? Living among one of the tribes?" The question sounded as incredulous as the twist to his voice suggested it was.

"That could be a possibility." Van Leyen reached down to retrieve something from his belongings, which were bundled tightly at his feet.

"She gave me this." He handed Sebastiaan a copy of the *Bible.* "Said it was a gift, it has her name in the front. She didn't know that I cannot read. I thought it a kind gesture, and so I kept it. But I think it will serve you better."

Sebastiaan took the *Bible* and flipped it open. *Danielle Van Aard, 1652* was written on the inside cover in black ink.

"Thank you, John." Sebastiaan nodded and turned his back on the man lest he saw the effect the gesture had on him. "Choose one more horse. We'll need two each."

***

Mid-January 1654

Another soul-scorching pain tore through her body, this one so strong it pushed Danielle onto her hands and knees. The scream that followed less than a second later rang through the cave.

This morning, as she'd finished her ablutions by the stream, she'd felt a sharp, clean stab a few fingers below her breast. It was like a thin glass pane neatly breaking in two. The pain was there and then gone but acute enough that she'd gasped for air. Then a wave of nausea had hit her like it did in the first couple of months and not yet since.

She had dreams of late – vivid dreams of Koba sitting next to her as she slept, rubbing her round belly and speaking strange, soft words. The old healer had died shortly before Danielle had joined the tribe. She knew that this day would not see its end without the birth of her child. Slowly, she'd turned from the stream and carefully, with one hand beneath her heavy belly, she made her way up the steep incline to the safety of her cave.

The first serious pain had started some time in the mid-afternoon, and now, as the sun was melting the African horizon, the pains were coming one after the other. Feeling the pressure on her lower back, she forced herself into a squatting position. Maheena, the young Hottentot woman, knelt behind her and firmly pushed her arms beneath Danielle's armpits, letting her lean back and holding her upright with surprising strength.

Maheena had been her faithful friend ever since the two of them had left the Cape of Good Hope nine months earlier – Danielle fleeing after murdering her husband, and Maheena to escape her cruel father and to marry the chief's brother. The tribe had offered them safety. Maheena's sunny disposition and patient heart had won them over one day at a time, for the Cochoqua had no love for the Hottentots from which she hailed. As for Danielle, her medicinal skills and close friendship with their chief, Kai, had secured her a revered place as the tribe's healer.

Xhitha, a young mother herself, was vigorously washing her hands in the scalding-hot water near the fire. The two women were Danielle's tribal sisters, bound by the hardships life had sprinkled over their paths, and she was grateful for their steadfast presence now. She'd been coaching the women for weeks on what to do should the labor take a bad turn. The unpleasant knowledge had left poor Maheena pale and shivering, for her own belly was beginning to swell with her growing child.

Another sharp contraction focused Danielle, and this time, she followed her instincts and pushed with it.

"I can see the head," Xhitha announced in a voice tight with concern as she lowered herself onto her knees and positioned the thick sheepskin underneath Danielle.

Danielle took a deep breath and waited for the next contraction's call, knowing that the next push would be the final one. The intense burning, pressure and pain eased almost instantly as the child slipped from her body and into Xhitha's waiting hands.

She had prayed relentlessly for months, hoping that God would bless her with a boy who would grow into a strong man, capable of facing the harsh realities of this world and not be crushed beneath the foot of another.

Her husband's cruel words on their wedding night had seemed to find a place of truth: *'By morning, you will carry my child. Whether you do so willingly is of little concern.'* Six weeks later, when her courses didn't come, she knew she did. At first, the idea of carrying Elias Coopman's child had filled her with revulsion, but she could not bring herself to drink the purple flower tea to end the fragile life growing inside her.

The child was innocent in all that had taken place in its creation. It was not their fists that had nearly beaten her to death and left her crawling from her marriage bed a bloody mess. It was not the child that had chased Danielle up the mountain, running in fear for her life. She wondered whether Elias would still have wanted to push her off the cliff had he known she was carrying his child? Perhaps not, but it was neither here nor there, for the past remained as it was, and only the present demanded attention.

She was lost in an ocean of confusion, fear, and anger as she'd tried to carve out a new life for herself. The first flutter of movement inside her had brought the peace she'd thought would never come. Maternal love had budded like an early spring flower, and the closer it came for the baby to be born, the more excited she'd grown to finally have somebody of her own – a family. Would fate allow her to keep it? It was a question she'd pushed to the back of her mind, determined not to be ruled by her fears and to live just for the day that was given to her.

"It's a boy!" Xhitha cried as she cut the cord and placed the little pink body in Danielle's arms.

Danielle lowered herself onto her back and raised the child to her breast, and as the final stage of the birth ran its course, she watched her son greedily latching on and demanding his first mouthful of sustenance.

It was too dark in the cave to see the color of his eyes, but she gently touched her fingers to the fine, dark, golden hair that lay wet against his scalp – her mother's hair. He was beautiful. His eyes were closed and puffy, his nose delicate and pink with a deep crease running horizontally at the top, giving him an angry old-man appearance. She smiled at the serious expression as he vigorously tried to fill his belly.

A single tear traced a path down her cheek as she remembered the man whom she wished had fathered her child, the man who had taken her heart and soul to the grave with him. *He will be our son, Sebastiaan,* she vowed with her eyes closed. *I will raise him in your name and your image. From this day forth, Elias Coopman will cease to exist in memory and thought.*

"Have you decided on a name?" Maheena asked as she reached for the babe to clean him. He let go of his mother with a smack of his lips and instantly took offense at the unwarranted deprivation. His screams drowned out the lullaby Maheena sang as she washed him. With a smile, Danielle watched the flailing arms and legs before Maheena gathered them and gently wrapped him in a soft deerskin.

A name; she had months to think on the matter but had made up her mind shortly after she'd discovered her pregnancy. If it was to be a girl, she would have named her after her mother – Senna. Senna De Vries, for there was no other last name she would ever give her child. In her mind, she was Sebastiaan De Vries' wife, and she would live every day of her life as such. However, if the babe turned out to be a boy, the choice was more difficult. She could not name him Sebastiaan, the name belonged to one man only. Instead, she'd named him after the men who held the most significance in both her and Sebastiaan's lives: his uncle and her father.

"Davit Aard De Vries," she answered Maheena's question.

"Such a long name for someone so small," Xhitha said as she gently washed Danielle's battered body before covering her with a clean *kaross.* "My tongue will take its time to learn the sounds. But we will speak his name with pride. Kai will announce him at the great fire tonight."

As if hearing his name, the tribe's chief entered the cave. The birthing of a babe was a private affair, and usually, only the women assisting and the father were permitted near the mother and newborn at first, but since Danielle had no husband, Kai had assumed the role of her protector and the guardian of her child.

A fire was burning near the entrance to the cave, bathing the space in a warm orange glow. Kai took the small, wrapped bundle from Maheena. The baby's cries dimmed to soft keening sounds.

"I heard you all the way from the clearing, little one." He laughed, holding the newborn to the firelight as a pensive look stole over his features. For a moment, his eyes lost focus, as if he were staring into the past.

"I've only once before seen hair like this, like the sun had left some of its light to play in it." His voice rumbled soothingly as he raised the child in both hands, looking him square in the face. "We will call you Kwala.""Sun child," Danielle echoed.

"Does the name please you, Little Flower?" Kai asked. It was a beautiful name.

"Yes," she said with a tired smile.

Chapter 1

17 years later – 1671

Three o'clock in the morning was a very discourteous time to be killed.

Sebastiaan gave the twinkling stars of the Southern Cross another glance and then nodded to John Van Leyen, who crouched next to him in the shadows of a yellowwood tree. In truth, it was more of an overgrown shrub with drooping branches, but excellent for providing cover as they surveyed the small beach lining the cove in which the slave ship rested.

"Aye, they've been quiet for some time now. Well soused and fast asleep," Van Leyen whispered.

Sebastiaan nodded, a futile gesture swallowed by the dark. A twig snapped, and he smiled at the deliberate sound. A moment later, the shadows stirred and Dakarai slipped under the branches.

"Thought I'd be catching you two napping," he murmured, his low baritone African voice lending the words a melodic quality as they blended with the night sounds.

"How could any decent human being get a moment of rest with you stomping about like an elephant in heat?" Sebastiaan returned.

Dakarai softly chuckled, wholly comfortable in the knowledge that he could move undetected and as quietly as a shadow over any terrain, affording him the moniker *Al-Shabah*, the ghost, among the Ottoman slave traders of the African east coast.

Sebastiaan wrinkled his nose, then leaned toward him, sniffing the air in short, staccato bursts while staring at the young man's face.

Only the whites of Dakarai's eyes were visible as they moved to avoid

Sebastiaan's gaze.

"The bastard pissed on me," he confessed mutely.

"How?" Van Leyen asked.

"Well, you know. He took his– "

"We know the mechanics of the deed. We are more concerned with your proximity to it," Van Leyen interrupted before Dakarai could launch into a detailed description.

"You should not have crept so close, Daka. If they had seen you, we would be dead in the water, and I don't mean that figuratively," Van Leyen admonished.

"But they didn't," Dakarai defended without a hint of remorse, and his white teeth shone as his lips peeled back in an arrogant smile.

The two could bicker like newlyweds, never revisiting the same point of contention and, as far as Sebastiaan knew, never resolving the current one either. For five *wonderful* years, Sebastiaan had been subjected to their colorful verbal sparring which had started on the night he and Van Leyen had liberated yet another Ottoman slave camp. Sebastiaan and Van Leyen had come upon the burned-out village. They'd seen the corpses littering the ground between the charred huts and followed the tracks that led them to the campsite. Chained together, Dakarai, along with many others, had sat in a hopeless heap as they watched with hollow eyes as their slave masters celebrated their bravery and good fortune around the campfire.

Sebastiaan had quietly freed the slaves, while Van Leyen had selected and armed the strongest to help with the impending fight, and once the pirates were lying dead and dying, all but one of the captives had disappeared into the darkness.

The young African had approached Van Leyen, incorrectly assuming the older man was the leader, and in broken Arabic, had pleaded his case. Van Leyen hadn't understood a word, but the wild and desperate fire burning in his eyes and his bleeding back had crossed the language barrier clearly enough.

"We are not an orphanage. Cut him loose," Sebastiaan had growled from where he was adjusting his saddlebags before Van Leyen had even uttered a sound.

"I don't know what he's saying. You speak this heathen tongue, just listen for a moment," Van Leyen had pleaded on the slave's behalf. Van Leyen was above average in height, with a formidable exterior crafted and chiseled by years of brutal hand-to-hand combat; however his soft heart acted as the counterweight. There was not a creature in need that did not call to him, and without fail, he seemed compelled to answer.

Sebastiaan had listened to the boy. It was a story he'd heard a thousand times before. The pirates had killed his family during the raid on his village, whipped him, and then clapped him in irons before leading him by the neck for the better part of a week. His name was Dakarai, and he claimed to be a Luo warrior of sorts. Sebastiaan was unimpressed and had shooed him away.

"Go home, boy," he'd snapped.

"You've freed me. I owe you a debt," Dakarai had stated, but it was not the words so much as the tilt of his chin and the squaring of his shoulders. In that moment Sebastiaan had seen a flash of himself in his youth – angry, bloody, and brimming with hatred, he understood the need to shed blood – still did. Staring into the unflinching black eyes, he'd made his decision.

"On one condition," he'd said to Van Leyen in Dutch and then repeated himself in Arabic. "You," pointing to Dakarai, "will learn to speak Dutch." Then turning to Van Leyen, "and you will learn to speak Arabic, or we part ways now. I will not be the bloody middleman, translating every thought the two of you deem worthy enough to wrap words around." With that, the negotiations were concluded.

Soon, Sebastiaan had learned that Dakarai had an inability to lie and an over-inflated tendency to understate circumstances and events, especially when the stakes were high. For example, had he known that night how proficient the lad really was with a *knobkerrie* and *assegai* – a short, heavy club with rounded head and a metal-tipped spear – he would have recruited him with a lot more enthusiasm. On the other hand, had he known how long it would take the African to learn to ride a horse, he would have tied him to the nearest tree, wished him the best of luck and left him there. Either way he sliced it, he'd rolled the dice on Dakarai and come out on top.

Shaking his head to free it from the past, Sebastiaan pushed away from the tree trunk and moved to the edge of the black shadows. A virgin white beach, fringed by dense shrubs and tall trees, shimmered under the silver sheen of a half-moon peeking through broken clouds. The secluded cove before them was the most stunning scene he'd ever witnessed in all his years: a narrow opening flanked by sharp cliffs, guarding calm, deep waters. It was a place of fantasies and dreams, were it not for the slave ship anchored less than fifty yards off the shore and the twenty-three drunken pirates sprawled around smoldering fires along the shore. This close, with no breeze to soften it, the ship's stench was a noxious blend of human misery, death, filth, disease, and decay, proclaimed the cruelty and brutality of the slave traders.

"Portuguese not Ottoman. Judging by the amount of droppings in the goat pen and chicken cages, I'd say they've been here a few days." Daka reported softly.

"Muskets?" Sebastiaan asked.

"Only five, poorly kept and unprepared. They all have cutlasses, and I am guessing daggers too, but I couldn't see those. Not a sober one among them. Bad teeth, and some have sores on their bodies."

Disgust pulled at Sebastiaan's upper lip as he turned his head to look over his shoulder at Daka.

"*Jesus*, how close did you get?"

"Close enough," Daka returned, missing the warning in Sebastiaan's voice.

Sebastiaan let the matter go, feeling the familiar sizzle in his veins as his body prepared for the confrontation ahead.

They could easily slip past the sleeping crew and swim the short distance to the ship. By his reckoning, there should not be more than fifteen sailors aboard the slaver. The odds were not good, yet they'd faced worse. However, once they freed the slaves, their chances would improve drastically – if they got that far.

"We can kill them all while they sleep," Daka offered his hushed strategy. The lad was disquietingly bloodthirsty.

"The snot from your birth is not yet washed from your ears," Van Leyen grumbled. "Go sit down and let the grown-ups talk."

"What are you thinking?" Van Leyen asked as he leaned into Sebastiaan, who was staring vacantly at the gray outline of the ship.

"We approach from the east."

It made sense. That part of the beach was rocky, and few had chosen to set their cooking fires there. The boulders would also effectively conceal their presence.

"At least this isn't a trap," Van Leyen blandly observed. As time passed, the slavers had become painfully aware that their fellow traders were being culled and their merchandise set free all along the African east coast. For more than a decade, dead slave traders dotted the landscape in a steady but unpredictable pattern from south to north, then back again. As a result, many had tried, but failed, to ensnare this *djin* that moved so stealthily and with seemingly no natural predator.

Daka had found no scouts or lookouts guarding the beach or the surrounding area. They were at the edge of yet another ancient forest, dense enough to hide in when one didn't want to get noticed but not dense enough to elude Daka's keen eyes and exceptional gift for tracking anything that moved be that on foot, hoof, or wing.

"I'm guessing there will be about ten to fifteen remaining on the ship. If we are lucky, half will be asleep." Sebastiaan's eyes scanned the decks of the ship, but the clouds were obscuring the faint moonlight, and it was too dark to clearly discern any movement.

"Still leaves us with plenty to sink our blades into," Daka piped up again.

"Yes, and when their mates wake up, things might get a bit busy," Van Leyen answered.

"We'll leave the ones on the beach, unless we have no choice, and once onboard we start real smooth and quiet. Take as many as we can without causing a ruckus. Daka, you will free the slaves. Make sure we don't leave anyone behind and encourage those who can, to fight. John, once all is clear, you will set the charges and light the fuses. I want nothing to remain of that hellhole. If separated, we'll meet back at the horses." With silent nods from the other two, Sebastiaan secured his saber in its scabbard, strapped it to his back, and covered his blond hair with a neckcloth before soundlessly stepping from the hiding place to blend into the night. Gripping his dagger in his right hand, he skirted the beach, crouching low to stay in the shadows of the shrubs and trees. Behind him Van Leyen and Daka moved soundlessly with a few seconds' gap between them.

All around, night critters chirped, passing important messages while scurrying about in their everyday grind. Sebastiaan and his two companions moved like dark omens from one shadow to the next. They reached the rocky part of the beach without incident, carefully creeping around the large boulders near the water's edge.

Sebastiaan rounded the last boulder and would have run straight into a giant of a sailor had the wind not whipped the faint whiff of pipe smoke in his direction. The man was leaning against the rock at his back, leisurely sucking on his pipe, his eyes staring at the nearly imperceptible opening of the cove a few hundred yards to the south.

There was no time to flatten himself against the boulder or dive back into the safety of the shadows. Sebastiaan knew the instant he crossed into the man's peripheral vision. The sailor tensed, straightening, his eyes narrowing as he peered into the darkness. Like anyone might, instead of reaching for his weapon, he searched for somewhere to put down his pipe.

Sebastiaan turned the clouded sky to his advantage. Twisting his body slightly to conceal the dagger in his hand, he slouched his shoulders and shuffled his feet like a sleep-heavy drunk. Bending his head but still keeping his opponent in his sight, he fumbled with the front of his breeches. Daka's unfortunate experience earlier served as inspiration for the ruse to lull the big man, giving him no reason to reach for the cutlass swinging at his hip.

The man barked an order and pointed to the dense line of shrubs behind them. Sebastiaan's Portuguese was nowhere near proficient, but years of exposure had sharpened his ear enough to nail down the basics.

Seeing the approaching man was set on relieving himself against the boulder mere inches from where he stood, the sailor retreated, if not to avoid a direct hit, then the subsequent splatter. "Go piss over there, you drunken idiot," the man growled his last words.

The sentry's feet sank into the loose, thick, dry sand as he retreated a few steps. His right hand still clutched the bowl of his pipe, which he used to add direction to his words. The other hand rested on the cutlass's handle, the gesture more habitual than lethal, and Sebastiaan dismissed it. The man was clearly right-handed and his left hand could not effectively draw the blade from its scabbard.

Without warning, Sebastiaan closed the distance between them, raising his dagger to sink it deep into the pirate's broad neck. He kept the blade level as he shouldered past, slitting the throat from ear to ear, leaving a wide arc of blood and a gurgled hiss in his wake.

The man's eyes and mouth remained open, frozen in horrified surprise. He did not topple, but rather crumpled from the bottom up. First, his ankles gave way, then his knees buckled, and finally, his head lolled. Before he could slam into the sand, Van Leyen appeared, helping Sebastiaan quietly lower the large Portuguese sailor to the ground, smothering the last of the noise escaping his severed esophagus in the sand.

With his boots neatly stowed between two boulders, Sebastiaan casually strolled toward the black water of the cove, dragging his feet in a lazy, uneven gait. He entered the water and sank to his shoulders, reducing his silhouette. Anyone from either the beach or the decks bothering to look would see nothing out of the ordinary.

From this close, Sebastiaan had a better view of the activities on deck. Two lanterns swayed gently back and forth at either end of the upper deck. A sailor was standing with his back against the bulwark next to a rope ladder hanging down the outside of the hull. Two men were stationed on the quarterdeck, deep in conversation, while another stood at the bow. None carried the rigid alertness of someone on guard. Days of ennui, a secluded location, and a boring, humid night with nothing left to stare at but their shipmates drinking on the beach had dulled their senses.

Sebastiaan allowed himself a slow smile. The men were coming to the end of their shift, their bodies already relaxing as they anticipated their sleeping hammocks. Those who would take over would still be groggy and heavy with sleep, and if luck played any role tonight, might even sport a few headaches. Tucking the dagger's blade between his teeth, Sebastiaan swam gently as the sandy shore gradually dropped away beneath his feet. This time, his companions stayed close and they moved as a tight unit through the water, barely disturbing the surface.

Sebastiaan reached the ladder first. Keeping his movements even and smooth, he tried not to jostle the ropes too much. A slight tug on the ladder was the only sign that the other two were following close behind.

As Sebastiaan climbed, he saw the head and shoulders of the guard drawing closer. The man was partially blocking the ladder, and as he neared the top, he overheard the sailor speaking to another. He paused his ascent. The ladder stilled beneath him. Glancing down at Van Leyen's upturned face, he signaled his observations. Van Leyen nodded, then relayed the message to Daka.

The conversation on deck ended, and it seemed the sailor was left alone. In his solitude, he felt safe enough to mumble a filthy curse to his shipmate's back.

Sebastiaan climbed the last few rungs until he was close enough to reach comfortably over the bulwark. He rose like a leviathan behind the unsuspecting sailor, his left hand snaking silently around the man's head to clamp firmly over his mouth. With a sharp tug, he pulled the head back and to the side, exposing the neck. His right hand swiftly drew the dagger from between his teeth and drove it into the vulnerable flesh until it met the resistance of the spine. With a final push and twist of the blade, he severed the spinal cord, ensuring no cry could escape his stifling grip. The attack ended between one heartbeat and the next, without a single gesture of resistance.

The sailor went slack in his grip, and Sebastiaan smoothly rolled over the side of the ship, following the body to the deck planks, where he stayed in a low crouched next to it. Behind him, Van Leyen and Daka climbed over the bulwark and immediately moved into the shadows.

Sebastiaan signaled for Daka to pull the ladder up, cutting the pirates on the beach off from those on deck.

"You there!" A shout rang out and Sebastiaan could feel the words rolling across the deck like a smoking cannonball ready to explode – *so much for smooth and quiet.*

Seeing two strangers crouching next to his fallen shipmate and a brutish African with primitive weapons strapped to his back, pulling up the ladder, the newcomer quickly came to the correct conclusion that something highly irregular and exceedingly detrimental to his longevity was afoot.

The call drew the attention of the scout high in the lookout's basket, for in the next instant, the deep, resonating sound of a battle horn disturbed the balmy night.

The sailor advanced on Sebastiaan while drawing his cutlass in a tight motion. His battle-worn body was heavily muscled, marked by a deep scar across his face and numerous others crisscrossing his bare chest. This was no new recruit showing off his skill by hacking away at a dead tree stump. The man's feet were lightning-fast, every movement well trained and highly coordinated.

More sailors flooded the deck and somewhere to Sebastiaan's right, Daka and Van Leyen met their first opponents. He heard the clash of Van Leyen's blades, followed by a dull thud and a sharp hiss as Daka found his first kill of the night.

The pirate closing in on Sebastiaan bared his teeth. Murderous intent was coming off him in waves. With his back pressed against the bulwark, Sebastiaan had no room to maneuver. Wasting time switching the dagger to his left hand to draw his saber could spell his end; best to slice and stab his way out. He flipped the dagger's blade against his forearm and sprang to his feet. By the time his legs straightened, the brute was upon him, his raised cutlass already traveling in a perfect downward arc to cleave Sebastiaan's head from his shoulders.

Sebastiaan was already moving, lithe and instinctive, sidestepping to the pirate's weapon. In a fluid motion, he shoved the man's arm across his body, the cutlass slicing uselessly through the warm air. Sebastiaan's dagger flashed in his grip, and with a surge of force, he drove it upward, plunging the blade into the man's neck just behind his Adam's apple. The steel bit deep, and with a savage pull, he ripped it forward, tearing through flesh and cartilage. The gurgling noise erupting from the obliterated throat barely registered as Sebastiaan reversed the motion, plunging the dagger into the back of the wide neck, jamming it between the vertebrae before yanking it free.

Tossing the dagger to his left hand, he drew his saber, its blade swiftly finding its mark. With a downward stroke, he cleaved the next pirate from collarbone to kidney, then stepped back sparing only a parting glance at the writhing body.

They had not been on deck for more than three minutes, and already the planks beneath their bare feet were slick with blood and gore. The air was thick with the tang of spilled blood; its weight heavy and pungent on the back of Sebastiaan's tongue while death grunts filled his ears. It was like standing in the eye of a storm, and for a fantastic moment, he was experiencing the events unfolding around him as if through the eyes of another far removed from the present. Blinking to dispel the untimely sensation, he focused on the next opponent as another sailor rounded the mainmast. His body became a lethal collection of weapons; arms swinging in a familiar rhythm, slicing, stabbing, parrying and lightning-fast riposting. His feet stayed sure, legs driving forward in lunges and flexing low in retreats.

He'd lost count of how many lay dead as he moved forward across the deck, claiming ground he never intended to keep.

Glancing over his shoulder, he saw Van Leyen moving almost parallel to him, swinging his twin sabers in crisscross motions, much like a farmer with a scythe sweeping through a wheat field, leaving only flattened stalks in his wake. Daka was nowhere in sight. He'd either reached the slave hold, or was in the forecastle, dispatching those still sleeping. Sebastiaan hoped for the former.

Thoughts of Daka's actions vanished as a tall, lean man with sleep-mussed dark hair and hawklike features stepped from the quarterdeck companionway, his booted strides sharp with authority. The creased linen shirt, sloppily tucked into his breeches, suggested he had dressed in a hurry.

He radiated arrogance, a seasoned lord brimming with swagger. Sebastiaan pegged him in his early thirties, his confidence shining through in bold, fluid, easy strides. This was no drunken sailor, but a captain who likely relied on cruelty and brutality to maintain his grip on power.

The man possessed the elegantly chiseled features, of a French noble – almost too pretty to be a pirate. His sharp eyes swept the deck in a quick assessment, his jaw set in a hard line. Yet his face showed no trace of the emotions he surely felt, seeing his dead sailors littering the deck. Instead, he focused his intense gaze exclusively on Sebastiaan, like a hawk spotting a field mouse.

At first glance the man had only the rapier in his hand which was lunging toward Sebastiaan's heart with blinding speed. But there was little doubt he had a blade or two tucked in his boots and a sizable dagger hidden in the small of his back.

Sebastiaan widened his stance and twisted his body. Raising his saber, he blocked the captain's rapier, letting it slide nearly two-thirds down his blade before flicking it aside. With a slight push off the balls of his feet, he countered with a swift, powerful downward cut. The captain leaped back, saving his shirt from the viciously curved steel, the ghost of a smile touching his lips.

Sebastiaan knew the hint of emotion had nothing to do with amusement. The captain had caught sight of the saber's unique curve and the extended double-edge tip. Sebastiaan had had the weapon custom-made in Algiers. The sabers he'd claimed from pirates over the years were efficient enough, but never quite right. Either the handles were too short or the blades too straight. The captain's keen eye had instantly noted these alterations, realizing that against such a weapon, his rapier was sorely outclassed. If he wished to survive this lethal dance, he'd need to fight dirty, and Sebastiaan would be deeply disappointed if he didn't. There's no sport in killing an honorable man.

Tossing the rapier tauntingly between his hands, the captain's smile broadened and a shrewd light flared in his cold eyes. Sebastiaan knew the movement was not for show but to confuse the opponent while he covertly pulled the dagger from the small of his back. As far as diversions went, it was not badly done, but hardly original.

There was no need for Sebastiaan to clutter the situation with theatrics as he circled his opponent. Best to give the captain the room he needed to bolster his sense of superiority. Comfort and complacency were the key ingredients of the recipe for ending up dead fast.

After a few minutes of feints and thrusts, they had established a rhythm of forward, backward and sideways movements. The captain was always the first to strike and with each riposte, Sebastiaan made sure he maneuvered them away from the open space on the deck and closer to an area littered with barrels and rigging.

Once more the captain thrust toward Sebastiaan's chest and once more he flicked the blade away with a small twist of his wrist. It was time to sow a little doubt in the cracks of the captain's confidence. With every flick, Sebastiaan tightened his bottom three fingers around his saber's handle, disengaged his blade and pulled it back into the guard position, sacrificing the opportunity to deliver a powerful cut.

Irritation caused a slight groove to form between the captain's brows. He was not used to being challenged in this cat-and-mouse fashion. Judging by his aggressive and overly powerful thrusts, his experience was born from facing opponents relying on brawn rather than anything else. Coming face-to-face with an enemy that physically promised an all-out brawl but moved with the elegance and grace of a dancer was a unique experience.

The captain altered his approach. Abandoning the cavalier full-frontal assault, he grew more careful in his lunges, all the while extending the dagger in his other hand to shield his flank.

It was unwise to allow any opponent time to readjust too often. With an unexpected sideways stride, Sebastiaan evaded the captain's rapier.

Turning his wrist upward, he brought the tip of his curved blade down to cut neatly across the man's knuckles, exposing the delicate pale sinew and bone beneath the tawny skin.

Sebastiaan had pulled his strike at the last moment, ensuring he did not sever the fingers; no need for the blackguard to go dizzy at the sight of his fingers staring back at him from the deck planks.

A guttural growl accompanied the sound of the dagger clattering to the deck. The captain kicked it away and clutched his now useless left hand to his belly, smearing the once white shirt with blood.

Sebastiaan exploited the fleeting opening. He extended his weapon; the moonlight giving the flat blade a dull sheen as it curved toward the captain's throat, the tip hovering a mere pulse beat from the bulging vein in his neck.

As the captain looked down at the menacing saber his body stilled, chin lifted, lips thinned, and his nostrils flared. Sebastiaan knew he was resisting the urge to swallow, but the brief pause was not meant to give the man time to think or regroup; it was an unspoken promise of what was to come.

"Sebastiaan, stop playing with that fool and finish it!" Van Leyen's voice rang out amidst the chaos as he ran across the deck.

Even though the captain's rapier had a longer reach than Sebastiaan's saber, he knew the slightest twitch would mean the severing of his neck, and so the rapier remained by his side. Dark eyes that showed hints of pain, but an abundance of cunning leveled at Sebastiaan.

"Retract your blade, sir. No need to spill civilized blood over chattel. There's plenty more where those come from." The captain's refined French seemed more suitable to the ballrooms of Versailles than the decks of a pirate ship.

"I don't trade in human life," Sebastiaan replied mordantly. If this man thought he was in a position to negotiate, he was sorely mistaken.

"Those are not humans, but heathens, I assure you. Good only for hard labor."

There was something in the words that catapulted Sebastiaan back to his days as a galley slave under the pirate Yavuz, now so many years in the past. The feeling of being at another's mercy, treated as mere property, a beast of burden rather than a man, burned through his mind. The years melted away and Sebastiaan felt the licks of the bullwhip as it cleaved his skin, the never-ending hunger, the oppressive heat, the blinding hopelessness. He'd fought countless men, each battle reinforcing the wall he'd built around his past. Yet this man, with a single cutting phrase, had penetrated that barrier. That slight breech brought the loss of Danielle anew, the pain as raw as if it had just happened. The force of it so powerful that it made his breath falter.

Had the captain the gift of seeing only a second into the future, he would have reacted differently to the slight glazing of his opponent's eyes. Instead, he used the minuscule reprieve to shift his foot backward, creating distance from the saber blade and room to raise his rapier.

With a firm mental shake, Sebastiaan caught the spark of hope in the captain's eyes as his body tensed to dodge the saber's cutting edge. *Enough.* Sebastiaan flicked his arm down, the saber slicing deep into the unguarded belly, cutting past the tense stomach muscles that valiantly tried to guard the vital organs behind them.

The rapier dropped to the deck, bounced three times before coming to rest a few inches from its owner. The captain sank to his knees, both hands frantically clutching at his spilling intestines as he tried to push them back into the yawning cavity of his abdomen.

Moments earlier, Van Leyen had still been fighting with the vigor and tenacity of a prized bull, cutting limbs and dealing death blows, but now there was no sign of him. Sebastiaan was alone and with more sailors flooding the decks, he knew he would soon be surrounded. Even if he, Van Leyen and Daka were fighting back-to-back, there were still too many to defeat. He'd miscalculated. There were close to twenty men emerging from the forecastle. Some were still groggy from sleep, but all were armed.

As Sebastiaan counted his adversaries, a new sensation demanded his attention. The deck beneath his feet began to tremble, then the vibration grew into a pounding as more than two hundred slaves rushed up the companionway, escaping the hell they'd been living in below decks.

The dynamic shifted in a spectacular moment and it was as though a dark freak wave was crashing on the deck. With a deafening roar, the men emerged into the open night air, the promise of freedom hindered only by their tormentors blocking their way. Driven by desperation and rage, the slaves ripped into their captors with their bare hands, collecting weapons as they went.

Sebastiaan watched as the wave rolled across the deck, leaving the mangled and mauled bodies of the pirates in their wake and then it disappeared over the bulwark. He had every faith that the men on the beach would soon suffer the same fate.

Chaos and destruction rained down around Sebastiaan. A chill began at his feet and gradually rose until it covered his entire body. This was his life. Nothing but bloodshed and violence. Looking at his hands, he was surprised to find them not dripping with the blood of his enemies. His limbs felt heavy as exhaustion washed over him. What a life he led, its burden reaching deep inside him to where the long-forgotten threads of his soul hung. An overwhelming desire to go home surged - but where was home? He had no home, no family and the emptiness was oddly liberating. This is the end. No more. No more fighting, no more searching for Danielle. No more trying to kill the memories of his past. Even as the slaves came pouring from the hull earlier, he couldn't resist the years-old habit of searching for her white face among them, her slender body, her long dark hair – it was over.

"Sebastiaan!" Van Leyen's voice reached him from across the deck. "The charges are set. She is going to blow!" Van Leyen had a cut on his arm and blood was oozing over the torn edges of his sleeve. Another smaller red line marked his cheekbone. "Daka led them all from the ship. Let's go!"

"That's good," Sebastiaan answered in a detached voice, his eyes looking through Van Leyen. "You go along. I'll be right there."

He had no desire to follow his friend off the ship, but Van Leyen did not need to know. As the decision took root in his mind, peace folded around him with the comfort of an embrace. Letting go of this life and all its trappings was as easy as opening your hand to let go of a feather you'd thought you'd treasured for eternity.

Van Leyen had set the charges in the hull and although he'd made the fuses as long as he could, there was barely enough time to get off the ship. He'd warned Sebastiaan to run, but the fool was standing in the center of the upper deck with his weapons sheathed and his eyes staring off into the black nothingness of the night. There was a finality to the scene that sent a shudder through him.

"Sebastiaan!" Van Leyen shouted again. The reality of the moment crashed into him, and a jolt of panic speared his throat, forcing his friend's name to emerge like a strangled scream. Sebastiaan showed no signs of hearing him. His face was frozen in an almost transcendent expression. Urgency and fear lengthened Van Leyen's strides.

Sebastiaan closed his eyes and tilted his face into the breeze brushing his cheeks. He heard the rush of blood in his veins and knew with euphoric certainty that when he opened his eyes next, Danielle would be standing before him, welcoming him home with her vibrant green eyes and her brilliant smile.

But Van Leyen rudely interrupted his plans by barreling into him and clamping his arms around him. Sebastiaan had no time to resist as the impact drove him back and over the ship's side. Only when the cold water closed over his head did his mind veer from the self-destructive path it was so thoroughly set on moments before. He was still tangled in Van Leyen's crushing grip.

As soon as Van Leyen felt Sebastiaan's body tense to swim, he released him. They dove beneath the surface when the powerful explosion sent a wave of hot air and shards of wood over the water above.

***

By the time they reached the beach and retrieved their boots, the freed slaves had dispatched the sleeping pirates as easily as they had those onboard. Many had died by their own cutlasses, some of which remained embedded in their now-lifeless bodies.

Sebastiaan and Van Leyen picked their way through the thicket and reached the stream where they'd tethered their horses. After leading all the slaves out of the hull, across the beach, and far enough inland to be sure of their safety, Daka had returned to their rendezvous point.

"Why would a seemingly cultured French prick be sailing with a Portuguese crew?" Van Leyen wondered as he sank his teeth into the soft flesh of the freshly hunted and roasted small antelope.

They hadn't eaten for a full day, stopping only to water the horses, desperate to distance themselves from the cove, uncertain how many sailors had survived the slaves' onslaught, though Sebastiaan doubted any had. If a few were lucky to have escaped with their lives, Africa herself would kill them off soon enough. Being alone and wounded in the harsh wilderness of the continent was not conducive to a long and fruitful life.

Not hearing Van Leyen's question, Sebastiaan stared mutedly into the flickering flames, unaware of the silent command Van Leyen gave Daka.

"I'll check on the horses," Daka announced unnecessarily and disappeared into the darkness.

The night sounds were a balm to Sebastiaan's restless thoughts. He wished he had the willingness to examine the black melancholy that had settled over him. He needed to be alone for a while and wanted to get up and wander off into the darkness as well, but somehow, his legs lacked the strength to do so.

"Sebastiaan, look at me," Van Leyen ordered.

Instantly irritated by the authoritative tone his friend adopted, Sebastiaan raised his eyes from the fire and leveled them at Van Leyen. It had been a long time since anyone had dared to address him in such a tone. In fact, the only person who ever did was his uncle. He'd not laid eyes on him in seventeen years and tonight the longing for his kin felt like a pit in his soul.

"What?"

"We're done. No more fighting. No more bloodshed. None of it!" Van Leyen's hand cut through the air as his voice rose with his declarations.

Sebastiaan stared at him with a mutinous expression. The outburst was so unexpected that it took him a good few seconds to bring all the ends of the conversation together. Van Leyen was clearly not in the mood to afford him the time to collect his thoughts and thundered on.

"I am sick to my bones watching you try to throw your life away. It's draining my soul. There will come a day when I won't be there to watch your back and the thought haunts me."

His hulking form and the fire blazing in his once-tranquil, now-furious eyes gave him a feral intensity. Is this what his enemies saw when he came charging at them with his twin blades swinging? – *Impressive.*

"You were not going to follow me off that ship last night, were you?" He did not wait for an answer. "Somewhere between gutting that French popinjay and the slaves leaving the deck, you had decided to end it all." He lifted his hand when Sebastiaan tried to say something, demanding silence. "Save it. I am not judging you. I know what it's like to have your life ripped away. When my wife and baby son died, I descended into a hell so deep that not even the sharpest light could find me. The very same thing happened to you when you realized Danielle was dead."

The words struck him like a bucket of cold water in his face and Sebastiaan bolted to his feet. No one had mentioned her name in over ten years. When they had reached Algiers and found no trace of her, he had forced himself to face the grim reality that he would never find her, that she had perished somewhere. He had grieved for months, drunk himself into oblivion every night and fought like a monster by day with the blind hope that every time he went into battle against the slave traders, one of them would end him. And through it all, John was there, unwavering and without judgment, guarding his back, listening to him retch and dragging him to his sleeping pallet, never once speaking a word of caution or admonition. Offering a quiet harbor for Sebastiaan's storm to crash into.

Glaring at his friend, seeing only understanding in his eyes he settled back down, swallowing the scathing words he'd been ready to hurl.

"For seventeen years you've fought the ills of this world and heaven knows the earth stands still to watch every time you raise a blade but ruthlessness and recklessness have been your bedfellows for far too long."

Sebastiaan wished Van Leyen would stop talking. Hearing his friend put words to the thoughts that had plagued him since that moment on the deck of the slave ship made his stomach roil.

"I understand the thing that is eating at you and well you know it. Not even the time I spent as a slave at the Cape was as painful as losing my family. Nothing can compare. But that morning I first saw you in Van Riebeeck's stables, I saw a lifeline, an opportunity to – " his voice trailed off and he raked a hand through his hair. "I don't know, perhaps a chance to start over. Later I realized that in our friendship I had found my purpose."

Sebastiaan wasn't looking at Van Leyen any longer but he was listening.

"What was that blessed purpose?" he snarled.

"You." The simple admission drew Sebastiaan's attention. "You became my purpose. Doing this noble thing we've been doing, freeing the slaves, giving life back to so many. That became my purpose." Letting his words sink in, Van Leyen waited a few breaths before he spoke again.

"It is time to put this to rest. We are but a few weeks' ride from the Cape of Good Hope. Let's start anew. Be it there or somewhere else. You need to build something. Leave a legacy. It is what Danielle would have wanted for you."

"Don't speak her name," Sebastiaan wanted to scream the words, but he could manage no more than a whisper.

"It is time to find peace, brother."

Chapter 2

He did not have a good rapport with the large black ostrich currently guarding the nest. For days, he'd tried and failed to get even close to the eggs, let alone see them. With the morning sun not yet touching the waters of the ocean and the female ostrich foraging near the rocky edge of the distant escarpment, he was ready to implement his latest plan. Why the pair had nested in the middle of the flat plateau was a mystery to him. It was as if they'd walked for miles and then suddenly stopped to settle down with no thought whatsoever to the safety or the suitability of the location.

Today marked his third attempt at stealing an egg. The tribe had their own ostriches, but collecting an egg from the enclosure was far from sporting and something even a small child could do. Stealing one from under the plumes of an overprotective, over-aggressive, wild male was quite another matter altogether.

Approaching the bird from behind and with no large shrubs to use as cover, he had to be silent and fly-footed. There were few weaknesses in an ostrich to exploit. It had exceptional eyesight, and while its hearing was slightly less acute, it was far from deaf. The bird was blindingly fast, given that the path of its journey was fairly straight, but when confronted with tight corners, its balance was abysmal and to that one small weakness, the boy had pinned his hopes for success.

His plan was brilliant in its simplicity which, to his thinking, was the surest way to victory, keep the wind in his face, stay as low as possible, move as quietly as a whisper and poke the male with the nearly five-foot-long stick he'd found the day before. Hopefully, the startled bird would abandon the nest in the direction it faced, affording him the time to grab an egg and make a run for the edge of the hill where the sharp drop to the ocean below was interrupted by a ledge. If he was fast enough, he would reach the edge and make the jump before being split in two by the bird's vicious claws. Then it was just a matter of waiting for the ostrich to grow bored and head back to its nest. Only then would he climb to the top, head back to the tribe and still be in time to break his fast with his mother.

With the stick firmly gripped in his hand, and the cool morning breeze in his face, he crouched low and tiptoed closer to the nest. Every step was a delicate negotiation with the ground below, each footfall as stealthy as the silent flap of an owl's wing, the imprint of his bare feet the only evidence that he'd ever been there. The excitement coursing through his body agitated his muscles and prickled his skin. Breathing evenly through his mouth, he tasted the salty cool ocean air as it wafted over his tongue. All around, insects were buzzing and below, the waves were crashing against the cliff face. His senses came together in perfect harmony, turning him into the lethal hunter he was so often praised to be. His heart pounded with a steady primal beat, the force tapping rhythmically against his breastbone. Casting a swift glance over his shoulder at the female, he ensured she was still happily feasting on her selection of seeds and insects.

The male, however, had made his first mistake of the morning: facing into the wind, instead of the other way, from which a predator might approach. The boy shook his head at the bird's complacency. He was almost there, only a few more strides.

With the unfailing sixth sense of a mother, the female bird intuited that something was amiss and chose that moment to look up from her meal. She instantly realized the impending danger and let loose a scream that rent the peaceful morning air, ripping his carefully constructed plan to shreds. Her shriek had the same effect on the large black male as the boy had envisioned for the stick. The bird leaped from the nest with disturbing alacrity, and, for an exhilarating moment, darted off in the wrong direction.

Abandoning all pretense of stealth, the boy hightailed it to the nest.

Confusion ruled over the ostrich as it charged straight ahead into the open field, spotting no apparent danger, despite his female's screams still reverberating across the distance between them. Speed was his ally, but balance was a matter that needed to be handled with finesse, and turning at a tight and sudden angle was the surest way to lose one's footing and tumble down in the most undignified heap of neck, feathers, and limbs.

The boy saw the instant the bird realized he was defending the wrong front and was turning around. The nest was within reach, but he was now painfully aware of the other ostrich charging toward him from behind. Perhaps not the most enviable position to be in. Not daring a glance over his shoulder to judge the distance between him and the advancing female, he relied on his hearing. The thumping of her feet was still a manageable distance away and he centered his focus on the hissing black cloud of feathers approaching him head-on.

The male ostrich spread its wings for balance, and barreled toward him. Its beak was open, and a cacophony of hisses and screeches was streaming from it.

The boy judged the distance to the nest, only three more strides, but then he needed to slow to a near stop, crouch down, and snatch an egg. His mind raced, calculating his chances of success, and grimly concluded he'd likely be knocked over, pinned down, and cleaved open by that mighty claw.

His primary plan was wafting into thin air, very much like the puffs of dust around the ostrich's feet. The male was charging him at breakneck speed, mindless of the innocent nest lying between them. The daft thing was about to trample his future offspring. It was time to implement his second plan.

With his dream of stealing an egg now thoroughly dashed, he waited until the ostrich was gut-clenchingly close and then he hurled the stick. There was no advantage in throwing it at the bird, for the mass of feathers would render such an attack moot. Instead, he threw it to the side, hoping to divert the attention of the avian, if only for the briefest of instances. His plan worked beautifully, as he knew it would, and the moment those large black eyes followed the path of the useless piece of wood, the boy sharply changed direction and sprinted for the safety of the cliff's edge.

The female ostrich was not so easily distracted and, with her maternal instincts completely transformed into raging fury, she ignored her hapless husband and instead kept the intruder dead in her sights.

She smoothly adjusted her trajectory without losing her footing and cut a straight line toward the boy. From the corner of his eye, he saw the gray mass grow larger. She was close enough for him to see her pink and white scaly lower legs as they pounded the dirt. He swallowed the unmanly scream that tried to escape him in a bid to find safety elsewhere.

He was close to the cliff's edge, and through the pounding of his heart and the frenzy of his escape, a spark of conscience broke through. He hoped the ostrich would stop in time and not follow. His next stride sent him over the edge. Having seen the ledge only once before and never actually attempted the jump, doubt skittered across his mind but vanished when his feet landed firmly on the solid rock slab twenty feet below.

His chest heaved as he caught his breath. There was no flurry of feathers or mangled limbs. He looked down to better assess the distance he would have fallen had he botched his landing. The sight below completely erased his concerns over the drop and the memory of the disgruntled ostrich above him. Bathed in the fresh rays of the morning light lay the most magnificent ship he'd ever imagined.

Not daring to breathe or blink for fear that the scene might vanish or be disturbed in some way, he silently stared at it, taking in every detail. Whispers of his mother's tales floated from his memory, tales of lands and places beyond the horizon, of great ships that sailed like mythical beasts upon the waves, guided and steered by brave captains and tough sailors, men like his father and his grandfather. The largest thing he'd ever seen floating on the water was a dead hippopotamus. It felt blasphemous to compare the magnificent beauty before him with such a grotesque sight.

The ship was sleek and elegant with a dark brown, almost black hull and decks that glittered white as the sun's rays bounced off them. Three proud masts stretched toward the blue sky. Her sails were tightly bunched up and tied to the crossbeams, as if she had pulled them up, afraid they might get wet.

His hands had gone damp with desire as he longed to run them along the smooth lines of her body, explore every curve and indent. He wished to circle his arms around the sturdy mast and fill his lungs with the smell of the wood. He wanted to feel the deck move beneath his feet, taste the wind, and listen to the sails as they snapped and strained. The creaking of the line that tethered her to the seafloor and the rhythmic beating of the waves against her hull reached him like a siren call.

An untamed wave of longing hit him square in the heart and his mouth went dry. Snapping it shut, he swallowed and forced some moisture back over his tongue. How was it possible to hunger after something he'd never known?

Possibilities and opportunities that were always there, but somehow hidden from his ignorant eyes, became clear. His imagination pulled free from its moorings and took flight. The feeling of being invincible, of wanting to chase the sun over the horizon and discover what lies beyond made his heart race and that ship was the answer. She would take him there. This wasn't just a ship; it was a symbol of freedom and hope. She was a promise waiting to be fulfilled.

Then understanding dawned like a new day. For the first time in his life, he was falling in love.

Was this what his friends felt when so many of them had gone soft in the knees, bleary-eyed and dim-witted at the sight of their sweethearts?

He did not know how long he stood on that ledge, staring down at the ship, but somewhere between jumping over the edge of the cliff and his next thought, the path of his life had shifted.

Men dressed in strange, cumbersome clothes hurriedly crossed the deck, shouted orders, and waved their arms, as if that would bring more clarity to their eager chatter. He shook his head in wonder. No matter who they were or where they came from, all people are intrinsically the same. In their actions, he could see his own tribe when faced with a dramatic or exciting event.

The boy watched with sharpened interest as the men lowered three small vessels before crowding into them. The boats glided over the water, urged forward by long pieces of wood that moved backward and forward in perfect timing. He followed their path until they passed through the narrow opening between the jagged rocks and disappeared behind the hills.

***

With sure-footed agility, the boy navigated the steep hillside, leaping from boulder to boulder, knowing which stones were firmly buried in the earth and which offered only the illusion of a stable foothold, lying in wait, ready to send the unsuspecting tumbling through shrubs and across the unforgiving rough spaces between.

He paused as he reached the bottom of the hill. Before him spread the vast inlet. Salt water from the ocean pushed in from one end just as the fresh water from the river tried to force it back out again. A small white beach curved like a necklace of seashells along the water's edge. Rugged hills covered in dense underbrush formed a tight barrier, stopping the ocean from claiming any more land than it needed.

Thin, white lines of smoke from several cooking fires were lazily curling their way upward. The smell of roasted fish reached him long before he deemed it close enough to hide in the deep shadows of the trees. Sailors were bustling about. Many were bathing in the fresh water of the river farther north. Others were heading back to the beach carrying large wooden containers, water sloshing over the brims as they walked. Three men were fishing with long lines instead of the sharp spear he used.

Skirting the narrow beach, the boy kept to the deep shadows of the underbrush. A cooking fire, some distance from the others, drew his attention. Two men were lounging by it. They looked and dressed differently from the sailors. Their bearing carried an air of authority. One, in particular, moved with the same smooth confidence and swagger as Kai, comfortable with the weight of power and responsibility. His gaze swept regularly over the men, noting their activities, while also searching for danger lurking in the unknown beyond where his eyes could see; he must be the captain. From the shadows, the lad watched as another man approached bearing several cleaned and gutted fish. The captain accepted the offering, thanked him, and turned to his companion by the fire.

Creeping closer, the boy grinned at the thought that this was the second time this morning he was stalking his quarry. Hopefully, this time it would not end in a near disaster. The fish sizzled over the fire and his mouth flooded with saliva at the smell of the food. He'd not eaten since last night and his insides were protesting the oversight.

Standing dead still, breathing quietly and moving only his eyes, he studied the two men. The captain's features were sharp and intelligent. Loose black curls, which couldn't decide if they wanted to be long or short, danced in the breeze. The softness of his hair was in stark contrast to the strong lines of his face. High cheekbones, shrewd eyes, thin straight nose, harsh, strict mouth and a crisp jawline covered in skin the color of mountain honey. Bending over the cooking fire, he tested the fish and then prowled toward the water's edge to wash his hands. Smooth, powerful movements lent him the graceful agility and unintentional confidence of a large leopard.

The captain was at ease, but far from relaxed. A sense of acute alertness crackled around him, as if he could smell danger long before it became a threat. For an intense moment he glanced past the other man into the shadows of the thicket. His eyes were not searching, but fixed on a definite place. The boy felt the heat of that stare scorching his skin. The moment lasted but a few seconds and then the captain looked away and continued talking to his companion.

The other man's skin was as dark as the night, and it gleamed like polished onyx in the places where the dappled sunlight touched it. Short, black, tightly curled hair grew close to his scalp, which was cut so short that it did not permit any movement at all. His body was large and scarred. Even at rest, lying on his back with his arm slung over his eyes, the ridges and valleys of his muscles were clearly visible. He embodied the raw power of an elephant bull in its prime. The lad felt his stomach tighten. The black tribes were strong and brutal. They loved war and bloodshed, and the Cochoqua harbored a deep fear of them and therefore avoided them.

"How long do you want to stay here?" the dark man asked in a low and soothing voice.

The captain tightened his lips and once more stared into the shadows of the shrubs.

"Three days, perhaps. Depending on how easily we can secure fresh meat."

A hum rumbled from the companion's chest as he contemplated the statement.

"Three days is not enough. The men need time to stretch their legs."

The lad was astounded that the man had the audacity to argue with his captain, but then he remembered that his mother frequently argued with Kai.

"Three days are enough. I don't like this place." The captain rolled his shoulders as if trying to shake something off.

"Orion, you don't like any place other than the deck of your ship." The black man sat up and rested his heavy arms over his bent knees. "This place is as good as any, if not better. It is secluded. There are plenty of fish and freshwater close by," he said and pointed toward the river. "What is setting your arse abuzzing this time? Or is it just the fact that you seem to have an adverse reaction to any piece of dry land?"

The captain cast his friend a dirty look before removing the fish from the glowing coals.

"Three days, Jiya. No more." His tone was tone curt and final and there was a stubborn set to his already tight jaw.

"How far up the coast do you want to sail this time?" the friend asked as he helped himself to the food.

"If I can have my way, we'll hunt and trade as far as Mombasa before heading south again. That should give my uncle plenty of time to reach the Cape."

The men were speaking Dutch, the language of his mother, which she'd taught him alongside the tribe's. Patiently, he watched as the captain sat down to eat, nodding at the cleverness of the man's choice – positioning himself with his back to the water, facing the shadows.

The boy had seen enough, and the longer he lingered, the greater his chances of being discovered became. He silently retreated until he felt safe enough to turn around and make his way back to the Cochoqua village. *Three days – he had three days to find his way onto that ship. Three days to convince his mother to let him go.*

***

"Davit Aard De Vries, where have you been?" Her words hit him the moment his head cleared the entrance to their cave. Danielle watched as her son ducked to enter and then straightened to his glorious height. He was the light of her life, but before said light could open his mouth to answer her question, she spoke again.

"I spent all of yesterday afternoon collecting berries for our meal this morning and then ended up breaking my fast by myself."

A cocky smile decorated his face as he watched her hand cut through the air. Experience taught him she was still at the outset of venting her frustrations, and he was not wrong. She had been particularly prickly the last couple of days, easy to rile, slow to smile, very much unlike her usual self.

"Then came the midday meal and," she paused for effect, daring him to say something, but he wisely kept his mouth shut, "yes, that's right; alone once more. I thought a lion had somehow gotten to you and deprived me of my dinner companion as well."

It was best not to mention that they almost never ate their noon meals together, for he was often out with the men hunting or tending the cattle, nor the evening meal, which they all shared by the great fire in the center of the village. Having reached the end of her rant, she stood with her fists planted firmly on her sides and her eyebrows raised in two neat arches.

Now she was done.

Davit scratched the few precious coarse hairs sprouting at random on his upper lip and decided not to defend himself. He was in no mood to explain his absence. What he had to say was far more important, but he would give her time to calm down first. The silence stretched between them as they stared at each other. She was waiting for him to speak, or at the very least to be the first to blink or look away, but he was determined to win this time. In the end, she sighed, pursed her lips and motioned for him to sit by the fire crackling near the entrance.

Davit smothered the smug sense of victory that bubbled from his core. A win against his mother was something to savor, for such triumphs were remarkably irregular. She handed him a *calabash* of sour milk and a bowl of nuts.

"Are you going to tell me what you did today, since I so carelessly abandoned my elderly mother?" he teased, then quickly ducked as she threw a bundle of rolled twine at his head.

"Careful, you little runt," she warned as she made herself comfortable and reached for a large pile of fresh herbs which she separated into smaller bundles. The afternoon sun was streaming through the opening of their cave, engulfing her in a gentle glow that gleamed off her hair. Here and there, a silver strand shone through the dark mass of her curls. Usually, she wore her hair in tight plaits, but she must have washed it this morning and left it to dry, for it hugged her shoulders like a mantle flowing down her back.

The years had not wrinkled and withered her like so many others. Her skin was now browned by the sun and her smile was bright and carefree. A few lines around her eyes marked her forty summers and a slight tilt to her lips hinted at a sorrow now long buried but not forgotten. The women of the tribe said she stayed this young because she was a witch and as such, the gods smiled on her. There was no venom in their words. His mother was, apart from the chief, the most respected and revered member of their tribe. She healed the sick and delivered the babies. She could speak to the gods and see what lay beyond the clouds of tomorrow, and she knew the secret powers hidden in the roots, stems, and leaves of the plants.

He watched as her hands tied the bundles of herbs seemingly with no instruction from her mind, her fingers nimble and sure.

When she spoke again, her voice was steady and without the earlier sharpness of her annoyance. "Today was the same as yesterday. Nobody died, nobody was born, and the ones in between are healthy and mostly happy. Pass me that bowl, will you please?" She dropped the neat little bundle in it as soon as he'd placed the clay bowl near her feet. "But there is a heaviness in the air from the moment you walked in here, and I'm just wondering how long it will take you to scrape your courage together and tell me what is weighing on your heart."

And there she was, straight as an arrow shot from a bow, never missing the target. It was the moment he had wished for, to tell her of his plans. He knew she would not be happy, but this was his life and the idea of staying in this village for the rest of it made him feel restless, trapped, and short of breath, like a heavy boulder pushing down on his chest.

In the eyes of the tribe, he was a man and old enough to choose a woman of his own. He figured if he had the right to be the head of his own family, he most definitely had the right to claim his future, but for all his manly bravado his throat suddenly felt dry and the words he meant to say to his mother had cowardly scurried off to the recesses of his mind.

Searching for a way to tell her of his decision, he let his eyes wandered over everything that had been his home all his life. He stared at their sleeping skins that lay in two neat bundles near the back of the cave, at the bowls of dried herbs that cluttered every flat surface and at the ancient drawings on the walls, made by tribes that had roamed these lands thousands of years ago – the Cochoqua's ancestors, not his.

Lately, he found himself often thinking of his father. The man was a mythical giant meticulously painted by his mother, strong, virtuous, and brave. He wondered what it would've been like to sit across from him, to hear his voice, to drink in his wisdom. Annoyed with the fruitless track his thoughts had once more traveled, he blinked hard and tightened his jaw.

He would talk to his mother in the morning. Tonight, he had to be among other men, sharing laughter around the fire, and later joining the group guarding the cattle for the first watch. He would loosen the ties that bound them together, cherishing his time with them, knowing it would be his last. The thought brought a pang of regret but also the undeniable spark of excitement for what lay ahead.

"We'll talk tomorrow," he said as he rose from his seat.

Danielle watched him leave and only when he rounded the bend in the narrow footpath did she release a deep sigh.

***

Davit had taken the first watch to guard the village and the cattle, and it was long past midnight when he'd quietly found his bed. He was still sleeping when Danielle left the cave before dawn.

She returned with an armful of dried wood. Not that she needed any, but the task required little thinking and kept her hands busy, leaving her mind free to work through her emotions and handle what was sure to come.

Stepping into the cave, she found Davit waiting for her. Her breath came a little faster than normal as she bent to lower the bundle to the floor. The path to the cave was steep, but it had never troubled her before.

Below, the Cochoqua village was waking up. Women's voices rose as they fed their families. Children laughed, a baby cried, soon followed by a man's soothing hum. What usually brought a content smile to her face and a sense of belonging failed to warm the coldness inside her this morning.

Watching his mother as she moved about, Davit noticed the tension in her shoulders and the tightness of her features. She was unusually busy this morning, fluttering from one task to the next, as if she were trying to avoid something. His idleness would not go unnoticed for long, and soon she would send him on some errand. Then, by the time he got back, there would be an endless string of people waiting for her attention. The need to speak to her about his future was burning like a coal in his belly.

"Can you *not* be busy right now?" Davit asked when it was clear that she would not stop of her own volition.

"Davit, I'm always busy. What is it you want, my darling? Are you hungry?" she asked over her shoulder when she knelt to straighten his sleeping skins.

Raising his eyes to the pocked ceiling of the cave, he reined in his impatience. Sometimes the only way to get her undivided attention was to shock her to a standstill.

"Mother, there is a ship lying near the cliffs. The sailors are camping by the peaceful waters. They will set sail again tomorrow and when they do, I plan to join them." His words were deliberate and measured, and as he spoke them out loud for the first time, he felt himself become lighter. It was as if a weight were lifting from him. He wanted to shout his relief to the heavens. The thrill of his excitement was rushing through his veins with enough force to make his ears ring and his hands shake.

Belatedly, he realized that the world around him had gone deathly quiet. Even the chatter of the birds outside seemed dimmed. His mother was wordlessly staring at him. Her ocean-green eyes resembled two large pools in her emotionless face. The color was leaving her cheeks and a pronounced white ring appeared around her lips. For a brief moment, he feared she would faint, but then her eyes narrowed, and her throat bobbed as she swallowed.

"What did you just say?" she whispered, but she might as well have shouted it.

He loved her more than life itself, but she was a force to be reckoned with when riled, and he could have chosen his words with a bit more care.

"I saw the ship yesterday at daybreak. It must have arrived during the night. When I went down to the peaceful water, I heard the men talk. They spoke Dutch, like you and me. One of them, I think he is their captain, said that he wanted to hunt and trade all the way up to Mombasa. I don't even know where that is, never heard of such a place."

His words pulled her from her rigid stillness. She went to sit by the entrance, her hair stirred in the breeze and, as if suddenly given their freedom, a multitude of emotions flitted across her face: wariness, suspicion, fear and – hope? The last was a surprise but it was gone in an instant. Had he not been watching her so closely or even blinked at that moment, he would have missed it.

What was it she secretly hoped for? Every year, on the same night, she went to the hill overlooking the ocean, built a fire, and sat with her *kaross* tightly drawn across her shoulders, as if to ward off the darkness, while she stared at the vast ocean. Then, at dawn when she returned, her face puffy and blotched from her tears, she would retreat into herself, where she would remain for a few days before allowing life to resume its normal rhythm. He knew the fire was for his father, but he never dared to ask. The ritual was too raw and private, even for him to intrude.

"There is a word written on its side," he continued. "*As-Sayf.*" Her color was coming back and she was looking more herself.

"*As-Sayf,*" she repeated the name, as if testing the strange words on her tongue, "it sounds Arabic." Adding a few pieces of wood to the fire, she watched it spark and crackle. "Tell me this though," she spoke without looking at him. "If you saw the ship yesterday morning, why did you wait until now to tell me?"

"I needed time to be sure it is what I truly wanted." Her shock was fading, and he felt relieved, as they could now speak calmly.

"And one day of thinking was enough for you to determine your future?"

Ah, judging by the sarcasm in her words, his hopes might have been a touch premature.

"I want to sail one of those ships. It's what I've always wanted to do. Ever since you told me about them and their brave crew. I've wanted that life for as long as I can remember. I can't ..." he searched for the right words. "I can't herd cattle, hunt antelope, and gather berries for the rest of my life."

She opened her mouth to object to his narrow view, but he spoke before she could.

"I *know* there is more out there. There has to be. This can't be all there is to life." His arm stretched toward the cave's opening where the ocean roared beyond the hills. "I want to see what lies beyond the horizon; live a different way, and then choose which I like best. Why else did you teach me to read and write, if not to prepare me for something greater?" Every morning of his childhood was devoted to lessons. When the other boys played, he sat with his mother, practicing his letters and numbers with a piece of charcoal on the large, flat stone by the river.

"Mombasa is far up the east coast," she said, ignoring his plea for a deeper and more meaningful life. "And if memory serves, it's Ottoman territory." His mother rose from her seat and paced the length of the cave before coming to a stop, staring vacantly at the wall. That look was not promising. She was trying to make sense of the situation, and wherever her thoughts were leading was not a good place.

"Something is not right."

He swallowed his sigh.

"Why would Dutch speaking sailors sail a ship with an Arabic name, and why would they even dare to enter Ottoman waters? It makes no sense at all. They could very well be pirates."

"I don't think they're pirates," Davit defended while trying to keep his tone neutral, but he must have failed, for she fired a warning glare at him.

"How would you know? Have you ever seen one?" his mother challenged in a tight voice.

"No mother, I haven't. Have you?" he snapped back and immediately lowered his eyes. He waited, fortifying himself against the tongue-lashing that would surely follow his outburst, but it didn't come. Why did they recently find themselves on opposite sides of so many arguments?

Instead of taking him to task for his insolence, she twisted her head and stared intently at his legs. He cringed as her eyes traveled up to pause at the scrapes and cuts on his chest, which she'd failed to notice the day before. His ascent back up the ledge yesterday morning was not as smooth as he had hoped. The surface was unexpectedly slippery from the early morning dew, and his first attempt at hoisting himself up and over the edge had seen his fingers slip free from their holds and him scraping down the sharp edges of the rock wall. Eventually, after several attempts and the foulest of curses, he reached the top. His only consolation at the time was that nobody was there to witness his clumsiness.

"What happened?" she asked, as she approached to better inspect his damaged skin.

"Nothing, really, I just slipped on some rocks," he deflected.

"And somehow you managed to cause injury to your chest?" Suspicion made her eyebrows pull together as if to drink from the groove between them.

"I went down to the ledge on the cliffside to see the ship below." It was not a lie, merely a half-truth.

"You could have seen that ship all the same, from the top. Perhaps this is not the best of times to lie to me. Out with it, Davit. Why were you on that ledge?" his mother demanded.

There was no point deceiving her. She had a way of knowing his best-kept secrets and if she didn't, she would whittle them out of him. He capitulated and told her about the ostrich nest and his attempt at stealing an egg.

"Why would you do something so foolish? Why would you risk your hide and life for an egg?" Confusion currently held sway, but her anger was not far behind.

"It wasn't as bad as you imagine it to be. It was just a bit of fun," he defended his actions.

"And yet, in order to escape, you had to jump off a cliff. You just said the rock was wet from the dew. What if you'd slipped when you landed? I've seen that ledge. There is no way you would have survived if you had fallen among the boulders on the beach below."

"But I didn't slip." A boyish smile dimpled his cheeks. "Besides, you always told me it is the journey that matters and not the destination."

His mother was decidedly unimpressed with his antics and his reasoning. "Child, how does your mind connect that wisdom to this fresh bout of stupidity?" She pinched the bridge of her nose while trying to fend off the imminent headache or sneeze. She usually sneezed when irritated, which only aggravated the situation.

"Davit, you could have been killed, and for what?" she continued. "Tell me what you have to show for your bravado?" She looked him up and down again. "Apart from a chest that looks like you'd been in a fight with a cat, what did you gain?"

"Mother, if you want an egg, I will get you one." He waved his arm toward the ostrich enclosure, his eyes dancing with mischief. "Just don't get so upset."

Danielle sighed and visibly tried to cling to her self-control, but her temper was well and truly lit by his cheap attempt at sidetracking the conversation.

"It is not about the egg!" she shouted.

"Then why are we arguing about it?" he returned and she steepled her hands beneath her chin, no doubt to stop herself from throttling him.

"See mother, this is why I need to go. I am bored. Everything here is easy and predictable."

This child was the center of her world and the reason for every beat of her heart. In those early days, when she was scared and uncertain, his tiny body had served as her compass and her anchor. She always found solace in his solid weight as she fed and rocked him to sleep. The bond between them had only grown stronger. Now he wanted to leave, and she was not ready.

"You have a vast and entirely misplaced sense of your own readiness and abilities," she said.

"Meaning?" his voice dropped to a deep rumble at her veiled insult.

"Meaning, yesterday you were still behaving like a child chasing after ostriches, and tomorrow you want to sail off into the sunset, with pirates no less."

Exhaling through his nose while staring at his feet, he decided to ignore the pirate reference for now.

"Mother, how will I ever be ready if nothing changes? How will I know my true abilities if not put to the test? How will I grow if there is no push to do so? Please be reasonable."

He watched as those last three ill-chosen words ignited the fire in her eyes. With his pointer finger extended, as if pleading for a pause, he scrunched his nose and tipped his head.

"I did not mean that." He stared into her face, hoping she would sense his sincerity. "Mother, I spoke without thinking. I take that back."

"That is precisely my point," she continued without missing a beat. "You do most things without thinking. You rush into everything and when you find yourself neck deep in trouble, you rely on brute strength or charm to get you out of it."

He tried, but failed, to suppress the sly, guilty smile that fought its way to his lips.

"Guilty, but the strategy has worked well so far." Drawing his shoulders to his ears, he raised both hands with their palms up.

"Davit, one day your luck will run out." Her voice had lost most of its edge and it stirred something in him. "Don't you understand? I can't afford to lose you too."

"You won't lose me. I *will* come back. I promise," he spoke softly as he approached her.

"How can you make such a promise? You don't know what the future holds," she countered with a defeated shake of her head.

"I don't, but you do," he soothed.

Danielle's hand closed around the small leather pouch hanging from her neck.

"The bones don't show me what I want to see. They show me what I need to know."

"Let me go. I will come back." The eyes that stared at him now were sad and misty, and he knew he'd won, but the thought that he'd brought her sorrow closed like a fist around his throat.

He was still a boy in so many ways, but Danielle feared that if he stayed, shrouded in the tribe's safety, he would never grow into the man he could be. She had raised him as the son of Sebastiaan De Vries, hoping that he would grow up in the image she'd created for him. But she was too successful. How could she have set him up in such a fashion and thought he would be content with a simple life? This was a mother's biggest fear, her most acute pain, and her proudest moment, to look at her son and know it was time to let go, even though in her heart she knew he was not ready.

"I want to do this, but I want to do it with your blessing." His eyes were pleading, but his words were strong and commanding.

They stood opposite each other, neither speaking nor looking away, but the earlier hostility was gone now. She really had no say in the matter. It was his destiny unfolding before her very eyes, and she was not foolish enough to stand in the way of such a powerful force. Her purpose was to protect and prepare him for what lay ahead, and she had done her best.

Closing her eyes, she sent a silent prayer to Sebastiaan.

'Please watch over him. Keep him safe and bring him back to me.'

Opening her eyes, she squinted at her son. He was a sight to behold: tall, strong, intelligent, arrogant and so very dear to her.

"There are conditions," she spoke at last, and his shoulders dropped as he released the breath he'd been holding.

"You will not reveal the location of this tribe. Not to anybody. You will *never* use your white name. And you will not mention me to anyone – ever. As far as the world is concerned, I died seventeen years ago. Never speak my name. All your life, I've watched over you. It is now your turn to protect me. Do you understand these rules and swear to live by them?"

He swallowed thickly, then nodded. "I do."

"Then you have my blessing."

Davit hugged her to him, and he felt the familiar warmth and safety of her arms as they locked behind his back.

"I love you," he said, planting a kiss against her hair.

"I love you too." Her voice sounded strangled, and her shoulders shook as she silently wept. "I will wait for you."

They held each other and when her tears finally stopped, she pushed away from him and took a deep breath to steady herself.

"You will have to tell Kai. Regardless of my boundless affection for you, I will not be part of that thunderstorm." She raised a finger to silence him when he tried to interject. "This you will do on your own. I treasure my peace, and don't need that man's bellyaching ripping it to shreds."

Chapter 3

Heavy, dark clouds blocked the early morning sun, making the day seem further along than it was. Orion didn't mind the weather, for it reflected his mood rather perfectly.

He usually slept onboard his ship. When they dropped anchor, his crew drew straws to determine which four would remain sober to row him to and from the *As-Sayf.* However, last night, he had placed a wager on a game of ombre against Jiya. Win, and he'd be ferried to the ship; lose and he'd remain ashore. He'd lost, trading his luxurious bunk, awaiting him in his cabin, for a hollow dug in the sand on the beach of the estuary, and his peaceful, amicable self for an insect-bitten beast in need of a dunk in the river. Scratching his head, he let out a colorful curse as a shower of fine beach sand rained down his back and past the waistband of his breeches, which rode perilously low on his hips under his untucked shirt.

"Rough night?"

"Fuck off."

Jiya's booming laugh scraped across his already bruised nerves much like a dull blade over a three-day-old beard. Spending the night listening to every sound produced by human, insect, and animal was not conducive to a stable constitution come sunrise. Jiya, on the other hand, looked as fresh as a daisy, already washed, and dressed in a crisp white shirt, black breeches and shiny boots, ready for the day ahead.

After giving his shirt another firm shake, Orion abandoned any further attempts to rid himself of the sand. Instead, he narrowed his eyes at the gathering bank of clouds, then looked back to where Jiya crouched stacking fresh logs with painful precision over the previous night's cold ashes.

"What are you doing?" Orion asked.

"Surely you've seen me build a fire before," Jiya said without looking up from his task.

Orion slowly lowered the bridge of his nose into the tight wedge of his thumb and forefinger. His impatience and headache raced at equal speeds to the pinnacle of his spine. Breathing audibly through his nose, he massaged his temple and ardently tried to keep his frustrations from hardening his voice.

"Jiya, we are not staying. Look at the clouds." Orion snapped his hand toward the gathering storm without opening his eyes. "I have no wish to spend the rest of the day waiting out the rain under the shelter of a tree. Nor do I wish for the ship to be smashed to nothing larger than crate planks against the rocks when that storm reaches us, which, by the look of it, is in precisely one hour."

Jiya deftly struck the flint against a piece of iron and then bent forward to gently blow the small sparks into the dry grass he had nestled in the space beneath the logs. He waited for the fire to catch, and at the first satisfying crackle, turned around and looked at his friend with a serene expression.

"First, the storm will come close, but it will change its mind when it nears the land, and then it will head back out to sea. We will not suffer at its whims this day. It will, however, leave us to enjoy a firm breeze to aid our departure. Second," he said, and raised his eyebrows as Orion was readying himself for a cutting retort. "You will feel a lot better once you've freshened up a bit and have food in your stomach."

Orion's lips tightened over his teeth, and he kicked at a sizable pebble that peeked through the sand. However, he had misjudged the size, and the rock remained firmly in place while a sharp pain radiated from his booted toe. The combination of the stab of pain and the welcoming news that something would aid their departure was already working to push his black mood into the background.

"How do you know the storm will shift? I don't sense any change in the wind," he challenged.

"I was born on this continent. No matter where I am, I can sense her moods," Jiya said.

Orion did nothing to hide his eye roll from his friend.

"That is hardly a scientific rea-" Orion fell silent as the sight before him pushed the breath from his body and caused his words to waft away like thin smoke.

Jiya noted the slackness in Orion's jaw and the frown that gradually deepened between his confused eyes.

"What's wrong?" he asked.

Orion was consciously applying himself to blinking. He squeezed his eyes shut, then forced them open before repeating the ritual. It was as if he were trying to clear his vision, like one would after receiving a blow to the head.

"*What*, are you doing?" Jiya asked when the condition seemed to persist, his own face now mirroring his friend's baffled expression.

"If I blink hard enough, will that go away?" Orion asked.

"What are you talking about?" Jiya spun around to follow Orion's stare. "*Puta merda*," Jiya muttered in Portuguese, his preferred language for profanities, curses, and expletives.

"Indeed," Orion concurred.

"*What* is *that*?" Jiya asked.

"I have no idea." Orion angled his head and slitted his eyes. Silent moments passed, filled only by the far-off sounds of the crew going about their morning routines.

"Do you remember that one time in Kilwa?" Orion asked softly.

"Yes," Jiya answered, knowing exactly what his friend was referring to. "When we saw that thing that looked like a donkey from the front but a zebra from behind."

"Yes," Orion breathed.

Jiya opened his mouth to explain, but finding no credible piece of knowledge to hand, he shut it again. He preferred simplicity and a clear understanding of all things, but there was no forthright or compact way to describe the scene before them.

The apparition was standing motionless about thirty feet away where the underbrush met the sand. When it took a few steps closer, Orion and Jiya's shoulders tensed, and as much as they instinctively and collectively wanted to take a step back, pride, dignity, and stout-heartedness compelled them to hold their present position.

Orion kept his eyes fixed on the young man before him, then slowly bent to retrieve his cutlass. As his fingers closed around the familiar handle, feeling its comforting weight, he straightened, aware that his eyes and mind were deceiving him this morning. They were justified in their joint efforts when he remembered the unholy amount of grog he'd consumed the night before. No wonder he'd lost that silly card game to Jiya.

Davit was losing his patience with the two men. He'd politely waited for the captain to wake and rise from his sleep before he'd stepped from the underbrush. He'd even deliberately stepped on loose leaves, snapped a twig, and dislodged small pebbles to announce his presence. His plan was to introduce himself calmly and politely to the captain, then argue his case for joining the crew. Now, the captain had armed himself and there was a dangerous glint to his narrowed eyes.

He took another few steps toward the men, thinking that if he could get close enough to shake hands with one of them, things would improve. His mother had taught him the comical custom, and he understood the gesture was a signal for friendship and trust among her people – their people.

"Avast!" the captain barked.

By the tone of his voice and the hardening of his eyes, Davit knew it to be a command of sorts, but he'd never heard the word before, and the meaning failed him.

"What?" Davit asked, forgetting his manners and polite intentions.

The one-word question had an almost identical effect on the two men before him. Two pairs of eyes widened simultaneously, both heads pushed slightly forward as if to hear or see better, and both faces looked like they'd just bitten into something unpleasant. Neither took their eyes off him and the heat of their dark stares rooted his feet in place. He opened his hands and stretched them out, showing that he meant them no harm. The dagger his mother had given him, when he'd said goodbye to her, pressed against his side, as if calling for him to reach for it, but he ignored it.

"It speaks," Jiya said in a hushed tone.

Orion studied the man's contradictory guise, cataloging the curious collection of attributes. He'd always thought Africa a strange and mythical place, and here was yet another testament to its intriguing nature. Blond hair stirred in the gentle morning breeze, which, regardless of Jiya's prediction, carried the scent of heavy rain. The skin, fair at some point but now bronzed, foretold of a life living in the open. Sea-green eyes, alive with curiosity and intelligence, stared back at him. Orion was willing to bet another night under the stars that this boy had not yet reached his second decade, but for all that, he was powerfully built. Lean muscles corded his outstretched arms, and his chest, stomach, and legs displayed a strength that was deeply ingrained and honed over time. He might be young, but he was far from soft, and the stubborn tilt to his chin and the resolute set of his jaw signaled confidence and assertiveness. Admirable traits were they distributed in controlled quantities, but one did not have to be a learned scholar to see that it was not the case in this instance.

The boy was also almost completely naked, except for a soft leather loincloth shielding his modesty. A round-headed club, short spear, and bow rested snugly against his back, while the tip of a quiver filled with arrows peeked over his right shoulder. The out-of-place eight-inch dagger hanging from his hip completed the perplexing ensemble.

"You speak Dutch?" Orion asked as he extended his blade in a universal gesture for the boy to stay where he was.

"I do. Now, lower your weapon. I mean you no harm."

Pure, unadulterated astonishment made Orion's arm drop to his side. He had just been issued an order. Squeezing his eyes shut, he shook his head to rid himself of his incredulity. The wormling thought himself a threat. He was rarely at a loss for words, but this day appeared to be an exception, and that it was still fairly early in the morning did not give him hope for the evening.

Orion was the first to recover from their initial disbelief and subsequent fascination. Whatever this boy was or wanted would be beyond his power to alter or enable. Though clearly of European descent, he had chosen to dress in the manner of the native tribes. He seemed healthy and well cared for, and quite adept in his environment. There were no obvious signs of need, or desperation, and whatever had brought him about could carry him back again.

"I don't have time for this. I need to wash, and we need to leave," he said to Jiya and stared at the gathering clouds once more before turning toward the river. The weight of his sleepless night was becoming an uncomfortable burden.

"Wait. Please," Davit pleaded as he heard the captain's dismissive words and hurried closer, but the large African's hand shot out and he froze in his tracks.

It was the flash of fear in the boy's eyes, when Jiya raised his hand, that gave Orion pause. Then he noted the tension in the lad's shoulders, the pulsing of the vein in his neck, and the muscles jumping and twitching on his upper legs – all tells of a strong current of nervousness running beneath the cocky facade. Curiosity niggled at the back of his mind. If ever he had a weakness, it was the lure of a riddle.

"What do you want?" he barked at the boy.

This was not at all how Davit had envisioned this conversation would go. He had hoped to sit down with the captain and discuss his future, the way he had with Kai last night. Instead, now he was flapping and floundering like a fish on dry land. His mouth was sticky, and his feet were heavy. No glib words sprang to mind, and he felt oddly ill at ease.

"When you set sail, I want to go with you. I want to become part of your crew," Davit blurted out his desire, cringing inwardly as his voice cracked awkwardly, making him sound like a small child begging for a treat.

Orion shot Jiya a look of pure disbelief.

"Out of the question." He turned and once more tried to head toward the river for his bath but stopped abruptly, feeling his offense set in before turning back to the boy with a scorching glare. Best to scare him off now and get the morning back on track.

True to his nature, Jiya remained silent as he studied the boy.

"You want to join my crew?"

The boy nodded, mistakenly thinking it was a question that needed an answer.

"Every member of my crew was handpicked. By me!" Orion's voice rose as he stabbed himself with his finger in the chest. "Why would I possibly want *you*? What do you have that is so special that it deserves a place among some of the finest sailors out there?" Orion was beginning to warm to this conversation. It was the perfect outlet for his frustrations.

Taking a step toward the boy, he continued: "What do you bring? What use are you to me? You've clearly never set foot on a ship. Therefore, it would be safe to conclude that you will spend the next two weeks hanging over the side, vomiting your insides out. Soon after, if you are still able to remain upright, you will no doubt piss yourself with fear when bad weather churns the waters of the ocean like a witch's cauldron and the wind strong enough to blow you off the deck. Mind you, should that happen, I will not come for you. I will leave you right there in the middle of the ocean and the choice will be yours whether to swim for land, which is a fool's errand, or give up and drown."

Orion looked the boy up and down with an expression that made it abundantly clear he was spectacularly underwhelmed by what he saw. The increase in humidity brought on by the impending rain made the fine sand, misting from his shirt every time he moved, stick to his skin. The chafing of his clothes was only exacerbating his discomfort and shortening his temper.

Davit listened to the tirade; it was not too dissimilar to the chief's reaction the night before. The chief was also quick to react when angered and then words flowed from his mouth without pause, much like the captain's did now. Over the years, he'd learned it was a way to vent frustrations and organize thoughts. As he had not spent enough time in the captain's presence to have done something to frustrate him, he decided to not take the words too personally.

Orion was feeling much better after delivering his set-down. Yet, there was something about the boy that appealed to him, whether it was the adventurous glint in his eye or the way he stood motionless in the face of Orion's anger. The lad had something, and he silently hoped that he would not cower. If he backed down or showed fear, Orion would send him on his way, but the smallest hint of defiance and grit could save him and perhaps grant him his wish.

"It's not about what I bring, but what I can do once I'm there," Davit replied in a deep, confident voice. "I'm strong, a good hunter, and a hard worker," he continued, then swallowed and spoke in a tone that was near sacramental. "And I want to sail that ship." His outstretched finger stabbed the air in the precise direction of where the *As-Sayf* was anchored.

Orion had hoped for a pinch of grit and perhaps a sprinkle of defiance, but this lad seemed to be filled to the brim with both.

"You want to sail *my* ship?" Orion asked in a low and ill-boding voice as he closed the remaining distance between them.

It did not escape his notice that their eyes were level. He was well pleased with the boy's temerity, but cockiness and arrogance were traits best earned and not spewed. Whether or not this boy joined his crew, he could use a lesson in humility. Orion's body tensed with hostility and the air between them thickened with the demand for violence, but to the boy's credit, he remained calm, kept his hands by his sides and stood his ground, not blinking or looking away.

"I do," he said, and his throat bobbed as a dry swallow traveled down its corrugated length.

Orion stared into the unusual green, guileless eyes before him, finding no trace of malice or deceit in them, just youthful stupidity. He could practically feel Jiya's thoughts from behind him. They were short on hands. Their most recent battle had been a bloody one, and he'd lost seven valuable men. This boy could be a handy addition. It would take a lot of work to tame and train him, but the crew would set him straight, given the lad was malleable.

"Do you know how to sail a ship like that?" Orion growled as he raised his eyebrows, knowing full well the answer to his question, but he wanted to cut the boy down a peg or two.

"No," the lad replied, "but you can teach me."

"Do I look like a governess to you?" Orion shouted, then winced as his headache protested the intensity of his question.

"I," the boy cleared his throat and shook his head in a tight, nervous movement. "I don't know what that is. But it sounds bad. So… no?"

At that, Jiya threw his head back and roared with laughter, neatly shattering the tension in the air.

Shortly after Jiya had been rescued from a slave compound in Muscat, Captain De Coninck had hired a governess to see to their education. Mrs. Schoonover was a formidable widow in her fifties, with wide hips, ample bosom, and dark gray hair never not strangled into a tight ball at the base of her head.

Orion had always thought Captain De Coninck ran a tight ship, and he did. That was until he'd met Mrs. Schoonover. That woman had educated him and Jiya with the efficiency of a military general. Her sense of humor was as nonexistent as her charm, which had made her the recipient of many a prank. However, for all her cold, rigid strictness, she had never raised her voice nor her hand at them and never had she taken note of or mentioned the color of their skins.

De Coninck had hired her for a duration of five years which the tenacious woman had seen through to the bitter end. On the day she had left for her new post, she'd departed from their lives with the same sense of order and dignity with which she had entered it.

The boy reached over his shoulder, and the movement drew Orion back to the present. When he brought his hand back he held two freshly killed rabbits, tied with a strip of leather, out to Orion.

Orion regarded the offering, and Jiya's laughter died away. The boy had not come empty-handed. Rabbits were rare in these parts, and taken as a percentage of the lad's belongings, it demanded respect and consideration.

Orion nodded and reached for the rabbits, and the boy's body deflated as the tension flowed from his muscles.

"What is your name?" Orion asked.

"Kwala," the boy replied.

"Where are you from, Kwala?" The boy was an enigma, and Orion's curiosity was stirred more than he would care to admit.

"I lived with a tribe north from here," Kwala replied. Noting the vagueness of the answer, Orion pressed for more.

"Which tribe? And this time, don't hide your answer behind vague words. I have yet to decide what to do with you."

"I lived with the Cochoqua about a day's walk from here." The lie slipped easily past Davit's lips. Even though he wanted to sail with these men, he did not want them anywhere near his tribe.

Orion watched the boy as he spoke. Only a slight flutter of his eyelid finked on the possibility that the truth was either twisted or stretched. He had no desire to run into any of the native tribes; they were aggressive, unpredictable, and formidable, and he was in no mood to kill innocent men, and so he let the lie pass.

"How is it you speak Dutch?"

"I am Dutch. My father was a sailor and when we got sick, the others left us behind. Soon after my father died, the tribe found me on the beach and took me in."

The muscle beneath the boy's left eye was fluttering like the lashes of a flirtatious girl. The lies were a concern, but nothing that could not be ironed out in the future. Everyone had their secrets and trust was earned, not demanded. Worst case, Orion would slit his throat and toss him overboard, but most likely, if the boy turned out to be too contumacious, he could just dump him on the nearest beach.

Orion had made his mind up somewhere between the boy not backing down from the threat of violence and offering the two rabbits. There was nothing, apart from his obvious strength, that promoted him, but Orion's gut was not objecting the decision. If the boy had the stomach for a life at sea and was given the right guidance, he could be shaped into a fairly efficient sailor. Orion cast Jiya a long and pensive look.

"I like him. He's cocky and gutsy," Jiya spoke in Arabic, not taking his eyes from the boy as he answered Orion's silent question. The boy showed no signs of understanding, rather a few wrinkles appeared on his forehead, clearly annoyed at being excluded from the conversation.

"Yes, but I need men, not boys, and I have no desire to teach him the difference between his brains and his balls," Orion replied.

"We can work and train some common sense into him. There is nothing like the deck of a ship to humble and harden a man."

Orion gave his friend a crisp nod and then completely ignored Kwala as he purposefully strode toward the river.

Jiya regarded the boy before him. Kwala was unsuccessful in hiding his fear and Jiya wondered at the source of the distress. He would have thought it made more sense for the lad to be fearful of Orion, and yet his anxiety seemed to have elevated at the captain's departure. Perhaps it was best to ignore the emotions and put the boy to work. The sooner he settled into his new routine, the better. Over time, he would learn that the captain was the last man he should feel comfortable with and that Jiya was the least of his concerns.

"I am Jiya, first officer, and navigator of the *As-Sayf*," Jiya said. "And that is Orion, her captain."

The boy hesitantly extended his hand. Jiya ignored it; instead he clasped Kwala's forearm in a firm grip, guiding the boy to do the same. He noted the slight tremble of the muscles beneath his fingers.

"Will he allow me to join the crew?" Davit asked.

"He will, but if you want his trust, refrain from lying to him in the future."

Jiya watched as the boy's eyes widened, and a blush rose from his neck to his face. Then, for the first time since they noticed him standing on the edge of the beach, the boy lowered his eyes.

"There are some truths that are not mine to tell," Davit said, silently pleading for understanding.

Jiya did not respond. Instead, he pointed to the two cleaned rabbits lying beside the fire.

"Roast those. The captain will want to eat when he returns. You can keep one for yourself."

"I'm not hungry," Davit said and shook his head.

An unbidden image of Sebastiaan instantly filled Jiya's mind as he watched the boy's golden curls move in the wind. Sebastiaan De Vries was a brother to him in every sense but the natural. The ever-present ache in his chest, caused by his absence, intensified at the thought and he turned away, leaving Kwala to his task.

Chapter 4

25 March 1670

It was early morning when Sebastiaan, Van Leyen, and Daka rode into the village of the Cape of Good Hope. The sun had freshly risen over Table Bay, casting the water in a silver-blue sheen. The transformation the tiny settlement had undergone since Sebastiaan and Van Leyen had last seen it was breathtaking. Everything seemed to have shifted on its axis. A sense of hardened determination had replaced the once undercurrent of desperation, evidenced by the fortified structures visible at strategic locations.

A lane lined with oak trees led to the entrance of the Fort De Goede Hoop and its extensive gardens. Three streets now separated the neat, whitewashed brick houses, built in the Dutch style with steep roofs covered in tarred tiles or thatch, each with a sizable vegetable garden stretching in front and extending further at the back.

Amidst all the robust progress, some things remained unchanged. Table Mountain and its hills still protectively hugged the small settlement in its folds. The forest at the mountain's foot was still there, albeit the edge no longer reached the beach but had pulled back in retreat. The beach was still white, the rocks still black, and the waves still boisterous.

They clopped down the dirt road, and like in any small village, the locals noted all newcomers with curiosity, avarice, or weariness. Daka marked every face and detail. His black eyes studying the new environment with the prudence of a battlefield commander. Van Leyen's back was ramrod straight and his expression inscrutable, while Sebastiaan's attention was firmly fixed on the ship, *De Parel* – The Pearl, lying at anchor next to a long and wide jetty that fell into the *new-additions* category.

"John," Sebastiaan called, and Van Leyen pulled alongside him so their knees were almost touching. "Get us the lay of the land and a place to sleep." He gave his old friend a meaningful look.

Van Leyen answered with a single, curt nod and turned his horse around, back the way they'd come.

"Daka," Sebastiaan spoke without looking at his companion. "Find comfort and safety for our horses."

"You know this place better than I ever will, but I hate leaving you here." The African's voice rumbled low, yet Sebastiaan caught the taut thread of tension running through it.

Sebastiaan dismounted and handed the reins to Daka.

"There's no need to be afraid. You're all grown up and well trained. You'll be fine." He shot Daka a sly smile, deliberately misunderstanding the lad's meaning. Daka responded with a sideways glance and a vulgar insult referring to Sebastiaan's inadequate manhood and his father's lack of common sense, all delivered suavely in Arabic. Feigning temporary hearing loss, Sebastiaan gave his horse a good-natured pat on the rump and headed for the jetty.

The bustling crew, hurrying across the decks to secure ropes, stow gear, and ready barrels and crates for offloading, indicated the ship's fresh arrival in the harbor. Sebastiaan tilted his gaze toward the masts, where sailors were yet furling the sails upon the yards.

"Commander Hackius." A voice heavy with authority, that could only belong to the captain, called to a well-dressed gentleman in his late fifties, where he stood near a swing suspended at the ship's side, ready to lower him safely to the jetty below. "Are you ready to go ashore, sir?"

"No, Captain, the sick will go first, followed by my wife, like I've told you several times over the last three days."

"But sir,"

"But Captain, now that we are at the Cape of Good Hope, it is *my* word, and *my* word only, that will hold here. The sick go first."

Sebastiaan watched the exchange with smothered amusement. The captain cast his eyes to the heavens, spotted with tufts of harmless clouds, then barked his orders across the deck. Soon eighteen stretchers were lowered, one after the other, and hastily carried toward the fort, followed by a stately woman in a dark green dress.

Commander Hackius refused the swing and made his way down the ladder with unpracticed but resolute steps. On the last rung, his knee buckled, and his foot slipped. Sensing the catastrophe in the making, Sebastiaan crossed to him in swift strides, slipping his hand under Hackius' elbow to steady him. To all those watching, it looked like an everyday occurrence. As soon as Hackius' balance was restored, Sebastiaan removed his hand and stepped back.

The commander straightened and smoothed his disheveled hair. A slow smile softened the lines of exhaustion around his mouth while his eyes shone with amusement and gratitude as they made a quick study of the man who'd came to his aid.

"Pieter Hackius," the older man introduced himself, and then, with a deep sigh and a quick glance toward the fort, "the new commander. That is, as soon as I inform the current one of the change to his status." A breathy titter accompanied the last statement.

"Sebastiaan De Vries, at your service." Sebastiaan took the hand already extended to him. The other man's grip was firm, but a tremor rippled beneath the surface of the cold skin as he wiped away the sweat beading on his forehead with a white, linen square.

The commander's amusement and gratitude vanished in an instant, replaced by utter bewilderment. His eyebrows shot up together, widening his eyes into near-perfect circles, while his jaw went slack.

"Sebastiaan De Vries?" Hackius repeated. "The long absent owner of De Vries Enterprises in Batavia? I thought you were but a myth, sir, and yet here you stand, the spitting image of your uncle, whom I hold in very high regard, I might add."

Sebastiaan tried to reclaim his hand, but Hackius was still absently clutching it, his mind occupied elsewhere. "Who would have guessed that I would find you here at the Cape of Good Hope of all places, and all this time …" his voice trailed off in wonder. The commander clearly preferred to treat symptoms of surprise with a hearty dose of verbiage.

"I arrived this morning. Not a mere half an hour ago," Sebastiaan said and, with a firm tug, reclaimed his limb.

"Via boat?"

"Via horse."

"There is a tale here, one I am most eager to hear." Hackius' surprise had somewhat worn off, and his curiosity was piqued.

"It is not much of a story, but I will answer any questions you might have, though not here," Sebastiaan said as he glanced down the busy jetty. Sailors and soldiers hurried back and forth, unloading cargo and shouting greetings to soon-to-be new acquaintances and sweethearts, yet not a single official was present to greet the new commander.

"There will, no doubt, be an elaborate dinner tonight at the fort, to welcome me and my wife. Join me as my guest. I will have a room prepared for you; one you may use for as long as you need." Hackius held his breath as Sebastiaan considered the generous invitation.

"I am honored, but perhaps …"

"I insist," Hackius interrupted, sensing Sebastiaan's refusal. "There are several reasons you cannot decline, and I will only enlighten you of the two foremost in my mind." Lifting his forefinger, Sebastiaan was unsure if the gesture was to signal his obedience or mark the count of the first consideration. "One, I wish to repay the kindness you showed me by saving me from certain embarrassment." Seeing that Sebastiaan was not yet swayed to his way of thinking, he lifted a second finger. "And second, I know your uncle well and would not let his nephew sleep in some seedy dockside establishment while I had the means to improve upon his circumstance."

And third, you need an ally, Sebastiaan thought, *and I'm the only person you know.*

"Very well. I accept, and I thank you for your generosity," Sebastiaan acquiesced with a small bow.

At that, the fifth commander of the Cape of Good Hope turned away from the conversation, looked to the fort, straightened his shoulders, patted the satchel hanging by his side and strode with resolve toward his new command.

No sooner had Sebastiaan turned to head back to the village, after meeting the commander, than he saw a woman running down the jetty in a dress of such bright pink that it made his eyes water. Her blond hair had come loose from their bindings and was streaming in her wake. Then, before Sebastiaan could add meaning to the chaos, she crashed into him and those very arms that had moments earlier pushed sailors and soldiers ruthlessly out of her way, wrapped around his body in a tight embrace.

The last woman to have put her arms around him was Danielle, and he thought the ache of that act and the loss thereof lived only in his heart and mind, but the memory sent a burning sensation over his skin as if he had rolled in stinging nettles. It took every ounce of his self-control not to peel the woman from his person and fling her into the water below.

She must have felt his distress, for she released him slowly without stepping back. Sebastiaan waited patiently for her to catch her breath, regain a measure of composure, and come to see she had mistaken him for another.

"It's you!" she huffed, with her chest heaving and her face flushed. Finally, she stepped away from him, straightened her bodice, and then raised both hands to frame his face. "I saw you ride into town earlier. For a moment, I thought it was your uncle, but then I realized it couldn't be. It must be you."

"Little Elsje Boom." Sebastiaan's scrambled thoughts managed to arrange themselves into a workable order. "The last time I saw you, you were sixteen years old."

"Well, you're wrong on two accounts. I'm not so little anymore and go by the name of Elsje Waterman now, have been for nearly fourteen years. And the last time I saw you, you were leaving the settlement, hanging onto your horse for dear life, with John Van Leyen in tow." She hooked her arm warmly through his and led him back to the village.

"Come to my house. I'll make you tea and give you some of that sinfully delicious fruit bread my husband is famous for. It's coming out of the oven as we speak. I can practically smell it from here." It wasn't an invitation, but an order wrapped up in a sunny smile, just like her mother used to do. "Gijs is the settlement's only baker, and I am the seamstress. There is little we do not know, and much I need to tell you before you take another step or breathe another breath in this town."

***

The front room of Elsje's house matched her in every way, from the canary-yellow front door to the multitude of colorful bolts of fabric stacked against the walls and across the long workbench that dominated the center, to the bright red oriental rug that covered most of the floor. A Bengali girl was busy with some task related to sewing, and had Elsje not spoken to her, she would have completely gone unnoticed.

"Rutvi, I'm going to be in the kitchen for a while. Will you see to any clients, please?"

"Of course, mistress," the girl answered in flawless Dutch, giving Sebastiaan a shy smile before returning to her task.

The house was oddly built; it was as if one room gave birth to the next as the need arose. A wide, low arch connected the kitchen and the bakery, and through the back door of the latter, an herb garden spread in all directions. The smell of freshly baked bread and rosemary filled the room and most of the street leading up to the house.

Gijs Waterman commanded the space and his assistants with a calm presence and a deep voice, the type that could hum a baby to sleep.

Introductions were made and for the first time since entering adulthood, Sebastiaan felt small standing next to another man. The hand that engulfed his delivered a firm but gentle grip; the other left a dusting of flour on his wife's cheek.

"How are your parents?" Sebastiaan asked once settled with a steaming cup of tea and several slices of fruit bread that could make a man forget his manners.

"They are well, returned to Holland in '63. Nothing was ever the same again after Van Riebeeck left. They live near my sister Leesa; you'll remember her? Turver passed away some years ago, and Leesa recently remarried. Her new husband is a secretary for the VOC."

"Why did you not follow?"

"We have things keeping us here." A shadow flickered across Elsje's face, like a lone cloud blocking the sun. "Gijs' parents are buried here, and I waited for Da…" She bit her sentence off and raised the cup to her lips to stop herself from saying the rest. Suddenly, Elsje couldn't look Sebastiaan in the eye. She lowered her cup and her finger absently traced the edge of the table. Gijs coughed once, as if to dislodge something sticking to his throat, and a heavy silence settled between them.

"You waited for Danielle," Sebastiaan said after he too had swallowed past the tightness in his voice.

"Every day. Every day I watch the road." She stared out the kitchen window to where the road snaked its way up the side of Lion's Hill. "You know, when I saw you leave all those years ago, blind with rage, so determined. I knew you would find her. I knew." Elsje wiped a tear from her face. "And when I saw you this morning, I've never felt such joy and heartbreak at the same time. I nearly stumbled twice in my haste to reach you, when all the while I wanted to run in the opposite direction."

The silence thickened and once more lay like mud between them.

"How long are you planning to stay?" Elsje asked.

Sebastiaan leaned back slightly, his eyes wandering to the window, "I think I'll stay for a while."

The answer was far too vague to satisfy Elsje, and her husband knew that a thorough interrogation would soon follow.

"You are welcome to stay with us for as long as you need. You and your companions," Gijs said, cutting Elsje off before the next question could escape her. "It's tight. We have three boys all under the age of ten, but we'll make it work."

"Thank you. It is most generous, but I've been invited to stay at the fort."

"Who was the man you spoke to on the jetty?" Elsje asked.

"Elsie-love," Gijs objected to her upfront prying. She deftly ignored his admonition.

"The new commander," Sebastiaan answered, "his honorable Pieter Hackius."

Elsje's eyes shot wide, and Gijs let out a low whistle. "A new commander? That is bound to shake a few things up," Gijs said. "It would explain the order I received not long before the two of you walked in here." Seeing them staring at him, he continued. "Fancy treats and fresh breads for a dinner for eight tonight at the old fort."

"The *old* fort?" Sebastiaan asked.

"Aye," Gijs answered. "You no doubt have seen the new fort, built on the old clearing where the tents used to be?"

Sebastiaan nodded.

"The old one is falling apart around their ears and about six years ago, they started construction on a bigger and sturdier one. They call it the *Castle*." Gijs pronounced the name with exaggerated eminence. "However, the inside is not ready to house the commander just yet. So now everyone refers to the buildings as the *Old Fort* and the *Castle*."

"Sebastiaan," the concern in Elsje's voice drew his attention. "If you have dinner at the fort tonight with seven other people, you need to know what you're walking into. First, tell me. Do you like the new commander?"

Sebastiaan shrugged, "Too soon to tell, but I'm leaning toward 'yes' for now."

"Well, the old one, Jacob Borghorst, is an arse of the first order. He is rude, conceited, obnoxious, and has all the arrogance of a magpie but without the cunning. He is convinced that everyone hates him... well actually, he's not wrong on that account." Gijs cleared his throat with a soft huff, but Elsje continued. "He thinks everybody is always talking about him behind his back or trying to make him look the fool. Not that he needs any help on that front. He's doing a fine job all by himself and needs no assistance." Gijs' chin dropped to his chest, and he shook his head at his wife's point-blank description of the most powerful man at the settlement.

"Then there will be the pastor, Adriaen De Voogd, and don't let his sweet name fool you; he is a nasty bit of work," Elsje continued in the manner of a schoolteacher reciting the times tables. "He is not yet thirty years old but has taken it upon himself to be the guardian of neglected and bastard children, the definition of which depends on his mood of the day. And by 'taking care', I mean he takes them from their mothers and gives them as indentured slaves to other families. In January he gave the three children of a Hottentot woman named Eva to the brothel, after banning her to Robben Island, but that is a story unto itself," she said with a wave of her hand. "He is dangerous, and he can do whatever he wishes because he has the weight of the church at his back and the commander's left tit in his mouth."

"Elsie-love!" The last statement made Gijs' head snap up, and he speared his wife with a warning glare, the effects of which were completely ruined when he gave her a wink. "Have a care, will you?"

"What?" Elsje returned, "It's the truth. But," she went on and once more her face tightened in a stern mien Sebastiaan did not think her capable of, "here is the real threat at the Cape. Alain Du Bois arrived here shortly after the second commander departed. You will remember him?" she asked.

Sebastiaan felt the hairs on the back of his neck rise at the mention of the name. It was the name of the man his uncle would kill on sight without a second thought; the man who'd murdered Danielle's father and escaped without a hint of accusation, and the half-brother to her husband, who was found dead the day after their ill-fated wedding. The very same man who tried to overthrow Van Riebeeck and take control of the Cape, and now he was here and Sebastiaan could not shake the feeling that his goals had not changed.

Elsje continued to describe the man's business influence, noting his role as the most prolific slave trader indirectly tied to the powerful VOC in Holland. Though the Netherlands had banned slavery, the VOC ensured their overseas settlements were well-supplied with free labor, with Du

Bois covertly facilitating a significant portion of that operation.

"He smuggles everything the commander has forbidden us common folk to trade in. We are not allowed to trade with the Hottentot tribes or the incoming ships directly. Forcing us only to trade with the fort, which buys at the lowest possible prices and sells at the highest. But, Du Bois, no, he has the run of the land. He can do whatever pleases him because he is lining Borghorst's very empty pockets; makes him look the other way and influences every law and policy that governs us."

Sebastiaan absorbed the information and listened as Elsje and her husband explained the inner workings of the settlement and how things had gone downhill since Van Riebeeck's departure.

"So, you be careful tonight," she warned, as he rose to take his leave. "And Sebastiaan?" she called after he'd clapped forearms with Gijs. "Some single women at the Cape are struggling widows while others are young and calculating. Tread lightly. They will do anything to have their bellies filled." She stared at him with both eyebrows raised, waiting for him to acknowledge the double meaning of her statement.

"Thank you, Elsje," he said and stooped to kiss her cheek.

At the door Elsje handed him a neatly wrapped parcel containing two new shirts and the order to bring his things in the morning so she could see to his laundry.

Soon after he left the Watermans' house Van Leyen pulled him into the tavern. The words 'The Heart' and a symbol to match were burned into a wooden sign, nailed above the door. They'd opted for a table in the far corner at the back, affording them a clear view of the door and the rest of the establishment without having to look over their shoulders.

Van Leyen told him the pieces that Elsje could not. Who worked for whom and when, along with their estimated income and gambling debt. Who smuggled what, how and from where. Who beat his wife and tupped his slave, and by the end of their late lunch, Sebastiaan knew the workings of the small town as if he had been born there. In return, he told Van Leyen of his meeting with the new commander.

"How is it you've learned so much in such a short time?" Sebastiaan asked between bites of stew and sips of beer. He wasn't hungry and was loath to wash the pleasant aftertaste of Gijs' bread from his mouth, but the beer was surprisingly good.

"This tavern is owned by a woman called Barbara Geems. Do you see the woman over there in the yellow dress?" Van Leyen asked and pointed with his eyes. Sebastiaan followed the gesture to where a woman of middling age and medium build with a sensual sway to the hips was serving a table of off-duty soldiers.

"She looks experienced," Sebastiaan mused.

"That she is and well informed too. She runs the tavern here at the front, and down that hall at the back, a brothel. If you continue right through and out the back door, you'll find her distillery."

"Industrious."

"Indeed."

"So, the question remains, how did you learn so much so quickly?"

"It is surprising how much a small amount of coin, patience, and a willing ear can buy you. Most men come in here needing drink, food, and women, and not necessarily in that order. Very few are interested in talking and even less in listening. While you were at the seamstress's, I offered to fix the stove in the kitchen. It had been blowing smoke all week, and while I worked, she talked." Sebastiaan shook his head and smiled at Van Leyen's methods.

"I can arrange lodging for you and Daka at the fort."

"No, thank you, my friend. We will stay here, and if need be, we'll sleep at the stables. There is not enough money in this world to lure me back to that building anytime soon, if ever at all."

Sebastiaan noted how some serving girls cast the officers and themselves looks of fake innocence laced with coquettish invitations. Others were much more forward and aggressive. Both methods seemed to work with equal success and when the first sailor entered, the entire energy in the room shifted from mildly civil to outright predatory.

"Careful you don't leave here with more than what you entered with."

Van Leyen dismissed Sebastiaan's concerns with a carefree smile. "I don't have the heart for such things."

"It's not your heart I'm worried about."

This time Van Leyen barked with laughter. "I don't take what is not freely offered, and for that, you need a heart. Mine was buried a very long time ago."

"Alright," Sebastiaan said, moving the conversation back to practical concerns. "We need a warehouse, large and close to the water. See what you can find. We'll meet by the horses, first thing tomorrow morning."

Van Leyen scratched his chin, and Sebastiaan dropped a few coins on the table, nodded to the proprietress, and shook his head at a serving girl who rubbed against his arm like a cat soliciting attention. By the time he walked through the stone arch of the old fort, he was already late for dinner.

***

The double doors to the dining hall swung open, announcing the late arrival of the last dinner guest. A profusion of wax candles illuminated the unanimous mixture of curiosity and expectation on the six faces turning toward the mysterious latecomer.

Pieter Hackius, the Cape of Good Hope's newest commander, rose from his seat, walked to the door, and extended his hand. "Good evening, Mister De Vries."

Sebastiaan returned the gesture and, like this morning, the faint tremor belying the commander's troubled health passed between their hands.

Commander Hackius addressed Sebastiaan in front of the dinner company as if they were old friends.

"I'm so glad you could join us. Please," Hackius pointed to the empty chair and place setting to the right of his own. He did not immediately take his seat, and so Sebastiaan remained at his side, noting the seating arrangements. Hackius had been offered the head of the table, as befitted his position, but it was a veiled insult for his back was to the door, placing him more at the foot of the table with the ousted commander at the other end – a petty power play at best.

Sebastiaan's eyes took in the fine attire of those around the table. All the men were choked by the height of fashion, with lace cravats cascading from their necks and cuffs that were going to be in dangerous peril should the entrée be a soup of sorts. In contrast, the shirt he received from Elsje hugged his shoulders comfortably. Its collar was soft and open at the neck, allowing him to breathe and move freely. By all standards, he was dressed like a savage: white shirt, black breeches, boots, and a dagger tucked in the small of his back, no jacket, no lace, no wig, and absolutely no powders of any kind. He relished the contrast.

Hackius pointed to the far end of the table. "May I introduce Mister Jacob Borghorst, our very competent and able former commander?"

The two commanders were of a similar age. Sebastiaan held the man's eye for a few seconds. Even from across the length of the table, which could easily sit twelve, he could see suspicion dancing in Borghorst's eyes. Borghorst made no attempt at civility and slouched deeper in his seat, letting one hand dangle over the armrest as the other toyed with the dull blade of his butter knife. A wrinkling of his long upper lip and a lift of a single eyebrow were the only response Sebastiaan received to his crisp bow.

This was the man who'd lost his entire fortune, forty thousand pounds' worth of precious stones, to the marauding English two years earlier. No wonder he was sour. Losing such a fortune at his age, when he was clearly looking forward to a comfortable retirement, could leave one vulnerable to corruption. An event such as that had the potential to suck the decency right out of a man, should his decency be so idly tethered.

Borghorst was deeply disliked by all - even the surrounding Hottentot tribes had given him the nickname of Siekum. Anything that was ugly, sickly and despicable was called 'Siekum'. Sebastiaan concluded that the loss of one's fortune did not strip away one's character or breeding, it merely shone a light on the fact that it was never there to begin with.

Commander Hackius moved to the next guest, Borghorst's wife, Cornelia. She was not sitting next to her husband but between two other guests and opposite another woman, whom Sebastiaan recognized as Hackius' wife. Borghorst's eyes snapped from Sebastiaan to his wife, judging her reaction to the introduction. However, Cornelia never lifted her eyes from her empty plate, with tense shoulders she kept her head down and her hands in her lap.

"My pleasure, Madam." Sebastiaan received a barely perceivable nod in response.

It was about to get interesting. The next person to be introduced would be the most powerful man, after the commander. Would it be the businessman, the pastor, or the surgeon? Sebastiaan had placed his bet on the businessman, whereas Van Leyen had put his money on the pastor, but, thanks to Elsje, Sebastiaan was privy to information Van Leyen was not. Just like never walking into a room without knowing who was inside, he never placed a bet he was not sure of winning.

Hackius raised an outstretched hand to Du Bois – and there he was, the one who, until that morning, had held the commander's strings tightly wrapped around his fingers.

"Mister Alain Du Bois," Hackius announced.

Sebastiaan caught how the blood had drained from Du Bois' face the moment he'd stepped into the room. A vein at the man's neck bulged and pulsed with rapid beats, as though, in an unguarded moment, he believed Davit De Coninck had strode into the dining hall, rousing his instincts of caution and self-preservation to clamor in alarm. But years of cunning and deceit kept Du Bois deathly still, trained to avoid attention when cornered. When Hackius presented Sebastiaan as De Vries to Borghorst before all others, the name sounding naught like De Coninck, Sebastiaan noted a soothing calm settled over the old crook. He'd probably realized it could not be De Coninck — the man across the table was twenty years too young, perhaps the result of a careless night decades ago, a consequence De Coninck was likely not even aware of. Yet, as that thought took root, another weaseled its way through the cracks in his logic. Sebastiaan, heir to De Vries Enterprises, a fact no soul in the room could ignore, with Davit De Coninck at the helm in his absence, saw all prospects of Du Bois' tranquil self-assurance evaporate.

A faint crease worked its way between Du Bois' eyes, his lips thinning, his rattled senses the sole cause of his vexation.

At their introduction, Du Bois rose from his seat and, interestingly enough, so did the rest of the men at the table. Sebastiaan ignored them and kept his attention on Du Bois, who was in the throes of a deep and gracious bow.

"It is my honor, sir," Du Bois said as he straightened. His shoulders relaxed, and his chin tilted at just the right angle, allowing him to look down his aristocratic nose at Sebastiaan despite being a few inches shorter.

Sebastiaan greeted Du Bois with a pleasant yet neutral expression. Years of fighting, gambling, and negotiating with men far beyond Du Bois' reach and capabilities had given him firm control over his emotions and reactions. Sebastiaan's brow was smooth, with not the slightest wrinkle or crease to express his thoughts. He kept his jaw relaxed, ensuring not a single muscle dared to flutter. The corners of his lips were slightly tilted upward, suggesting the beginnings of a smile or simply the play of the candlelight. The look in his eyes was steady, without being interested or bored. He could see the calculations and deductions flashing through Du Bois' eyes, but he gave him nothing of himself.

Then Hackius pointed to the man at Borghorst's left, opposite Du Bois, who must be Adriaen De Voogd, God's representative at the settlement, if his pious face and self-righteous posture were any indication.

"Adriaen De Voogd, our esteemed pastor," Hackius said and Sebastiaan offered a nod in greeting, receiving the same in return.

Hackius turned to his left. "Pieter Walrandt, our capable physician." Sebastiaan smiled at the way Hackius praised each man like they were children who needed to be treated equally but individually. The surgeon mistook the gesture and visibly preened at being the only one to receive such a warm expression from the mysterious latecomer.

"And last, but far from least, my dear wife, Alida." Mrs. Hackius openly showed her pleasure at being introduced to her husband's new friend.

"Mister De Vries." He took the raised hand and kiss the air above it.

"Your servant, Madam." Taking his seat between the new commander and his wife, he realized he was unwittingly placed in mirror position to Du Bois.

Borghorst snapped his fingers at the servant by the door, a sharp command to serve the table, but the servant stood unmoved, his face a mask of indifference. Hackius waited until a deep flush colored Borghorst's face at being ignored and then he calmly turned, addressed the man by his name, and asked him to serve the entrée.

One-nil in favor of the new governor – two, if he counted his own invitation – Sebastiaan quietly thought as his eyes drifted to the two lion skins draped upon the wall. Their pelts gleamed a muted gold in the candlelight.

The first course arrived, and delicate bowls of turtle soup were placed in front of each guest.

"Turtle soup, sir, made with a little Madeira," the head servant spoke to Hackius as if he were the only person in the room.

"Thank you, Joseph," Hackius replied, dipping his spoon, and closing his eyes as he took his first mouthful. The rest of the table took their cue, and the dinner commenced.

The soup was exceptional. Clearly Mrs. Boom was no longer commanding the fort's kitchen, Sebastiaan thought with a suppressed grin. If it was up to her, they'd be dining on a generous piece of flatbread washed down with a mug of pea soup. He couldn't imagine that force of nature being bothered with turtle soup, much less adding Madeira to it, no matter how much it enhanced its depth or added to its complexity.

Once past the introductions and the entrée, conversation at the table found an easy rhythm. Most of it centered around the new commander, but now and then minor issues or points of interest regarding the settlement arose as well. Nothing too serious or demanding, simply seeds sown for future harvest. Borghorst seemed to be the only oddity jumping from one conversation to the next, ensuring nobody was talking about him or trying to pull the wool over his eyes.

Alida tried a few times to engage Cornelia with light remarks, but failed at every attempt to raise the woman's eyes from her plate or her lap, and so she settled on exchanging a few pleasantries with Sebastiaan, before realizing just how hungry she was and just how good the meal was. After that, she paid little attention to the men at the table.

"Mister De Vries," Borghorst called, effectively ending all other conversations. "Rumor has it you've spent the bulk of your adult life traveling up and down the African east coast."

Since it was a statement rather than a question, Sebastiaan did not reply. Instead, he cut a decent portion of venison from his plate, loaded the morsel with currants and berries, which he scraped from the thick sauce covering the dish and shoved it in his mouth. Only then did he look at Borghorst while leisurely chewing, creating an uncomfortable hitch in the conversation, which he knew would heighten the man's already frazzled state.

Borghorst harrumphed and continued, "I can imagine that such a pursuit would hold appeal since your late father worked tirelessly to secure your future and your uncle is currently doing the same to maintain it."

Again, no question, so he took another bite. The discomfort at the table rose like the temperature in a burning building. The physician shifted in his seat, Alida snapped Sebastiaan a quick, sideways glance, and Commander Hackius looked ready to put an end to Borghorst's rudeness.

"What I meant to say was," Borghorst continued, and Sebastiaan good-naturedly leaned forward in anticipation of the long-awaited point to the random observations. "Did you set out to learn anything new, in the form of an interesting scientific or anthropological discovery, or were you simply indulging your boyhood fantasies of adventure? I hope it to be the former rather than the latter. It would seem a terrible waste of effort otherwise."

Oh, the joys of being an idiot. One never knew when one was going too far, Sebastiaan thought as he wiped his mouth with the white, stiffly starched linen napkin and gently laid it in his lap again. By now, everyone at the table was looking at him with varying degrees of sympathy, all except Du Bois, whose eyes had frosted over, gleaming with condescension and specks of glee at his lapdog's performance.

"Well, Mister Borghorst, if you put it that way, it does sound rather frivolous, doesn't it?" Sebastiaan huffed a self-deprecating laugh and raised his glass. "To boyhood enthusiasm and often pointless pursuits!" he called. Hackius burst out laughing, then echoed the toast.

"To pointless pursuits," Hackius rose from his seat and lifted his glass to Borghorst.

The insult landed precisely where it was aimed, leaving Borghorst resembling a chameleon in a flower patch. His mildly pale skin turned bright red, then a sickly shade of puce, before it arrived back at the start and went as white as a bedsheet. Everybody at the table was aware of Borghorst's loss of fortune, and should anyone have forgotten, their memory was now refreshed.

All except Borghorst and his wife stood and raised their glasses to the toast.

"Mister De Vries," Hackius drew Sebastiaan's attention as they settled back in their seats and laughter died down. "In your travels, have you ever come across a place called Monomotapa, the famed city of gold? From what I understand, several of the commanders who came before me have sent expeditions to the interior, trying to locate it, but all have failed. Now, we are beginning to suspect that the place is more myth than reality. A mere figment of the imagination on the part of the Portuguese. What is your opinion?"

Sebastiaan had been to Monomotapa twice and had been warmly received and richly rewarded on both occasions. The first time, he'd helped defend the city against an attack from a neighboring tribe and on the second visit he'd returned the chief's youngest daughter, the apple of his eye, after she'd been taken as a slave. Monomotapa was currently a tribe in turmoil, plagued with infighting, rapacity, and strong interference from Arabia. Adding the greed of the VOC to the mix would not aid in a peaceful conclusion to their troubles. Sebastiaan had no desire to disclose any knowledge about the place or its location, for it would only lead to one end, and that was, come morning, he would find himself on horseback leading an expedition for the better part of a year.

His head was shaking long before he could utter his thoughts. A sip of wine gave him time to formulate his answer, and when he spoke, he sounded bored and nonchalant.

"I've heard many stories of such a place, Commander Hackius, but in all honesty, those stories are often the result of too much drink. Personally, I believe it is a myth and nothing more."

Hackius curled his lips as one would upon discovering that the last slice of cake was already taken. "I would have loved to be the one who discovered it." He sounded no worse for the loss of the opportunity.

Sebastiaan chuckled and raised his glass. "To lost treasures," he said and then drained it in one gulp.

***

"I did mention we were looking for a warehouse, right?" Sebastiaan squinted at the dilapidated shack teetering on the edge of an equally fragile jetty. "How is it still standing?" he muttered.

"How was your dinner?" Van Leyen asked.

"Insightful. How was yours?" Sebastiaan returned.

"Insightful," Daka, instead of Van Leyen, spoke absently causing both men to stare at him with identical questioning frowns.

Realizing that the dreamy look on his face and the out-of-turn answer revealed perhaps a touch more about his evening than he would have liked, Daka coughed and pointed to the deficient structure.

"Seems rather small, doesn't it?"

Sebastiaan narrowed his eyes at the younger man.

"It was the only thing I could find that was reasonably close to the water," Van Leyen defended his find.

"Well, if we don't do something about it, a mild southeaster will blow it straight into the water." Sebastiaan crouched to peer beneath the jetty and gauge the work needed to make it usable.

"Never mind the southeaster, a firm fart would see the job done," Daka added his assessment. Van Leyen frowned, then slapped him upside the head. Sebastiaan laughed.

"We'll have to rebuild it." The location was excellent, an hour's ride from the settlement, and secluded enough for a ship to rest unmolested by the high winds and waves. The forest provided further privacy and shelter, and for what Sebastiaan had in mind, both would be a requirement.

"Aye, back to the fort you go," Van Leyen said as he kicked a large pebble into the water. "Secure us this gem. I don't think you'll have a hard time convincing whoever owns it to part with it."

Sebastiaan stared out over the ocean. Something about the place felt right; he could find peace here.

Chapter 5

avit's body folded inward. His arms flew out to the side, and he lunged back, narrowly escaping the swinging cutlass, as the African advanced on him spitting lightning and growling thunder. The severed air whispered across his naked chest, and his skin puckered in the wake of the passing blade. His own impotent weapon was glaring up at him from the deck planks. He cursed the useless thing that had, only moments earlier, been knocked from his hand. The laughter and cheering of the surrounding sailors ennobled the foul deed.

The speed of the crisscrossing blade left him no room to sidestep or concoct a scrap of defense. Davit felt trapped and panic was beginning to take its toll. Twice he'd bumped into a sailor at his back and on both occasions, he was ruthlessly shoved back into the path of the blade he was hopelessly trying to escape. He had been set upon by Jiya the moment his feet hit the deck after jumping down from the shroud, having won the race against three other sailors, to see who could descend the fastest. At first, he'd thought it was just another unexpected training exercise, but he'd swiftly been dispossessed of that misconception. This fight was primal and raw.

A murderous light shone in Jiya's black eyes, and each swing of the cutlass was becoming more powerful, more deadly. The fight was lost the moment Davit had lost his weapon, but still Jiya advanced, giving no quarter, no advice, and no words of encouragement. Hatred made Jiya's nostrils flare and his lips pull back, exposing white teeth shining in the dark face. Every feature was contorted with savagery.

This was his friend, his mentor. It had taken Davit nearly two months to learn to trust the mountain of a man. He'd been raised on tales of black-skinned devils. Jiya had just proven them true. The suddenness and brutality of this attack were proof that he'd made a grave mistake in trusting this man.

Davit's mouth was dry, and his feet felt heavy and sluggish, like every stride was trudged through gory mud. He saw the laughing faces of the sailors as they cheered Jiya on, but no sound reached him, only the infernal hammering of his heart and the rushing of his blood mixed with his wheezing breath as it bounced back and forth between his ears. Then his foot hooked on an uneven deck plank. He lost his balance and fell backward. The wall of the bulwark slammed across his shoulders, keeping him upright, and still Jiya advanced. The last Davit saw before he closed his eyes was the sunlight glinting off the blade as it descended toward him.

The blow landed full on his nose, snapping his head back. White-hot pain blossomed in his face, forcing his eyes wide, and blood gushed from his nose.

A few sharp barks from the boatswain dispersed the sailors, leaving the combatants to their one-sided duel. Jiya retreated to where Davit's cutlass lay. With the tip of his blade, he nudged it up and flicked it to Davit. Catching the weapon mid-air took an embarrassing amount of concentration.

"*Never* close your eyes in a fight!" Jiya roared.

Humiliation, pain, and confusion coalesced into a noxious sludge of rage that pulsed like a war drum through Davit's veins, but common sense prevailed, and he firmly pushed the emotions back into the bilge of his guts. The time would come for him to dredge it up and put it to good use. He would not be the runt forever. He wiped his face, which did nothing to better his condition and only resulted in him smearing his forearm with blood. It was as if a cork had been pulled from a keg, and blood kept pouring from his nose.

Jiya walked toward him, and the relaxed casualness of his gait made the banked inferno inside Davit flare. Ignoring the metallic taste in his mouth and his speckled vision, he pushed himself away from the railing and raised his cutlass, but the blade was once more knocked from his hand as if he were a helpless babe.

Two large hands reached for his face and Davit tried to slap them away. "Easy."

Jiya's calm voice drilled through the ringing in his ears. Then he felt the thumbs pressing firmly on the twin dents in his lower jaw.

"I will kill you," Davit vowed through clenched, blood-stained teeth, as the pressure on his jaw increased. "By all the gods, I will kill you."

"Aye, that is a good start," Jiya said, as he kept the pressure on the pulsing veins, choking the blood flow to Davit's face. "A man must have a vision. But first, such a man must learn to keep control of his emotions and retain his weapon." The last three words were spoken individually and clearly. "Then he can embark on foolish missions, such as killing his tutor and the ship's best navigator."

Removing his hands from Davit's face, Jiya stood back and studied the young man's nose until he was certain most of the bleeding had stopped.

"Tomorrow we will try again," he said with a pensive look then extended his hand. "I am not your enemy, Kwala."

Could have fooled me, Davit thought, but swallowed the dismissive scoff that came so easily when his hackles were up, and clasped forearms with Jiya.

Movement caught Davit's attention and, to his chagrin, he found Orion staring at him from across the deck. The captain stood with arms folded across his chest, eyes hard and cold, face stark, revealing nothing of the disgust and disappointment he must surely be feeling.

Orion's gaze traced the streaks of blood running from the boy's upper lip down his chest to the thick, dark puddles pooling on the deck at his feet as he approached them.

"Are we still out of sight?" Orion gingerly stepped over the blood to stand beside Jiya while studying the ocean.

"Aye, she is still bobbing just over the horizon. She changed direction twice since yesterday, but those were merely course adjustments and not evasive maneuvers. Her handling is sloppy and uncertain, making me think she is being handled by an unfamiliar crew," Jiya answered.

"What are we talking about?" Davit asked.

"*We* are not talking. Go wash your face and get a bucket and brush to clean up this mess," Orion barked and watched with satisfaction as the boy's spine straightened with the intended offense.

"How is he doing?" Orion turned to Jiya once Davit disappeared into the forecastle.

Jiya contemplated the question, his attention fixed on the clear blue sky. The wind was dying down. Hopefully, there would still be enough of it left after sunset to push them closer to their quarry. If the wind dropped too soon and the distance to the galleon was too great for the rowboats, the attack would have to be postponed. Still, he had faith in the 'blacks.' They would deliver even on an ocean as smooth as satin. Years ago, Orion had commissioned the creation of the black silk sails, with no thought spared to the cost of such an extravagance. Jiya still experienced the odd chest pain at the memory of the king's ransom they'd paid for the set. However, they very quickly proved to be an invaluable addition, for they rendered the ship near invisible at night and could bulge on the pique of a brittle cough.

"Are you going to answer me, or do you need me to repeat the question?" Orion demanded, his voice tight with pent-up frustration. It had been months since their last raid and the ennui brought by the normal day-to-day grind was becoming unbearable. There was a similar restlessness among the crew. The men needed to vent their choler. Their blades had been dry for far too long.

Jiya exhaled slowly through his nose.

"He gets on well enough with the crew. There were a few scrapes early on with some of the younger sailors. Nothing serious, just a flexing of the muscles and a test to see who could piss the furthest."

"Did he win?"

"Might have. The men broke things up before a winner could be decided;

no need to have anyone grow an untimely ego."

Orion nodded.

"He helps out in the galley a lot."

"He aspires to be a cook?" Orion spat. He had nothing against the occupation, but he definitely had had a different path in mind for the boy.

"No," Jiya huffed his amused denial, "I think Harja let him snitch morsels from the food stores."

Orion did not object to the offense and remained silent as he listened to Jiya's report. It was disconcerting how the boy's antics amused him. Never before had he felt anything more than obligation and responsibility for his men. Jiya was the exception. They had grown up like brothers and the bond had only strengthened over time. But there was something about this half-tamed, barely civilized boy that nagged at a long-forgotten memory of himself – a familiarity, an inexplicable feeling of kinship. Orion shook his head to clear his mind. In a few years, he would turn thirty. Perhaps he was becoming sentimental in his old age.

"He's good at rigging, has no fear of heights. Can dance up there with the best of them, even in high winds. With the understanding of navigation and the calculations involved, the boy could do with a bit more struggling. He's shite at carpentry though. I swear Orion, he does not have the sense the Almighty gave a flea when it comes to carving and mending. How Niccolò hasn't killed him yet is a question I would like an answer to."

"He lacks patience, not sense," Orion unwittingly defended Davit's shortcoming.

"Aye, that could be it," Jiya conceded, "his Italian is improving, though. The boy has a sharp ear and a quick tongue."

"How is that possible? I've yet to hear Niccolò speak more than five words at a time."

"He speaks to Kwala."

"How is he with a blade?" Orion asked and watched as concern crept over Jiya's face.

"He's not ready," Jiya replied.

"Why the hell not?" Orion barked. "It's been months."

Orion followed the boy's path as he crossed the deck at a crisp pace. Davit had a natural agility and in the months since he came onboard, his body had undergone a dramatic change. The youthful frame had hardened, his shoulders stretched a few notches wider and the groove hiding his spine had deepened, but none of that meant anything if he could not hold his own with a blade in his hand.

"Something is stopping him from advancing. I can't put my finger on it," Jiya said. "He has the ability, I know he does. He's got balls bigger than he needs at his age, but he is not used to losing or being humiliated." Seeing Orion's deepened frown, Jiya scratched his head in agitation. "Once he realized the others were watching, his mind raced in all directions, causing him to lose his focus." Jiya shook his head and ran a frustrated hand down his face.

Orion had a fairly good idea what the root of the problem was. He'd noticed the boy's struggles to fit in with the crew. That he still slept every night on the upper deck, and not in his hammock, was a testament to his status as an outsider. No doubt he'd been an outsider all his life, what with his blond hair and green eyes and being raised by an African tribe. Orion's crew was a patchwork of Babylonian proportions, with nearly every race this planet offered. The cook was Javanese, his boatswain Slavic, his carpenter Italian, and the smattering continued down the ranks. Despite this, Kwala's peers continued to shun him for being a savage.

Orion climbed the steps to the quarterdeck, his hand gliding over the intricately carved banister. The banister itself was an exquisite piece of art, with its newel sculpted in the lifelike shape of a woman, reaching no higher than his lowest rib. The wood was shaped and polished to resemble sheer fabric clinging to her body, as if caught in a strong breeze, outlining and emphasizing every hollow and curve. The rest of the fabric, along with her hair, flowed behind her to create the smooth surface of the handrail, and the individual balusters. It was but one of Niccolò's masterpieces that decorated the *As-Sayf*.

A gentle breeze blew from the African mainland, warm and pregnant with moisture. Orion closed his eyes and drew a lungful of the sweetness.

The gradually diminishing ghost of the moon that haunted the daylight hours was nowhere in sight. Tonight would be as dark as sin. There was nothing better for an attack than a windless night with thick and heavy sea fog closing in around them, muffling sound and obstructing visibility.

***

Orion stared at the four faces before him. They were a frightful sight. These were hardened and disciplined men who lived by the sword. Sailing was merely a means to an end. This never-ending pirate plague that devastated the Mediterranean and threatened every European ship that dared to cross the oceans had ravaged each of them in some form or another. They all had a score to settle, and Orion felt pride swell inside him as he gave each man a hard look. Dressed in black from head to toe, their faces and exposed skin smeared with a mixture of fat and soot leaving only their eyes and teeth to shine white in the dark. No one spoke a word. Their breaths were even and controlled as they leaned back and forth in perfect unison, propelling the rowboat over the quiet water. Another three boats followed in their wake. The sides of the boats were rimmed and padded with rolls of tarred sails, ensuring their meeting with their target was as soundless as could be. It was only the soft scrape of the oars that signaled the galleon's impending doom.

They'd snuck up on the ship close to midnight. Leaving the As-Sayf a mile behind, shrouded in fog and nearly invisible, they'd rowed to their prey in under ten minutes. The sea fog had closed in and lay like a woolen blanket over the water and, together with the new moon not yet born, lent an eerie sense of foreboding to the black night. On nights like these, Orion preferred to stay far away from the coastline and doubled the guards in the lookouts, but the Ottoman pirates took no such precautions.

Until a second ago, there was only one man in the lookout's basket high on the mizzenmast, but he now draped over the side of the crow's nest like forgotten laundry on a rainy day. The bolt from Niccolò's crossbow neatly struck between his eyes, the shaft propping his head away from the basket's side, leaving him to stare sightlessly at the puddle of blood dripping from his mortal wound onto the deck below.

The four rowboats surrounded the galleon like ducklings would their mother. Each carried four two-man teams armed with two crossbows, one man tasked to fire the grappling hook – muted with cotton – and the other to fire a bolt at an enemy, should one threaten his mate as he climbed the newly secured rope.

Orion felt Jiya stir behind him as their rowboat kissed the side of the galleon. A fraction of a second later, grappling hooks traveled in straight lines to sink into the unsuspecting gunwale of the upper deck bulwark. They latched on with a few dull clunks. Orion gave the rope a firm tug, ensuring it was securely fastened before he became a mere shade moving up the side of the ship.

The first four men slithered over the bulwark within a breath of each other. Crouching low, they melted into the shadows, weapons drawn as they waited for their teammates to emerge. Less than a minute after the rowboats touched the side of the *Vlieland*, thirty-two heavily armed and highly trained assassins had spread over the unfamiliar upper deck, searching for targets.

The theme for the night's attack was stealth, rather than the usual shock and awe in which his crew excelled. How long their presence would go unnoticed was still an ongoing bet between him and Jiya. Orion had his four reals on a solid thirty seconds whereas Jiya was more optimistic and had stretched his faith to about two minutes.

Orion won the bet when a panicked *"Ya Allah!"* preceded a gurgling noise as the next warning words were cut short by a blade to the larynx.

They had estimated there might be double the usual number of combatants to deal with, since a single Ottoman galley could not overpower a galleon with the *Vlieland's* firepower. They were not wrong in their assumptions. Pirates oozed from every crevice, and soon the decks were crowded with flashing blades and leaking bodies.

At the start of the fray, Orion was aware of Jiya fighting by his side, but they soon became separated, and he found himself alone and fending off three attackers. Not a bad scenario, considering the alternative. One-on-one fights tended to take a turn toward the tedious fairly quickly. He was handed an unfair amount of battle sense, the ability to read and sum up a fight or an opponent immediately and accurately. There was not much to it; he could take the measure of his opponent within the first few swings of the arm, then a few shuffles of the feet usually confirmed his suspicions, and from there it was a simple matter of waiting for an unguarded opening in which to end it all. It was rare to find an opponent who offered a few surprises and added a bit of spice to the fight. Those occasions were rare enough to count on one hand. But three opponents, now that made things interesting, so many more variables to consider and strategies to test.

Orion deliberately hastened his breathing and rounded his eyes. He even went as far as dragging his back foot, as if plagued by fatigue. His thespian enervation did not go unnoticed. Victory lit in his opponents' eyes at his signs of panic. He was laying his trap, and it was working beautifully. Soon they would grow complacent, thinking him an easy kill. The tells were already there in the way the one in the middle sported a cruel smile, flashing teeth that really should not be put on display.

Orion slowed his movements, drawing them closer as bloodlust pulsed through his body, fueling his daring, sharpening his mind, and numbing his heart. His need for violence was a never-ending demon scratching the inside of his belly, clawing and groaning to be heard – always goading and haunting him.

He was playing a teasing game of tactical maneuvering with the three men who were trying to circle him like a pack of hungry dogs. He kept them at bay with his blades, sidestepping and shortening the arc of his swings, herding them into a cramped corner of the deck. There, they would be neatly boxed in by the shrouds and overturned barrels, leaving very little room to launch an effective attack without harming each other.

Too late did the leader of the three realize he needed to break free from the others if he wanted to draw first blood or, better yet, claim the kill. Fate and Orion's careful manipulations forced the man to step over a coil of rope. Seeing the man's mental machinations play out on his face, Orion opened his guard slightly, balancing himself neatly on the balls of his feet, and waited. The moment the man's foot stepped over the coil, Orion delivered a short kick dead center between his legs, with enough force to have him choke on his balls one after the other. The man involuntarily hunched over as the muscles in his abdomen and thighs contracted in response to the radiating pain, inconveniently impaling himself on the short blade of Orion's dagger as it swung upward.

With the death of the first and the hasty departure of the second, the third man was now facing Orion by himself. The confidence that had shone so brightly from him before, now drastically dimmed with the blood of his fallen comrade warming his bare feet.

"Were there women on this ship when you took it?" Orion growled his question in Arabic. Surprise flashed across the pirate's face at hearing his own language spoken without the blemish of an accent.

"Answer me!" Orion roared. The man nodded. "Did the men rape them?" The question was softly delivered, only enhancing the deadly intent behind the words. The man breathed hard but kept his mouth shut and his head still.

Orion stepped closer, caressing the underside of the man's jaw with his cutlass blade.

"They did," the man breathed, too afraid to nod or shake his head.

"Did you participate?" Orion asked and his voice held a hint of consolation, soothing the man's jitters.

"No," the man whispered.

"Don't lie to me," he pressed as the man failed to mask the guilty look on his face. "Answer me truthfully, and I will spare your life." The man nodded. "Say the words," Orion demanded.

"There were three women. Two are dead, one still lives," the man spluttered. Hope was giving him courage and his tongue a mind of its own. "She is in the hold with the crew, I swear."

Orion had once seen the body of a girl raped to death. Both hips were broken. It was a sight that had stayed with him to this day.

He nodded at the confession, softening his mien and reaching out with his right hand as if to embrace the man and, with his left, he drove his dagger deep into the man's belly, ripping him open from his navel to his breastbone. Orion closed his eyes for a moment as his own blood found a measure of peace.

Orion wondered what had happened to his second pirate. The man seemed to have vanished. It was a concern, for he had little desire to have his Achilles tendons severed by a blade licking out from the shadows where the bastard could potentially lie in wait. He softly stepped over the bodies at his feet and moved to where the deck was open and uncluttered.

Searching the shadows for a disturbance, Orion noted the out-of-place water droplets hanging on the inside of the bulwark, suggesting that something wet had made its way over the side and onto the ship. Curiosity made his brows twitch together as he stared at the moisture dripping onto the deck. A muted disturbance sounded to his left, and he spun in its direction, in time to see the body of a pirate sink to the floor, revealing the boy with his primitive round-headed club. *Kwala!*

Disbelief and anger vied for dominance; anger won out. How is it possible for his word to have been so blatantly and casually ignored? He had ordered the child to stay behind and help guard the ship. The discordant glint in the boy's eyes at the time had amused him. Never would he have thought that the little shit stain would defy him. There was not a man on his crew who'd dare to do so, for he would flog the flesh from their backs until the ridges of their spines sparkled in the sunlight.

Orion opened his mouth to shout at the boy just as Kwala engaged another pirate. A man came at him, swinging his powerful cutlass. The blade flashed in the flickering light of the lanterns. The pirate was *not* of insignificant size. He stood a good head above Kwala and easily weighed twice as much. Orion's anger took a step back to let alarm propel him forward. He vaulted the barrels that, moments earlier, had played so well into his hand, but were now an obstacle, and sprinted toward Kwala.

Distracted, Orion came to a halt, his arms swinging ineffectively at his sides while his eyes were fixed on the scene before him, not too different from the canonical David and Goliath. Silently, he prayed for a similar outcome.

Kwala swung his round-headed club in a movement so fast it didn't register until Orion heard the crack of the pirate's knee. The man stumbled as his balance was instantly compromised, his hand opened to cushion his fall, but before his blade could clatter to the deck, Kwala was already pulling his dagger free, dark with the blood from the man's shredded liver.

The boy did not spare the man a second glance, not even blinking to see if he was dead or dying, instead he moved on to his next adversary. His strides were cocksure and decisive, leaving wet footprints in their wake. Orion watched as the muscles on the boy's legs bulged and flexed when he lowered himself to move more efficiently. Droplets gleamed on his bare torso, his soaked pants clinging to his frame.

Kwala must have swum the distance from the *As-Sayf*, meaning the boy had swum over a mile, climbed the ropes, landed on the deck of the enemy ship and still he showed no signs of exhaustion but fought with the economy of a seasoned warrior. Once more the sound of a snapping bone reached Orion, and again he watched as the boy crouched low, reached under the pirate's guard and delivered an inerrant deadly strike. Not a single strike of his blade was wasted on non-lethal cuts. Each was perfectly aimed at either the groin, the throat, or the heart. A few found their mark in the liver, leaving the victim writhing at his feet before being delivered from his agony by a deathblow to the head.

Orion could feel the fight starting to shift. Soon the ship would be theirs. Kwala was fighting with cold calculation and intense focus. He was closing in on his next target which, in the current instant, was a group of pirates circling Jiya. Two of the men had their backs to Kwala, blissfully unaware of the impending devastation bearing down upon them. Orion did not doubt that Jiya could hold his own against the men and was in no immediate danger, but the addition of Kwala would make for an entertaining spectacle.

Orion moved into the deep shadows with his back protected against the bulwark as he watched the boy fight; it was like seeing a symphony come to life. Every part of the boy's body moved independently, and yet the result was a work of art complete in its perfection and purity.

Kwala drove the perfectly round head of his *knobkerrie* into the temple of one man, cracking the skull, then moved on to the next, his arms moving without pause, delivering blows and simultaneously driving his dagger forward.

Shaking his head with incredulity, Orion studied his every action. Kwala favored small movements, conserving his energy, keeping his limbs tight and controlled. He was remarkably nimble and light on his feet.

A blade swung perilously close to Orion's left ear. Frowning at the unexpected attack, he sidestepped and found the pirate he had completely forgotten about. Panic was burning in the man's eyes and his attack was more frantic than tactical. Orion killed the man with two powerful swings of his cutlass and a quick stab of his dagger before returning his attention to Kwala.

***

Davit had swum a mile through black water and still breathed easy. He scaled the hull to its midpoint, gun ports giving him purchase, then spotted the blackened rope. Latching onto the rope, he'd practically run up the side. One clean pull vaulted him over the rail—feet never touching wood— dagger already half-drawn before his soles hit the deck.

He stilled for a moment as he took in the scene before him. The pocket of darkness where he stood were quiet and for a sour heartbeat panic whispered that he was too late.

Lanterns swung overhead, spilling light across the *Vlieland's* decks, the air already heavy with the smell of blood. He searched the shadows before daring to move forward. He had boarded the ship blind with no idea what he'd find once he cleared the bulwark, but luck was on his side and so far, his presence went unnoticed.

Dead ahead, Orion was engaged by three men. Davit saw no signs of distress. In fact, Orion looked downright bored. He moved away from the lopsided fray, knowing that if Orion spotted him, his corpse would hit the deck before being joined by the three pirates, currently grinning at their executioner. Also, interfering in Orion's fight would be the highest form of disrespect he could pay his captain – best to find his own prey.

Adjusting his eyes to the faint orange light, he detected movement to his right. A man was crouching low and closing in on the *As-Sayf's* cook, who was already heavily engaged, swinging his cutlass like he was preparing a carcass for the pot. Davit's left hand closed around the handle of his club and his right had a firm grip on his dagger. As the man straightened, he closed the distance with a few quick strides, stepped onto a crate which launched him the extra few inches he needed to bring his club down on the back of the man's head. The wet crack of the skull suggested an injury that would most likely have been lethal, but the head tilted at an odd angle, which gave Davit the opportunity to reach across and sink his blade where he knew the jugular vein pulsed beneath the skin.

Finding his first kill had opened the door to the rest of the battle. Davit had been in battles before when neighboring tribes had tried to steal their cattle, but never had he seen a battle like this. The carnage of it was astounding in its speed and brutality. The sound of blades clashing was so much harsher than the muted wood-on-wood sounds he was used to.

A large man took the place of the one he'd just felled and came at him with a feral, blood-splattered face. The man was fast but overconfident in his size and obvious physical superiority. He rolled the heavy blade across his knuckles with lazy precision, letting the curve flash once in the lantern light. He was an overeager attacker and Davit allowed for a large gap to stretch between them, wanting the brute to thrust. The man took the bait and pounced; his meaty arm swung out in a powerful arc. Davit took a quick step to the side, slamming the round head of his club neatly into the man's kneecap, a sharp crack signaling the success of his strike. He brought the club up again and blocked the oncoming blade, the force of the impact rattling his shoulder blade. Wasting no time, he drove his dagger into the man's torso, aiming straight for the liver. The blade came away with a sucking sound, covered in black blood.

The unease of not knowing what lurked in the shadows at Davit's back sent a warning ripple up his spine, motivating him to keep moving forward.

He crossed the rest of the upper deck, finding no foes worth the effort, and bounded up the companionway, taking the steps three at a time to the quarterdeck. He immediately spotted Jiya surrounded by no fewer than six men. Jiya was standing like a proud lion surrounded by hungry and hopeful hyenas. The sight drove the breath from Davit's chest. Once, he'd feared this man, but Jiya's gruff lessons had forged a strong bond between them. There was no doubt in his mind that Jiya was perhaps the most skilled warrior he'd ever known, but six against one was a cruel mismatch and he would be damned if he was going to stand by and watch him fall.

With slow and deliberate strides, the men tightened the circle around Jiya. Davit lowered his body, hiding himself from the ones facing in his direction, and sped toward the nearest man. His blood was running high, and he wasted no time on planning or forethought as to which one would be the best to attack first. It was simply first come, first served. He flipped his blade into a reverse grip, cutting across the back of the first man's knees before driving it into the side of his neck as he sank to the deck. Then Davit's club found its target in the sweet softness of the man's temple. He moved through the opening he'd created in the circle and caught a flash of Jiya's smile before finding himself back-to-back with his mentor.

Jiya and Davit moved in perfect unison, their feet stepping in time as if performing a well-practiced dance. Hours of training with Jiya had accustomed Davit to his movements. They anticipated each other's shifts and strikes, pivoting together, creating a whirl of arms and weapons flashing out to deliver and parry attacks. It was frustrating their opponents, for there seemed to be no opening to exploit. Earlier, the pirates had worked together, closing in on Jiya. Now they lunged forward at irregular intervals, trying to break Davit and Jiya's rhythm. The change in strategy was unsuccessful and fatal, for Jiya felled the first one to step from the tight circle, with a thrust to the heart.

The rest were slow to learn, and as one after another lunged from the circle, they inevitably made themselves the perfect targets for either Jiya's cutlass or Davit's club. When the last man remained, there was a moment's hesitation as neither Davit nor Jiya could decide who should kill him. It seemed the fool had forgotten to run. Jiya, ever considerate, met his vacant gaze before running him through with a clean strike.

Orion's rallying cry rang out across the deck and the men answered as one. Davit and Jiya turned toward each other. Their eyes were ablaze with battle fever and both their arms were shaking with the remnants of the fight when they clasped forearms.

"He'll skin you alive," Jiya said, even though his face and voice belied the pride he felt for the boy.

"I know," Davit panted, a grin breaking through his exhaustion.

***

"We should have kept that ship," Davit bemoaned the loss of the magnificent vessel as he and Jiya stepped around yet another pile of stacked oak logs, counting and entering the amount in the logbook. The iron chest filled with ducats and guilders was already counted and stowed in the stateroom.

"She was old and riddled with woodworm, and she is slow, probably why she fell into the Ottomans' hands so easily," Jiya mused, and pointed to where the barrels of brandy were still waiting to be counted and recorded.

After the battle for the *Vlieland* had drawn to an end, the surviving twelve pirates were made to kneel in the middle of the upper deck, their hands bound behind their backs. One hundred and twenty-seven souls were released from the hull. Most were the original crew of the *Vlieland*, including her first officer. Her captain had perished during the Ottoman attack more than two weeks prior.

Orion's initial plan was to claim the ship, but seeing the number of survivors and the state of the hull, he'd thought it best to return the ship to its crew, leaving the food rations, but removing the cargo – payment for services rendered, before sending it on its way.

"Then why did we go after her, if we knew she was slow?" Davit doggedly followed Jiya as he counted the barrels.

"One hundred and forty-nine," he said to Davit, who made a note in the logbook. "We freed the captured men and woman, prevented them from becoming slaves."

"And got handsomely paid for our efforts, and I counted one hundred and fifty barrels," Davit returned.

Jiya gave him a sly smile and shook his head.

"You counted wrong." Their easy banter was interrupted when the cabin boy rushed onto the deck, skidding to a halt near the barrels, his glittering eyes gliding over the treasure.

"Are we one short?" he inquired in a too shrill voice, the direct and unfortunate result of his tender years and excitement over the brandy and the as-of-now missing barrel that would make its way below decks as soon as the sun settled over the sea.

"Indeed," Jiya answered.

"The captain wants to see you in the stateroom," the young boy said to Davit, his cheeks turning a blotchy mixture of ivory and red and his eyes sparkling as he relayed the order. After Davit's impressive debut on the decks of the *Vlieland,* his nickname of 'Savage' was now spoken with respect and admiration rather than derision, and he found himself the idol of many a young cabin boy and apprentice.

Orion had yet to mention Davit's offense of disobeying his orders of the night before, hence he had spent a fitful night in anticipation of the captain's wrath.

Best to face whatever was to come head-on and as quickly as possible. Davit gave the stateroom door a firm knock and entered when he heard the rumble of Orion's voice.

He hesitantly stepped over the sill. He'd never been to the stateroom. It was a room like he'd never seen before. Rich, dark furniture was grouped together in the generous space. A thick rug the color of oxblood spanned the entire floor. A wide bed, covered in a blanket of deep blue, with crisp white sheets, stood against the starboard wall.

Gamora was basking in a puddle of sunlight on the foot of Orion's bed. The cat was a sweet-looking thing with powder gray fur and stormy blue eyes, but a bigger menace to society was yet to be discovered. The creature hissed, clawed, and bit at all but Orion. She was terrible at catching mice. For some reason, she'd deemed the act beneath her and had no other occupation but to amuse the captain, who seemed to be completely blind and ignorant of the blasted fiend's uselessness.

Orion returned his violin to its stand, ensuring the bow was neatly stowed, before acknowledging him. Davit had lain many nights on the deck listening to the music flowing from the stateroom. Sometimes it was lively, other times haunting and beautiful but, mostly it was dark, demanding and powerful.

Orion's stare was distant and cold, and Davit's skin turned clammy under its power. His feet seemed to have grown roots, keeping him fixed firmly to the floor.

"You disappointed me," Orion said, his voice low and measured.

Davit swallowed thickly, his insides dropping, leaving behind a ringing in his ears and a hollow feeling in his chest.

"What were you thinking? What were you trying to prove?" Orion demanded, his tone even but turning colder with every word uttered.

"I," Davit exhaled and tried to stare back into Orion's dark eyes, but after a second, he found it unbearable and dropped his gaze to his bare feet. He refused to wear a shirt, regardless of having been ordered to do so many times, and he suddenly missed its protection. "I wanted to prove that I am not without skill or worth."

Davit sounded pathetic to his own ears and, for the first time in his life, he wished not to speak, to neither explain nor defend himself. Enduring the captain's disappointment was worse than being flogged. He would trade his newfound place among the crew in a heartbeat if it meant winning Orion's approval.

"And you thought disobeying my orders would prove your worth and skill?" Orion's eyes were sharp and unyielding, ensnaring Davit.

"I am so– "

"If it happens again, you are off my ship regardless whether there is land nearby or not. Is that clear?"

"Yes, Captain," Davit breathed, waiting for his punishment to be announced. Flogging was the standard and the crew was already taking bets on the number of lashes he would get.

"Get out of my sight," Orion barked.

Davit's feet carried him swiftly to the door; in his haste to leave the room he missed the smile that plucked at Orion's mouth.

Orion's own fire had sparked around his sixteenth birthday. While others were driven by greed, lust, or the convictions of their beliefs, he had been motivated by a profound yearning for vengeance. His uncle's capture and torture at the hands of Ottoman pirates when Orion was a young boy had provided the justification he needed. Preventing others from suffering that same fate had become his life's purpose, but he was not delusional enough to believe that was the only reason. Walking the path of a vigilante, operating without the protection of a flag, with only his conscience to guide him, was a balancing act. It took tremendous discipline and restraint to behave in a manner affording him the equanimity to face himself in the looking glass and keep feeding the beast inside him in a way that would not cost him his soul.

A faint purr drew his gaze to Gamora, curled on the bed, her gray fur catching the sunlight in a sooty halo. Orion reached over and stroked her curved back. His thoughts turned to Kwala's fighting in the raid. The boy struck with surgical precision and calculated intensity, favoring smaller, tighter movements. That might be the reason why he struggled with the cutlass's sweeping style. Jiya's training had given him an edge, but perhaps it was time for Niccolò to step in.

Chapter 6

They were at the tail end of a long, wet winter, and the morning air still carried a raw edge. A cold gust pushed toward the slumbering continent. It coursed through the roof's exposed skeleton and ruffled Sebastiaan's hair. Feeling the chill, he lifted his head, then closed his eyes against the rising sun as it climbed past the clouds that bruised the horizon.

Please God, guide my feet and light my path. And above all, keep her safe.

The words of his silent prayer joined the rising sun every morning since the day he'd left her on the beach. The details of Danielle's features were not as sharp anymore. However, the brilliance of her eyes remained as vivid as always, her nearly black hair sparkling in the sun was still there, but the rest were fading into more of an idea than an image.

The picture Maria Van Riebeeck had sketched of her long-ago was now just a smudge, the paper worn and friable. He didn't carry it any longer; it rested peacefully inside the *Bible* Van Leyen had given him on the morning their lives had collided; he didn't read that any more either.

Sebastiaan raised his hand to soothe the ache in his chest, and opened his eyes.

"Beautiful morning," Van Leyen said, sitting across from him on a thick beam twenty feet above the floor of their newly constructed warehouse, dubbed *The Shack*, his long legs dangling and his woolen cap pulled low.

"How would you know? You haven't looked up since we sat down."

The two of them had climbed the scaffold when there was just enough light to locate the lantern, wanting to use every available hour this day could afford them to finish constructing the frame for the roof. Daka had left the day before with the wagon to cut thatching reeds. They'd discovered a marsh, about twelve miles inland on a hunting trip a few weeks prior where plenty of reeds grew. Actually, it wasn't a reed at all, Van Leyen was quick to point out, but rather a leafless, grass-like perennial, but it worked just as well, if not better than the thatch used in Europe. Sebastiaan could not care less if they had raided the Garden of Eden and covered the roof in fig leaves and apple peels; so long as it kept the elements out and his future cargo safe, he would be content.

Van Leyen only smiled and kept on hammering at the nail he was currently driving into the wood with envious precision.

"When do you expect Orion?" Van Leyen asked around the two nails clutched between his lips.

"A fortnight ago," Sebastiaan replied, and a worried crease worked its way between his eyebrows.

"Two weeks either way on the open ocean is not a long time. No need to fret."

"I'm not fretting," Sebastiaan fired back, not bothering to conceal the thick layer of irritation in his voice.

"Aye, you are. You've been staring at the ocean for days, as if that would bring the lad quicker. It's a wonder your arse isn't full of splinters from all the chafing and twisting you've been doing on that beam. Move," Van Leyen said as he hopped forward on his arms to continue his neat line of nails.

Sebastiaan shuffled backward, then he snuffed the lantern, its faint orange light made redundant by the brilliance of the morning sun. He preferred almost anything to construction, but they had enough meat, fresh and cured, to last them until the Lord returned and a pile of firewood to match. The wagon was in good working condition, and every palm at the fort was sufficiently greased. He had bought furniture from the local joiner, a man of small stature and thin, oily gray hair by the name of Dieter Girten, a Frank turned nomad. The furniture was sturdy but lacked imagination and currently huddled together at the back of the *Shack* under a section of the roof covered by an old ship's sail Sebastiaan had bartered from a fisherman. The three of them could at least sleep in comfort, though occasionally at the mercy of the weather. Therefore, there was nothing left for him to do but to fish, wait for Orion and hand tools to Van Leyen.

"Why don't you get down and see who is coming?" Van Leyen suggested and pointed with his chin toward the two-track road leading to the cove.

"It's probably Daka," Sebastiaan said as he reached over to hand Van Leyen three more nails, one for the hand and two for the mouth.

"No, it's not the wagon," Van Leyen's voice sounded bored. "Two horses, easy gait, no hurry."

"Gijs then. Is it Wednesday already?" Sebastiaan asked.

"Wednesday it be, but who is with him, I wonder?"

Elsje's husband had shown up, soon after construction on the *Shack* had begun, with a basket of freshly baked bread and pastries, professing that Elsje had nagged him into the deed to ensure that they were properly fed and to deliver their clean laundry. It soon became apparent that Gijs craved the company, which the three of them were happy to provide. What was perhaps intended as a quick visit had turned into a day of hard labor and a weekly ritual. Gijs was difficult to dislike and easy to talk to. He was a wealth of information, since he'd been at the settlement from the age of twelve. He was also a wealth of muscle power. The man was as sturdy as an ox and skilled with his hands and could shape and mold wood as easily as he could dough.

"If you are spending the day with us, who is looking after your bakery?" Daka had asked, his mouth ringed with crumbs, a result of the indelicate abandon with which he'd devoured the treats.

"Elsie," Gijs' answer was immediate and confident. Sebastiaan, Van Leyen, and Daka's heads had snapped up in unison, each face undiplomatically displaying varying degrees of concern. "Relax," he'd laughed. "She'll do fine. Besides, it's the middle of the week. The charred scent of burned bread is usually gone by Friday."

Sebastiaan stepped from the jetty, instinctively moving away from the dry, loose sand to where the earth was more compact underfoot. Van Leyen's unholy ability to hear and see things long before anyone else could, proved correct once more. From around the bend in the road, two riders came at an easy pace: Gijs, and a man Sebastiaan had not yet had the opportunity to meet.

Gijs dismounted and gripped Sebastiaan's hand in a firm, familiar shake.

"Wouter Mostert," Gijs said without preamble. "He wanted to speak with you. Friend of mine. A good man."

Sebastiaan had heard the name spoken often within the walls of the fort. Wouter Mostert was the leader of the militia, burgher councilor, and the most successful and wealthiest of the free settlers at the Cape, which wasn't saying much, seeing that the lot of them seemed to walk a tightrope over a chasm of starvation, but still the man exuded a soft air of authority.

"It's a pleasure to meet you, Mister De Vries," Mostert greeted with a curt bow after Gijs purposefully strode toward the sounds of construction with a mouthwatering whiff of fresh bread curling around his feet. Mostert was a slender man, perhaps on the downside of forty, with hawklike features, weary eyes, stern mouth, a deep bronze skin hard-baked by many hours under the unforgiving African sun, and hair the color of cold ash from a fresh fire. His clothes were well-worn, of good quality and clean, his boots were recently resoled but freshly polished. Sebastiaan detected no apparent weapons and no excess physical strength beyond that required to perform his day-to-day tasks.

"Mister Mostert," Sebastiaan returned the greeting. "I understand you wish to talk to me. Do you want to do so in private?" He despised lengthy greetings. Best to get to the heart of the matter quickly. That way, the rest of the day was free to work on the solution to whatever problem had driven this pillar of society his way so early in the morning.

"I would like to keep the audience to our conversation small, but whether you tell your companions later or they hear it now makes no difference." Mostert's voice held a dry graveled tone, like it, too, had been brittled by adversity.

"Very well." Sebastiaan pointed toward the *Shack*, afraid that his stomach would soon start demanding out loud the promises his nose was feeding it.

"It is remarkable what you've accomplished in such a short time," Mostert paused and stared with obvious admiration at the building, before lengthening his strides to catch up with Sebastiaan.

The *Shack* had grown from a frail, gray skeleton, poised to collapse into the surrounding waters, to a sturdy building with its frame now forty feet long, and its roof, when finished, rising over twenty-five feet. Its doors, window frames, and shutters shone black as the sunlight bounced off the glossy paint and the chalky scent of the fresh whitewash still clung to its walls.

The jetty, though initially sturdier than the *Shack*, was by no means usable. It too had undergone a growth spurt, doubling its width, stretching much longer, and now boasted the robustness of a well-bred yearling.

"Most of the praise should go to John," Sebastiaan replied. "Dakarai and I were more hindrance than help."

Mostert chuckled, "He is a talented builder. I remember him from when I was a young man."

They crossed the honey-color floor, each reinforced with a pastry in hand, setting a course to where the tall, double back doors were flung open, framing the perfectly calm, deep waters of the cove and the loading deck beyond.

Sebastiaan dragged one of the straight-back chairs from their collection over and gestured for his guest to make himself comfortable. Not wanting to subject himself to the same level of discomfort, he opted for an upturned crate. The morning sun was warming his back and irritating Mostert's eyes, but to the man's credit, he endured Sebastiaan's tactics at expediting the meeting.

"What is it I can do for you, Mister Mostert?" Sebastiaan asked once settled.

"Just Wouter," Mostert said. "And in truth? I am not sure at all. My hopes were that you would listen and perhaps offer advice or a different perspective. When one is stuck in a storm, it is often difficult to see the land, even if it is not far off."

"What makes you think I am qualified for the task?" Sebastiaan made sure no warmth tainted his words. Instead, he kept his voice cool and indifferent.

"You came highly recommended by Gijs," Wouter said and lifted his chin to where Gijs was already hard at work. "Our friendship is an old one. He is perhaps the only man I completely trust." Wouter was quick to add when he saw the cloud of concern cast a shadow over Sebastiaan's face. "Gijs keeps his affairs close to his chest, but knowing the hardships we face, he thought it wise to arrange this meeting." Sebastiaan nodded his consent and Wouter began.

"I was among the first released from my service agreements with the Dutch East India Company years ago, back when Van Riebeeck was still governor. We were granted land to farm along the Liesbeeck. At first, the Company provided rations, tools, and seed, but that support dwindled soon after, especially once Van Riebeeck left. The VOC declared they had invested enough time and money in the settlement's development, and from that point henceforth the farmers were on their own."

"That sounds fair enough. It has been, what? Ten years? Surely, that has been enough time to establish oneself," Sebastiaan observed.

"In theory; yes. In reality, it has been a different situation altogether."

Wouter explained how commander after commander had tightened the laws and regulations around the free settlers until the only thing free was the title of the term under which they lived. Farmers were required to protect their own land from attacks from the native tribes, with the VOC using them as a buffer to safeguard the settlement, thereby saving money by employing fewer soldiers. Trading with the local tribes was permitted in items no larger than ostrich eggs or tortoise shells. Anything of more substance, such as rhinoceros horns, ostrich feathers, and ivory, were to be brought to the fort directly, where the officials would negotiate with the tribal leaders. Should a settler be caught with any of the items on the list of prohibited goods, the settler was fined, and the goods confiscated.

Only one man was allowed to hunt for ivory and rhinoceros horn, and trading in whatever he could lay his hands on — Alain Du Bois.

Nobody was allowed to trade with the visiting ships directly, all transactions were handled by the fort alone. This meant the fort had the monopoly over grain and seeds and sold them to the farmers at exorbitantly high prices, while purchasing the same farmers' produce at disgracefully low rates. The fort then resold these goods to the ships at eye watering prices.

The farmers realized that carving a living off the land was not possible and supplemented their income by keeping canteens. Although the fort, and by extension the VOC, frowned at the practice, it soon found a way to profit from it, and these canteen owners were compelled by law to operate under a liquor license that would be bought annually from the fort. These licenses were expensive, and few could afford them. The ones that could, had to buy their alcohol from the VOC and also pay an excise on it. To make the endeavor remotely profitable, the desperate canteen owners adulterated the liquor to the point where it was hardly strong enough to intoxicate a house cat. The alternative was to keep the liquor strong and to run a brothel on the side.

"I don't have to explain the social problems born from that point onward," Wouter said.

"And yet there are four pregnant slaves working in your inn; my guess is you know all about the social impact of slavery." Sebastiaan spoke quietly, but the intended notes of accusation hung like icicles from his words.

Wouter's eyes searched his for a few heartbeats and when he spoke his features were calm, if not a bit melancholy.

"Slavery is a necessary evil that seems to rule the times we live in. We cannot function without it, not at the rates the VOC is charging and paying for our produce, and we can only farm the land given to us by the fort. Expansion is forbidden."

"Does the VOC own the whole of Africa that it so boldly assumes it may dole out land as it sees fit?" This time Sebastiaan's words were not nearly as measured as before.

Wouter breathed a wilted laugh. "How could we stand against a giant like that when even the smallest of protests end with a week's stay in the *Donker Gat?*"

Sebastiaan had been unfortunate enough to have seen the *Donker Gat,* or the *Dark Hole,* on a tour of the newly constructed *Castle.* He had accompanied Hackius when the new commander invited him along to familiarize himself with the enormous structure. So far, the *Castle* was a work in progress. The result promised a thirty-five-feet high fortified pentagonal structure with each point drawn into a bastion armed with cannons peeking through embrasures, swearing menace and a quick deliverance to the hereafter to any advancing enemy, be that over land or sea. The view from the curtain wall was breathtaking, spanning from the rugged mountains to the unobstructed view of Table Bay, but it was the *Dark Hole* that had made Sebastiaan's skin crawl.

In the few seconds before the heavy door slammed shut, plunging him into darkness where he couldn't see his hand before his face, the chains hanging from the walls dragged his mind to the edge of a long-forgotten abyss. The shackles dangling from them called to a part of him he wished not to be disturbed. His breath had hitched. Cold sweat had beaded his brow. Were it not for the commander's ceaseless chatter, he might have lost his wits as old memories bubbled up like fumes from a cauldron.

The *Dark Hole* was meant as a *rehabilitation* room for unruly slaves and petty criminals, where the offenders would spend the night contemplating their misdeeds. A week in that hellhole was unthinkable.

Even the mere memory of the torture chamber was enough for Sebastiaan's hands to dampen, and his heart to race. Silently, he stared at his guest, not daring to speak for fear that his heightened emotions would somehow betray themselves in his words. Wouter mistook his silence for judgment and reached for the topic that still hung unaddressed between them.

"And you are misinformed," he said without a hint of remorse. In fact, the point-blank statement was delivered with a healthy dose of defiance. "I do not have four pregnant slaves. I had six, counting the two that gave birth earlier this year."

"Many at the Cape, town folk and farmers, cannot afford to buy slaves. So, Du Bois, who is the chief slave trader, rents them out. Now, you don't need to be a philosopher or gypsy to see that some of the women are rented as *kitchen* slaves. When such a slave becomes pregnant, she is returned, having lost her value because of her unfortunate condition. Du Bois then puts her up for sale at a very low price. Her new owner, more often than not, works her hard, forcing a premature delivery. If the woman and child survive, the church steps in the very next day to remove the child from what they deem an immoral mother. The child is then sold to brothel owners or childless couples as an indentured slave." For a moment Wouter's voice broke, and he took a few breaths, staring at the serene cove.

"So yes, I buy them. My wife cares for them, helps them through the birthing and then we give them the safety of our home where they can work and keep their child until they can find suitable husbands. At which time they are given their freedom."

"Du Bois," Sebastiaan whispered. He was a snake that had slithered into his life almost two decades ago and had wreaked havoc upon it ever since.

"Alain Du Bois. Have you met him?" Wouter asked.

Sebastiaan nodded.

"He arrived at the Cape shortly after the departure of the second commander, spreading his influence and power like a fog in the night, silent but traitorous. He owns everyone at the settlement, from the commander to the tavern wenches. Even me," Wouter confessed.

That unwelcome statement drew Sebastiaan's attention, and his eyes locked with Wouter's.

"How?"

"If I were to defy him, how long would my liquor license, inn permit, mill contract, or canal construction contract remain valid? If I lose even one of those, I cannot support the people who depend on me. Du Bois has worked himself into the management and government of this settlement like a weed. He influences every law that is passed, every restriction that is enforced and every transaction that takes place above or below the table. In a way, I am more vulnerable than anyone else. Du Bois whistles a tune, and I don't stop dancing until he runs out of breath." Wouter reached for another pastry but forgot to raise it to his mouth.

"He owned Commander Borghorst in the most literal sense, having funded most of his lifestyle and secured a somewhat decent means of retirement for him. The man did not even dare to venture as far as the privy without Du Bois' blessing. Everybody has borrowed money, a favor, or influence from him at some point. Du Bois is holding my life in the palm of his hand, and the only reason it hasn't been snuffed out is because I bow, smile, and toe the line." A strange emotion flittered across Wouter's features, swift as a thief, before it was gone and weathered honesty reigned supreme once more .

Sebastiaan scratched the edge of his jaw, wondering if the man's amiable bowing and toeing extended past the observant eyes of the authorities.

"Mister Mostert, you've woven a touching tale, but how is it any of my business? What is it you want from me?" Sebastiaan asked callously, his voice flint-hard and challenging. If Mostert should cower or beg, this conversation and any future considerations would end abruptly. He had no time for soft-spined do-gooders who dripped with virtue and benevolence publicly, but privately were as rotten as the best of them.

Wouter leaned back in the intolerable chair and tipped his face to the sun, took a deep bite from the pastry, chewed with obvious delight, and then swallowing the morsel down he gave Sebastiaan a lazy smile.

"I came this morning to introduce myself, enjoy the beautiful view, and extend an invitation to a quarterly meeting with the free burghers. As a free man yourself, I thought you might be interested. The next one is at the end of this month on my farm. Gijs knows the way." With that he rose from his seat, dusted his hands, touched his forehead, tipping an imaginary hat, and left.

Once inside the dark building he swung around to face Sebastiaan, still seated on the crate.

"It was a pleasure meeting you, Mister De Vries."

"And you," Sebastiaan replied as he watched Mostert's departing form. The man had brains and balls; not as common an occurrence as present company might suggest.

By the day's end, Gijs had returned to his wife, and Daka had arrived once more with a dreamy look in his eyes that made Sebastiaan wonder if all the time away was spent collecting thatching reeds. As soon as the sun dipped behind the mountain, Daka pleaded exhaustion and took to his bed. Sebastiaan took a bottle of Madeira, two earthen cups, and walked to where Van Leyen sat on the beach next to a stone-ringed fire. His arms dangled over his bent knees as he watched darkness coloring the water a deep, unsettling shade of pewter. A pot of meat stew was happily bubbling on a bed of white-hot coals to the side.

"I don't think that will go well with the carrots," Van Leyen said the moment he identified the bottle.

Sebastiaan lowered himself next to his friend. "Care for a cup?"

"*Jesus*, if we must. It gives me a frightful headache, though. The Portuguese should stick to pirating and leave the finer things in life to the filthy French." Van Leyen's hand reached out to accept the cup with the words of protest and condemnation still decorating his lips.

"It's all we have left," Sebastiaan said by way of apology.

"Orion better bring something decent, and soon," Van Leyen grumbled and took a healthy sip, chased it between his cheeks a few times, and swallowed noisily.

"So, you had a visitor today," he said, not bothering to look at Sebastiaan. "And I'm guessing the man came bearing the weight of the world on his shoulders, looking for someone to help him carry it."

"I'm bored." Sebastiaan drained his cup and poured another.

"I can see that. Let's get drunk, or better yet, let's find someone in need of a thorough thrashing. I hear there are bare-knuckle fight nights in the cellar of one of the taverns in town. It's strictly by invitation only, but I'm sure I can get us entry."

"People are suffering, John."

"People have been suffering for eons before you were born, and they will continue to do so long after your bones turn to dust."

"I need my life to be something other than just a blood-drenched mess."

"I understand that, but why don't you focus on this new idea of yours? Extend your shipping routes to Europe, like you've planned." After a pause, Van Leyen continued, "Why don't you go back to Batavia for a bit and visit your uncle? Daka and I will see to things here."

Sebastiaan leaned back on his hands and stared off into the darkness. Van Leyen drained his second cup, got up to stir the stew, and then took to breaking a dry twig into small pieces, which he aimed at the coals, creating tiny volcanoes of sparks every time one hit the mark.

"There might be a way for us to do both," Sebastiaan said after a long silence.

"Dear God. Please don't," Van Leyen protested. "Who put the idea in your head that it is your responsibility to fix every wrong this world puts before you?"

"Perhaps it is because I can."

"This is about Du Bois, is it not?"

Sebastiaan only stared at Van Leyen. Neither spoke, but a silent conversation passed between them, one of understanding and undying loyalty.

"I'll stand by you, no matter what you decide to do. But I beg you, think long and hard about this," Van Leyen finally said. "You might not want to shed blood anymore, but if it involves Du Bois, there might not be a choice."

Chapter 7

"There," Van Leyen announced definitively and pointed to the faint horizon where it vanished into a hazy fog.

Another week had passed during which Sebastiaan had ridden every day to the edge of the escarpment that formed the eastern point of the potbellied cove. The ride was not long but made arduous by the dense forest that filled every inch between his warehouse and the end of the continent. It took him most of the morning to reach the point and then most of the afternoon to get back to the *Shack*.

With work on the building completed, he didn't mind frittering away the hours in his vigil of Orion's arrival. Each time he took a different route, one no less beautiful than the others, all filling him with a deep sense of peace.

Sebastiaan raised the spyglass to his eye. Pinching the other shut, he searched the smooth skyline.

"I don't see a damn thing," he protested after scouring the pale horizon.

Leaning over from his horse, Van Leyen delicately took the instrument between his forefinger and thumb and adjusted its position. Sebastiaan sat motionless for a while longer, and then his gaze sharpened when the flicker of a sail appeared. It disappeared almost instantly, but he kept his focus steady. After a few breaths, it showed again, this time more solid.

"It could be anyone," Sebastiaan said and collapsed the telescope.

"It's the *As-Sayf*," Van Leyen returned over his shoulder from where he was loosely tying his horse to a tree.

With a slight shake of his head, Daka gave Sebastiaan a long-suffering look and dismounted. Years of experience had silenced their incredulity and doubt. John Van Leyen was an unassuming force unto himself. They had questioned him one night around one of many and often deeply philosophical campfires, about his strange ability to hear and see things no other human could. Stretched out on his back, not bothering to open his eyes, he'd artlessly said that if Sebastiaan were to pull his head from his arse and Daka his from the clouds, they too might hear and see the obvious.

"Let's hope he remembered to change the name. Are we guiding him into the cove?" Daka asked as he gathered dry pieces of wood for a signal fire.

Over the years, they had developed an effective messaging system. Sebastiaan and Orion's occupations were two sides of the same coin. Where Sebastiaan had raided Ottoman slave traders by land, Orion had done so by sea.

In the beginning, they had communicated via encoded letters left with trusted acquaintances, alluding to one another's plans and future whereabouts. Then they'd endeavored to meet up as often as they could. Orion would bring fresh supplies, medicine, food, news, and letters from De Coninck in Batavia. Sebastiaan for his part would find a secure cove or safe harbor for the *As-Sayf,* which would change her name to the *Sword of Orion* depending on the geographical location and political climate.

They would light a fire and send simple smoke signals, guiding the ship to a secluded bay, the nearest harbor, or sent a warning not to come close to land and rather proceed to their next rendezvous point. Orion responded by flying a pennant from the top of the mainmast: yellow to confirm or red to signal an emergency.

"The boy wasn't born yesterday, he would have changed the name," Sebastiaan replied as he dragged a large piece of wood to the growing pile. "He needs to dock in the harbor. I don't want it to look like we've got something to hide."

"We might not have something to hide right now but when that ship drops her anchor, I would bet my best pants that that statement might need revision. Do you plan to declare everything on board the *As-Sayf* to the fort?" Daka's voice held a hint of laughter.

"You assume Orion would have something illegal on board?"

"Few things are illegal these days," Daka called back, "but it's a stone-cold fact that Orion will have wares in the hull of that ship that would set mouths watering and palms itching at the fort. So, my question stands: how much are you willing to divulge?"

"Only what is necessary," Sebastiaan replied to Daka's pestering.

"Hmm," Daka gave a sly grin, "very little then. I like it. How long before he reaches the harbor?"

"If the weather holds, no later than Tuesday morning," Van Leyen replied and threw the last few branches on top of the hip-high pile.

Sebastiaan dug the tinderbox from his saddlebag. Striking the flint against the steel, he sent a spray of sparks into a cluster of dry leaves they'd stuck in the gaps between the branches. It took to flame in a single whoosh and soon a robust fire was roaring. Fresh greenery, added on top, produced a thin but sturdy column of white smoke. Using a thick woolen blanket, Daka and Van Leyen intermittently disturbed the smoke: two bursts, a pause, then two bursts again – "proceed to harbor". They continued the pattern until the yellow flag unfurled from the topmast.

"It's him," Sebastiaan confirmed excitedly, lowering the telescope and staring unaided at the faint outline of the vessel. A small knot in his chest loosened, as if Orion's arrival signaled a homecoming of sorts.

"We already knew that," Van Leyen grumbled. "Did he see the smoke?"

"Yes. Damn, I've missed that boy." Sebastiaan lingered a moment longer with a sweet smile on his face, staring at the growing sails.

Orion had become the son that Arent, Sebastiaan's closest friend, had always wanted. Sebastiaan had known Orion since the boy was a toddling little creature of only two summers when Arent had bought him at a slave market. Stepping into the role of uncle had come naturally. Orion was wild, eccentric and loyal and had it not been for his stalwart support, Sebastiaan would not be alive today. Orion always seemed to be close at hand when disaster bore down upon them.

About five years ago, Sebastiaan's thigh had caught an Ottoman blade during a raid. The wound was minor enough to be ignored, but when it turned sour, Sebastiaan had developed a fever that nearly took his life. They had previously arranged with Orion to meet at an inlet a few days' ride from their skirmish, but Orion was not due for at least a week. Daka had built a fire and signaled the emergency for days without pause while Van Leyen had done all he could to keep Sebastiaan alive. On the morning of the third day, Orion had materialized in the firth, seemingly out of thin air. Sebastiaan was rushed onboard, where he'd stayed under the watchful eye of the *As-Sayf's* ancient but highly skilled Hindu surgeon. He was forced to endure the old curmudgeon's prodding, stinking ointments, and sweet-smelling smoke until Orion was satisfied that he could mount and sit a horse well enough not to embarrass himself or the horse.

"I need to go into town. If I don't come back tonight, I'll meet you on Tuesday." Daka's face was still alight with excitement, but a few hard lines around his eyes belied the seriousness of the unmentioned reason for his departure.

"Are you in trouble?" Sebastiaan asked.

"No, of course not," Daka assured him and with a loud noise of encouragement, he pushed his horse past Van Leyen.

"It's a woman," Van Leyen stated, concern and suspicion creasing his forehead.

"Who's, I wonder," Sebastiaan added.

Daka had had many dalliances in the past, all with women belonging to other men. His theory was simple: the women were bored or neglected, meaning there was very little they would not happily consent to. All the entertainment a man could want without the threat of attachment or tearful melodrama when he left their village or city.

"You want the boy to dock in the harbor first? I take it we're playing this one above board?" Van Leyen switched the topic of their conversation to a matter they could actually control.

"As much as we can."

"You'll have to make a sizable donation to the commander's retirement plan."

"Whatever the going rate for a blind eye is, I guess."

"We might need more than just one blind eye. If my gut is correct, we'll want the man's entire faculty of senses occupied elsewhere."

"I'll find a way."

"Aye, you always do."

***

The *Sword of Orion* lay low in the water, pulling at her anchor, her waterline completely submerged and her sails furled. It had taken her the better part of the night and the following morning to reach the safety of the harbor and even at rest she looked skittish and ready to bolt. Orion would spit fire if he knew Sebastiaan owned a perfectly calm cove not a day's sailing from where they were currently bumping against the jetty.

The wind had picked up overnight, leaving Table Bay in a foul mood. Though the swells were not high, the water was dark and choppy. Rain slanted down from heavy clouds that lapped at the ocean with long white tongues. Earlier this morning, Sebastiaan had taken shelter under the eaves of a lean-to attached to one of the dockside buildings. With one shoulder resting against the log wall, his ankles crossed, the collar of his coat flipped up against his neck, and his hands tucked into his armpits, he had watched the *Sword of Orion* battle her way into the harbor. It was cold and his breath pushed little white clouds with every exhalation.

She was an English-built pinnace, and almost half the size of the cargo ships in Sebastiaan's fleet, but she was fast and agile; built for exploration, speed, and piracy. The fore-and-aft rigging gave her maneuverability that could make a man's heart shake. He'd once seen her do a turn that had defied logic. She had been locked in a close-range battle, her enemy ruthlessly peppering her larboard side with anything that could be blasted from a cannon. Having had enough of the abuse, Orion had raced past the other ship, loaded the starboard guns and then, digging her prow into the water he'd swung her stern about, turning her like a ballet dancer on a small stage, and sent the offensive galley to the bottom of the ocean with a battery of well-aimed and perfectly timed shots.

Sebastiaan had watched the nerve-shredding drama unfold from the beach through the narrow view his telescope afforded him. By nightfall his, Van Leyen's, and Daka's voices were raw and wispy from the vigor of the orders and advice they'd shouted from the beach. Daka was permanently damaged by the ordeal. With his nerves pushed beyond breaking point, he had declared right there that he would think carefully before ever again setting foot on anything that floated, and *never* if captained by Orion.

Orion was almost nineteen when he found himself on the African east coast, an incident that remains unexplained to this day, while serving as the captain of one of the De Vries trading vessels. Whenever questioned about that deviation from his sailing route, Orion developed immediate and acute hearing loss and a worm-eaten memory. Nonetheless, he'd spotted the pinnace riding her anchor in shallow waters awaiting her captain and most of her crew's return from raiding yet another sleepy African village.

Orion and a few of his best men had boarded and liberated the vessel, leaving the returning Ottomans and their traumatized loot staring at nothing but an empty ocean. Jiya had turned the De Vries ship back to her intended trading route, leaving Orion to inspect his new acquisition. This inspection inevitably had led him to the hull, where he discovered the original crew tied up like hogs awaiting Christmas Eve.

Arguing that the only thing worse than an Ottoman pirate was a British sailor, and even though he could have used the manpower, he had refused to violate the tenets of his belief. Finding the nearest strip of dry sand, Orion had set the English sailors free. He'd supplied them with provisions, weapons and a pouch of coins, pointed them roughly toward England, turned on his heel, and boarded his freshly plundered ship.

No sooner had his feet touched the weathered deck planks, than he'd christened her the *As-Sayf* which translated into the *Sword of Orion*, in honor of the ship that had rescued Sebastiaan from Ottoman slavery a decade earlier, and also to soothe and appease the demands of his ego.

Some would argue that it was not a christening, but a marriage. Orion did not dispute the point, the heart of the matter was that she was his and he immediately set sail for Batavia where he rebuilt the entire vessel from the bilges to the lookout's baskets and then set out to begin a lucrative career as a privateer or pirate, depending from which side of the law one approached the matter.

A faint bell sounded, and Sebastiaan saw one of her two heavy anchors slowly lowered into the water with the same gentleness a mother would lay down a sleeping child. After this, the ship approached the welcoming jetty with catlike hesitation and slow precision. Orion was many things, most of them questionable, but recklessness with his ship and the lives of those onboard was not one of them. The bell sounded again, signaling that the maneuver had been successfully executed and the vessel was securely set.

Sebastiaan stepped from his shelter and strode down the jetty in long, measured strides. A sailor appeared near the railing and flung the mooring line out. Sebastiaan stooped to lift the familiar weight in his hands and deftly tied it around the post on the platform. He reached for the lowered rope ladder and scaled it with far fewer steps than there were rungs, swung his legs over the side and embraced his nephew.

"That took you long enough," Orion greeted as he backslapped his uncle.

"Good to see you too, whelp." Sebastiaan laughed and returned the greeting. Stepping back, he regarded the young man standing before him and felt unbidden and fierce pride rise inside him. The excitement of their reunion caused them to speak at the same time; both laughed and tried again but the thoughts and sentiments were lost when Sebastiaan was abruptly folded into a smothering embrace from Jiya.

"Effendi," Jiya's deep African voice vibrated with the power of his emotions. He held Sebastiaan for a long moment and when they parted, he shamelessly dried the tears from his face.

"Let's talk in the stateroom. It's warm, dry and exceedingly more comfortable than the open deck." Orion slung his arm across Sebastiaan's shoulders. The two of them were of a similar height, but Sebastiaan was broader. Orion's only hope to win that silent competition was to wait for old age to bend and twist the other man into a manageable size.

"Sold," Sebastiaan said.

"You go ahead. I want to look in on the lads in the hull. They are setting aside a bit of timber to unload." Jiya clasped hands with Sebastiaan. "My heart shines with joy at being with you again, Effendi."

"And you," Sebastiaan said, receiving Jiya's brilliant smile just before he lowered himself through one of the open hatches of the upper deck.

"How are you, uncle?" Orion asked once they were both comfortably seated in his private cabin. "And are Van Leyen and Daka still with you?"

"Well, and yes," Sebastiaan answered. "Now tell me, what do you have down in the hull that is making this bucket of woodworms ride so low in the water? Also," Sebastiaan continued when Orion was about to voice his indignation at the woodworm reference, "I smelled fresh oak when I stepped onboard. Did trouble come so close that you were forced to repair the deck?" Sebastiaan knew he was prying into affairs that did not belong to him, but the sight of the new deck planks had instantly sparked his concern.

Orion was holding his finger in the air, waving it about long before Sebastiaan had finished his question.

"First," he began, "calling this beautiful ship a bucket is crossing the line. For that offense alone, I should dilute your brandy." Orion's eyes sparkled with mock annoyance. "Second, no, we did not run into trouble, but a captured Dutch fluyt called the *Vlieland* did. Are you familiar with her?"

Sebastiaan shook his head.

"After liberating her, we handed her over to her crew, whom we'd freed, and then emptied her hull as payment." Orion's articulate fingers unfurled one after the other in a gesture reminiscent of one bestowing benevolence on the less fortunate. "However, I miscalculated the size of our hull and by the time we had transferred the cargo of oak logs and brandy, we were a touch short on storage." Sebastiaan nodded with quiet understanding. "Seeing that we had all that wood conveniently close at hand, I thought it wise to free up some space below and resurface all the decks and replace the paneling on most of the cabin walls." Orion raised his glass and took a small sip. "Not that it is any of your business, but I do appreciate your concern." The neat little barb caused Sebastiaan to release a burst of laughter, leaving him to wipe droplets of brandy from his chin.

"Well, at least your balls have grown quite nicely since we last met."

"The size of my balls had never been the issue," Orion returned, his tone dripping with insouciance.

Amen to that, Sebastiaan thought, leaning back in his chair, and closing his eyes in contentment.

"It's good to have you here," he said.

They sat in silence, simply enjoying each other's presence, listening to the rhythmic drumming of Orion's fingers on the leather cover of the ship's ledger lying at a precise angle before him.

"Something is brewing behind those closed eyes of yours," Orion remarked. "Care to tell me what you're plotting or what you've already done? I saw you standing under that lean-to, when we came in. You were as relaxed as an unlit line of black powder."

Sebastiaan opened his eyes, leaned forward to rest his forearms on his thighs and rolled the glass between his open palms.

"Oh, shit. That bad," Orion breathed and mirrored his uncle's previous position by leaning back in his chair and dropping his head against the backrest while staring at the wooden ceiling.

"Not entirely." Sebastiaan breathed a half sigh and then laid out the events of the past few days, starting with Wouter Mostert's visit and his subsequent plan.

By the time Sebastiaan fell silent, Orion was pacing the back of his cabin, the thick rug absorbing his footfalls. Rain was pinging off the windows lining the back wall. Gamora made a sound deep in her throat, as if sensing the turbulence of her master's thoughts.

"You want to undercut the VOC?" Orion's voice rang low with surprise and disbelief. "That is a mighty big bear to poke." He ran a hand through his hair, leaving the black curls in disarray.

"I'm not aiming to enrage the VOC or invoke its wrath. The plan is–"

"Uncle," Orion's voice held a sharp edge and he spun around to face Sebastiaan, continuing as if Sebastiaan had not spoken at all. "You plan to convince the farmers to sell their produce to you instead of the fort, for which you will pay a fair market price, then load the stock onto your ships and sail it to Europe or Batavia."

"In essence, yes," Sebastiaan confirmed, "but the plan needs refinement."

"Well, there's an understatement if ever I've heard one. Most of the cargo will rot before it reaches either destination. You will be forced to trade with the visiting ships, if your plan is to turn a profit, and that brings us neatly back to my previous observation of pissing off the VOC."

"Are you planning on being an arse the whole time, or is this a temporary condition?" Sebastiaan asked, barely concealing his annoyance.

"Strictly temporary, until I can wrap my head around the brilliance of this plan," Orion retorted without a hint of apology. "We are going to need money and quite a bit of it. My guess is those few pouches of gold you carted about in your saddlebags must be nearly empty by now."

"We?" Sebastiaan asked, unable to hide his excitement.

"Yes, we. Did you think I'm going to sit this one out?"

Sebastiaan narrowed his eyes at his nephew. This was the result he was hoping for, but he was no fool. "You are short on crew, aren't you?"

"Very." Orion gave Gamora an affectionate scratch under her chin before sitting down in his chair again. "I've lost seven and gained one, whose serviceability is still unknown."

"How so?" Sebastiaan asked.

"He's young and only half civilized."

"So," Sebastiaan drew out the word as he tried to see the downside. "From that statement alone, I'd say he's a perfect addition to your crew, would blend in flawlessly."

Sebastiaan looked at the feline, where she lay curled in a tight bundle at the foot of the bed, ignoring the indignity that tensed Orion's shoulders and pulled at his face.

"Would you behave like a lady and not claw me to shreds if I pet you?" he asked the ill-tempered cat.

"She's mellowed quite a bit," Orion defended his pet.

Sebastiaan reached out a hand to glide over the silky fur, but halted his movement when she flicked her steely eyes at him, bared her puny fangs and produced a minatory hiss.

He gave the cat a dirty look and retracted his hand.

"I wrote to your grandfather some months ago, informing him of our whereabouts and my intentions to settle at the Cape of Good Hope. I also discussed my ideas of extending our shipping routes to Europe and asked the *Danielle* be sent here. Obviously, I've also requested funds. But that was long before my meeting with Mostert, and I'm afraid the funds I've requested would not be enough to secure this new venture."

Davit De Coninck, Sebastiaan's uncle on his mother's side, had become a solid grandfather figure to Orion. Sebastiaan missed him deeply; the man was more father than uncle to him. De Coninck had raised him from the age of twelve and had, more than once, saved his life in the most literal sense.

Orion was listening but did not look troubled in the least by Sebastiaan's concerns, causing him to wonder if the boy was fully grasping the scope of his plan.

"We can start small: approach only a few farmers at first and build from there," Sebastiaan continued, but Orion was already shaking his head in disagreement.

"No. If we start small, we'll give the authorities time to adjust and counter our initiatives. We need to go at this full bore or not at all."

"I agree. That would be ideal. In the end, though, should we succeed, our plan will cause panic at the fort. There will be nothing to sell to the visiting ships once the farmers stop trading with them, which, lest we forget, was the very reason for settling at the Cape in the first place. The VOC will respond decisively. They will threaten the farmers, call in the loans on their land and remove the patrolling soldiers. The farmers will be homeless and vulnerable, and that would be enough to buckle them."

"Not if we advance them the funds they need to pay off their debts. And besides, from what you've explained, the soldiers are fairly worthless anyway, so their loss will most likely not be mourned. I, on the other hand, have battle hardened men collecting dust. My crew can easily take over the role and provide actual protection at no cost to the farmers, since we will be paying them." Orion countered.

"All fair points, but funding is still a problem," Sebastiaan returned.

Once more Orion extended an elegant finger, got up from his chair, then dropped to his knees before crawling halfway underneath his bed.

"Not necessarily," came his muffled voice from the darkness. Crawling backward, Orion grunted as he dragged a chest the length of a man's forearm, and just as deep, from under the large bunk.

Fumbling with the damaged lock, he flipped the lid and stood back to reveal its contents.

Sebastiaan stared at the tightly stacked towers of golden Dutch ducats that reached all the way to the top of the chest.

"Saints above," he breathed. "How much is that?"

Orion nonchalantly shrugged his shoulders, then scratched the back of his head while a mischievous light ignited in the depths of his dark eyes. "I'm not sure. I got bored and stopped counting after reaching thirty thousand and not even halfway through, but there are also silver guilders and Spanish reals in there."

Sebastiaan remained mute for many minutes after the revelation.

"How did you come by it?" he finally asked.

"Payment for–"

"Services rendered," Sebastiaan finished Orion's favorite line.

"Funding is not a problem." Orion flipped the lid back in place with his booted foot.

"That is your money. I will not touch it." Sebastiaan's tone was hard and final.

Orion released a deep sigh, looked to the heavens, sent a silent prayer for patience, and leveled his gaze at his uncle.

"You've harangued me for years to work for the company. Now I am. Yet here you are refusing me." He raised his eyebrows daring Sebastiaan to challenge his perfect rationalization.

"It usually works the other way round, you idiot. When you work for someone, you *receive* money, you don't give it."

"Then make me a partner, and consider this my buy-in." All humor faded from Orion's eyes. Sebastiaan realized the boy was dead serious, and that this was the moment he'd prayed for.

"Is this your way of giving up your pirating ways?" Sebastiaan asked, equally serious.

"Privateering," Orion corrected, "and yes. I can't continue. The price is too high. I've lost too many good men."

Sebastiaan abandoned his chair, rounded the desk and extended his hand to Orion. "Well then, welcome to De Vries Enterprises."

"Thank you, uncle." The words sounded like they were struggling to push past an obstacle in Orion's throat.

"What now?" Orion asked, when his emotions were firmly under control again.

"Now we go and meet the commander at the fort, do a grip-and-grin and depart for our private cove, complete with warehouse and jetty."

Slowly and with serpent-like focus Orion turned to face Sebastiaan.

"We have a cove?" he asked, the words low and measured. "And you made me drop anchor in this?" He stabbed a finger at the nasty weather and bubbling harbor outside.

***

"You could have gone a little easier on him with the timber. There was no need to drive such a hard bargain," Sebastiaan admonished.

Orion's laughter cut through most of the dockside noise. "I rose this morning from the comfort of my bed, a pirate. Ten hours later, you expect me to somehow morph into Sinterklaas, spreading cheer and good fortune wherever I go? I think not."

The meeting with the commander was short and to the point. Hackius had visibly relaxed when Sebastiaan had walked through the door of his chamber. The two had an easy friendship. The commander enjoyed

143

Sebastiaan's steadfast intellect and often creative perspective to most of the hardships facing their day-to-day troubles. In return, Sebastiaan found the man refreshingly untouched and unimpressed by corruption. Orion, for his part, was his usual arrogant and confident self, which the commander, for some inexplicable reason, had found entertaining.

Sebastiaan had not missed the way the commander had studied Orion upon meeting him. His eyes had twitched for the smallest fraction of a moment, as if he recognized something, but then couldn't find a foothold for the instinct and let it go.

The small matter of docking fees and taxes that normally applied to any ship not sailing under the Dutch or VOC flags was waived, since the *Sword of Orion* would only use the harbor for a few hours and would not require any refreshments from the fort. Sebastiaan was not aware that such a concession existed and was prepared to pay the necessary fees, but Orion cut him a sharp, quelling look when he'd hinted at such. Hackius had good-naturedly pretended not to notice the silent exchange between uncle and nephew.

"Shall we get something to eat?" Sebastiaan asked. "I promised to meet Daka at *The Heart*."

"Eat at a tavern? No, thank you." Orion longingly looked at his beloved ship bobbing against the jetty.

"*Jesus*, you're such a doily. Why the hell not?"

"Uncle, I do not employ a mere cook, but a chef. Why would I prefer the efforts of some poorly trained kitchen wench to that of a true culinary master?" Orion's upper lip twitched, and his eyes squinted as his overactive imagination conjured up images of gray gruel, thin ale, and stale bread. A ripple of disgust ran the length of his entire body, causing it to shake like a wet dog, before he continued. "We'll leave at first light. Most of my crew will be sober enough by then not to run us aground."

"I'll see you tomorrow." Sebastiaan gave Orion's hand a quick shake and turned toward the tavern.

Noise, warm orange light, and the smell of a hearty stew and good ale floated through the partially open windows of *The Heart*. Sebastiaan ducked his head as he entered, shook off his wet coat and searched the busy room for Daka. One of the serving girls called his name and approached him with lazy eyes and a coy smile.

"Your friend left a while ago. He said he was going back to the cove, and that I should save a table for you." She was pretty with large brown eyes and dark blond hair artfully arranged to enhance her many appealing features. Tilting her head toward the table, she waited for his reply.

"Thank you, Millie." Sebastiaan gave her a barely-there nod. She led the way, her hips swaying seductively with each step.

"What will it be this evening?" she asked. Each time he visited the tavern, he'd noticed she bullied the other girls out of the way, ensuring that she served his table, and each time she asked the same question. He knew she hoped that one day he would relent and give her the answer she wanted.

"Just a meal, thank you." It had been Sebastiaan's standard reply from his first visit, and would remain so until his last.

The table was conveniently placed out of the way, tucked into a corner. Positioning his chair so his back was protected by the wall, Sebastiaan studied the room. It was boisterously busy. Many patrons were off-duty soldiers, but the clear favorites were the newly arrived sailors who were generous with their coin and their affections.

A flicker of movement caught his eye, and he turned toward it. In the opposite corner, a lone young sailor sat at a table. His eyes darted from the kitchen to the serving maids — perhaps waiting for his meal, or for one to notice him. He was handsome with long, muscled limbs, sun-browned skin and golden blond hair. With such looks, it was a mystery as to why he was still alone, and Sebastiaan watched him a little longer.

Relaxing further into his seat, the boy pulled a dagger from his hip. With a well-practiced flick of his thumb and middle finger, he spun the blade on its tip in the palm of his open, sailor-hardened hand — a neat trick done not to draw attention but to combat boredom.

The blood drained from Sebastiaan's face, his lips turned to ice, and his head felt like it was rapidly filling with hot air. His body propelled itself out of the chair and only when his hand closed around the sailor's throat did his senses begin to feed his brain coherent information again.

"Where did you get that dagger?" he growled, his face mere inches from the boy's as he slammed him against the wall, not bothering to lift him from the chair first, leaving it to teeter precariously on its hind legs.

Panic, rage, and pitch-black sorrow coursed through his veins, blocking his ears and blurring his vision. He felt the boy's throat bob as he tried to swallow. The slight movement cleared some of Sebastiaan's vision, and he stared down into a pair of fearless, vibrant green eyes – the likes of which he had only ever seen in one other person: *Danielle*.

Chapter 8

Having been drunk once in his life, at the hands of Niccolò the carpenter, Davit had sworn a solemn oath that he would never repeat the experience. The evil that had lived in his stomach at first, which he foolishly thought he'd expelled after vomiting until his throat felt raw, had dug its heels in, and by morning had relocated to his head. Never before had he felt so miserable and received so little sympathy for his wretched condition.

Before disembarking this evening, Jiya had pulled him aside for a long, private talk, explaining the dangers and distractions that were the hallmark of every harbor town. Gambling, women, drink, and innocence were ingredients that could bake a very sorry pie.

Davit was not completely ignorant where women were concerned. His mother had informed him years ago about the private acts between men and women, and that a woman should be treated with respect and care, and never be ill-used. That, when he took a woman to his bed, she'd better be the one he intended to spend the rest of his life with, for she could end up with a child in her belly and no one to care for them. The wicked glint in her eyes that came only when she was deadly serious had warned him that should he break that rule, his longevity, and perhaps the ability to procreate successfully one day, might be in dreadful peril. Therefore, hearing Jiya explain about women selling their bodies, through their own choice or that of another, was a concept he'd found morbidly intriguing, but not enough so to explore.

His friends had deserted him earlier in pursuit of drink stronger than the mug of ale he was nursing, and women he would only allow himself to admire from afar. One of the girls was particularly beautiful. She possessed a smile that promised to light up the darkest of nights and round, wide hips that seemed to move like the swells on a lazy ocean when she walked. Davit had watched her covertly, or so he'd thought, but she'd caught one of his careful stares and had given him a mischievous wink that had caused a rush of blood to scorch his ears and flush his face well past his hairline.

"Sebastiaan," she called from near the counter. Davit's eyes followed the arch of her voice and landed on a newly arrived man, still surrounded by the weather from outside, shrugging off his wet coat.

Sebastiaan – it was a common name. There could be thousands of men who answered to it, and thousands more shaped to nearly the exact attributes and list of characteristics his mother had fed him since he could remember. If all those men were to stand in a line and Davit was given the choice to pick the one that most closely resembled the image he had created of his father, he'd pick the man who'd just walked through the door. A small bubble of hope floated from the pit of his stomach, like the single breath of a deep-sea clam. *My father died years ago,* Davit reminded himself and burst the fragile delusion before it could grow wings.

He watched the man's bland expression when talking to the girl – familiar but uninterested. The man took a table in the opposite corner, relaxed in his chair, and surveyed the room. Davit averted his eyes; his nerves were glowing with some unspoken awareness. He reached for his dagger, a recent habit, born from the need to guard against a surprise attack from Jiya, Niccolò, nerves, or boredom. He flipped it over and spun it on its tip in his open palm, finding the small prick of pain soothing.

Were he staring at the man dead-on, he might have seen him move, but doubted he would have had time to do anything about it. In the next brutal instant, he found himself pinned against the wall. A very large and impossibly strong hand closed around his throat, trapping the last thought in his brain.

In that parlous, unexpected moment, the only thing he could think about was that if that hand was somehow separated from the rest of the body, it would still be clutching his neck. The ridiculous image flashed before his eyes, driving all shock and fear from his mind.

"Where did you get that dagger?"

The man pushed the words through gritted teeth, his eyes flashing with frenzied violence, and Davit felt the muscles in the man's arm shake with raw, untethered rage. The pressure on his throat forced an unintentional swallow, causing the grip to ease by some small measure, affording him just enough air to answer.

"It's mine," he croaked.

That was apparently the wrong thing to say, for the man's eyes darkened, his fingers tightened, and this time Davit was given a thorough shake, hard enough to make his teeth rattle.

"Only two people have ever owned that blade, and one of them was *me*."

The man had reached the edge of his control, and the words were shouted down Davit's exposed ear, causing it to ring. Then, Davit remembered his hand was still clutching *the dagger*. Slowly, he lifted his arm, pressing the weapon's tip into the soft flesh between the man's ribs, just below his heart, which he could feel beating in the fingertips around his neck. It was meant only as a warning, a silent but deadly message to take a step back. It didn't work.

"Tell me where you got that blade," the man snarled, "and choose your words carefully – your next breath depends on my liking the answer."

He was becoming more savage and dangerous with every passing second. Davit had seen plenty of violence to distinguish a threat from a promise, and this angry beast was not slinging about threats. There was no talking or charming his way out of this death grip. He either had to kill the man or tell him the truth. Something deep inside him recoiled at the thought of striking down this magnificent being. It was the same defiance he felt years ago when Kai commanded him to kill a lion to prove his manhood. He had refused, creating a rift between them that had lingered for months.

On the day he'd left to sail with Orion, his mother had given him the dagger. *"This was your father's. It kept me safe, and it will keep you as well."*

He knew it had pained her to part with it. For some reason, she'd always called it Mary, a tradition he'd promptly ended.

"It was my mother's," Davit whispered.

The man's eyes were a muted green, like the moss growing on the rocks near the water, but there was nothing soft about them. They were cold and hard as they bored into his. His grip eased just enough for Davit to wheeze a droplet of air into his starving lungs.

"Who is your mother?" The man barked again, giving Davit another shake for good measure. He struggled against the oppressive hand, trying to wriggle himself free, but his efforts only brought him more misery, for the fingers tightened once more.

'Never speak my name.' His mother's words echoed in his mind. *'Protect me.'* He tried to look away, tried to think, but he could not breathe, and his vision was starting to blur.

"Mary," he said.

Sebastiaan watched as the boy battled with the truth and then settled on the lie. However, the name he'd throttled from the child had the notable effect of buckling his knees. He let the boy go and sank down into the nearest chair. The fight was slowly draining from him.

Mary – the silly name he'd given the dagger when he was no older than this boy. The first time Danielle had heard him refer to the vicious blade by the dainty name, she'd laughed at him and had teased him relentlessly. Could this be Danielle's child? Faint points of possibility were beginning to form, but he needed information before he would let himself entertain even the smallest glimmer of hope. He let time burn by simply staring at the boy.

"Why are you lying?" he asked, his voice rumbling across the table. "Of all the names to give, why did you choose that one?"

"I'm not lying," the boy defended, but a nerve flickered beneath his eye, signaling the opposite. This child would make a terrible card player, and Sebastiaan bit back a warning against gambling.

"Stop it. You're a piss-poor liar." Sebastiaan decided it was best to revert to growling. The boy seemed to respond better to aggression than gentle persuasion. "Your entire face is twitching like you just sat on a rusty nail."

Millie came to Davit's rescue, delivering their meals. Her eyes flickered between him and Sebastiaan, as if weighing whom she would favor if such a choice ever arose. The girl was smarter than most would give her credit for. She wisely gave them a noncommittal smile and took her leave.

"Let's see how you fare with my next question." Sebastiaan watched the boy closely. "What is your name?"

"Kwala." The answer came quickly and without any twitching – the truth then.

"I'm Sebastiaan De Vries," Sebastiaan said and extended his hand across the table. The boy did not return the greeting. Instead, his eyes shot wide and then froze roughly midpoint between shock and disbelief, his face turned the color of a day-old corpse, and a blue-green vein bulged on his forehead. Sebastiaan frowned at the reaction. Then everything happened all at once. Blood surged to Kwala's face, his eyes glowing a vivid green. He shot from his chair, sending it crashing into the corner behind him, and leaned forward on the table, his supporting arm shaking violently. Blind, feral rage had replaced the disbelief, or whatever it was that had stalled his mind moments ago. Sebastiaan watched the striking display of aggression with renewed interest, his attention riveted on those extraordinary eyes.

"You bastard!" the boy roared. "You are alive! You abandoned my mother! While she was carrying your child!" The shouts were deafening and rose above the tavern's clamor. The room fell quiet around them; and only the sharp patter of raindrops against the windows pierced the crypt-like silence. Sebastiaan resisted the urge to glance over his shoulder to see if they were alone. He let the boy vent his anger, a joy he hadn't thought he would ever feel again flooded him from his head to his feet.

"Don't you have anything to say for yourself?" Kwala was still shouting, the vein on his forehead now more pronounced than before. Sebastiaan prayed the thing would hold and not rupture under the pressure. He could feel the tension drain from his body, and his face relaxed into a gentle smile. Everything the boy accused him of, save for the fact that he was indeed alive, was untrue, but he did not care a wit. Between the raw shouts stood the silent truth: this was Danielle's child.

Much later, when questioned about this moment, would he admit that somewhere in the back of his mind the fact that Danielle had a child had struck him hard, but the knowledge that she lived was bigger than all other considerations.

The tavern stirred from its stunned hush as Millie nodded to the other girls to resume their work; a bottle clinked, hesitant conversations swelled in muted tones, and movement crept back.

"Would it be safe to assume that the child you are referring to might have been you?" Sebastiaan asked, trying to keep his voice as even as he could manage.

"Yes!" Kwala's self-control was shattered beyond repair. Sebastiaan nodded at the admission as he tried to make sense of the situation.

"Sit your arse down and let us talk like civilized men who are not hard of hearing."

"I have nothing to say to you." Kwala had a good voice that would carry well across a distance, for his volume was yet to lower, but it was somewhat dulled now that the others were slowly returning to their previous entertainments.

"Really?" Sebastiaan asked and cocked his head up at the boy who was still looming over him.

He was a beautiful child, healthy and strong, with an open face – its sharp, defined lines a striking masculine echo of his mother's, now even more vivid with his temper ablaze. Yet those blue-green eyes, like the ocean on a warm day, so vividly hers, pierced him with their identical gleam. Many times, Sebastiaan had seen that same fiery gaze in Danielle, paired with the same reckless curl of the lip when the fuse to her short temper caught fire. He wanted to laugh at the magnificent sight but controlled the impulse. The boy would most certainly take that unwanted expression of emotion the wrong way, and he was in no mood for a brawl.

"Kwala." The warmth inside Sebastiaan inevitably spread to his voice. "Sit down."

The boy was not easily placated, and his raging temper refused to be doused so handily.

"My name is Davit," he spat. "Davit Aard De Vries. Your son." The name rolled off the boy's tongue with the ease that could only come from years of use.

She'd given her child his name. She'd kept him alive in her heart, made the boy believe he was the father, thereby killing off whoever had sired him. The act spoke of hope and hatred. Danielle was not somebody who hated easily. It would have taken an extraordinary event to cause such depth of feeling. An event like the assault she'd suffered on her wedding night. Sebastiaan watched the boy, still primed to avenge the long-ago wrong perpetrated against his mother. Only he was angry at the wrong man and for the wrong deed.

"Say her name," Sebastiaan spoke around the heavy lump in his throat.

"No," the boy refused stubbornly. "You don't deserve to hear it."

This had to end. There was too much information Sebastiaan needed, and this boy's stonewall attitude was not helping matters along.

"Say her name or I'm walking out that door." Sebastiaan pushed from his chair. For the first time, he and Davit were standing face-to-face, their height evenly matched. Sensing the spiteful response dancing on the boy's tongue, Sebastiaan continued before Davit could deliver his ill-conceived retort.

"Don't say the words burning your insides right now. You will regret them, because they will be spoken in a moment of anger. Now hear me well." Sebastiaan's voice was low and only loud enough to drift between the two of them and not beyond. "I'll leave if that is truly what you want. But I promise you this: I *will* find her."

Sebastiaan let his words linger, giving the boy time to absorb and understand them, before he turned to leave.

"No, you won't," Davit said, his vehemence still clear but much more controlled.

The softly spoken words halted Sebastiaan, his back still to Davit.

"She's dead," Davit said ruthlessly.

The words hit him like a thousand daggers, and only by some miracle did he remain standing. The rush of joy he'd felt moments earlier, butchered in its infancy, obliterated by the short statement. Inside him, the last flicker of light coughed and spluttered. Here was the proof of his darkest nightmare. All the years of searching had come to the end he'd always feared.

With his eyes shut tightly, he bit into his bottom lip until he tasted blood. He'd lost her so many times in the past: when he was taken slave, when he'd visited her house, when he'd returned after years of searching and been forced to face the obvious. Each of those times, he had survived, and he would survive this one too. The regret and guilt he felt for having left her on that godforsaken beach that fateful day was a burden he would carry until his last breath.

A vital spell of clarity forced itself through the thick fog of his sadness, like a shard of sunlight piercing dense thunderclouds. All those times before, he was left with nothing but a vast, soul-destroying emptiness; now he had something. This child was his link to her, and he would not let him go. He would not fail her again. He would make himself into the father this boy believed him to be. If that meant taking the secret of his true paternity to his grave, then so be it.

Davit watched the words strike Sebastiaan, the broad shoulders before him dipping faintly, as if bearing a sudden weight, while his back stiffened, bracing against collapse. He was eternally grateful that Sebastiaan was facing away when he'd spewed that desperate lie, for even he could feel the muscles in his face dance beneath the skin. He had spoken in anger, and a small measure of regret already gnawed at him, but he would not let this man near his mother until he was sure of his measure. Her perspective might have been clouded by youthful infatuation. Sebastiaan might not be the man she remembered from her youth. He could very well have turned into a cruel and ruthless bastard since she'd known him. Too many questions remained unanswered, too much still to be explained. Despite the yearning in his heart, Davit could not yet bring himself to trust Sebastiaan De Vries.

Sebastiaan turned to face Davit. Both had undergone a visible change in the last few heartbeats. The fight no longer burned in Davit, and the joy no longer in Sebastiaan. They reached for their seats and sat down again. Sebastiaan looked at his bowl of stew and pushed it away, his appetite lost. Davit, on the other hand, had no such qualms and devoured his with noisy appreciation.

Sebastiaan wordlessly stared at the boy. His heart felt wrung out and deeply bruised, like someone had severely and repeatedly punched the organ with a bare fist.

"How did she die?" he asked quietly.

Davit kept his head bent over his bowl when he answered. "Fever." His mind was racing as he tried to find some truth to which he could stitch his story. Last year, Grandmother Hari had died of a fever. She was the oldest woman in the tribe; his mother said she'd been old even when she'd come to live with them. Her death came very fast. One day she had a cough, the next she took to her sleeping skins, and before the break of the new day, she was gone.

Sebastiaan narrowed his eyes and studied the boy further.

"When did this happen?" he asked.

"The winter of last year."

Sebastiaan nodded. "Were you with her?"

"Yes," Davit replied without looking from his food.

When there was nothing left in Davit's bowl, he used his finger to scoop up the last bit of sauce from the bottom.

"Davit," Sebastiaan said, "look at me."

The boy slowly raised his head; his eyes were wary. "I don't want to talk about my mother," he said, almost pleadingly. "It is difficult. She is – *was* all I had."

"I understand." Sebastiaan had so many questions, but he understood how hard this conversation was on Davit. "One last request," he said, and held Davit's gaze.

"Tell me how she lived. Please." This time, it was Sebastiaan's turn to beg. If he could have at least that much, he would be satisfied.

Davit released a deep sigh and slumped back in his chair. "We had a good life," he said, and watched some of the tension leave Sebastiaan's face and shoulders. "It was nothing like this." He waved his hand at the tavern at large. "It was simple and peaceful. She was the tribe's healer, which is a revered role." He shrugged, not knowing what more to say, but when Sebastiaan remained silent, he felt compelled to go on. "It was always just the two of us. I grew up with the other boys, and she had a constant stream of people needing her attention. We lived within the safety of the tribe and always had food." He huffed a small smile, realizing how odd that must sound. "You see, compared to the other tribes, ours was wealthy. We had a large herd of cattle and sheep that sustained us. We stay close to the rivers and the ocean, moving less than the others. Kai, our chief, said it was my mother's fault that we didn't move around as often. We only shifted between two locations. My mother was forever trying to make things grow, always coaxing some seed into sprouting or persuading a plant she'd plucked from somewhere to grow in her garden, which was something the tribe never had before but now does, and that was also, according to Kai, my mother's fault." A melancholy smile tugged at Sebastiaan's mouth, crinkling the corners of his sad eyes. Davit stopped talking and scraped his spoon across the bottom of his empty bowl.

Sebastiaan slid his food to Davit, who accepted it without a word, eating eagerly as if to shield himself from a past he struggled to revisit. Sebastiaan raised his hand, signaling for a tavern girl to refill their ale mugs. When she left, a long, comfortable silence stretched between them as Davit finished his second meal. It gave Sebastiaan a moment to imagine the life Danielle had lived, picturing her days spent with her child, working in her garden, tending the sick, offering comfort to those in need. He could see her sitting by a small fire, cooking their meals before settling down to sleep. Knowing she'd been safe and cared for soothed him, but the thought that a year ago he'd been near Mozambique, only months from her when she died, ignited a fury that made him want to tear the world apart with his bare hands. Closing his eyes, he waited for the swell of bitterness to subside.

Danielle's death had always been a possibility, but it was a thought he'd brutally pushed to the back of his mind. In his heart, he had been certain that he would one day find her, but now the words had been spoken out loud, and he had to accept them – she was dead.

"Danielle," Sebastiaan whispered.

"Yes," Davit said softly, and Sebastiaan realized the boy had been studying him.

"Why did you leave the tribe?" Sebastiaan asked.

Davit's face turned guarded, his voice impassive. "I needed a different life." Shadows danced across him as he stared out the black window, rain easing beyond.

"I never abandoned your mother," Sebastiaan said after a while.

Davit turned away from the window, looked at Sebastiaan, and waited.

Releasing a sigh that felt like it could implode his entire being, he continued.

"While on my way back to her from Batavia, our convoy came under attack. I was taken as an Ottoman slave that night." Sebastiaan looked down at the scarred tabletop, wondering how much to reveal. "I spent months in captivity until my uncle Davit found and rescued me." A slight look of confusion creased Davit's brows but Sebastiaan ignored it and continued. With careful broad strokes, he recounted the years from that fateful night to meeting Orion this morning in the harbor.

"My mother told me I was named after her father and yours," Davit said.

"She was not wrong," Sebastiaan murmured. "After my mother passed, I was sent to live with my uncle Davit De Coninck. He's been more like a father to me than my own ever was." His fingers tightened briefly around the ale mug and then relaxed. "My father's illness was one of the reasons why I had to leave your mother behind at the Cape."

"What were the other reasons?" Davit pressed, leaning forward.

Sebastiaan shook his head. "They matter little now."

"They matter to me," Davit insisted, his voice low but firm.

Sebastiaan's gaze drifted to the coals in the fireplace, glowing with liquid heat. "Many at the settlement were sick with dysentery and your mother was the only healer." His words carried a weary edge, dusted with age-old traces of resentment, bitterness, and hard-won acceptance. "So you see, I couldn't stay, and she couldn't go."

With a forced breath his eyes settled back on Davit, his tone shifting as he regarded the boy's sun-bleached hair and weather-bronzed skin.

"You have the look of a sailor. Is it safe to assume you arrived on board the *Sword of Orion*?" The room had grown quiet, many of the customers had left, leaving their conversation to fill the stillness.

Davit nodded.

"How did that happen?" Sebastiaan asked.

Davit gave him a brief and painfully distilled summary of how he'd met Orion and Jiya. Sebastiaan believed every word of the story, but he wondered about the ones that were so carefully tucked away. There were secrets aplenty in Davit's life, that much was clear, but to push the boy now would be a mistake. He would take his time, win his trust, then slowly and carefully piece it all together.

The tavern door opened and the candlelight shivered in its sconces. The rain must have stopped, for only a flurry of leaves accompanied the newcomer.

"Effendi." Jiya's deep voice cut through their conversation as he approached their table.

"I see you've met Kwala," he said, landing a good-natured punch on the boy's shoulder.

"Kwala, this is the man I've told you about. The one that saved my life when I was but a boy." Jiya's face was alight with affection and adoration when he looked at Sebastiaan.

"I know," Davit said. "He is my father."

Jiya's gaze snapped to Sebastiaan. He had been with Sebastiaan through some of the darkest moments of his life after they'd been freed from slavery, the only one who truly understood the depth of depravity Sebastiaan had endured. Their bond was rooted in honesty, and what he saw now in his friend's face confirmed the truth of Kwala's words. Jiya went rigid. The easy warmth drained from his face, replaced by complete stillness. When he finally breathed again it was shallow and careful.

Chapter 9

My father. The words rang sharp and clear through his head. They made his skin feel too small, too tight as if his body couldn't contain the truth. He had met the man who'd shaped his childhood, the myth his mother had woven into every lesson, every prayer – a figure he'd carved in his mind to rival the gods themselves.

Twice a year, the tribe celebrated the solstices, honoring the longest and shortest nights that marked the turning seasons. They danced around a large fire in the center of the village, calling to the gods for blessings and offering their devotion. He'd danced too, but instead of the gods, he'd called to his father, asking for his guidance, for his wisdom. When he was a young boy, he had spent hours in endless one-sided conversations with him, pulling him along in his imagination when he played by the calm waters of the inlet, believing with the innocence of a child that the water was the thread connecting them across the barrier of time and reality.

Tonight, those fantasies and dreams had crashed together in a solid form when the man he'd thought long dead had stood before him. Granted, the onset of their acquaintance was not entirely in accord with his fantasies, but the incident, taken as a whole, was rather magnificent. Walking next to Jiya, he felt as if a thick layer of air lifted him above the pebbled, uneven road, cushioning his every stride. The thought that it was not all that difficult to fly flittered through his mind. Sebastiaan De Vries was everything he'd imagined him to be: fierce and wise, though perhaps a bit shorter than the proxy he'd dreamed up.

Jiya's interruption had been supremely untimely. He would have liked nothing better than to sit at that table until sunrise talking to his father. When they'd left, Sebastiaan had given Jiya's hand a steady shake; then he'd pulled Davit in for a hug and a backslap that stung pleasantly for long minutes afterward. The embrace had the singular effect of reorganizing everything inside him. It was like a line that wasn't fed properly through a deadeye suddenly found its groove and then the entirety worked a bit better, smoother.

Jiya seemed oblivious to the jubilant tempest raging inside Davit as they left *The Heart*. Once outside, he'd asked Davit about his mother, the shock from the revelation still fresh on his face, to which Davit had responded with a one-word answer meant to quell any further prying: "Dead." The brief shield forged in an instant had hung sharp in the air. After that, Jiya talked about the cove, their plans for an early departure, and all the unsavory places they would have to scour and crawl through this night to round the crew up. Jiya's voice droned on unceasingly until they reached a dull gray building that looked like just another dockside warehouse.

The only sign that the place was not deserted and locked up for the night was the flicker of pale-yellow light that wavered in thin, broken lines through the slats of the tightly closed, weather-beaten shutters. According to Jiya, it was a canteen of sorts; meaning drink, but no food. Davit thought the owner of this establishment was plainly disenchanted by his chosen path in life, for the place held less charm and warmth than a pauper's coffin.

The interior held no airs of being any better than the disparaging exterior, for it was equally cold and inhospitable. Four tattered old men, as gray as their surroundings, were sitting at a table playing cards and drinking something resembling week-old piss. Jiya had given the derelicts a nod in greeting and leaned in to drop a few coins on the table. Not one pair of eyes was drawn to the money. Instead, they fixed on Jiya and Davit; assessing, measuring, judging. After a long evaluation, in which not a single word was spoken, one leathery, skeletal hand, charted with purple veins, crept forward to cover the coins. The other rose lethargically from the table and held up four fingers, accompanied by a faded tilt of his head, which seemed to pull at his thorny eyebrows. Jiya nodded his understanding and led Davit to a narrow set of stairs at the back.

There were no tapers lighting the staircase and they gingerly made their way down the uneven and too-short stone steps. At the bottom, a heavy wooden door signaled the end of their journey. Jiya struck the door four times with the side of his fist. It opened promptly but only wide enough for them to squeeze through sideways.

It was like being born. One moment everything was dark and silent, and the next, the absolute opposite confronted them. Caged lanterns hung high along the walls, flooding the room with light. A throng of jostling and excited men filled the underground cellar, which stretched to twice the size of the room upstairs. The air was heavy with the smell of sweat, blood, spilled ale and many unwashed bodies, Davit concentrated on breathing through his mouth. His ears rang from the roar of the shouting and cheering crowd.

A man mindlessly spat out the excess tobacco chew and Davit narrowly sidestepped the sour squirt of brown spittle. He gave the offender a warning glare, but the man ignored him and continued to elbow his way deeper into the crush. Perhaps if the clot saved the fetid content of his mouth and used it more pointedly as a weapon, he might have better success in clearing a path to his intended destination.

Jiya recognized someone, and he angled them toward a tall, dark-haired man with brawny arms folded across his chest, standing near the center of the room. The man looked completely at home amidst the chaos, and his head turned in a lazy arc toward the sound of Jiya's voice. Recognition flashed across his face, followed by a warm smile and a rich, pleasant laugh. They met in a forearm-clasp and a crushing embrace, ending in backslaps hard enough to stagger most men.

"John," Jiya greeted laughingly. "Good to see you. How are you, my friend?"

"Always good. Better now." John shouted back, and his gaze drifted from Jiya to settle on Davit.

Davit felt a prickle of unease when the older man's sharp pewter-gray eyes shadowed as they studied every inch of his face. He looked like a man close to his fifties, with a body that had absorbed the years in the form of brute strength.

"This is Kwala," Jiya said. The slight pause in Jiya's introduction drew John's attention to a needle point. "Sebastiaan's son." Davit felt the room recede, the noise, the people – everything became vague and muted. Only the words remained. Jiya, unaware of the effect his introduction had on Davit, turned to him. "Kwala, this is John Van Leyen, one of your father's closest friends."

Davit gripped the man's hand and in that instant every instinct screamed that this was a man to fear. John's expression shifted — swiftly but subtly. A lethal and calculating light flashed through his eyes, yet his smile remained as relaxed as it was when they'd approached. Neither spoke. Once again Jiya broke the silence.

"I need to gather the crew. Back soon."

John proved to be a man of few words. Not that a conversation was possible with the ambient noise, but the air between them crackled with some unidentified sentience. Jiya was pushing his way to one of the crew and leaned to shout in the man's ear before moving on to the next. A spectacle in the center of the cellar drew Davit's attention, and he moved away from John.

Inside a chalk square, two men were doing an admirable job of beating each other to a bloody pulp. Both fighters' knuckles were raw. One man's eye was purple and swollen shut, yet he showed no sign of capitulating. The other's nose was freshly broken, and his lip split. Blood flowed into his mouth when he opened it to breathe, and he spat a glob to the side. Determining the favorite was impossible, as each blow received loud cheers and encouragement while coins changed hands eagerly.

Meeting his father had set Davit's blood on fire; it throbbed through his veins as his heart hammered against his ribs. He felt like a wildcat in a tight cage. His hands itched and his feet twitched, the pent-up thrill threatening to tear him apart if he didn't unleash it. This place – the blood, the sweat, the raw chaos – promised an outlet. He shouldered through the crowd, eyes locked on the chalk square.

There appeared to be no clear rules for selecting the fighters; the next simply had to step over the line once the spectators dragged the previous loser away. Davit didn't have to wait long, for the man with the swollen eye received an uppercut to the jaw that sent him sprawling onto his back. The bloodied winner collected his coins and stepped away, clearly done for the night.

Unfazed by who his opponent might be, Davit shoved the man to his left aside and stepped over the three-fingers-wide line, fists raised, ready for whoever broke from the crowd next. A fresh wave of excited cheers erupted, but the opponent never came, for a powerful hand clamped behind his neck and propelled him backward into the thick of the onlookers. The crowd roared their disappointment, hurling protests, curses, and lewd suggestions, as they were denied the excitement of the fight the fresh, young sailor had promised.

"Let's go," Jiya growled in his ear and dragged him like a kitten by the scruff of his neck, up the stairs, through the morbid canteen, and out into the cold night before releasing him with a push hard enough to send him tripping over his feet.

"That place was amazing!" Davit exclaimed once his feet were firmly supporting him again.

"What were you thinking crossing that line?" Jiya shouted, sounding none too pleased.

"I would have won," Davit countered. However, his words didn't sound as firm as he'd wished, for the fresh air was rapidly clearing his mind and cooling his blood.

"You could also have died," Jiya returned. "That place is a meat grinder. None of the fights are fair. I've seen men, bigger, stronger and tougher than you, lose their lives in places like that."

In hindsight, and with the uninvited return of his senses, Davit privately admitted that it was perhaps not his finest idea, but it was going to be a long night if Jiya was waiting for him to apologize for his lapse in judgment.

"Come on," Jiya said, once more his usual good-natured self. "We need to talk to Orion."

"About tonight?" Davit asked. He despised feeling like a child, and his behavior down in the cellar now seemed foolish.

"Which part?" Jiya asked.

Davit tilted his head toward the canteen, trying but failing to hide his humiliation.

"No."

They boarded the *Sword of Orion* and walked side by side across the quarterdeck. Jiya noticed how Kwala was dragging his feet as they neared the stateroom door.

"I'm going to find my bed," Davit said and pointed with his thumb over his shoulder toward the stairs they'd just ascended. "Tired. Long day."

Jiya laughed when he saw Kwala taking a few steps in retreat.

"Coward."

"You have no idea," Davit agreed. Touching his forehead in a hasty salute, he made a crisp turn and left the deck at a brisk pace, contradicting his previous claims of exhaustion.

Jiya knocked and entered on Orion's command. Several candles filled the cabin with warm light. Orion was lounging in his chair behind his desk, his feet resting on the painstakingly organized and meticulously polished surface. One hand draped idly over the armrest, the other stroked Gamora's back in long, slow caresses.

"What are you smiling about, and why did Kwala run away?" he drawled and rolled his head against the back of the chair to look at Jiya.

"He's tired. Had a long day," Jiya repeated Kwala's lie.

Orion lifted the cat from his lap, planted a soft kiss on her head, and gently lowered her to the floor before removing his feet from his desk.

"Fascinating," Orion quipped. "Now tell me the truth."

The joy of finding Sebastiaan's child had filled Jiya with such exuberance that it felt like the sun had risen inside him. He had met Sebastiaan when he was nine years old. At the time, they were both slaves struggling to survive at the hands of their Ottoman owners. Sebastiaan had been his protector and he in return had been his faithful shadow. He had spent most of his childhood in Sebastiaan's presence, yet they never developed a father-son relationship. What they shared was a deep and enduring friendship.

In all his years, Jiya had known just one person who occupied Sebastiaan's heart: Danielle. His devotion to the faceless woman had left a vast emptiness inside Sebastiaan that had only expanded rather than contracted over time. Jiya hoped Kwala might be the cure, his presence a solace for Sebastiaan's heartache.

"Jiya," Orion's voice was laced with irritation as he called his friend back to the conversation.

"He's your cousin," Jiya said, and watched as confusion creased Orion's face. With any other person, tact in delivering such delicate news would be advisable, even required, but with Orion, it was best to open with the sharp end of the matter.

"Who?"

"Kwala."

"What?" Orion was having trouble coming to a reasonable conclusion fast enough. "How?"

"He's Sebastiaan's son."

Orion had never been rendered speechless; his viper-quick tongue and razor-sharp wit could rise to any occasion. Yet now he stared at Jiya with a vacant expression, his senses scattered into a brief hiatus.

"Who's his mother?" Orion asked after a moment.

"Who do you think?"

"Danielle?"

"I don't know. It could be," Jiya replied.

"*Jesus.*" Orion slumped in his chair, his eyes darting across the room as his mind raced to make sense of the revelation.

"She might be. It would make sense, the boy's age, the blond hair." Orion fell silent for a long while, then added. "I knew Danielle when I was a small boy, but I can't remember what she'd looked like. Sebastiaan sometimes spoke of her extraordinary green eyes. If she's the mother, I guess they would be the same as Kwala's." Orion stared at Jiya, who'd made himself comfortable in the chair across his desk. "Where is she? Do you know? Did he say?" Orion shook his head as he considered all the implications of this new development, not expecting Jiya to provide the answers to his questions. "My uncle will tear the world apart to find her. He will not rest. It will be the last seventeen years all over again."

"I don't think she is alive," Jiya stated softly, remembering Kwala's curt reply when he'd questioned him about his mother. It was clear the boy did not want to talk about her, and he'd let it go.

The statement lifted Orion's eyebrows in two neat arches. "Does Sebastiaan know?" Jiya nodded. "How did he take it? The news would devastate him."

"I think it did, though he hid it well," Jiya said.

"That would explain so much." Orion stared at the freshly paneled wall. "There was something about that boy that had crawled under my skin from the start. Something I could not explain or reason away."

"Aye," Jiya added, "I think we both saw hints of Sebastiaan in him."

"Perhaps," Orion replied ambiguously. Perhaps it was Sebastiaan's blood echoing in his veins, or perhaps it was something else. Time would tell.

***

Parts of the forest were still in the grips of the fading winter, the air slow to warm. Tendrils of fog snaked low to the ground, winding around the black, fern-covered trunks of the old trees. Sebastiaan slowed his horse. When he'd set out this morning, he had no destination in mind and almost immediately gave the horse its head, letting it choose the direction they would travel in. Horse and rider alike seemed to enjoy the tranquility of the forest. With heavy, unrushed, steps, the animal found its way through the thick underbrush, snorting now and then in reply to the call of a bird.

There was a place, dead south, where the continent's southernmost tip curved into the sea like a gnarly finger. He'd once made his way to the very end of the rocky point, at times forced to steady himself on all fours to avoid slipping and tumbling into the churning waters below. The grueling climb had led him to the most stunning phenomenon. A thin, white scar of clashing waves ran from the rocky tip toward the horizon as far as the eye could see, marking the collision of the Atlantic and the Indian Oceans. The two bodies of water came together in eternal disagreement, rubbing and chafing but never mixing. One side the color of ditch water, the other a deep sapphire blue.

Sebastiaan thought it a fitting resemblance to his current emotional state. One side of him was mourning the loss of Danielle, the other alive and overjoyed at finding her child.

The horse came to a halt near a tree that seemed to defy every rule nature had set for it. Its roots and branches were indistinguishable from each other. Both were thick and unruly as they curled and climbed over the forest floor. Many herbs had found a haven between the knee-high roots. Small purple, white, and yellow flowers playfully dotted the area. Sebastiaan filled his lungs with the sweet, earthy smell of the fragrant plants. There was something about this place that called to him, and he dismounted. Finding a comfortable place to sit, he lowered himself onto one of the large roots, tilting his face to the warm burst of sunlight that struck through the thick canopy of leaves.

Memories floated from the depths of his mind, behind his closed eyes. He watched as his dreams played out their unfulfilled possibilities, and then he watched them fade away. He did not halt their retreat. It was time to bury the past and start looking to the future, time to move on. The recognition released a visceral pain that radiated from his chest, searing through every nerve until he felt numb and raw, as if his skin had been turned inside out.

Leaning forward, he hung his head, letting sorrow shudder through his shoulders in silent sobs. Time passed without marker or meaning.

It was the sharp, clear twitter of a pair of waxbills that pierced his solemn state. Slowly, he opened his eyes and searched the branches. His movements were duly noted as the sound instantly died down. Sebastiaan remained motionless, waiting for the birds to show themselves. A flutter drew his eyes upward, and he spotted the pair staring down at him from their lofty perch. The male locked his black beady eyes with Sebastiaan's in a stare that promised the fiercest of retributions if Sebastiaan dared to threaten his mate. She, on the other hand, had long since decided that, despite his appearance, he posed no danger and renewed her argument in crisp, demanding tones.

Sebastiaan felt no particular sympathy for the male. *May you never learn the silence of her absence*, he thought and gave the feisty bird a half smile. He stared at the small pair a while longer and then stood up with the vigor of a man twice his age.

After gathering an armful of herbs, he led his horse east. The area pulled at a long-forgotten memory. The sound of water and the smell of wet soil drew him deeper into the dark shadows. When he reached a waterhole with a large flat rock in the middle, the memory fell into place. It was the spot where he had taught Orion to swim when he was a small boy. He could still remember how Orion had clung to his neck, too afraid to let go. That was the day Danielle had met one of the tribal chiefs. Sebastiaan wasn't there when it had happened, but that evening she'd casually informed him of the event. His heart still quaked at the countless ways that moment could have ended in disaster.

Kneeling by the water's edge, he cupped his hands and lifted the small puddle to his face. He repeated the motion until his skin stung from the icy water and then set about building a fire. He patiently waited for it to grow in strength before committing the herb stems one by one to the flames. Surrounded by the stillness of the forest, he spoke to Danielle as if she were sitting next to him, his voice in perfect harmony with the sound of the water as it gently pushed past the rocks to fill the rocky pool. He told her that her son had found his way to him and how he planned to be the father she'd wanted him to be. He spoke to her about his plans for the future and then he spoke about their time together, recalling every instance, of which there seemed to be precious few. When there were no more words to speak and no more herbs to sacrifice, he could not bring himself to douse the fire and so he stayed until it had spent itself, staring at the smoldering pale red coals until they, too, turned to ash.

It was near sunset when he reached the *Shack*. Van Leyen and Daka were sitting on the platform outside the double back doors.

"Lads," Sebastiaan greeted, and heavily sat down on one of the three crates that permanently furnished the loading platform.

Van Leyen gave Sebastiaan a long, hard stare. His eyes were dark and troubled before he looked away to where the sun was about to touch the top of the mountain. Soon it would dip behind and then darkness would come swiftly. Daka reached over to hand Sebastiaan a plate of fried fish and a mug of ale. They sat in comfortable silence, each deeply submerged in his own thoughts. Sebastiaan ate his food with neither pleasure nor disagreement.

"He'll have a hard time getting in." Daka winced and stared at the cove's narrow opening in the distance. The wind was still bothersome after the heavy rains of the day before.

"Aye, he might have to wait until morning." Van Leyen gave a slight shake of his head. "Those rocks are not for the faint of heart."

"I've never known Orion to be either patient or faint of heart," Daka said and whistled softly as he watched the *Sword of Orion* nearing the jagged opening.

"It would be nice to have something decent to drink." Sebastiaan flicked his ale with a neat arch into the water.

Van Leyen shuffled his feet, rubbed his hands together as if they were cold and drew a deep, steady breath through his nose – all tells that something bearing considerable weight was crowding his mind.

"Spit it out," Sebastiaan ordered.

"The town is abuzz with news of your son's arrival," Van Leyen responded after carefully measuring his words. His voice droned evenly, as if it were nothing more than a whiff of gossip, while his eyes remained fixed on the approaching ship, its sails catching the last of the day's light.

"You have a child?" Clearly, Daka had not been exposed to the news, and the surprise drove him from his seat. He stared Sebastiaan down with his feet planted wide and his hands fisted on his hips. "How is it I have not known about it? We have breathed the same air, broken bread and spilled blood together for years and all the while, you've been keeping secrets."

In battle, the man moved like a leopard, silent and lethal, but surprises of any kind were always loudly and explosively absorbed and analyzed. Sebastiaan silently waited for the newest development to settle in Daka's mind. Then, in a steady tone, he recounted his meeting with Davit.

Van Leyen's head slowly turned to Sebastiaan. "Where is she?" he asked, his voice barely above a whisper, but heavy with the weight of the question.

Sebastiaan's head moved in one slow, grievous shake, his eyes falling to the planks beneath his feet. The silence carried the truth he couldn't voice.

Van Leyen's stare drifted back to the horizon, his jaw clenched, as he tried to hold back the tremor in his breath. His face carried a quiet fracture as he said a silent prayer for her soul. They had suspected she was dead, had lived with that thought for ten years, yet clung to a faint flicker of hope that one day, somewhere, they would find her. Van Leyen wiped a hand over his face, taking with it the moisture from his cheeks.

Daka had quietly sunk to his haunches, his back to the water, one hand dangling forgotten over his knee while the other clenched into a fist against the deck planks.

Sebastiaan studied his friends: John's face crumpled with raw sorrow, while Daka's burned with a quiet resolve. Yet, Sebastiaan felt a strange distance from their pain, as if shielded by a divine hand. He recognized it for what it was – purpose."

"I have Davit now." His words broke the oppressive silence.

Van Leyen nodded, but Daka spoke first, his voice unwavering with quiet calm. "I pray he's the spark to reignite your heart again, my friend, for grief has dimmed your light too long. This place," Daka said, gazing at the cove and the forest beyond, "is the closest I've seen you to peace."

"I think we can build a good life here," Sebastiaan agreed, deliberately steering the conversation into easier waters. He had promised Danielle to care for her son. He would love her always, but he would mourn her quietly; her child did not deserve his darkness.

"Your son, what does he look like?" Daka asked and watched as

Sebastiaan's face soften.

Van Leyen answered without looking away from the approaching ship. "Spitting image of his mother, he is."

"How do you know? Did you meet him?" Daka asked, once more peeved at finding himself the last to the new development.

"I saw the lad last night at the *Slaughterhouse* when he and Jiya came to round up Orion's crew. My heart stopped cold when Jiya introduced him." Van Leyen slowly turned to face Sebastiaan.

"What were you doing in that filthy place?" True to his nature, Daka ignored the core of the matter and focused on the point nearest to his ears.

"The fights were good, and the sailors bet big," Van Leyen answered but kept looking at Sebastiaan. "Now, we both know that the boy is not yours."

"He's not yours?" Daka asked, his eyes darted from Van Leyen's bruised and skinned knuckles back to Sebastiaan's face.

Sebastiaan's lips thinned, and his face hardened.

"Who is the father?" Daka demanded.

"Elias Coopman," Van Leyen answered, and Sebastiaan's stomach turned sour at the mention of the man's name.

"That animal who was her husband for but one day?" Daka's outrage and disbelief were driving his voice to new heights with every word uttered.

Sebastiaan nodded, his throat too tight to speak.

"There is more, though," Van Leyen said. "I met a man last night, by the name of Martim Fernandes. He had an interesting story to tell. All about how he had survived a pirate attack roughly six months ago when their ship was anchored in a cove up the coast. Crawled on his hands and knees back to the Cape and straight to Du Bois." Van Leyen's eyes closed for a long moment as he sighed deeply. "He claimed that a horde of pirates had boarded them, killed the captain and the crew and set the slaves they were transporting free. Through sheer luck and the help of local tribes, he had managed to make his way back. Apparently, the shipment of slaves was destined for the Cape of Good Hope and the ill-fated captain was Du Bois' only son."

"*Tomba*," Daka whispered. Low waves sloshing beneath them and slamming against the wooden piles, filling the silence after the filthy curse.

"The incident sounds awfully familiar," Sebastiaan said, squinting his eyes in confusion.

"Aye, it does. However, this arsehole padded it a little to make it less humiliating."

"Did he recognize you?" Sebastiaan asked and rubbed his temples to ease the sharp stabbing pain that flared behind his eyes.

"I don't think so. We spoke for quite some time and there was nothing."

"How drunk was he?" Daka inquired.

"Just enough to loosen his tongue and color his memory. Du Bois is not taking the news too well. He's already plotting revenge; however, he is a little short on suspects."

This was a complication Sebastiaan could not afford, not with so much at stake. Du Bois was his enemy, but he had planned on waging a subtle war, not a full-frontal assault that would only end in a bloodbath. The epiphany that he now had something to lose hit him square in the chest like a battering ram at a city gate.

Van Leyen was waiting for Sebastiaan to respond, but when he didn't, he continued.

"You do realize the implications of all this?" Van Leyen pressed.

"He doesn't know it was us, and as long as that remains, we are fairly safe to continue with our plans," Sebastiaan replied.

"No." Van Leyen's voice was tight with urgency. "Don't you see? Davit, being Coopman's son, makes him Du Bois' nephew. If Du Bois discovers that fact, especially considering his recent loss, he might lay claim to the boy, in the most literal sense of the word. On the other hand, if he believed him to be yours, and he finds out that we are responsible for his son's death, he might kill him to even the score."

Sebastiaan's stomach dropped with a suddenness that left him light-headed and nauseous. The possibility of losing Danielle's son to the man who'd murdered her father was unbearable.

"Davit De Vries is my son," Sebastiaan spoke with the authority and conviction of a man who would fight until his dying breath to defend what was his.

"Jiya introduced him as Kwala," Van Leyen interjected.

"It is his tribal name. He hadn't given them his real name. More importantly," Sebastiaan said as he battled to keep his rising fear at bay, "we are the only ones who know the truth of his paternity and that knowledge dies here today. We will never speak of it again. It is the only way to keep him safe. Is that understood?" Both men nodded their agreement.

The Sword of Orion had made her way through the mouth of the cove and was heading toward them.

"Can your heart truly accept another man's child?" Daka asked, his face cast in shadows, but his eyes gleamed with a panicked light.

"Yes." Sebastiaan's response was immediate and without a hint of doubt. The pride in the boy's voice, the night before, when he'd declared him his father, had taken to the ice around his heart like a hammer to a glass pane. "I don't care who fathered him. I loved the woman who brought him into this world. She believed me dead and kept my memory alive by raising her child in my name, and I will not forsake her or abandon him. If that means living a lie, then so be it."

"Du Bois is a despicable human being." Daka's words dripped with dark vehemence.

"But a shrewd one. We should closely guard the secrets we keep from him and be grateful there are no more," Van Leyen said.

The wind was howling around the corner of the *Shack* and the lone, rabid screech of a bat lent an eerie note to the disturbance.

If only that were true, Sebastiaan thought, turning his gaze to the *Sword of Orion* as she crept closer.

Chapter 10

For once, the air did not smell of sour wood stoves and putrid harbor, as days of rain had left it fresh and clean. Walking through the rows of olive trees, Alain Du Bois barely noticed the small green fruit hanging among the silvery-green leaves. Since receiving the news of his son's demise, the color had vanished from his world. Where once a forest of hope and possibility grew, now only the blackened stumps remained, the ground covered in a thick layer of ash.

He and Lucien had never been close. The boy had inherited the worst of both his parents: his mother's volatile nature and his father's lust for the forbidden – not that the latter was such a negative trait to possess should one have the wherewithal to nurture and hone it into a virtue rather than a curse.

Alain had not thought of his long-deceased wife in years, but his son's death had been like a shark thrashing about on the seabed, dislodging and disturbing that which should have stayed buried. Lucia was a woman of quiet beauty with a tranquil exterior: tawny-blond hair, oval face, lips that knew not how to smile or frown, neither full nor thin and eyes that fluctuated between a muddy green and an overcast brown. Her mercurial temperament, conversely, supplied the variety and turbulence her subtle exterior lacked.

When sated and coddled, she was bright and effervescent, her laughter ringing through the gardens and the halls of their estate. But like a bauble blown from the thinnest glass, the slightest upset or obstacle could shatter her jubilance into lethal shards that cut and marred indiscriminately, leaving the recipient confused and reeling from the assault. Most often, that victim was her only child. One moment she'd cradle the boy against her breast, and the next have the child fleeing the room with a bloody nose or a cheek aflame from a stinging slap. Her screams and vitriol would then be heard for days as they rained down on servants, child, and spouse.

There were signs of her instability early on. However, it was greatly overshadowed by her enormous dowry. Alain had tried to be an adequate husband, but her strict rules and ever-increasing expectations had, after the first month, driven him to the peaceful arms of his mistress. After Lucien's birth, her condition had worsened. At first, he'd thought the trauma of childbirth was to blame, but after six years without improvement, he'd stepped from the house one cloudless spring morning, softly shut the black-lacquered front door behind him, and never returned.

On Lucien's eighteenth birthday, Alain received a letter announcing that his time at the *Sorbonne* was coming to an early but inevitable end, for he'd found neither joy nor passion in his studies. Regrettably, what passion he had was found in the bed of a young *vicomte* from a powerful family. Lucien had requested a position in his father's shipping empire to avoid scandal to both families after their liaisons were discovered. It was more ultimatum than request, to which Alain had relented.

The rift between them was apparent from the beginning. Despite the strain, Alain had sought to nurture the Du Bois blood in Lucien, a lineage teeming with business acumen, zeal, and striking aristocratic looks.

Lucien was a deeply complicated young man. His father's blood might have flooded his veins, but his mother's demons held supreme dominion over his heart and mind. He had often wielded cruelty for sport rather than profit, and his favorite target was his father. He viewed Alain as the solitary creator of the sum of his failures, misfortunes, and shortcomings, having abandoned him to the whims of his mother at a tender age.

Alain had believed that elevating the boy to captain and providing him with a ship of his own would settle his unstable nature. Despite Lucien's flaws, he proved a boon to the Du Bois enterprise. The boy was brave, daring, an exceptional swordsman, and wickedly clever. Soon the slave trading, which had always been a steady component of Alain's activities, had turned into the backbone of his ventures, transformed and driven by Lucien.

His son's entry into Alain's venture came at a fortuitous moment. It coincided perfectly with the arrival of Governor Jan Van Riebeeck's letter and affidavit accusing Alain of murdering Aard Van Meerhof, the father of his future sister-in-law. Not that the troublesome connection held any claim over their family at the time of Van Meerhof's death.

Van Riebeeck's letter had released a calamitous storm around his ears, a storm he'd weathered, but only by the skin of his teeth. Alain had managed to escape the noose, arguing that although the accusations against him were unflattering, they resulted from a simple case of misunderstanding brought on by mistaken identity. However, the matter could easily be remedied should the honorable governor be kind enough to provide a witness to Alain's alleged crime. The governor could not, but the accusation was enough to taint Alain's reputation and shroud him in a cloud of suspicion. He was relieved of his captaincy of the VOC merchant ship under his command and ordered by the courts to leave the Netherlands and never to grace her shores again, casting him into a life of neither title nor consequence.

Having Lucien at the helm of his shadowy industry was a blessing. While it gave Alain the time to outlive the ghosts of his misdeeds, the constant excitement and rigors of life at sea had helped quiet his son's inner tribulations.

The fresh sunlight glinted off two slaves' bare shoulders as they cleared the path ahead. They kept their heads bowed and their eyes downcast as he passed.

For as long as Alain could remember, he had craved autonomy. Being the second son of a moderately influential French aristocrat had robbed him of the opportunity to inherit the village and surrounding farmlands over which his family had ruled for generations. That honor was passed to his opium-soaked brother. Where his brother had inherited the land

and title, Alain had inherited his father's cunning.

His father had taught them from a young age to only play by the laws they could not skirt, break, or make. Alain had learned to look at the world through a unique lens of opportunity and innovation and as such had discovered the only laws he had to follow were the laws of physics. The rest were merely suggestions and anyone who did not have the spine to live his life by those terms irritated him beyond the bounds of his forbearance.

Alain's jaw clenched; his mouth settled into a grim, determined line.

Man was not born free. Freedom was not, as so many assumed, a birthright, but the prize of hard work and strength. Those who lived without it did not deserve or earn it and therefore must be ruled by those who had.

His years working for the VOC had furnished him purse and pretext to thrive beyond its reach. The Company was an enormous entity that cast a vast shadow, and in those spectral places beyond the piercing light of legitimacy, Alain had woven a network that spanned much of the globe. Exotic, rare, and illicit goods found their way onto his private fleet of swift vessels, and from there into the eager hands of his discerning, refined clientele.

Alain was a prosperous man. Though he had wealth enough to live in comfort and bribe his way into Heaven, he still fell short of buying his dream: to be a landowner with a population bending its knee to him, abiding his laws and heeding his call. It was an aspiration not gained by tossing one's name in a hat and hoping for the best.

"Good morning, Mister Du Bois," a gardener called from somewhere among the many garden beds. He gave the man a crisp nod but did not break his stride. Casting his eyes over the vast gardens, he wondered how long it would take his future farmers to rival these gardens for variety. The sooner the fort was completely reliant on sourcing its produce from outside, the better. He shook his head and forced his thoughts back to the matter at hand.

The Cape of Good Hope posed a unique opportunity. It was unblemished by previous occupants, offering a fresh start.

The settlement at the southern tip of Africa had always held a special allure. At first, it was an ideal port for transferring and storing his more questionable cargo. However, as more VOC employees chose to be released from their commitments and become free settlers, eager to forge their own paths and build new lives on this wild and unforgiving continent, new opportunities for prosperity began to emerge.

Where the good, honest Dutch men and women had settled and resigned themselves to a life of strife, their government, comprising VOC officials, did not. Alain had arrived at the Cape and immediately set about to soften the circumstances for these pampered bureaucratic puppets with their constantly empty pockets.

After fifteen years, he had bought and bribed himself into a position where he influenced and manipulated every law and regulation passed at the Cape of Good Hope. His was the hidden hand on the chessboard, moving pieces in and out of play. By design, he'd crippled the farmers to near breaking point, and soon they'd come begging for his salvation – which he'd grant. He would buy their land, exact their rents and mold them into a high-functioning force.

The arrangement would satisfy all. The VOC could shed the burden of supporting the struggling peasants, who in turn would trade their hollow freedom from the Company for Alain Du Bois' rule. He would create a close-knit community. Instead of trying to survive on their own, failing, and drowning themselves in liquor and sin, they would support each other, lift each other up, united in their common goal of serving one leader, one master.

It was a dangerous notion to allow for too many independent voices and ideas. It would only lead to sparks of innovation and disproportionate prosperity, as in the case of Wouter Mostert. The farmers were on their knees. Du Bois had to act now. He could not afford for any more rats to swim to safety, serving as examples to the others and undermining his plans.

To be in a position of power at the birth of a settlement was a situation that did not present itself often, and Alain was fortunate enough to be alive during this time. He would not waste this God-given opportunity. Throwing this gift to the wind would be tantamount to blasphemy.

The question that kept him awake these past few nights pushed to the forefront of his mind once more. What good was a dream if there was no one to pass it to? Even after all the years at sea, away from France and its many distractions, Lucien could never trust or tolerate a woman's touch, and his tastes had stayed with his own sex, killing the hope of ever producing an heir to his father's empire.

His death had not come as a surprise, but it was a shock. In the days following the news, Alain allowed the settlement's demands to consume him, immersing himself in his duties as an antidote to the emptiness that grew with each morning.

***

"She weighed anchor before sunrise," Hackius said tiredly, tapping at the sweat on his forehead with a stained linen square before pinching his eyes shut fighting off another wave of dizziness.

The old fort was falling apart, in the most absolute sense of the word. Another section of the east wall had collapsed during the early hours of the morning, waking the occupants and forcing them out of doors, dressed as they were in their nightshirts and caps, for a quick headcount. Fortunately, the fort was not hosting any guests, for once again the guest quarters were strewn about the open space in an untidy heap of clay and timber after losing the battle against the downpour of the past few days.

Hours later, Alain had found the commander, respectably clothed amidst the rubble, assessing the damage. The man was swaying on his feet and looked as if, at any moment, he too might join the debris scattered around the courtyard. Hackius had arrived at the Cape already stricken with yellow fever, and over the months the disease had entrenched itself further. Lengthening his strides, Alain reached Hackius, pulled him from the mess, then all but dragged him up the stairs to the commander's chamber, where he'd firmly seated him in his chair before releasing his arm. Duty had compelled him to pour a restorative measure of whiskey, but Hackius seemed to lack the strength to lift the glass to his lips, and Alain drew the line at playing nursemaid. If the man could not lift it, it would remain untouched.

Du Bois frowned at the man across the desk, currently clutching his forehead. Hackius was deteriorating at an alarming rate. Over the past week, his skin had turned turmeric yellow, sporting scattered blooms of broken veins and clusters of black bruises, a sure sign the illness had reached its final stage and was now ruthlessly attacking his liver and, judging by the swelling around his wrists, likely his kidneys too.

"She left without replenishing her stores? No fresh water, no fresh food?" Alain asked, unsuccessfully hiding the note of disbelief in his voice. Hackius nodded faintly without opening his eyes as another wave of heat flooded his already battered constitution.

Alain waited for the man to recover enough to explain the events of the previous day. He'd left for his estate, the first time in a month, only to return and discover the fort had entirely forgotten that trade was the sole reason for its existence. The situation was too indigestible for Alain to fathom.

Another of Du Bois' ships, *De Feniks* – The Phoenix, would arrive soon, which was what had prompted his visit to the fort that morning. With the best intentions, he'd hoped to find the commander and inform him of the second inbound shipment of slaves, as the first was now confirmed lost. He'd also hoped to assess the commander's health and perhaps recommend his retreat to his vineyard, Rondebosch. Instead, they'd entered the commander's chambers with Hackius on the brink of collapse, when his eyes landed on the bill of sale. The commander was a creature of untidy habit, and his desk closely resembled the state of the courtyard this morning, with debris scattered as far as there was surface enough to support it. The new document shone in its crispness where it lay atop its fallen antecedents.

He lifted the parchment, and his legs failed him so suddenly that he dropped into the chair behind him, trusting blindly it was still there.

The receipt was plain enough. One hundred oak logs, bought yesterday, at a price so monstrous that Alain reeled at the amount beside the entry. Five guilders per log, set down in a steady, almost artistic hand. In total, the rounded sum of one hundred and sixty Dutch ducats had been paid to the *Sword of Orion*.

Why pay for Dutch oak when every valley here groaned with timber ready to fell?

In Amsterdam the self-same logs sold for a fifth of what Hackius had squandered.

"Commander, with all due respect, you *are* aware we are surrounded by forests as far as the eye can see?"

Hackius waved his hand weakly in front of his bowed head as if to swat away a lazy fly.

Alain inhaled slowly and noiselessly through his nose, concentrating on the cool air at the back of his throat until his heart slowed to a measured pace.

Du Bois had served and survived four commanders, each vying to reach the highest rung of incompetence, all succeeding. Had it not been for his steady hand, balancing fresh produce for the fleets against seed and grain for the farmers, the VOC would long since have abandoned this leaking money-pit to its well-deserved grave.

The winter past was one of the fiercest Alain had encountered in all his years at the Cape. Storm after storm had ravaged the coast, turning Table Bay into a death trap, forcing no fewer than seven ships, two returning to Holland and five en route to the Far East, to forgo the promise of fresh food and water and find relief elsewhere.

Du Bois could, by some force of discipline, stomach the losses of those ships, since they were due to nature's fickle and violent humors, but this latest development was unacceptable, incomprehensible, and thoroughly avoidable.

He stared at the commander and wondered briefly if the man was going to spare him the effort of delivering the richly deserved dressing-down by simply dying where he sat. Alas, Hackius opened his jaundiced eyes, which floated like pale dumplings in a thick sauce.

A draft wheezed its way through the closed windows, now miserably misaligned as the building sagged and moved with the unstable soil on which it was built. The air was not cold, but Hackius shivered and Alain bit back the tongue-lashing he was about to unleash.

If he had to endure the sour stench of vomit clinging to the air around the man, then Hackius had better come up with an explanation that would at least sound like it had made sense at the time.

A low grunt, much like a purr but leaning closer toward menace than pleasure, gurgled its way up Du Bois' throat as he listened to Hackius blathering on about how the *Sword of Orion* was not to set sail again but would remain at the Cape for the foreseeable future as it belonged to De Vries. With extreme control honed by years of walking a thin line between lawful and questionable, Alain relaxed his upper lip, where it twitched over his teeth in its bid to curl in disgust.

He returned the offensive document to the desk with a flick of his wrist and leaned back in his chair. There was nothing to be done for it now. He had a warehouse full of rotting food, starving farmers who cried foul every second day of the week, slaves running off in the depth of night, no doubt only to be eaten by the nearest lion, but too stupid to realize, and a man he did not trust who'd just finished building a warehouse and jetty of his own and as of last night, had added a ship to complete the ensemble.

"If we want the favor of the VOC to shine on us for any future length of time, we must show a profit," Du Bois said, his words clipped and cold. "Buying timber which we can easily supply ourselves, and not selling so much as a single onion will not secure that goal."

To his endless disturbance, Hackius seemed unperturbed. Instead, he rose from his seat on trembling legs.

"I am retreating to my vineyard for some time. Everything here is under control and should the need for my guidance arise, De Vries will send word."

It was as if some malevolent evildoer had poured frigid water down Alain's back. Since when did De Vries hold such a vaunted place at the Cape that he could know anything, let alone when the commander's presence was needed or not?

"De Vries?" Du Bois asked. "He is a good hour on horseback from the settlement. How would he manage? Surely you do not expect him to ride out here every day to maintain law and order?"

"That is precisely what I expect. As my friend, I know he will oblige. I have prepared rooms for him upstairs." Alain nodded his agreement, but behind his thoughtful, understanding black eyes, his mind was scrambling for a grip on this fresh development.

"Is that the letter informing him of your intent?" Du Bois asked as he read the upside-down words of the hastily scribbled note now creased beneath Hackius' shaking hand.

The commander frowned at the mess he'd made of the correspondence.

"Ah, yes." Hackius reached for his quill to scratch his signature at the bottom. The act started strong, but the last few lines barely left a mark on the parchment. Very much like the man himself, Du Bois reflected.

"That is very prudent," Du Bois said. "Can I offer my services and deliver the note to him personally? Rumor has it that he's finished construction on his property, and I have been wanting to pay him a visit for the longest time. This will give me the perfect excuse to make the journey."

"It would be much appreciated," Hackius agreed and looked at the door, when a soft knock was quickly followed by the keening of the hinges as it slowly opened.

"Would you like to go upstairs, sir?" Hackius' countenance brightened by a good half a shade at the sound of Joseph's diffident voice.

He stumbled away from his desk. The slave quickly stepped to his side and held out his arm, like a gentleman leading his dance partner onto the floor, and escorted Hackius from the room.

Du Bois remained in his seat and listened to the shuffle of the commander's receding steps. He rose and impatiently snatched the note from the desk, rolled it in a tight ball and slung it into the fireplace. The weather was fine, bringing the first warm day in weeks, with no need for a fire, but the fever had rendered Hackius interminably cold.

Alain had no aspirations to be the next commander of the settlement. Such a position would only shackle him to the VOC once more. He was an independent businessman and wished to remain as such. Those he could not soothe with money had committed enough crimes to allow him to threaten, blackmail and extort them into compliance.

There were exceptions, of course - Hackius for one and De Vries for another - but every man had a weakness, that which he wished to keep safe or hidden. Hackius' was his health and De Vries' would soon be discovered. No man's life was that unblemished or robust.

"Well, at least he has enough wood now to burn till the end of his days," Du Bois murmured to himself as he watched the ball of parchment glow bright and burst into flames. If Hackius were to die at Rondebosch, and all evidence pointed toward that conclusion, Du Bois would discreetly select a temporary replacement from the available ranks. Pushing De Vries into that position was a thought that did not even merit consideration. It was out of the question.

Alain exited the commander's chamber and stepped into the sun-drenched courtyard. Shouts were coming from the pile of rubble where slaves were filling buckets of debris to be carried away. His strides were sure and quick as he made his way out of the chaos and toward the newly built *Castle* where his horse was stabled.

Perhaps the captain of the guard would be a suitable candidate? He discarded the idea almost as soon as it sparked to life. He was easy to control, good at following orders, but he did not have a strong enough standing in the community. Then there was the physician, Pieter Walrandt, whose fingernails were perpetually caked with blackened grime, and Alain's mind recoiled at the picture of those blunt, filthy fingers rummaging through festering wounds. The prospect of advising and guiding such a repulsive figure daily was an ordeal Alain's sensibilities could not endure.

Adriaen De Voogd, the young pastor, however, was a notion worth contemplating. He was well respected, pious, and ambitious. The latter was proven when he had sold his sister to the previous commander's secretary as a wife in a bid to secure his position at the settlement. What was even more attractive than the man's scheming were the many skeletons rattling in his closet, a closet to which Alain held the key.

Yes, it was time to move the bishop into play, Alain thought, and for the first time in days, the sun warmed his face.

Chapter 11

"Damn, I'm getting old," Van Leyen complained, straightening his back.

He and Sebastiaan had been piling logs since the small hours of the morning. With all hands needed to empty the *Sword of Orion's* hold, the two of them had taken it upon themselves to stack the logs in neat piles along the inner walls of the shed. Where once the space was empty, save for their meager belongings, it now felt tight.

They had fallen into an easy rhythm, each taking hold of an end of a log, swinging it back and forth a few times before letting it fly in a neat trajectory to land at the top of the pile. As the stack rose higher, their endurance took the opposite direction, and slowly but surely, they fell behind.

"We're not old," Sebastiaan said with a grunt, enjoying the feel of his vertebrae snapping back into place after a thorough stretch. "We're stupid. Leave those." He waved at the pile of timber yet to be stored. "There are more than enough hands on that bloody ship to do this."

Van Leyen dropped his side of the log as if it were on fire. "I'm going to find something to eat," he said, and with his shoulders slightly slumping and an audible scrape to his stride, he headed for the beach.

Sebastiaan's thighs and shoulders were burning, and he could feel the gray cloud of a headache gathering right in the center of his skull. All early signs of starvation, he diagnosed. The firm clipping of approaching steps interrupted his self-examination.

He squinted at Orion and Davit as they sauntered through the *Shack's* double back doors, glaring sunlight pushing at their backs, casting their faces in deep shadows and bouncing off the hardwood floor in a haze of dust motes. Their footfalls were in perfect harmony, as if marching to the beat of a drum only they could hear. One was swarthy, the other fair, but that was where the disparity ended. They shared the same gait, the same swagger, and the same breadth of shoulder. If one were to ignore the differences in their coloring, it would be easy to imagine their bodies cast from the same mold.

"Uncle."

"Father."

The first greeting was accompanied by a deep scowl, the second by a blush that managed to show through the sun bronzed skin. Both caused Sebastiaan's chest to swell and his heart to beat just that little deeper. His smile was slow in coming but, once fully developed, stuck to his face like a wet feather to a windowpane. Contentment, satisfaction, and a feeling of immeasurable wealth smoothly warmed his insides.

"Good morning lads, you're just in time for breakfast," Sebastiaan greeted and slapped each on the shoulder as he turned them toward the front door.

Their dining area was a few hollow, washed-up logs arranged in an open square. A portly man with a stern face shuffled between three precisely spaced cooking fires a short distance away, while Van Leyen sat atop the center log like a scolded child. His mien was dark enough to curdle sunshine and his gray eyes stabbing at the cook's back.

The aroma of fried fish, melted herb-butter and roasted flatbread wafted through the air. Sebastiaan swallowed several times as his mouth flooded and his stomach rumbled at the promise of food. They'd been unloading the *Sword* since the morning star ruled the night sky, with no break in their labor.

Why the unloading could not wait for a godlier hour was a question only Orion could answer. The crank and pulley system stored in the ship's hull was constructed en route from Table Bay. No sooner had the anchor touched the sandy bottom of the cove than the contraption rose on deck.

Swinging back and forth, it lifted timber from the hull and lowered it into neat piles along the *Shack's* loading dock. Now, eight hours later, with the sun almost halfway to its zenith the *Shack* was beginning to look and smell like the warehouse it was intended to be.

"You've stolen my chef," Orion accused as he, too, struggled to suppress the uproar of his empty stomach, briefly clapping hands with a smiling Daka as they passed each other.

"*Our* chef," Sebastiaan corrected and steered them toward the disgruntled Van Leyen.

"What gives?" Sebastiaan asked, once seated and after witnessing another crease jostling for a place on Van Leyen's already crowded forehead.

"How difficult do you think it is to build a fire and fry a fish?" he asked, twisting his upper body toward the freshly arrived company, elbow out and fist planted on his knee. "Not that hard," he answered his own question, and Sebastiaan bit back a smile. "But *Saint Lawrence* over there," he continued, referring to the Roman deacon who was martyred on a hot gridiron somewhere in the third century, "turned it into a ritual of precision. I swear he examined every stone before deeming it worthy to encircle the coals. At this rate, we'll be lucky to enjoy our first bite by sundown."

Harja, Orion's Javanese chef, divided the fish among three pewter trenchers, carrying them effortlessly while struggling through the thick, loose sand. Offering the first to Orion, he paused, awaiting his captain's approval, before handing out the rest.

Orion inhaled the flavors drifting from his breakfast: roasted fish dripping with a butter sauce delivered on a crusty piece of flatbread. Closing his eyes, he took the first bite and gave a deep, satisfied groan as the flesh melted in his mouth.

The chef's eyes followed every move Orion made, from lifting the food from the trencher to the moment his lips closed around the first bite. By the time Orion's throat dipped, signaling the morsel had passed its critical test, Harja was leaning forward, eyes sharp and chin tilted, awaiting his captain's verdict.

"Thank you, Harja," Orion said with a nod. Harja's shoulders dropped and a triumphant smile split his face. With a respectful bow, he served the rest to Sebastiaan and Van Leyen.

"*Jesus*, all this song and dance," Van Leyen muttered, but wisely waited for Harja to turn his back before retrieving a small pouch from his belt, opening it, and bombarding the dish with salt.

Davit laughed under his breath, tossed a quick word of excuse over his shoulder, and hurried to Harja's side. The two of them fell into the old rhythm: Harja spearing chunks of sizzling fish straight from the grid, slapping them onto slabs of flatbread, Davit ferrying the loaded trenchers to outstretched hands. Sailors spilled from the shack, their steps lazy and loose, shirts stained with sweat, voices rising as the smell of food hit them.

Jiya emerged last from the building, drawing Harja's attention, who promptly dispatched Davit with a trencher heaped specially for their first officer. Jiya accepted the offering, thanked Davit with a grateful slap on the back, then drew him off toward Sebastiaan and the rest, talking low and earnest as they walked.

"Andreas," Orion called to one of his younger crew members. The man whipped around and hurried to his captain, knuckled his forehead, and stood at attention, awaiting his orders.

"You will assist Harja today," Orion ordered in a voice like soft leather over cold iron, the lazy tone failing to hide the notes of authority.

"Aye, captain," the young sailor replied eagerly, spun around and raced toward the chef.

"Cousin," Orion called.

Sebastiaan saw the moment that small truth hit Davit's mind and trickled down his spine, pinging every bone as it went. His shoulders tensed, and his head snapped in Orion's direction.

"Come sit down," Orion instructed.

Davit returned to the log on stiff legs. He sat bolt upright, fists clenched so tight the knuckles blanched. Sebastiaan watched as the boy's warring emotions played across a face trying to remain still. With a single command, Orion had drawn Davit into a family. Sebastiaan opened his mouth to say something soothing when Orion's sharp voice struck first.

"Where the hell is your food?" Orion barked, completely oblivious to the boy's newfound distress. Davit's eyes darted past Sebastiaan to Orion and then dropped to stare at his empty hands.

"Ah," he said, and shot off toward the cook again.

This time Sebastiaan could not contain his laughter.

"Don't laugh," Orion mumbled, and pointed his eating knife toward Davit's retreating form. "That boy has a predilection for disobedience. Believe me when I tell you uncle, having him run in the direction I've ordered is a novel experience for both of us."

"Are you telling me that you are having trouble taming him?" Sebastiaan asked, laughing harder when he caught Orion's disgruntled expression.

"Not anymore," Orion returned. "He's all yours now."

"All done, Effendi," Jiya cut in, as he found a comfortable spot to sit, one long leg extended, the other bent. "I've covered the brandy barrels with a thick tarp, but they are still a major fire hazard. There really is no other way to protect them."

"Other than drinking it," Daka chimed in as he joined them, his plate supporting more than double the portion of the others.

"What?" Daka responded to Van Leyen's frowning judgment then shuffled over to make room for Davit. "Harja gave me extra after I promised to go hunting today. He is in the mood for boar."

"Does he know there are no boars at the Cape?" Van Leyen asked.

"Does he know about your little salt-pouch rebellion when he wasn't looking?" Daka fired back, lifting his eyebrows and tilting his head toward Van Leyen's meal.

"Aye, fair point," Van Leyen conceded, "your secret is safe with me." Satisfied over his rare victory, Daka tilted his head back and dropped one entire glistening fillet into his mouth then chewed with gusto before licking the butter from his fingers.

"Speaking of secrets," Van Leyen looked to Sebastiaan, after rearranging his features, which were warped by disgust at Daka's lack of manners. "We have our meeting with the farmers tonight."

Sebastiaan grunted his agreement and scraped the last morsel from his plate.

"I think I should go alone." He gave Van Leyen a meaningful stare. Van Leyen's eyes narrowed, and he responded with a barely perceptible nod, understanding Sebastiaan's unspoken request.

"I don't like the idea of you going with no one to watch your back," Orion offered his opinion, which was promptly met with a dark scowl from Sebastiaan. "Besides," Orion bravely continued in the face of the brewing storm. "I am a partner now, and if we are to replace the soldiers with my men, I think it would be wise for me to be there and assure the farmers myself." Sebastiaan inhaled deeply and compressed his lips. The last thing he wanted was to overwhelm these poor, battered people with a show of force.

"I'll watch over the both of you," Daka said and spat a small fish bone to the side.

"I'm coming too," Davit joined in. That drew Sebastiaan's full attention, and he slowly turned his head toward the boy.

"Have fun with that one." Orion slapped Sebastiaan's knee, rose from his seat and stepped away from the group to call for his carpenter.

"You don't even know where we're going," Sebastiaan teased, noting the stubborn glint that sparked in Davit's eyes.

"It doesn't matter," Davit said willfully, his jaw tightening adamantly, as if preparing to receive a blow. Sebastiaan smiled softly, for he'd many times seen that same tenacity on Danielle's face. He knew if he pushed back too aggressively, it would only result in a tug of war, one he would eventually concede out of pure affection and not reason. But the stakes were too high for him to capitulate. The longer he could keep Davit hidden from prying eyes and the less Du Bois knew about his vulnerabilities, the better.

Once again, John Van Leyen came to his rescue. "Davit, I want you and Daka with me tonight. We need meat for the pot. There are a lot of mouths to feed and what we have will not last." John cast a lazy look at Daka who, for once, understood the subtle message.

"Aye," Daka added, his voice gruff, "it's time you learn how to fend for yourself." That gauntlet landed with an echo. "I heard you're not too shite with a short blade. Let's see how you fare with a bow and arrow." Daka knew that tribal boys could nock an arrow almost as soon as they could walk, yet he prodded the lad's pride with a sly grin, stoking that sensitive young male arrogance he understood all too well.

The taunt almost worked. Davit's mouth tightened as he struggled to hold back the scathing retort that was champing at the bit to be released. The vein at the center of his forehead throbbed into view and Sebastiaan shifted his gaze to stare at the calm water of the cove, biting the inside of his cheek to stop himself from laughing. Daka could pester a saint out of his senses, but Davit was not so easily baited and resolutely remained silent.

"Can you ride?" Van Leyen asked, and Davit shook his head. "Then how will it look when you arrive at the meeting tonight stuck to your father's back like a tick? Hmm? No, a man must know how to ride a horse. We'll use our little outing to teach you." Nobody mentioned the ordeal a few years ago when, during one of their meetups, Orion was forced onto horseback. It was an incident that had scarred all involved, none more so than the poor horse. Only under Van Leyen's persistent and gentle hand had they achieved a marginal measure of success.

Davit's cheeks colored once more, as the suggestion that he might be a source of embarrassment to his father carved a fresh notch out of his pride. Sebastiaan felt a flicker of pity, then crushed it. Sacrifices needed to be made, and the boy had pride enough to spare.

"Fine," Davit grumbled and dropped his gaze.

Thus, the matter was settled with nary a drop of blood spilled. Van Leyen and Daka would take the boy away from the settlement and keep him safe, while Sebastiaan and Orion would set out to undermine the mighty VOC.

"Niccolò," Orion called, not seeing his carpenter right away but knowing he would not be far. He searched the beach and then scanned the deck of the ship.

"Capitano," Niccolò's soft voice spoke from behind Orion, causing a gut-clenching flinch. Damn, the man was stealthy.

Niccolò stood at an even six feet, his body elegantly toned and lean, not an ounce of fat to spare. From a distance, he posed no threat nor drew the eye, but up close, the flatness in his gaze and muted confidence betrayed hidden depths – a silent catalog of lethal skills he could sift through like pages in a tome. He moved without sound, neither crunching of sand beneath his feet nor the creaking of planks when on deck, floating from one place to the next like the early morning mist.

Niccolò had planted himself an arm's length away, close enough to make Orion's skin itch for distance. His voice was never more than a soft murmur, yet he refused to repeat himself. Easier, it seemed, to crowd others than to waste a single extra word.

Niccolò had joined Orion's crew, scarred and tormented, with blood-clotted, blond hair and haunted ice-blue eyes. He'd simply boarded the ship as it had lain at anchor in the Port of Muziris and never left. Striding into the captain's cabin, he'd declared himself in crisp Italian, though Orion soon learned that he understood Dutch as well as any cheesehead from the fatherland.

Over the first couple of months of observing his new carpenter, Orion concluded that there was much more to Niccolò than met the eye. His speech was refined, as were his eating habits, hinting at a gentle, if not privileged, upbringing. His deft handling of a rapier and ease with a horse confirmed this suspicion. He was a talented artist who found solace in carving and molding wood in awe-inspiring creations that could knock Michelangelo on his arse and keep him there.

Where all other sailors owned one sea-chest, Niccolò owned five, brimming with the disguises of half a dozen nations: European and Indian court garb, priest's robes, vibrant kaftans, embroidered tunics, and beggar's rags. Orion had taken one look and known exactly what manner of man had walked aboard his ship.

Orion had offered him a rank and cabin of his own. Both were respectfully but firmly declined. Though the man rarely spoke a word to anyone, he seemed to relish the sailors' presence around him, as if the rhythms of their day-to-day lives brought him peace.

Niccolò stood motionless while Orion explained the consequences of tonight's meeting and the role the crew would play in the days to come.

"Choose your men," Orion said. "Familiarize yourself with the area, and determine a defensible perimeter. Take a few days if you must. I want to know the location and size of every ditch, anthill, and outcrop."

"I take it we are to stay out of sight?" Niccolò all but whispered.

"Above all else."

***

"I was not sure you would come," Wouter Mostert said as he wrapped a thickly calloused hand around Sebastiaan's.

"Are we late?" Sebastiaan asked, looking around the deserted yard of Mostert's handsome stone house and its outbuildings. The farm lay a fair distance from the settlement; too close for a secret meeting, in Sebastiaan's mind, yet far enough to go unnoticed if they were careful.

"No," Wouter said, "we heard the horses, and the folks thought it wise to make themselves scarce. They are waiting in the barn."

Wouter Mostert's congenial smile did not fade, but his body tensed slightly as he turned to Orion.

"Captain Orion Van Jeveren, my nephew, and business partner," Sebastiaan said by way of introduction, "Mister Wouter Mostert." The two men studied each other as they shook hands. Wouter's thoughts were carefully hidden behind the warmth of his eyes, and Orion's distrust behind an inscrutable expression.

"Your servant, Captain." Wouter's polite greeting was met with the barest of nods. Sebastiaan made a mental note to, once again, remind Orion that it was a form of greeting and not a statement of intent.

Wouter seemed unaffected by Orion's aloofness and with the ritual of introductions observed and obeyed, he turned to Sebastiaan.

"Did you come as a bystander, or are you here with a solution?" Mostert was obviously not one for beating around the bush.

"A *potential* solution," Sebastiaan said.

"Care to enlighten me now, or do you want to keep it a surprise?" From his tone, Sebastiaan gathered it was not a question per se, but a polite demand for information. The message was clear: this time they were standing on his land, his territory, and they were going to play by his rules. Sebastiaan and Orion spent the next ten minutes explaining to Mostert the plan they had put together.

"Much will depend on their commitment," Sebastiaan said. "If they don't *all* agree to this, it will not work. We can't have half of them sell to us and the other half to the fort. It will lead to a bidding war, and that is something I am not prepared to engage in."

"Let's put it to them. Have them decide their own fate. Shall we?" Mostert said and pointed to the barn.

It was a solid stone building with a thatched roof that housed not only farm tools and necessities but also larger equipment used for brick-making. Passing between the two dome-shaped kilns, Sebastiaan stepped inside. Bags of sand and sawdust were piled shoulder-high by the door; deeper in, farm tools, molds and drying-racks were pushed against the wall. Those who had come for the meeting filled the open space in the middle. A few hay bales had been appropriated as seats for the women; the men stood. The children drifted among the adults like restless little lost ghosts.

The air inside was stale and heavy, weighed down by the press of too many bodies into a confined space, vibrating with the drone of subdued voices. Casting Sebastiaan a brief look as they stepped through the door, Orion carefully separated his lips just enough for his breath to pass. Oil lamps, scattered throughout the makeshift hall, suffused the room with a warm yellow hue, but even the flattering light could not hide the shallowness of the gaunt faces before them.

Wouter stepped onto a wooden crate, elevating himself, and effectively drawing everyone's attention. Conversations died down by degrees.

"Good evening all, and welcome," Wouter started in a voice deep with authority cultivated from years of leadership. "We are gathered here in good company, and I pray that our meeting shall be fruitful. Let us start with the Word of God, and then bow our heads in prayer, asking for His blessing and guidance.

"Deuteronomy twenty-six," he read. *"But the Egyptians mistreated us and made us suffer, subjecting us to harsh labor. Then we cried out to the LORD, the God of our ancestors, and the LORD heard our voice and saw our misery, toil, and oppression."*

Wouter was smartly paving the way for the ideas Sebastiaan was about to bring forward. Sebastiaan let Wouter's voice drift to the background and used the somber moment to study the bedraggled group. There were about twelve families present, all farmers with patches of land along the Liesbeeck River.

One man was standing like a dead tree stump in the middle of a body of water, one row from the front, half a head taller than the rest, arms folded across his broad chest. There was something familiar about him, yet Sebastiaan could not put his finger on it. The farmer wasn't the sort you'd meet and soon forget. Large and burly, with short brown hair shot through with iron-gray, high cheekbones, a prominent nose broken more than once, and firm lips half-hidden by a close-cropped beard. Two deep lines furrowed where his eyebrows met. It was not just financial hardship that had carved those lines. Then Sebastiaan saw it; not the man, but the helpless anger and desperation burning in his eyes. Something held his heart in a death grip, and that unseen hand was squeezing hard.

There had been a time when Sebastiaan had carried that same look. Not caring for the similarity, he turned his focus to the front row, where an old man with a stern, deeply lined, and sun-weathered face stood. His long gray hair, more salt than the original pepper, glimmered defiantly in the lamplight; one hand was pressing a sweat stained leather hat to his chest, the other was resting on the bony shoulder of an equally old woman sitting by his side. With her head held high, she stared at the back wall, her sharp eyes momentarily frozen as her thoughts wandered beyond the demands of the present. Her long silver hair was neatly rolled in a thick bundle, and her gnarly fingers absentmindedly played with the stitching of a patch on her dress. An air of dignity wrapped around the aged couple, most evident in their clean faces and clothes. They were tired and starved, but not broken.

The old woman sat with her back straight, slightly turned from the younger one sharing the hay bale. The other could not have been older than five and twenty. Hardship had taken its toll, and he would bet good money they were all younger than they appeared. The way the young woman was looking at him made him think she'd been doing so for a while. Her eyes, almost too big for her delicate face, fixed on him with open interest.

Without breaking the connection, she raised a slender hand and with one finger hooked a strand of light brown hair from the side of her face. The rest she'd knotted into a tangled mass at the back of her head. The advanced state of her pregnancy caused her full breasts to strain against the confines of her dress. She was undeniably lovely, but far too skinny for a woman in her condition. A grubby, barefoot little girl with bright red hair, which hadn't seen a comb in many a month, if ever, stood by her side. She, too, was looking at Sebastiaan with unguarded curiosity.

Realizing he'd been staring at the young mother, he searched the group for her husband - someone showing signs of jealousy or possessiveness. He found none; not even the brooding cumulus cloud behind her so much as twitched in his direction. In the back, though, a few men stole glances her way with the same unguarded hunger she had aimed at him.

"Let us bow our heads in prayer," Wouter said, closing the *Bible*. There was a rustle among the attendees as those standing shifted on their feet and mothers pulled their young close, trying to keep them still.

Years of living by the sword had left their mark on Sebastiaan and no matter how devout or respectful he was, there was no way he'd closed his eyes in a room full of people he did not know. Instead, he lowered his head and stared at his boots, trusting his peripheral vision to feed him critical information.

His skin pricked with the niggling sensation that the young woman was still looking at him. Lifting his head, he met her gaze; they were the only two people in the room who had not closed their eyes.

That raw, unconcealed stare woke a dull ache in his chest as he saw the promises flickering in her eyes. For a heartbeat he let himself imagine her round-cheeked and wrapped in a soft dress; he felt the impossible weight of a child in his arms, saw himself caring for a woman and being cared for by one. Then Danielle's image filled his vision - her dark curls whipping in the wind, eyes bright with laughter, skin flushed warm and alive.

A faint smile stole onto his face before he could stop it.

"Amen," Wouter said, and the word snapped Sebastiaan from his reverie. The young woman was still staring at him, unaware of his thoughts, hope shining in her eyes, for he'd not looked away and she'd noticed the softening of his features.

Bleeding saints, what the hell was wrong with him?

Wouter let a hearty silence descend on the room, just long enough to send a message that this meeting would be different from those that came before. The man was a born leader, confident, strategic and enigmatic. All eyes were fixed on the small stage.

"Friends," Wouter began; no warm smile followed the agreeable address. Instead, his face hardened, the outer tips of his eyebrows lifted as the front ends dipped into a deep frown. "For too long we have been taken advantage of. We have been exploited while we labored in the harshest conditions, being used as mere tools by those at the fort." He stabbed a firm finger in the direction of the settlement. Many exchanged startled glances. Clearly, this level of bellicosity was an uncommon occurrence. Wouter paused, letting the premise of the meeting sink in, before he continued. "They use us to make themselves look good for their VOC masters, as they conveniently turn a blind eye to our suffering." Heads nodded in agreement. A low "Mm-hmm" drifted from the floor. Wouter's eyes darted over the faces before him, touching each, if only for an instant.

"It is no accident or coincidence that the land we've been granted is at the far corners of our settlement. The mighty VOC is cutting expenses by deploying fewer soldiers, instead using us as a shield to keep the settlement safe from the aggressive native tribes. We are the lifeblood of this settlement, and yet we live like shadows in our homes, many without furniture, sleeping on the cold floor. The clothes on our backs, often the only garments we have." Wouter's voice was gaining volume with every statement and soon rang through the audience like a Sunday morning church bell, loud and crystal clear. "But make no mistake, these conditions are not a sign of poverty or indolence. They are the result of the cruel negligence of those in power."

Many strong "Yeses" sounded, and one man punctuated his agreement with a raised fist. Shoulders straightened in defiance and many backs stood a little firmer as forgotten pride pushed to the surface. Wouter let their blood simmer for a moment.

"But by the grace of God, there could be a better way to meet the future." The barn fell deathly quiet.

"This evening, I have invited a man whom I believe can tip the scales in our favor." Sebastiaan found himself the subject of many curious but wary stares. "This man comes as our ally, not our savior. He stands before us with an opportunity, a new path forward. One we must accept unanimously or not at all, for going at this halfway is not an option. We must stand together to reclaim our dignity and our future." There was no clapping or cheering, just a weighted, anxious silence.

"Allow me to introduce Mister Sebastiaan De Vries." Sebastiaan bowed his head in greeting and graciously ascended the wooden crate as Wouter stepped off to the side.

Foregoing the pleasantries of customary small talk, Sebastiaan decided to cut to the heart of the matter. "I stand before you not as a friend, or a savior, as Mister Mostert so generously phrased, but as a businessman with a proposition."

The statement was met with a shuffling of feet and the start of a low buzz as the attendees murmured their agitation and distrust. One man shook his head and dropped his chin to his chest. Sebastiaan's left eyebrow climbed at a sharp angle and he rubbed his bottom lip in contemplation, then lifted that same finger to silence the room and quell the budding mutiny.

"My proposal is simple: Sell your produce to me instead of the fort," he said with a shrug of his shoulders, "I will pay you a fair price."

His words were met with deafening silence. He knew they were expecting a lengthy, persuasive monologue, and so he gave them none. Patiently waiting for them to start their objections. People in distress will always find a problem for every solution. They cling to their troubles like a dog to its vomit, not because they love the taste, but because it's familiar.

"Who decides what a fair price is?" the old man in the front row asked, his voice brittle with suspicion and years of broken promises.

"I will buy your produce at a hundred percent increase over the cost of your production," Sebastiaan answered immediately.

"What does that mean?" the old man persisted.

"It means," Sebastiaan explained, "that I will buy your … what is it you produce?"

"We produce whatever the fort allows us to grow. This season, it is wheat."

"It means I will buy your wheat at double the cost of producing it."

The old man fell silent as the buzzing in the room increased.

"So, where do we buy our seeds from? You?" a young farmer in the back asked.

Sebastiaan shook his head before he spoke. "I have a ship en route, and I have requested tools, seed, and saplings, but I don't know what is onboard nor when the ship will arrive. Therefore, it might be best if you continue to buy from the fort for now."

"If we stop selling to them, they will stop selling to us," the young man returned.

"Not necessarily," Sebastiaan replied. "Why should they?"

"They will do it out of spite," another shouted. A hum of agreement rose, and once more feet scuffed the straw-strewn floor.

"The governor is not an idiot. At the end of the day, the fort's bottom line and ultimate weakness is to show a profit. If they don't sell to you, then what would they do with the seed and grain they received from the VOC? Send it back? I think not. Besides, that problem will go away once we've established a regular supply with reliable incoming shipments." This time the drone of voices took on a more discontented undertone.

"It's a rich man's solution," a man shouted. "We don't have the luxury of time. If something doesn't work, we can't simply sit back and wait for a shipment of unknown seedstock to arrive from God knows where." Many heads nodded in support.

"Batavia," Sebastiaan clarified the latter.

"Either way, it will take months," the farmer persisted, sounding agitated and not without reason.

"Look, I can't guarantee the fort would keep selling to you, but I can't see any other path for them to take."

"Aye, they will sell to us," a man standing in the middle row said, "but they will sell at an even higher price than they do now."

"Then you turn them down and walk away. But you must do so as a group. None of you can afford to buckle under the pressure. No matter what," Sebastiaan advised. That statement was akin to letting a snake into the henhouse. Everybody started speaking at once. Some even tried to leave and would have succeeded were it not for Wouter, who brought the group under control.

One farmer pushed his way to the front and stabbed a finger at Sebastiaan. "The kind of courage you speak of can only be shown if there is coin under the bed. Like we said, it's rich man's talk. It will not work." The man's voice was deep and heavy, rising easily above the other objections.

"We appreciate you coming down here from your high horse to talk to us and flash your fancy plan like it's common sense." His lip curled with equal measures of defiance and desperation. "But we know who you are. We've heard the rumors. You come from wealth and clearly have never suffered or toiled a day in your life." A challenging glint lit the man's eyes as he looked Sebastiaan up and down. Sebastiaan smiled. "We don't begrudge you your life, but please, go back to it, and leave us to solve our problems on our own." He finished with a flick of his hand, as if he wished to swat Sebastiaan from the room.

"How much?" Sebastiaan spoke in an even tone.

"How much what?" the man asked, taken aback.

"How much money will it take for you to solve *your problems on your own?*" Sebastiaan regarded him with the detached tolerance of a priest reassuring a sinner of his salvation.

"I don't understand your meaning," the man said as Sebastiaan's un-affected attitude drained some of the wind from his sails. "We are all indebted to the fort. Each season, they pay less for our harvests and ask more for tools, grain, and slaves. Many of us are now at the point where our harvest barely covers what we owe, and then we have to borrow again for the next season. If we don't sell to the VOC, they will take our land as payment for our debts. Just last week, two families were forced to sell their land to Alain Du Bois for the mere sum of their debt, reduced now to tenants under his thumb."

Sebastiaan exhaled deeply and looked at Orion. Not missing a beat, Orion walked to the side of the barn, grabbed a small, wobbly wooden table and with one hand dragged it across the uneven floor in a series of skips and scrapes to flank the 'stage'. Then he reached into his satchel and produced a heavy leather pouch, which he dropped unceremoniously on the table. Without delay, he reached into the pouch, extracted five silver coins, which he neatly stacked in a small tower, and then topped it off with a gold coin. He did it eleven more times until twelve stout towers glittered on the table.

The air in the room underwent a rapid shift in the face of the growing stacks of coins.

"I've come to the realization that I can stand here and speak until I sprout feathers and it will not make a dent of difference to your perspective." Looking to the table and then back at the group, Sebastiaan made certain he held the eye of every one of them.

"That," he said, pointing to the table, "is a rich man's solution to a poor man's problems. But that is not what this is about. I have no intention of starting a vendetta against the authorities. I am offering an alternative which would hopefully be the foundation for a free market in the future.

And I am not above buying your attention." They all reacted to his statement with stunned faces and slack jaws.

"If money is the problem, then there it is," he said. "But it is not and we all know it. The VOC's governance of the Cape is flawed; it is an unsustainable system. How can it work when any higher-ranking official on any ship docking in the harbor can override the commander at the fort? How can it work when these men spend two weeks at the Cape and then introduce policies and laws they brought with them from Batavia, India, and even Japan with no regard for the unique conditions of life in Africa?" Most in the group were fidgeting, their eyes glazed over and fixed on the table.

"We need to look past the obvious, which is money," he said, "and start looking to the future. To the land your children will inherit." That got their attention, and he pushed his advantage.

"Tell me, what does victory look like for you?" Once again, the group offered nothing but silence. Sebastiaan's temper was starting to tug at the threads that held it in place. He pointed to the old man who'd spoken first.

"What is it you want?" he pushed.

"Fairness," the old man said decisively.

"Protection," a woman with a child on her hip called.

"They don't care for us," her husband added. "We are nothing but slaves to them."

"Yes, I don't doubt that," Sebastiaan agreed. "But let's not look for someone to blame. And instead, focus on ways to strengthen your position so their actions don't affect you so catastrophically."

"Grave crimes have been committed against us," the burly farmer in the middle spoke for the first time. "Someone must be held accountable."

"Enough!" Sebastiaan's voice cracked across the room like a whip. "This is not a Sunday service." His voice dropped, but the edge stayed cold. "So how do you want to go about this? Shall we hunt for the sin first? Demand repentance, recognition, whatever will finally placate you?" He let the silence stretch, then gave a thin, humorless smile. "And after that fruitless little dance, will you honestly believe the world has magically turned into the paradise you deserve?"

He drew a slow breath, the only outward sign he was reining himself in.

"It is utter nonsense because it does not solve the problem." He spoke every word in single file. "It solves nothing. It only deflects. You want a villain to string up so you can feel something has been done, while the actual problem sits there untouched."

The room fell into dead silence.

"I will ask one simple question and will keep asking it until I get the right answer. Tell me: what is the problem?" he demanded.

After many moments passed, a hesitant voice offered. "The governor–"

"No," Sebastiaan ruthlessly interrupted, ending that lament in its infancy.

"Tell me," he repeated softly. "What is the problem?"

"Alain Du Bois–,"

"No."

A flicker of something close to pity crossed his face, gone before it fully formed.

"You don't know what the problem is?" he asked with raised brows. "Well, that is a problem. How can you solve something if you don't know what is wrong?"

"The VOC is–," a thin voice tried, but Sebastiaan only tightened his lips and shook his head.

"The problem is," a sharp-faced Bengalese man, perhaps in his early thirties, spoke Dutch with a heavy Japanese accent. The collision of traits made Sebastiaan's mind stumble for an instant, and he simply stared.

Swallowing once, the man valiantly pressed on. "The fort has a monopoly, that gives them the power to kill every opportunity before we even know it exists." He pulled a young boy with shining black hair close against his leg as he waited for whatever judgment would follow.

"Exactly," Sebastiaan praised. "You cannot fight them, and nor should you, but I am suggesting a different path. I am offering to buy your next three harvests in advance tonight," he said and pointed to the stacks of coins. "That should be enough to settle your debts with the fort and to buy grain for the foreseeable future. And if you work smart, there will be enough left to ease your most pressing burdens and even furnish your homes. Once you've settled your debts, they can't take your land, and whatever you produce from this point onward comes to me."

"What will you do with the produce? The VOC does not allow anyone but the fort to sell to the visiting ships," the old man asked.

"Haven't we established that you have enough problems of your own? Do you really want to adopt mine?" Sebastiaan smiled and the man conceded the point.

"Our crops are almost ready for harvest. What is to stop us from taking your money and selling our produce to the fort?" a young opportunist asked. Sebastiaan's smile widened.

"You are a farmer, right?"

"Yes," the young man said, sparks of humor hiding in his answer.

"Your honor would stop you from doing so," Sebastiaan replied. "Also, had you actually seriously considered this wicked course of action, you wouldn't have told me." Small eruptions of laughter followed the statement. "Trust is a fragile thing. But I have every faith that this will work."

"There is one more concern," the Bengalese man said, somewhat dampening the light-hearted mood. "Currently, there are soldiers patrolling the border. Granted their efficiency is questionable, but it is better than nothing. If we stop selling to the fort, they will remove that thin layer of protection to force our compliance, and that would leave us more vulnerable."

"That is not a concern," Orion spoke for the first time and, like hatchlings waiting for their meal, all heads turned to him. "We already have men in place, safeguarding the border. They are effective, highly trained and disciplined. No one will be left vulnerable as long as we reside at the Cape. That is final." With that Orion effectively ending the discussion and, by extension, their part in the proceedings.

Sebastiaan took his cue and stepped from the crate. He'd done his best. The rest was up to them.

Wouter came over and leaned in to whisper in Sebastiaan's ear.

"How do you wish to proceed?" he asked.

"Put it to a vote. If they all agree, we proceed. I will pay them each in advance here tonight. If they don't agree collectively, we go back to the *status quo.*"

It took less than five minutes for all hands to rise.

"I thank you all for coming," Wouter said. "Before we adjourn, I would like to offer our deepest gratitude to Gijs and Elsje Waterman for providing enough bread to feed all and a few items of clothing for the children." Once more, the beehive stirred in unified gratitude. "My wife Hester will distribute the items while one family at a time comes forth to introduce themselves and conclude their business with Mister De Vries."

Judging by where the Southern Cross hung in the sky, Sebastiaan guessed it was nearly midnight by the time he, Orion, and Wouter stepped out of the barn.

"It came together rather well in the end," Wouter said.

Sebastiaan studied him for a moment in silence. It was time to lay the rest of his cards on the table.

"Wouter," he said and Mostert's face tightened. "This is only a temporary solution."

"I know," Wouter said. "I wish it wasn't."

"We are poking a very large bear with a very short stick. It will work for a while, but in the end the VOC will squash it. However, it will buy you time and leverage. With no debt hanging over their heads and the taste of success fresh in their mouths, you can unite them and negotiate from a position of strength. I am simply a means to an end, a way for them to find their own salvation."

"Why are you doing this?" Wouter asked.

"I have my reasons, but for now, they shall remain my own."

"You are a godsend. Offering relief the way you did, answered many prayers."

Sebastiaan accepted the compliment with a dip of his chin. He and Orion mounted their horses, said their farewells, and took their leave at a leisurely pace.

"You know, something occurred to me," Orion said after a long, contemplative silence.

"And what is that?" Sebastiaan asked.

"Every now and then, sporadically, if you will, throughout the course of my life– "

"Get to the point."

"I've heard the name Alain Du Bois mentioned. It always went along with a string of profanities and some very serious oaths."

Sebastiaan remained silent.

"It is not a common name, and I was wondering if it could be the same man mentioned in the meeting tonight."

Sebastiaan stared off into the darkness. Their path was dimly lit by bright stars and a healthy portion of the moon, their horses' heavy footfalls the only sound.

"You wouldn't be doing this just to piss him off, would you?" Orion persisted.

"Would you still support me if I did?"

"Oh, hell yes."

Chapter 12

ijs had brought the news early that morning; Commander Hackius had passed away the day before. The funeral was to be held at two o'clock that afternoon, as per the decree of the acting commander, pastor Adriaen De Voogd. There was hardly enough time for Sebastiaan to wash and dress before he had to leave with Gijs. He thought it best to attend the funeral alone to keep a low profile. Davit wanted to accompany him but once again he had to refuse the boy. This time the denial was not so easily brushed aside.

"Is it embarrassing for you to be seen with me?" he asked, and Sebastiaan's heart almost stopped at the naked hurt in the boy's eyes.

"Come with me," he said and took Davit into the forest to a private spot by the stream where he'd bathed not ten minutes earlier. Not caring if he'd be late for the funeral or that Gijs was waiting by the horses, he sat down on a large boulder and motioned for Davit to join him. The stream was narrow but fast-flowing as it gurgled its way to the cove. Pools of sunlight warmed the forest floor. The gentle breeze rustling through the low-growing ferns held a hint of moisture, signaling that the day might not end as amicably as it had started.

Sebastiaan inhaled the earthy smell of decaying leaves and wet soil, letting the ethereal beauty of the forest settle around them. He could feel the tension coming off Davit where he stiffly sat next to him. In the few weeks since their paths had merged, the boy appeared to have lost his bearings. Outwardly he was content, filling his days with hard work, especially now that the farmers' wagons rolled in heavy with harvest, but there were moments when he seemed caught between two worlds, where uncertainty and some heavy weight deep inside brought a panicked look to his eyes, and then Sebastiaan would watch as he withdrew and disappeared into the forest alone.

"I am not ashamed of you," he said.

"You just don't want to be seen with me." Davit kept his eyes on the water, rubbing his hands slowly together. "I understand." There was nothing pitiful in the statement; rather, Sebastiaan's insides twisted at how resigned Davit sounded.

"You understand nothing," Sebastiaan returned.

Davit pulled his gaze from the stream and stared at Sebastiaan, studying his face, waiting for him to expand on the incomplete statement.

Sebastiaan carefully weighed his words before confessing. "I have a powerful enemy." He did not want his troubles to become Davit's, but the boy was surprisingly perceptive and shielding him from the dangers surrounding them was unwise. Sebastiaan often had to remind himself that Davit was not a defenseless child and the more he knew, the safer he would be.

This fierce urge to shield him warred constantly with the boy's hard-won independence. If Sebastiaan had his way, he would bundle him onto the first ship and send it far out to sea until every threat had been hunted down and ended.

"There is a war between us that goes back to before I knew your m– " Sebastiaan bit the rest off. It dawned on him then that Du Bois had killed Davit's grandfather. It was that solitary event that had pushed his mother on a path that eventually had led to his birth. "We have a long history," he said at last. "To cut it short, I killed his son earlier this year, and that has significantly muddied the waters."

Davit's eyes rounded with alarm.

"Why?" he breathed and Sebastiaan watched as surprise and confusion were gradually replaced by something infinitely more devastating – caution.

"I did not know it was his son. We came upon a slave ship further up the coast," he said, pointing with his chin toward the east. "She was lying in a cove much like this one. We killed some of the crew, including the captain, and set the slaves free. The night you arrived, John told me he'd discovered the slain captain was Alain Du Bois' son. I didn't kill him because he was my enemy's child. However," Sebastiaan sighed, "I don't think it would have made a difference had I known the truth of his identity."

"Alain Du Bois," Davit repeated, committing the name to memory.

"Davit, listen to me." Sebastiaan did not continue until he had the lad's full attention. "I don't want you anywhere near him. I don't want him to know your face or your name. That is why I don't want you to come with me. Not because I am ashamed of you, but because I am afraid for you."

Davit's hands hung between his knees, his thumbs tapping a silent beat against each other as if he could drum some sense from the tangle inside him. Over the past weeks, he'd grown to trust Sebastiaan's word, his character, and his judgment.

"I hate the idea that I make you vulnerable," Davit said after a long stretch of silence.

"I don't," Sebastiaan replied at once. There were a thousand things he still needed to say, but somehow, they all found a resting place when he drew Davit close and kissed his sun-warmed hair.

"I know you're not a little boy anymore but I wish I could have done that when you were." He looked at Davit and ruffled the shaggy hair at the back of his head, then smiled.

The gesture, given so easily, unlocked a door Davit had kept firmly shut.

He thought of his mother often, but never for long. She was safe, and if fate was kind he would see her again, but he never allowed himself to dwell on her for too long.

Yet now the childhood memory came anyway. The two of them would be about a menial task, collecting berries or cleaning some small animal they'd caught in a snare, when she would pull him close and kiss the top of his head. Afterward, she would swipe the curls away from his forehead and give him the warmest, loveliest smile that always made him feel wanted –

treasured.

Longing flared so fiercely he had to clench his teeth to keep it in. For one reckless second he wished he could tell Sebastiaan about her – tell him that she was alive, that she had not forgotten him, that she lit a fire for him every year. He knew the words would take the deep sadness from his eyes, but Davit also knew without a doubt he would lose his trust. If Sebastiaan knew he had been lying to him, he would never forgive him.

His heart whispered that Sebastiaan would understand.

His mind screamed that the risk was too great.

Pushing the troubling thoughts aside, he resorted to humor, his old and trusted tactic that worked so well on his mother.

"I don't think I've ever been kissed by a man before." Sparks of mischief danced between his words. "I don't know how I feel about it."

"That was scarcely a kiss," Sebastiaan countered, utterly unrepentant. He stood, offered his hand, and hauled Davit up.

"Your lips connected with my head. It was most definitely a kiss." Davit insisted, brushing grass from the seat of his breeches.

"Fine," Sebastiaan sighed with mock annoyance. "I will try not to do it again."

"There's no need to overreact. I didn't say it was unpleasant, merely unexpected."

Sebastiaan shook his head. He was about to comment on the boy's arrogance, but he rather enjoyed it and so he held his tongue instead. Their walk back to the *Shack* was colored with Davit's relentless teasing and the low, helpless sound of Sebastiaan's laughter.

Low, uninspired clouds were drifting in from the ocean. The last of the harvest, mostly stacks of wheat, was due to arrive today and tomorrow. Sooner rather than later it would have to be carted to Wouter Mostert's mill before the damp set in and the whole lot began to rot. The farmers were as good as their word and over the last few weeks, all had brought in their crops. Storage was becoming a problem and if the rain set in, it would be disastrous.

"I expect five more farmers to bring their harvest this afternoon."

"Where will we store it? The *Shack* is almost completely full," Davit replied. Orion had insisted that Sebastiaan, Daka, and Van Leyen move from the *Shack* to sleep onboard the ship, freeing up some space inside. Daka had flatly refused, and Van Leyen had agreed but only on nights when the wind and rain were making sleeping in the open uncomfortable. Sebastiaan had happily traded his thin reed pallet for the comforts of a proper bed with clean linens. Orion had also emphatically entreated that they donate their meager and unsightly furniture to the farmers, as it would find no resting place aboard his ship.

"Move the oak logs outside. That should give us ample room," Sebastiaan said.

"That is not an insignificant task," Davit protested, as he searched the beach and deck for idle hands. Most of the men were on daily patrols and only a few remained to maintain the ship and provide security for the *Shack*.

"At least it will keep you out of trouble until I return." Sebastiaan's smile widened at Davit's immediate scowl.

"We can use the wood to build another warehouse," Davit teased.

"Good idea," Sebastiaan agreed. "Talk to John about it. I'll see you tonight."

"I was joking."

Davit was speaking to his father's retreating back, knowing it would not make a speck of difference, for Sebastiaan could fake hearing loss better than Gamora on her worst day. He watched as Sebastiaan exchanged a few words with Gijs before swinging onto his horse.

***

It was not a stately funeral. Hardly anybody knew that commander Hackius had passed away, and those who did, now stood around the open grave with expressions ranging from sorrowful to indifferent.

Alida, the late commander's wife, was flanked by Sebastiaan and Joseph. Now and then she dabbed at her cheeks and under her nose with a small lace-edged handkerchief. She was not overly emotional, but sadness drooped her shoulders and the skin under her red-rimmed eyes was heavy and dark. Joseph was openly weeping, and it occurred to Sebastiaan that those showing the most grief at the commander's passing were the slaves that stood in a tight group off to the side. A few villagers and a handful of soldiers were mostly indifferent, having never met the commander or only seen him in passing. Of all those in attendance, Du Bois and De Voogd were the most interesting to watch.

Du Bois stood with his hands clasped behind his back, staring at the rough coffin as if willing the man inside to stay dead. He did not look like a mourner. He looked like a carrion bird studying a fresh carcass for unwanted signs of life.

Adriaen De Voogd was racing through a *Bible* passage that was completely unrelated to the occasion, and Sebastiaan wondered if he'd simply opened the book and started reading at random. He was rushing through the ceremony in a flat monotonous voice and had he not slammed the book shut with such force, no one would have been aware that he had started to mumble an inaudible prayer.

The haste of the funeral was understandable, but the lack of grace and dignity was not.

With a twirl of his finger, De Voogd motioned to a slave. The man stepped forward, drove his shovel into the pile of fresh earth, and began to fill the grave.

As the first clumps of dirt rained down on the wooden lid, Alida flinched, closed her eyes and twisted her shoulders in an effort to turn away from the cold sight, but her feet seemed to have forgotten how to move. A small sound escaped her, and she pressed her fingers against her lips. Sebastiaan closed his hand under her elbow and pulled her away with him.

"What are your plans for the immediate future?" he asked softly after they'd walked a distance. He was leading her away from the grave, but without a destination in mind. If she had nowhere to go, he would take her to Elsje's.

"Pastor De Voogd requested I travel with the coffin this morning from

Rondebosch along with our belongings. I am to leave for Amsterdam on the first available ship. For a small fee, he has graciously allowed me to remain in our apartment at the fort." The far away lilt of her voice made Sebastiaan want to spit a filthy curse at the pastor's feet.

"I am truly sorry for your loss. If there is anything I can do to ease your burden, you need only to send word." He released her arm slowly, ready to catch it again should her step falter.

She stopped as they reached the stone arch leading to the inner courtyard of the fort.

"My husband always spoke highly of you, and I thank you for your kind words. But I will be alright. This day did not come as a surprise. My only hope was that I could bury him with his family."

"Of course," Sebastiaan said. After a somber moment, Alida gave his arm a gentle squeeze, then turned toward the building looming in the background. He waited until she had reached the heavy front door and closed it behind her before he walked away.

He'd neglected Gijs and Elsje over the last few weeks and blindly walked toward their house. A few days after Davit's arrival, he'd taken the boy to meet them, and it was such an emotional ordeal that Davit had refused to set foot near Elsje again. Not that he blamed the boy. She'd given him one look, grabbed hold of his hand and did not let go until Sebastiaan had announced that it was time for them to head back.

Elsje had the door open before he could knock. "Say you'll stay for dinner," she greeted, grabbing his hand and tugging him inside.

"Thank you," Sebastiaan said, letting her pull him through the warm chaos of the house toward the kitchen.

"How is that beautiful boy doing?" Elsje asked, planting both hands on his shoulders and lovingly forced him into a chair.

"Well enough," Sebastiaan said. Gijs slid a loaded plate in front of him without a word.

His friends had been at Danielle's wedding and had known her for far longer than he had. They understood that Davit was not his. Sebastiaan had broached the topic of the boy's true paternity with Gijs, sharing his fears for Davit's safety and the importance of keeping it a secret. The matter was silently and studiously avoided thereafter, and for the sake of all involved, Gijs and Elsje had embraced Davit as Sebastiaan's son.

"I swear, my heart nearly leaped from my chest and landed on the floor when I saw him," Elsje went on. "He's the spitting image of his mother, except for the hair, of course. I must have made the poor child daft with all my blabbering that day."

Sebastiaan was about to tell her that Davit had enjoyed her company but was saved when three boys tore through the kitchen. The first two were screaming at the top of their lungs as the third and smallest brandished a stick like a broadsword.

"I'll shove this up your arses if you call me puny again," he roared, his blue eyes blazing and his little face red with fury.

"Boys!" Elsje raised her voice, but to no effect. The back door slammed shut, and all was quiet again. It was like a flash storm that had come out of nowhere. One moment it was bright and sunny, the next a deluge drenched everything before the sun went on shining again as if the day had suffered no interruption at all.

Elsje's nose wrinkled in agitation. "I don't know what is wrong with that child," she said. "The first two are almost tolerable, but that last one …"

"Spitting image of his mother," Gijs said mildly.

Elsje's cheeks flamed, reminding Sebastiaan of the look on the little boy's face mere seconds ago, the resemblance was so uncanny that he shoved a healthy spoonful of pie into his mouth to choke his laughter.

"Let them play a little longer, and come sit down," Gijs soothed his wife's ruffled feathers. "I want to eat in peace tonight. We can feed them later."

Elsje settled herself, but then almost immediately shattered the dawning tranquility.

"There is trouble at the fort," she announced.

"Elsie," her husband warned, giving her the tiniest shake of his head.

"What? He needs to know."

"Know what?" Sebastiaan asked, his muscles instantly tight with concern.

"The farmers have stopped trading with the fort," she explained.

"That was the plan," Sebastiaan answered, forcing himself to relax. "I must admit I didn't expect them to keep to our agreement, but to a soul they all did."

"They are good people, Sebastiaan," Elsje interjected.

"I know that, but they are also battered like fish in a dockside eatery. I never thought they would band together."

"Well, they did, and now the fort has nothing to offer the visiting ships, except for fresh water. Most of the food produced in their own gardens goes toward feeding the soldiers and workers."

"Have there been many ships visiting in the last few weeks?" Sebastiaan asked.

"Only one," Gijs said. "The pastor sent slaves from the fort to scour the Wednesday market and buy every scrap of fresh produce they could lay their hands on. By the time they reached the third stall, the prices had almost quadrupled. They even went from house to house, begging to buy whatever was growing in our gardens. The next day Pastor Adriaen took his horse and did the rounds to get a handle on the situation."

"And?" Sebastiaan prodded when Gijs paused to chew.

Leaning in, Elsje picked up where her husband left off.

"The pastor found out the hard way just how complicated things had become. That flea-ridden horse's arse– "

"Elsie-love," Gijs warned around the food in his mouth.

She did not even spare her husband a sideways glance and continued. "Like I was saying, that worthless sack of horseshit stopped visiting the farmers months ago." Gijs groaned. "He refused to pray over the sick and dying because they did not pay their tithes. The farmers claimed they had no income to deduct a tenth from, but De Voogd did not care half a wit for their plight. He declared instead that, because of their selfish and greedy actions, the gates of Heaven would be forever closed to them. He even went so far as to curse them in church on Sundays." Elsje abruptly fell silent as she tried to regain the thread of the conversation, her eyes bright with righteous fury.

"Marcus Greeff, you would have met him at the meeting that night," Gijs said. "Large, burly farmer, honorable man, good husband, loving father. He lost his wife and daughter to a fever that took hold when they were already weakened by hunger and sleeping on the bare, cold floor. He had begged the pastor to visit his dying family, but the pastor refused. So, when De Voogd arrived at his door last week, Marcus nearly cut his throat. Would have done it, too, if the pastor hadn't run so sprightly for his horse."

"*Jesus,*" Sebastiaan breathed.

"I don't think *He* would have been the one waiting for the pastor on the other side," Elsje said. "But yes, that is the gist of it."

Sebastiaan could still see that broken, ragged group from the night of the meeting. He had never expected to find so much steel left in them.

"Does De Voogd know the farmers are selling to me?" he asked.

"I don't know. I suppose he might. It is not a closely guarded secret, but then the farmers are not a talkative bunch of late," Gijs said. "As far as we can tell, they are still buying seeds from the fort."

"What are you going to do with all that produce?" Elsje asked.

Sebastiaan exhaled slowly and stared out the window. The three boys were hanging by their knees from a low branch, arms stretched toward the ground. The youngest had his folded tight across his chest, a small, furious bat glowering at the world.

"I don't actually know," he answered at last. "So far, they've brought mostly wheat, which we will start carting to Wouter in the morning to be milled. We can ship the flour to Europe or Batavia and trade the rest along the African coast. I might even open a general store in the village. Whatever goes to rot can be mixed with manure and worked back into the soil."

Sebastiaan shrugged and leaned back in his chair.

"You would need a license for a store," Gijs pointed out. "That could be a problem."

"Every problem has a price," Sebastiaan said lightly. Gijs chuckled at the unshakable calm in his voice.

"Are you pressed for money?" Elsje asked and Gijs winced at the indelicate question.

"Not really," Sebastiaan replied, unaffected by her bluntness. After that, the conversation meandered in easy circles. No one wanted heavier talk tonight

As the light began to fade, Sebastiaan rose from his chair. He needed to reach the cove before full dark.

"Bring that boy around tomorrow if you get a chance," Elsje ordered as they walked him to the door.

"I will," Sebastiaan lied and kissed her cheek.

***

If his backside didn't need his feet to get around, it would have marched itself straight to this chair out of pure habit. Du Bois had lost count of the number of times he had sat in front of the commander's desk offering advice and guidance, listening to one idiotic soliloquy after another. At least the imbecile he was listening to now was of his own choosing, which somewhat blunted the crude edges of the stupidity falling from the man's mouth.

"You are spending too much time at your estate," Adriaen De Voogd began, voice already climbing toward a whine. "Since I've taken over as temporary commander of the Cape, I have been inundated with problems, and the Council has refused to get involved unless their Chair – you – approves of their decisions."

Alain listened in silence while the pastor vented his spleen.

"Over the last few weeks, the management of the settlement has consumed all my time, leaving my flock rudderless. I hardly have time to prepare for my Sunday sermons any longer," he moaned, as though being made to work seven days a week was some novel torture.

At least that explained the shambles of the earlier funeral.

"Surely it can't be that dire." Du Bois said, honestly believing the pastor was having a needless fit of the vapors. "It's been what, a little over two weeks? How much can go wrong in such a short time?"

"The warehouse is completely empty, and it's not as if we receive any advance notice from the VOC about when ships will arrive. We have to be prepared for an unexpected number to drop anchor in the harbor at any time of the year," De Voogd said. That made Alain sit a little straighter in his chair. He assumed the empty warehouse claim was an exaggeration. After all, the man was in the habit of spitting over-inflated threats at his congregation every Sunday for the past eight years.

"Yes, I know how it works," he snapped and bit down on his rising irritation. "What do you mean the warehouse is empty?" he asked, trying to gain a picture without actually having to ride over to the structure and count the number of wheat stacks on the floor. "It is the end of the harvest. It should be full."

"I am aware, and as such, I was expecting the farmers to bring their crops, but instead they all lined up, and only cleared their debts, not selling so much as a kernel of wheat. They bought seeds for the next season, but only after I agreed to lower the price."

Alain felt the blood leave his face.

"You lowered the price," he parroted in disbelief.

"I had no choice."

"Why?" he breathed.

"They refused to buy at the current price and I had to show a profit somehow."

"But they sold nothing, and yet they had money to clear their debt and buy grain?" Alain struggled to make the pieces fit.

"Yes," De Voogd confirmed.

"And you did not question this?"

De Voogd shook his head. "At the time, I was fairly overwhelmed with the situation, but afterwards I did wonder."

"Wonder what?" Du Bois asked, fingers flexing with the urge to close around the man's throat.

"I wondered why all the coins seemed new." He looked at Du Bois with a puzzled expression. "I still can't figure it out. The coins look like they've never been used. I mean, it makes little sense. Where would they have gotten them from?"

Du Bois' stared past him at the blank wall. Somebody was funding this little disaster. He knew everything there was to know about everybody at the settlement, and only two suspects came to mind: Mostert and De Vries. It was unlikely to be Mostert. He was financially stretched to his limits, which left De Vries. He knew absolutely nothing about the man, and it was eating at him.

"Have you investigated this anomaly?" he asked.

"At first I waited, thinking there was a delay of some sort, that perhaps they had trouble bringing in their harvests. But then five days ago, I sent a couple of soldiers to the Berk widow to question her, hoping to gain an understanding of what was afoot."

"Is that the pregnant woman with no husband?" Du Bois asked.

"Yes," De Voogd said. "But they have not returned, and so I've sent another four soldiers to search for them."

"And?" Du Bois' voice dropped to a whisper, for a chill had just crept up his spine and a tightness was forcing the air from his lungs.

"They could not find the missing pair. They also reported that the widow had moved from her farm and was now living with the Mostert family where she would remain until after the birth of her child. When they visited Mostert, he had refused them entry to his house and so they could not question her. Mostert himself had very little to say." There was an uncomfortable silence in the room and De Voogd nervously continued. "After that, I decided to ride out to the farms and talk to the farmers myself."

Du Bois did not prompt him. He simply leaned forward, eyebrows raised. At this point, he was not sure speech was still within his grasp.

"The farmers were reluctant to speak to me. Some were even violent. Needless to say, the harmony that once existed between us seems to have dissipated."

The man was delusional.

When De Voogd opened his mouth, Alain raised his finger and shook his head. He took a few seconds to think and when he finally spoke, the temperature of his voice had dropped dangerously low.

"This situation must immediately be brought under control." De Voogd eagerly nodded his agreement. "Let's focus on the money they've used to pay their debt. It could only have come from one source and that is Sebastiaan De Vries. Have you questioned him?" Du Bois asked.

"No," the pastor answered.

"Very well, arrest him and question him," Du Bois said without giving the order a second thought.

"Arrest him?" De Voogd's tone rose, signaling his resistance to the idea.

"Yes. At the same time, we will use a firm hand to force the farmers to change their ways."

"How?" De Voogd's suspicion was palpable.

"Send a few soldiers to burn down a few farms."

"Excuse me?" De Voogd breathed. "You can't be serious?"

"I most certainly am. You have created this mess and now you will clean it up. Start with the widow's place. Burn the remaining crops and the house. She is not there, so there will be no loss of life. That should get their attention. Then move to the next and do the same, make sure nobody dies. Soon, these peasants will realize the benefits of abandoning the current path they are on. By the time you get to the third farm, the problem will be solved."

"That is an extreme course of action." De Voogd mumbled as if talking in his sleep.

"You need to force them back to their knees; it is the only way to regain control of this. If you don't, this settlement is doomed. If we can't supply the ships, the Cape of Good Hope will cease to exist, and the entire failure will be hung around your neck."

De Voogd was beginning to see the full disturbing picture. Hard times called for hard action, and he would not fail this community.

"I can't arrest De Vries without a charge," he said as that obstacle just occurred to him. "Mostert will free him in a heartbeat. He knows the law better than anyone."

"You are mistaken. Mostert is not the expert on the law. *I* am." Du Bois' dark eyes grew black. "For *I* wrote it. As for De Vries, leave him to me," he said and stood from his chair. "Ready the soldiers. I want the attack on the farms to start at daybreak tomorrow." With that, Alain left the commander's chambers.

A plan was forming, and there was almost no time left to bring it to life.

Chapter 13

The solution to Du Bois' problem was moving around his kitchen in the form of a young woman, her dress brushing the stone floor as she bent to set a scrubbed pot on a low rack by the smoldering hearth. She'd been scouring pots every night for two months, ever since her last owner returned her at the onset of her pregnancy.

He should have tried to sell her at a much-reduced price, but he enjoyed having her around. She was quiet and efficient, rarely uttered a word, and when she did, it was always in hushed tones. Many times, he'd considered taking her to his bed, but the thought of sharing a woman with the pastor was uncomfortable enough to douse any entertaining notions. She had been in De Voogd's employ for less than six months and he could well understand why the pastor had used her so eagerly. She was exceptionally beautiful, with rich carob-brown skin and sharp, fine-boned features.

His instinct to keep the woman close had proven advantageous, after all. Since her return from De Voogd's, a healthy blush touched her cheeks, and her eyes held an irritating serenity. At first, he'd thought it was pure relief to be removed from the pastor's household, but Du Bois was no easy taskmaster and soon he'd suspected there might be more behind her tolerance for his demands and her persistent state of serenity. He'd also noted how eagerly she finished her chores in the evenings before slipping out the back door instead of lying down on her pallet in front of the hearth, returning silent as a whisper before the break of dawn to resume her duties.

Not one to have a question unanswered, he followed her. Night after night he watched as she met passionately with a young African whom he soon learned was one of De Vries' men. They always met in the lee of his stables, and then disappeared into the forest. Du Bois did not have to follow to know what was transpiring. Since she was already pregnant, he had allowed the affair to continue. He had planned to discuss the matter with De Vries, to blame his man for her unfortunate state and demand payment. Yet now the woman's value had risen far beyond anything he might have claimed in compensation.

He cursed himself for not having looked into De Vries sooner. It was out of the ordinary for him to have such a powerful entity in his sphere and not know all there was, but he had been distracted by his son's death, Hackius' illness, and the loss of one of his ships.

It was already dark outside, and he knew she was rushing through her chores, eager to slip away with her lover. She remained unaware of his presence as he leaned against the door leading to the rest of the house, and when he spoke, she was visibly startled.

"Take your clothes off," Du Bois said in a matter-of-fact tone, as if he were ordering her to clean a floor or make a bed.

"Sir?" She spun around, her face instantly taut with surprise.

He reached her in easy strides, and she retreated, her back hitting the pot rack. Raising his hand, he struck her cheek with a stinging slap that tore a small, wounded sound from her. She brought her hand to her burning face and numbly stared at him with horror slowly filling her eyes.

Her bewilderment was to be expected, for he'd never mistreated her in the past and she'd thought herself safe with him. Still, her stunned inaction irritated him. He struck the other cheek with the same deliberate force, seized a fistful of her hair, and dragged her face close to his.

"I can do this all night until you do as you're told," he said in a colorless voice.

She nodded against his grip and bent down to untie her shoes, her trembling hands complicating the simple task. He released her and took a step back. There was a time when his blood would spark to life at the sight and sound of a woman's terror, but no more. Now, it was merely perfunctory, a means to an end and for that end to be successful, he needed the results of his ministrations to be a touch more visible.

When she rose, he struck her again. This time he aimed the backhanded blow so the heavy stone of his ring split the soft cushion of her lower lip and drew a bright line of blood. She dropped to her knees, but he caught her by the upper arm and hauled her upright before she could sink fully to the floor.

"Get on with it," he said. "I have no wish to stand here watching you dawdle over a task that should come as second nature by now."

She dragged the shapeless brown gown over her head and stood in nothing but a threadbare shift. Her gaze darted across the room, searching for anywhere to settle except his face.

"Everything," he ordered and pointed to the ugly thing still clinging to her body. "I want you as naked as the day you were born." She whimpered and a few small droplets of blood dotted the floor near her feet.

An owl's soft hoot floated on the evening breeze, and Du Bois watched the muscles in her shoulders tighten.

"Is that him?" he asked. Her head snapped up, and she stared at him, eyes wide with animal panic, then slowly shook her head, trying to deny the truth of the secret she thought she'd kept so well.

"Just an owl," she replied, and swallowed thickly. Du Bois chuckled softly at her lie.

In the center of the room stood a small kitchen table and a single wooden chair. He drew the chair out, turning it so the back faced the back door.

"Sit."

She stepped from the heap of discarded clothing and crossed the floor on unsteady legs, each footfall small and reluctant. Perching on the edge of the seat, her back straight, feet, knees, and thighs tightly together, she folded her slender arms across herself in a futile attempt at modesty.

"No, sweetheart." He gave his finger a slow twirl. "The other way."

A faint crease of confusion appeared between her brows.

"Get up," he ordered. "Turn around. Straddle the chair. Sit down.

Place your chin on the backrest, and face the door." She obeyed his every command.

From his pocket Alain drew two lengths of thin cord and bound her ankles securely to the rear legs of the chair. Satisfied, he lifted the short horsewhip from its peg behind the door and swung the door wide. The candle on the table flickered, and he lit a few more until the room was bathed in warm light. The stage was set.

"Call him," he said.

Understanding slammed into her and the blood left her face, turning her skin an unsightly shade of ash.

"No," she breathed. One tear slipped free, then another, then a silent stream.

Du Bois drew the whip across her back, not hard enough to break the skin, only enough to raise a thick, angry welt. She screamed, and outside, the darkness stirred. Could it be the African moving closer, or the two men he'd posted on either side of the house?

"Call him," he spoke close to her ear, his voice barely above a whisper.

She did not reply, but resolutely clamped her lips shut and inhaled unevenly through her clogged nose.

The second stroke bit deeper, and this time it drew blood, forcing a sharp cry from her stubborn mouth.

"Call him, or I will turn you around and whip that child from your stomach." He gave her a questioning look, and another stinging lash forced her wail.

"Daka!"

Instantly the open doorway filled with the broad, enraged frame of the young African. The moment he vaulted the two stone steps and burst across the threshold, dagger raised, two cutlasses flashed from the shadows and crossed at his throat.

Du Bois' men stood motionless, blades steady. One reached over without haste, took the dagger from Daka's fist and the knife at the small of his back. Daka prayed for him to stoop and search for the blade in his boot, but the fool was smarter than that.

He hated this place. He had planned to talk to Sebastiaan about her, asking leave to take her away. But she was fearful of leaving, and had begged him to wait until her child was born.

Tonight, as he did every night, he had waited for her in the shadows of the stables.

Then he heard her scream his name, the single word was broken and full of pain.

The sight that met him now threatened to rip his guts from his body. Risha was completely naked and tied to a chair, her face swollen, blood dripping from her nose and a thin line running from a cut in her lower lip. Her eyes were large and swimming in silent tears, raw fear shining from their depths. Du Bois was standing behind her with a horsewhip in his hand.

A deep tormented growl rumbled in his chest. Everything inside him felt as if it was on fire. Three strides. Three impossible strides. He was helpless, and the knowledge twisted his heart.

"Risha." Daka's voice was thick and barely audible.

Du Bois flashed him a dark smile and pulled her head back.

"Show him your beautiful face, sweetheart," he cooed.

"You're a dead man," Daka hissed, his empty hands folded into tight fists.

"Yes, yes, my boy. We are all dead men. It's just the elusive date of our demise that separates us." Du Bois sounded like the devil on a Sunday morning stroll, calm and calculating, knowing he had the situation well in hand.

"Now, step inside and let us talk like the civilized men we pretend to be." He motioned to his men, and they pushed Daka deeper into the kitchen, closing the door behind them.

"I think you've met my kitchen slave, Margaret of Bengal, though she prefers Risha."

Du Bois watched the fire burn in the young man's eyes. Daka gave a terse nod, but remained silent.

"She has called you here because I would like to have a word with you."

"If it was my presence you desired, you could simply have sent for me.

There was no need for this." The anguish in Daka's voice made his words fracture.

"Oh, but there is every need," Du Bois said. "You see, my time is limited, and *this* will ensure an honest and swift discourse. I think you already know that the discomfort your woman here will experience will solely depend on how well you cooperate." Du Bois ran his finger down Risha's spine, tracing the ridge with idle ownership.

Daka despised power plays. On a battlefield everything was simple: find a throat, cut it, move to the next. Here, every word was a trap, every silence a noose. This was Sebastiaan's game – reading lies, twisting them, striking through the mask. All Daka had was the thin hope of staying calm.

"What is it you want from me?"

"Information," Du Bois replied.

Daka flicked a glance at the two guards. Their eyes kept sliding to Risha. The wooden slats of the chair's back did little to conceal her naked body from them. She was the perfect distraction and when the time was right, he would use that to his advantage.

"Untie her, and I will tell you anything you wish to know." He'd deliberately lowered his voice, hoping the sound would soothe her.

"Sadly, you are not in a position to negotiate. However, if you answer my questions truthfully and completely, I will release her to you, a free woman." He held Daka's gaze until the younger man gave a curt nod. The African's face betrayed almost nothing, and Du Bois felt a flicker of appreciation for the discipline.

"Don't, and she will pay the price for your misguided loyalty. Do not underestimate the weight of that price, for my patience is not what it once was."

Du Bois continued and his voice hardened, "You work for Sebastiaan De Vries?"

"I work with him," Daka replied immediately.

"I will tolerate that nugget of glibness only once. Consider that your first and only warning." Du Bois brushed the side of Risha's face with his knuckles. She recoiled, and a cold smile curved his mouth.

Daka swallowed and tried not to look at her.

"Usually, I am much more circumspect, but unfortunately, time is not on my side, thus forcing me to speak plainly," Du Bois said. "Sebastiaan De Vries is in dire need of incarceration and I am in need of a reason." Daka frowned; Du Bois continued. "No man with that much wealth and apparent power came to such position without breaking a few rules."

Daka remained silent, his mind working at a furious pace. How much information could be forced from him? He'd known Sebastiaan for more than a decade, shared every day with him, bore witness to every deed and spent countless hours around campfires sharing ideas and thoughts. The sad truth came quickly: a dangerous amount.

Noticing the faint tremor in Daka's tightly clasped hands, Du Bois pressed his advantage, his voice sharpening with intent.

"Let's talk about his arrangement with the farmers. Tell me about that."

"There isn't much to say." Daka replied, and Du Bois uncoiled the whip. "Except that he attended a meeting at Mostert's farm a few weeks ago where he'd purchased the yield of the next three harvests from the farmers."

Du Bois nodded slowly. That would explain the sudden influx of money.

"What does he plan to do with it, and more importantly, where did he get the money to take such a bold step?" Du Bois sounded as if he were talking more to himself, voicing his thoughts, but Daka was not fooled. The man had the charm of a snake, lulling his prey into letting its guard down before delivering the lethal strike.

"So far, it is mostly wheat that is coming in and we are planning on taking it to Mostert in the morning for milling. I don't know what he plans to do with the fruit and vegetables. Perhaps sell it at the market or open a store of some sort." Daka's shoulders rose and fell. "As for the money, I don't know where that came from."

The sound of the whip snapping across Risha's back came a split second before she cried out. The strike was delivered with such blinding speed that Daka had not even seen it coming.

"See what happens when you lie to me?" Du Bois asked in a smooth tone. "Now try again."

"I didn't lie!" Daka shouted.

"Don't raise your voice," Du Bois warned, as if speaking to a child on the brink of a temper fit.

"I didn't lie," Daka repeated more quietly. "His nephew must have brought it with him, for our money was almost completely spent by the time the *Sword of Orion* arrived."

"It is a touching tale," Du Bois said and readied the whip again. "However, none of that is cause for arrest."

Daka fell silent. He was just a boy when Sebastiaan had rescued him from Arab slave traders, and for years he'd fought by his side, learned from him, become a man under his guidance. He owed him his life but, in this moment, he knew he would sacrifice him for the woman he loved and for the child growing in her belly. Somehow he would have to betray him in a way Sebastiaan could survive.

To satisfy Du Bois, he would have to give him something substantial. There were only two options, and both threatened to burn a hole through Daka's heart. He could reveal Davit's true identity, which would give Du Bois enough leverage to bring Sebastiaan to his knees without having him arrested, but any harm to Davit would leave Sebastiaan a broken man. The least he could do for his friend was to protect his child. Confessing that Sebastiaan killed Du Bois' son was the only option left. It would leave Sebastiaan with a mighty battle on his hands, but one he might survive.

The whip struck again. Fresh, thick blood glinted on the leather cord. Risha choked on her pain and the stifling room swallowed her hoarse sobs. Exposed and broken, her hands hung limp at her sides. She was surrounded by men and yet utterly alone. For just a moment the room tilted and Daka had to blink hard to remain upright.

"Your silence is not appreciated. It also comes with a price," Du Bois said casually. "I apologize. I should have mentioned that rule at the beginning."

"Stop, please," Daka begged. "I'll tell you everything I know. Just please, give me time to think."

"No, lad. Time is the one commodity you do not have. For time is an evil that will only breed lies and deception. In fact, if the next words out of your mouth do not give me what I need, I will whip her to death right here, in this chair, while you stand there and watch. I will not stop until the deed is done, no matter if you should change your mind halfway through. Her life is in your hands." Du Bois' face had turned stone-cold, all traces of any humanity gone.

Daka knew his time was up.

"For years we've fought up and down the east coast. Raiding slave camps, setting the captured free, and killing the traders. At last, we ended it all and moved to the Cape. Our last raid was in February when we came upon a slave ship lying in a cove about three weeks' ride east." Du Bois went very still. Daka continued. "We boarded the ship, killed the crew and the captain and set the slaves free."

"What was the name of the ship?" Du Bois asked, his voice low and menacing.

"*Zuiderland*," Daka answered.

The name left his tongue like a death sentence. Something dangerous flashed through Du Bois' black eyes. Chilling dread flooded Daka. There was no guarantee Du Bois would release Risha, or that the men at his side would not run him through. Telling the man they'd killed his son was foolish in the extreme. Daka had gambled with their lives and he had the sick suspicion that he'd just lost. Bile rose hot and sour and he choked it back with a thick swallow.

The name hung suspended for a few moments. Alain Du Bois had been a father for thirty-five years, and then one afternoon came the news that his son was dead, slain defending his men and his father's ship. For the first time in all his memory, Du Bois' chest tightened and his eyes burned with the need to shed the tears that now threatened just beneath the surface. He could still see his boy's face, the black-haired babe with the large brown eyes; the arrogant and proud young man with an air of defiance that demanded to be noticed. He had vowed to find his son's killer, no matter how long it took, and now he knew. Sebastiaan De Vries had destroyed everything in one callous moment. The shock of the African's revelation was slowly ebbing, leaving the burning need for revenge to fill the vacuum.

De Vries would be arrested, and he would die a slow death befitting the crime he'd committed.

Daka saw the exact moment when the darkness inside Du Bois tipped the scales. The men flanking him had grown complacent, their eyes fixed on the naked woman before them. Daka took a small step back, away from the blades at his neck, and fell to his knees.

"Please," he begged, "I gave you what you wanted." Twisting his body to hide his right hand, he reached for the dagger in his boot. "Just let her go. You can kill me, but let her go."

His words unleashed a fresh torrent of sobs from Risha as she earnestly tried to pull her legs free. The attempt was futile and her helplessness pushed her over the edge of her control. If Daka dies, Du Bois would give her to his men before ending her life. Her sobs grew louder until she was screaming at Daka not to leave her.

In an instant, the kitchen was filled with the din of Risha's hysteria, Daka's pleading, and Du Bois' shouts for his men to cut his throat.

Pulling the blade from his boot, Daka cut deeply into the back of the knee of the man to his left, severing the thick tendons. The man roared in pain and sank to the floor. Blood smeared the stone floor as he tried to drag himself away.

An unexpected sound came from the front of the house. Someone was pounding feverishly upon the door, demanding entrance. The persistent hammering of a fist against the wood only added to the obscene chaos reigning in the kitchen. Daka jumped to his feet. The man on his right swung his cutlass, forcing Daka to leap back. His foot landed in the middle of the pool of blood and he slipped, crashing onto his back.

"Mister Du Bois!" a man shouted.

Du Bois ignored the door. "Kill him!" he shouted to his man, his whip viciously cutting into Risha's back. Her mouth opened wide before wet cries tore from her, but she stayed conscious, staring into Daka's eyes, begging him to stay alive and fight.

Daka flung himself sideways, rolling to his knees once more to evade the swinging blade. There was no time to rise; the cutlass was already descending for the death blow. The man had his feet planted wide, partly to avoid stepping in the blood but mostly to balance himself. Daka drove his fist into the man's unguarded groin. As the guard folded, gasping, Daka rose and plunged the dagger into the base of his neck, then yanked the weapon free as the body went slack. Seizing the fallen cutlass, he turned toward Du Bois.

His first attacker was still bellowing and the pounding on the door was more persistent than before. Risha was sobbing, blood pouring from her back and a thin stream of urine dripping onto the floor.

"Mister Du Bois!" The man had to shout to be heard over the hammering of his own fists, but he did not stop. "Fire on your ship, sir! You must come! Hurry!"

Du Bois kept the table between him and Daka as he stepped into the dark hallway.

"Leave now, or I will kill you," Daka growled, knowing it was an empty threat; Du Bois' blood on his hands would see him hunted down before dawn.

Alain Du Bois melted into the darkness of his house, his receding footfalls sharp on the timber floor, and Daka hurried to Risha. He knelt next to the chair and cut the rope from her ankles, then gently lifted her in his arms, trying not to touch the wounds on her back.

"My clothes," she whimpered against his neck.

"There is no time," he said and headed for the back door.

"Please," she begged.

He lowered her, and she stumbled to the door and clung to the frame. He gathered her meager belongings in an untidy bundle, handed it to her, then scooped her up again, exited the house and ran for his horse tied behind the stables.

For an insane moment, Daka thought to go to Gijs and Elsje Boom for help, but it was a fool's errand. The longer he stayed in the settlement, the greater the chance of his arrest for the man he'd murdered in Du Bois' kitchen. Risha was in a bad way, but her wounds were not life-threatening. He would care for her once they were deep inside the forest. He hoisted her onto his horse, then leaped up behind her.

"Where are we going?" she asked, still clutching her clothes to her bare chest.

"Into the forest," he said. She was shaking so fiercely that her teeth chattered and he gently pulled her close until her head rested against his shoulder. "You are safe now."

He needed to think. He wished he could return to the *Shack* and warn Sebastiaan, but even though he suspected Sebastiaan would understand what had happened tonight, he feared Orion and to some extent Van Leyen might not be so open-minded. Van Leyen might take his fists to him, but Orion would kill him without giving it a second thought. He had betrayed Sebastiaan. He had given Du Bois the evidence he'd needed to lock Sebastiaan in prison for the rest of his life and throw away the key.

Leaving the Cape of Good Hope was the only option for him and Risha, and he pushed the horse into a bruising gallop.

Chapter 14

8 November 1670

"We are going to need a much bigger cart," Van Leyen said when Sebastiaan stepped off the jetty. There was much to do but no rush to get it done, and so Sebastiaan had indulged in sleeping until the sun had chased him from his bed this morning.

Where the morning light once bounced off the bare floor planks of the *Shack*, there was now scarcely room to walk, save for a narrow path winding between bales and sheaves of wheat. It was an untidy affair, for no two bales were the same size and the sheaves ranged in girth from as thin as a poor man's thigh to as stout as a brandy barrel.

"We'll have to make at least five trips every day for the next week to get all this squared away," Van Leyen continued. He dropped two fat sheaves from his shoulders then waited for Davit to bring a large bale to a stop against the cart.

Sebastiaan and Daka had planned on delivering the first load to Wouter Mostert's mill today. It would be the first time in five years Mostert was going to get paid for the service.

"I still don't know how the man kept body and soul together with all the charity he is doing in the community," Van Leyen said, shook his head and spat the wheat straw he'd been chewing to the side.

Early on, the fort had seized the opportunity and charged a hefty fee for milling, which the farmers, of course, could not pay, and as such the cost was added to their growing debt, increasing the fort's control over their lives. Mostert had stepped in, offering to mill the wheat for free, but since the fort owned the mill and he merely rented it, that generous gesture was stifled the moment he proposed it. Undeterred, he'd found a way around the restriction by claiming the farmers paid through a bartering system – a claim that was entirely fabricated but difficult to disprove.

Sebastiaan opened his mouth to answer, but Van Leyen had already turned to the next worry. "We'll have a real problem when the fruit and vegetables start coming in."

Looking around the beach and the clearing beyond, Sebastiaan began to understand the reason for his friend's disgruntlement.

"Too much food is not a problem. It's a luxury. Where's Daka?" Sebastiaan asked, scratching at a bothersome spot behind his left shoulder and then raising his arms for a thorough stretch the low ceiling of his cabin on Orion's ship did not allow for.

"Yes, where is Daka?" Van Leyen grumbled, dropping more sheaves onto the growing pile next to the cart. "That is a good question. He went into town last night and has not returned."

"He knows we are going to the mill and probably thought to save himself a trip by waiting for me in town," Sebastiaan reasoned.

"Thus, successfully avoiding loading the cart," Van Leyen added under his breath.

A lukewarm wind was blowing in from the interior, bringing with it the musty smell of the forest and faint, sour hints of wood smoke. The morning was beautiful, not a cloud in the sky, and the cove's water shifted from pale green to cerulean blue where the sandy bottom fell away. It was easy to forget that a flurry of activity bustled beyond the thick rim of trees. If not for the crooked dirt road the wagon had carved over the months connecting them to the settlement, Sebastiaan could imagine living here and forgetting the world existed.

However, standing around, stretching his back and staring at the scenery, would not get the cart loaded. Sebastiaan took hold of the railing, swung himself over and landed on the empty cart with an agility that belied the pain in his knees. He reckoned there might just be enough room to fit two bales, with space left to wedge in sheaves. Without Daka, they were definitely short on hands. Most of the crew was patrolling the border, and the rest were getting ready to take over from the night watch, leaving only himself, Van Leyen, and Davit free.

"Davit," Sebastiaan called. "Bring the hooks so we can lift the bales." Seeing the confusion on the boy's face, he explained, "Four large iron hooks on the back wall. Go." Sebastiaan waved his hand toward the *Shack's* door. Davit disappeared into the blackness of the building, returning with Orion on his heels.

Orion, dressed in a crisp white shirt, black breeches and gleaming black boots, looked every bit the pirate he claimed no longer to be.

"Beautiful morning. What are our plans?" he asked by way of greeting.

"I am taking this load into town for milling. John and Davit are scouting for a spot to build the new warehouse, and Daka is not here yet," Sebastiaan replied. He took the hooks from Davit, slammed them into the sides of the nearest bale, like a timpanist striking a kettledrum, then pulled it onto the cart. "Where is Jiya?"

"He and his men went on patrol until late last night. I was planning on taking his place today, but I'd rather go to town with you," Orion said, lazily tossing a thin sheaf onto the cart with one hand.

"Are you planning on helping, or are you just here for decoration?" Sebastiaan grunted as he pulled the second bale into place.

Orion made a face when he accidentally tipped his head too far back and got an eyeful of bright sunlight. "Purely decorative," he drawled, unabashed, and flicked a patch of cat fur from his sleeve. Movement in the treeline drew his eye and his features hardened into the stern look his men had come to expect.

"Captain," the man shouted from a distance.

Sebastiaan also turned toward the voice. The man was covered in a mixture of ash and mud, with twigs and leaves sticking out of his hair and clothing in all directions. He could stand next to a tree and Sebastiaan would walk right past him, oblivious to his presence, his camouflage undoubtedly Niccolò's handiwork.

Orion waited as his mercenary jogged over the loose sand.

"Maxime," Orion greeted.

There was a nervous edge to the man, evident in the rapid, uneven blinking of his tired eyes and the tight press of his lips, forcibly holding back the words he wished to say. He offered Orion a habitual salute and awaited his captain's permission to speak.

Maxime belonged to Niccolò's team. Orion had not seen any of them for days, as Niccolò kept them in the forest, close at hand.

"Niccolò sent you?" Orion asked.

"Yes, Captain."

"Tell me."

"About a week ago, two soldiers came to the Berk widow's farm. We happened to be in the area. The soldiers were up to no good. They had that look about them, and so we figured it might be wise to move closer, just in case. You know how Niccolò gets these feelings, and he was right too. They questioned the slave working in the fields, although she didn't treat him as one." Orion shook his head, signaling for the man not to get sidetracked with matters that were not their concern. "When she came out of the house to see what they wanted, they grabbed her by the arm and dragged her back inside. Niccolò, Bas, and I followed them, nearly frightening the slave straight into the hereafter when we rounded the house. By the time we reached the kitchen, the men already had her bent over the table, her face red and swollen from their persuasions."

Anger simmered in Orion's gut. He'd promised to keep these people safe, but he'd thought he was doing so against an attack from beyond their borders, not from within.

"What happened next?"

"We don't know how much damage was done, as we didn't waste any time getting to her. Niccolò pulled one soldier off her, and I took the other. Bas was outside with the slave and the widow's little girl. Niccolò ordered Bas to escort the woman with her child and slave to the Mostert farm. Then we took the soldiers into the forest, one with his breeches still around his ankles, the other pissing himself all the way." Maxime wrinkled his nose in disgust, as if the pungent stench of urine was still sticking to the back of his throat. "I argued we should rough them up and let them go." Orion was already shaking his head. "But Niccolò said that making them dig their own graves and laying them to rest was a better way to deal with rapists." Orion nodded his approval. Had the situation not been so dire, he might have found some amusement in the man's choice of words.

"Why did Niccolò wait until now to send word? You said this happened a week ago?" Orion asked.

"Yes, Captain, it was perhaps less than a week. I don't know. We kind of lost track of time out there," Maxime explained. "Niccolò thought it might have been an isolated incident, at first, but this morning the situation changed and he sent me to bring word and ask for reinforcements." This dug a swift and deep frown between Orion's eyes.

"Explain how the situation changed," he commanded.

"A large group of soldiers has returned to the widow's farm, heavily armed and carrying torches. They've set fire to the fields and the house. Sat there on their horses and watched the place burn. Our scouts have reported that more groups are moving to some of the other farms. When I left, it was only the one farm that had been attacked, but that is sure to change, and we also had reports of soldiers attacking our crew."

Maxime reached the end of his report, Orion regarded the man for a while, his mind racing ahead. "Thank you, Maxime. Get something to eat and send Jiya out here, if you please," he ordered.

By the time Jiya reached the beach, Orion, Sebastiaan, Van Leyen, and Davit were standing in a tight circle as they discussed the latest development.

"Even when Hackius was half-dead, he'd still kept things together," Van Leyen said. "Now everything is spinning out of control."

"The fort is retaliating, and it is our interference that has brought this on these poor people," Sebastiaan added.

"They'd be far poorer without your interference," Van Leyen cut him off. "We knew trouble would come. We just didn't know what it would look like, and now we do."

Jiya arrived, looking disheveled and bleary-eyed. "What happened?" he asked, and Orion spent the next few minutes relaying Maxime's report.

"Father, I don't think it is a good idea for you to go into town alone," Davit said. "I know better than to volunteer to go with you, but I think somebody should."

Sebastiaan appreciated the boy's concern and his insight but took offense nonetheless. "I am not a damn child that needs to be watched." Davit dropped his head at his father's sharp tone.

"Aye, we know you are not a child," Orion said steadily. "No one is suggesting otherwise, but when there is trouble on the loose, you do have a knack for finding it. I will go with you. Just to keep an eye out."

"Keep an eye out for what?" Sebastiaan challenged.

Orion stared at Sebastiaan for many seconds, as if waiting for his thoughts to shape themselves into the words he needed. "You are going to Mostert's farm, and now we know the Berk widow is there. She's pregnant and roughed up, courtesy of a couple of overenthusiastic soldiers. I'm coming with you, if only to stop you from charging off and committing some act of violence in the name of her tattered honor that will land you in a cell at the *Castle*, eating prison gruel, living for the guards' amusement, and trading good behavior for sunlight. That, sir, I will not allow." Orion spoke without coming up for air and, when he was done, he promptly dismissed his uncle's murderous glare and turned to Jiya.

Sebastiaan was dumbstruck by the sheer inanity spilling from Orion's mouth, too stunned to protest. Orders were barked and arrangements were made while he struggled to form a coherent rebuke. The implication that he needed a keeper was galling beyond measure.

"Davit and I need to find a spot for the new warehouse, but we'll stay close," Van Leyen said, giving Sebastiaan a surreptitious nod. He would keep Davit safe and away from the *Shack* should a threat come their way. "It would be wise for the two of you to be seen in town going about your business. That'll give us a layer of deniability, albeit a thin one, should the fort suspect that we have a presence at the border."

"I'll take the rest of the men and see how we can assist Niccolò," Jiya added.

"Jiya," Sebastiaan said, relieved at having his thoughts back in working formation. "Send the men, but I need you and a few others to stay within easy reach to lend a hand should John need it. Understood?"

"Yes, Effendi."

"Right then, let's see how this thing plays out," Orion said, then looked to Sebastiaan. "Are we good to go?"

***

It was close to midday when Sebastiaan and Orion rode into town. The horse they'd chosen to draw the cart was not at all pleased with the demotion and it had taken them longer than expected to get it to submit to the task. After a few minutes on the road, Sebastiaan was of the firm opinion that the mare had deliberately, and quite spitefully, slowed her stride. With every step, she painstakingly lifted her leg, then let it drop to the ground as if the weight of her limb was too much to bear while snorting and huffing as she trudged on. He'd thought she would drop the act after a while, but she was determined to turn a trip of about an hour and a half into a half-day trial. They had planned to do more than one haul today, but at this rate he would be happy to reach Mostert by midafternoon. He resolved to choose a different horse tomorrow, then smiled, leaned over, and patted the animal's shoulder.

"Well played, darling," he said and gently pulled her ear. She responded with a snort that made her lips dance over her long, yellow teeth.

Usually, Sebastiaan carried a dagger in the small of his back and one in his boot. This morning, however, he and Orion had erred on the side of caution and had strapped their sabers and an extra blade to their sides as well.

Riding into town at a leisurely pace, he greeted one of Gijs' bakery boys. The lad gave him a bright smile, tipped his cap, and continued his trot toward the bakery at the end of the street. Most of the town had developed a fair distance from the shoreline, as if folks didn't trust the water of

Table Bay to keep its promise to stay behind the line of the white beach. By Sebastiaan's estimation, another village the size of the current one could comfortably fit in the open space between it and the beach. The distrust was warranted, for when the storms set in, the water level rose so dramatically that the *Castle's* entrance was regularly flooded. There were even rumors that prisoners had drowned in their cells inside the new fortress during a particularly high spring tide surge.

The townsfolk had built their houses south of the VOC garden, which stretched roughly forty acres inland and served as a lush green link between the industrious little village and the patches of farms beyond. The garden itself was a work of art. Stone-lined irrigation channels connected meticulously arranged vegetable beds bordered by thick, fragrant rosemary hedges, while orchards brimmed with fruit trees of every variety from around the world that could take to the soil and climate.

Mostert's industry and farm were west of the gardens, and as such Sebastiaan and Orion had to make their way down Olifant Street and then up the dirt road skirting the gardens to reach their destination. Had it not been for the cart, they would have bypassed the village altogether and cut through the thick forest.

The town was its normal weekday self. Nothing was out of the ordinary and yet it felt like an invisible hand was stirring the air, making it too thin in places and too thick in others. Shop assistants were hurrying back and forth, carrying crates on their shoulders or parcels under their arms, while others strolled leisurely, as if they didn't have a care or concern in the world and all the time to get where they needed to be.

The street was a peaceful blend of domestic bliss: on the right, white-washed brick houses staked their claim, while on the left, a new grocer's shop, signaled budding commerce. The bell chimed as the store's door opened, and a young slave exited, clutching a wooden crate filled with flour and a few glass jars with cloth-wrapped tops. He halted before stepping onto the cobbled street, glancing hastily up and down, wary of being trampled, then darted off toward his master's house. A dog barked, its low-pitched tone lacking the intensity of urgency, merely expressing curiosity or a greeting. Perhaps the passing slave was a familiar sight, and the two were periodic acquaintances.

Three women were standing on the opposite side of the street, enjoying the speckled shade of the oak trees, their laughing voices fading into silence as the passing cart drew their attention. One of them cupped her hand to whisper in her friend's ear. The friend nodded but kept her eyes locked on Sebastiaan, snapping her gaze away when he caught her staring.

"Is it just my imagination, or is there a tension in the air that was not here the last time I came to town?" Orion asked. They rode at a slow walk, keeping pace with the cart.

"I wasn't aware you visited town so often," Sebastiaan said.

"I don't. I came in once or twice with John, and I can well remember that it felt different then."

Was it the years of living dangerous lives that had turned him and Orion into men who, like wild animals, sniffed the air, and knew when to dart in a certain direction to avoid a predator? Would it ever fade? If they were to find normal lives, would the wildness inside them finally sleep and let them live like others do, oblivious and blind?

"See, this is why I prefer to stay on my ship," Orion grumbled. "This bloody feeling that something is about to crawl up my arse, it's insufferable. And it only happens on dry land."

"It will pass," Sebastiaan said. "You're just not used to being in one place for any length of time. I think you need to find something that interests you. Perhaps consider settling down. This place is as good as any."

"You mean with a house, wife, and children?" Orion looked like he had just drunk vinegar straight from the jar.

"Yes, that is exactly what I mean."

Orion's expression remained fixed on his face and Sebastiaan laughed. "Stranger things have happened."

"Uncle," Orion clipped, the word a verbal punch. "It is a well-known fact that man is foolish and, as a collective, we are not making any headway in our development." He shook his head. "If anything, we are stagnating, frozen and sometimes even devolving, some at a faster rate than others.

So why should I do as others have done and think the outcome would be different?"

"Because," Sebastiaan returned, "you differ from others. Therefore, the outcome might not be so predictable as you think."

"Fine," Orion ceded and gave Sebastiaan a jaded look. "Now tell me what's really on your mind, what lurks beneath this layer of horseshit."

Ignoring Orion's theatrics, Sebastiaan continued in a light tone. "I think we should start a brandy distillery." He pointed to a spot near the foot of the mountain where the valleys were soft and deep. The folds were covered by one of the largest vineyards at the settlement. "That farm produces the tartest grapes I've ever tasted. It would be perfect for such an undertaking."

"Now, why did you not start with that?" Orion asked.

"You would have found a way to disagree," Sebastiaan replied deadpan.

"Sour grapes to a nagging woman?" Orion tilted his head from side to side as if weighing the situation in his mind, tipping the scales one way, then the other. "It's a brilliant idea. Is it legal?"

"Yes."

"Damn," Orion said and exhaled loudly. "Nothing is ever perfect, is it? But I guess we can make it work."

Sebastiaan laughed softly, and they fell into an affable silence. Yet, he couldn't shake the uneasy feeling that made the small hairs on the back of his neck rise in warning. It felt like swimming in a calm ocean with a powerful undercurrent. Above, the surface was tranquil, but below, something was pulling and tugging at him. Everything was too loud and too quiet all at once, too calm and too tense. The women's laughter sounded sharper, but above, in the trees, the birds were dead quiet. Usually, the oak trees lining the cobbled street were alive with bird chatter, but today, not a single chirp or flutter drifted down. The wind was pushing the thick cloud of smoke from the burning farms inland, leaving Table Mountain shrouded in gray haze.

Ahead, a group of soldiers, perhaps ten or twelve, turned into the street. They were jogging in a tight formation. Sebastiaan pushed the carthorse to the side, and Orion fell in behind them to make room for the posse to pass. The man leading the group had the stature of a loosely filled grain sack; the contents shifting and bulging with his movements. His face was almost completely round, as if his creator had drawn inspiration from a dinner plate.

The group did not pass, but veered in their direction and came to a halt with a clatter of weaponry. The insignia on the grain sack's uniform informed Sebastiaan that he held the esteemed position of captain of the guard, but the sweat streaming down his red face suggested that the jog from the fort was a definite first. Sebastiaan's eyebrows dipped in a slight inward bend as he shot a silent query at Orion. He responded with raised brows and a slight shrug of his shoulders, while the pad of his thumb caressed the smooth edge of his saddle as if to soothe his rising ire.

Sebastiaan did not dismount, but kept his hands relaxed on the reins. His horse was outwardly calm, but he could feel the powerful muscles vibrate beneath him. Orion's horse did not appreciate the soldiers closing in and danced to the side and then backward. For once, Orion did not fight the animal, but closed his hand around his saber and let the horse's rump push into the nearest soldier, forcing the man to retreat or risk being trampled. The carthorse, already having a bad day, chewed the bit in her mouth and violently swung her head from side to side, her eyes wide and rolling with alarm.

"Easy," Sebastiaan spoke to the mare in a soothing voice, but she'd been ignoring him all morning and he had little hope that she would heed him now.

The captain's outfit might have been pristine at some point. At present, it sported dark patches of moisture under the arms and on the chest. It took the man a good few seconds to calm his over-tasked heart and draw enough breath to support his voice.

"Sebastiaan De Vries?" the captain panted.

"Yes," Sebastiaan answered calmly.

A crowd was forming. The three women on the other side of the street paused their conversation, turned their attention to the developing scene, and cautiously stepped closer. They could smell the trouble and wished to be close enough to see everything, but far enough that, should blood spill, they would remain unblemished. Others stepped from the surrounding buildings, and passersby stopped to watch, thrilled that an average Tuesday had taken such an unexpected turn. Necks stretched to see past inconsiderate spectators blocking their view. Others pointed to the soldiers, exchanging nervous glances. A man who'd been sweating more than his curiosity would account for melted into the crowd and disappeared down the street, his head low, his stride urgent but not frantic.

"By order of Commander De Voogd, you are under arrest," the captain wheezed and motioned for two soldiers to pull Sebastiaan from his horse. Sebastiaan had noticed the way the two soldiers had been twitching since coming to a halt. It was as if they had been informed of the role they were to play in this arrest beforehand and were eager to see it done. One was young, with the spotted face of a lad in his mid-teens. Sebastiaan removed his feet from the stirrups and relaxed his body in anticipation of what was to come. Resisting arrest would only lead to violence, and the odds were not in their favor. His mind flashed to Daka, briefly wondering if he was somewhere close by, watching. Hope sparked for a moment, but he tamped it down. One extra fighter would not make a difference.

"On what charge?" Orion demanded in the same voice he used on deck. It was a tone that could bring the hardest of men to yield, and the effect was not lost on the surrounding soldiers. A few took a step back, as if avoiding the scorch of a flame. Sebastiaan had seen Orion in battle, and the sight was something to behold, but it was not something he wished to see today.

"For the murder of Lucien Du Bois," the captain charged, loud enough for even the furthest of spectators to hear.

"Who the *fuck* is Lucien Du Bois?" Orion shouted and kicked an approaching soldier square in the chest. The man stumbled backward, his foot caught on the uneven cobblestones, and he went down with a rattling noise as his collection of weapons crashed with him into the gutter. "Stay where you belong," Orion ordered as he swung down from his horse and made to draw his saber.

Orion's face was hard and formidable with the power of his outrage. His near black eyes, usually smoldering with irritation and annoyance, turned piercing and cold. The tawny skin tightened across his sharp features, his lips thinned to a hard line. What Sebastiaan saw on his nephew's face sent a shiver through him. Orion would spill an impressive amount of blood on this day, and while it promised to be spectacular, he would end up in a cell all the same, and Sebastiaan needed him to remain free. Van Leyen would do everything in his power to rescue Sebastiaan, but Orion would succeed.

"Orion, no!" Sebastiaan shouted as he tried to push the restraining soldiers away. Whatever else he was about to say was cut short when the butt of a musket slammed into the back of his head. The pain was sharp, and a cluster of bright white sparks burst across his vision. He stumbled forward, and the soldiers clutching his arms seized the opportunity to stretch them out and push him to the ground. A heavy knee landed between his shoulders, most likely the captain's, and his face was pressed against the cool stone surface of the street. The soldiers pulled his hands behind his back, and he felt the familiar weight of iron shackles closing around his wrists.

Sebastiaan turned his head as far as he could in time to see Gijs stepping from the crowd and pulling Orion with him. From the intensity of his gaze, Sebastiaan knew Orion had already selected his first targets. When Gijs' hand closed around his bicep, Orion raised his arm to deliver a backward strike with his elbow. Gijs was no fool and had twisted his body out of reach before he'd touched the high-strung warrior. Orion whipped around, ready to eliminate the hindrance, but paused when he saw the baker's concerned face.

Gijs did not waste time, nor did he draw attention to them. Orion was already in trouble for kicking the soldier and he stepped between him and the unfolding scene in the street. Relief flooded Sebastiaan as Gijs pushed Orion back while urgently speaking in his ear, undoubtedly trying to explain the concept of a tactical retreat. It was a theory Orion could never quite wrap his head around. Sebastiaan did not envy his friend that impossible task. By the time the soldiers hoisted Sebastiaan to his feet, he was three daggers and a saber lighter, his hands bound behind his back, and his ankles shackled, connected by a too-short chain. A thin line of warm blood dripped down his neck.

The procession moved down the street toward the *Castle* at a silent, brisk march. The short chain reduced Sebastiaan's gait to an awkward shuffle, his feet staying low to the ground. He and the captain were walking side by side. The captain kept his eyes fixed on their path, never once diverting his gaze, and walked with the confidence of a man who had completed his job successfully. The soldiers were tense and alert, their eyes searching, their weapons at the ready.

Sebastiaan hadn't felt the weight of shackles in over seventeen years, and the sensation slid back into his memory with alarming lucidity. It brought a black wave of helplessness that momentarily choked his mind. His vision blurred, and his chest grew tight as his lungs contracted, making it impossible to draw air. The anxiety that only sporadically visited him in dreams bore down on him with the intensity of a lightning storm.

Small beads of sweat dotted his forehead, and he felt a faint tremor in his muscles, like when he woke from one of his nightmares. Years ago, he had found a way to cope with the terrors that haunted him in the depths of the night. He had taken to leaving an out-of-place object – something as simple as a pebble – next to his bed before going to sleep. That object served as a barrier between what was real and the mere ghosts from his past. When waking in the cold grip of a nightmare, he would find that object and focus on it until the world stopped spinning and his body ceased trembling.

Searching for something out of place to ground him, he looked to his own body. His clothes were the same as this morning when he'd dressed in the sun-drenched cabin on the *Sword of Orion*, but his boots were out of place. The soldiers had not removed them, perhaps in their haste, perhaps out of oversight, and the leather now cushioned the shackles from biting into his skin. He smiled inwardly at how powerful that small realization was. Next, he focused on the details surrounding him, searching for the familiarity of the everyday: the trees, the white buildings with their black roofs, and the comforting smell of Gijs' bakery drifting on the breeze. It wasn't much, but it was enough to keep the wolves of panic at bay. Enough for him to regain control of his faculties, critically assess his unexpected situation, and comb through the events that had led up to his arrest.

Lucien Du Bois – the captain of the slave ship he'd killed one dark February night earlier this year. There were only two others who knew about the events of that night, John Van Leyen and Dakarai. John did not betray him. Sebastiaan knew it down in the deepest pit of his soul. One could never know what drives another, but with John, he was certain the man had no motive. He never got drunk, he had no weakness to exploit, and most reassuringly there was nothing tethering him to this world except his loyalty to Sebastiaan.

Dismissing John from this context was easy, but that left Daka. Could Daka have betrayed him? If so, to what end? Money and power could not have swayed him; he had plenty of the former and held little respect for the latter. Sebastiaan chewed on his thoughts. Somehow, Daka was not that easy to dismiss.

As they traveled down the street, the crowd from his arrest trailed behind, resembling a carnival procession, marked by many relaxed conversations. Nothing like a public display of government-sanctioned thuggery to spark a lively round of gossip and an opportunity to catch up with a busy neighbor. The light breeze from moments earlier had intensified and changed direction. It was now coming in over the ocean and held a chill as it whirled the fallen leaves on the street and rustling the branches of the trees.

Sebastiaan's thoughts returned to Daka. His gut told him that some sinister ploy had lured Daka into a trap where he had no choice but to betray him. Did he have any vulnerabilities that could be exploited? The answer came quickly – the woman. Sebastiaan and Van Leyen suspected Daka was involved with a woman in town, and unlike all the others that came before, this one was not just a one-night wonder.

Sebastiaan allowed the scene to play out in his mind. He replaced the actors, putting himself in Daka's shoes and Danielle in the hands of an enemy. There was *nothing* he wouldn't sacrifice to keep her safe. Daka was neither stupid nor a coward, and it made him wonder how much he had divulged. Sebastiaan was thankful that Van Leyen was with Davit. But would it be enough? Once more, panic threatened to push to the surface, and he forced himself to think of something else. He hoped Orion would go back for their abandoned horses. There was a veritable fortune in those saddlebags, and he would rather it ended up back in their small chest or in Mostert's pocket.

Contemplating the murder charge against him, Sebastiaan knew his situation was bleak. With Daka as an eyewitness and the sailor from the *Zuiderland* to corroborate the claims, the case against him was as watertight as a shark's arse. The commander and Du Bois would almost certainly arrange for a swift trial, and by sunset tomorrow, he would likely be swinging from a noose.

As Sebastiaan and the soldiers entered the Castle's inner courtyard, the heavy doors guarding the archway closed behind them, halting the accompanying crowd and replacing their chatter with silence.

The *Castle* was a pentagonal military structure, destined to feature a heavily armed bastion at each point upon completion. Once finished, it would be more than just a defensive fortress; it would be a community of its own. Inside the wide walls, there were a church, bakery, workshops, living quarters, offices, and cells. The impressive building, painted saffron yellow to absorb the bright sunlight, boasted an open walkway paved with slate quarried from Robben Island. A durable mixture of lime, shells, and sand bonded the stones, creating a striking contrast between the porcelain-white cement and the deep black slate. The only jarring feature was the reddish-brown paint on the doors and window frames.

With the soldiers preoccupied at the border, harassing farmers, the place felt abandoned. A seagull flew overhead, its harsh call echoing off the walls. As the bird vanished, two builders rounded a corner, their easy conversation flowing as they discussed plans for the evening after their day's work. They shared a laugh, but their voices faded as Sebastiaan was hurried along. They were like ships passing in a storm, unaware of each other; one in full control, its sails taut and its bow angled precisely to the wind, the other with a broken mast and a leaking hull, deeply in trouble and drifting helplessly.

The soldier at Sebastiaan's back pushed him through an open door and down a whitewashed corridor with an arched ceiling. He knew where they were taking him, and the knowledge filled him with dread. Sebastiaan opened his dry mouth to suck in a rush of cool, musty air, but his breath caught halfway. He forced another, and it slid down, thick and sluggish. Could he survive the horrors that awaited him once more? The first time in Muscat had nearly broken him and it had taken years to return to a state that faintly resembled normality, but that was when he'd thought Danielle was still alive. Now? Things were not the same anymore.

The captain and another soldier escorted Sebastiaan down a narrow tunnel. It was dark inside, with only the light from the open door illuminating their way. A couple of wide steps marked the end of the tunnel. They took a sharp turn to the right, and the soldier deliberately shoved Sebastiaan forward. He tripped over his shackled feet, twisted his body, and fell onto his side on the floor of the *Dark Hole*, the *Castle's* notorious torture chamber.

The room, originally built as an arsenal, was repurposed as a soundproof prison cell after the first flood soaked the stored munitions. The square chamber featured thick stone walls, a stone floor, and a heavy door. It lay deep within the *Castle's* walls at one of the five points. A half-finished bastion stood at that corner, its completion now imminent. Only days earlier, John had brought news that the French had landed at Saldanha Bay and planted their flag. They hadn't stayed to defend their claim, and the flag was swiftly removed and burned to ash. The bold act had rattled the new commander, and construction of the *Castle,* no longer a task for spare moments at a leisurely pace, was now the top priority.

The first bastion guarded the mountain and much of the bay, while the second, once completed, would secure the rest, making an attack by sea nearly impossible. Sebastiaan wondered if the tension they'd sensed earlier in the street stemmed from fears of a French assault or the attack on the farmers. It seemed highly unlikely that the townsfolk knew about the plans for his arrest; if they had, Gijs would have picked up on it right away and ridden out to the *Shack* in warning.

Sebastiaan struggled to his feet, encouraged by the captain's boot in his ribs. The captain had little in the way of strength, but the kick stung nonetheless.

"Torch!" the captain ordered and landed another kick, which glanced to the side and Sebastiaan wondered if he meant for him to stand up quicker or struggle to do so longer.

By the time Sebastiaan had scrambled to his feet, the torch had arrived, and he closed his eyes, not to block the sudden influx of light but to avoid seeing the rest of the room. On an earlier visit to the *Castle,* and subsequently the *Dark Hole*, he had read the words carved into the walls by previous prisoners and had seen the small lines where they'd tried to mark the passage of time. Men and women had been locked in this cell without charge for months, an offense the fort vehemently denied. Only the words carved into the stone stood in opposition. The writer was either dead or put onto a passing ship to an unknown destination. A shiver ran down his spine. He could feel the ghosts of those who'd been here before him stir at the intrusion. The air smelled sour and musty. After the last flooding, no one had bothered to dry it out, and the water was left to seep into the floor and walls, leaving everything clammy to the touch.

Sebastiaan felt a firm tug on his arms as each was chained to the wall and he opened his eyes. His legs were forced apart, his ankles chained in the same unyielding manner. The chains linking him to the wall were too short to allow him to sit or draw his legs together, forcing him to remain standing. Once done, the guard gave the chains a final tug, ensuring all was secure. He locked eyes with Sebastiaan and released a glob of saliva that would have hit him full in the mouth had he not turned his head to the side.

"Wilhelm," the captain admonished mildly.

Sebastiaan felt the warm spittle drip down his cheek. Then the door slammed shut, and the lock ground into place.

For a while Sebastiaan felt nothing but the damp wall at his back, and the cold iron touching his skin. The silence stretched, broken only by the pulsing drip of unseen water. The room felt endless, and yet he knew it was only a few feet wide. The darkness was oppressive and time warped, a second stretched to a minute, a minute to an hour, and the void became more than just air. It coagulated and shifted, turning into something tangible – a living thing, multiplying and folding in on itself until it grew thick enough to touch. Its weight pressed down on him, suffocating him. Panic was setting in at an alarming rate, clinging to him like a second skin. He knew the only way to fight it off was to breathe, which presently seemed more difficult than it should have.

Instinctively, he pulled on his arms and legs, trying to cover his body and wipe his face. The actions were futile and resulted only in rattling the chains, the thick stone walls absorbing the sounds, muffling them and amplifying the mass of the darkness. It felt as if a heavy hand was closing over his mouth and nose. Shaking his head from side to side, he tried to dislodge the phantom obstruction. His chest was burning, and his head felt detached from the rest of him, which brought the image of him hanging by his neck to the forefront of his mind.

He heard a tormented growl, like that from a beast caught in a trap. The sound stunned him, for he'd thought he was alone in the cell, but it was dark when he entered, and in the moments before the door closed, he hadn't bothered to look around. Was there another? Was he restrained too, or free to move about? Was it another prisoner or was it his tormentor? He tried to listen, but there was nothing, just the sickening silence and the living blackness. He coughed. The effort was pitiful and shallow. A second attempt worked better and once a little air found its way into his struggling lungs, the next breath came of its own accord.

"Hello?" he called. With his pulse pounding in his ears and his heart thrashing like a trapped bird, hearing a reply was impossible. He called again, and his voice bounced back to him. He hated the sound. It felt as if the room was feeding off him, trying to peel strips from his body with long, cold fingers, scratching and clawing at his skin. He saw Yavuz's face and his shiny black boots. The Ottoman captain smiled at him before raising his arm to bring down the whip. He felt the bite of the bullwhip on his sunburned skin.

His inner demons stirred to life. Like roiling snakes in a pit, they shoved past one another, slithering to the forefront of his mind and dragging vivid images with them: Danielle's bloodied body, her screams, Davit floating face down in the river, his blond hair bobbing on the water. He saw his father frowning at him and his mother crying from somewhere in their house. Then the clamor from the slave market in Muscat drew him away from his childhood memories. Frowning, he realized they were not memories at all, they were lies; twisted falsehoods brewed by the snakes, that dripped poison into his mind. His parents loved each other. From deep inside him, a single thought struggled its way through the pain and the suffocating helplessness. *None of this is real,* it whispered, but the snakes were stronger.

Sebastiaan clung to the threadbare lifeline. Somehow, he knew to trust that faint instinct. His demons still howled, unwilling to crawl back into the basket where he'd kept them for so long. The small voice grew louder, and the lifeline steadier, as did his grip on it. *This is not Muscat,* he repeated softly. The words became a mantra, pale at first, but growing stronger with each repetition. When he felt sure enough of that, he moved on to the next: *Davit is safe.* The chant turned into a hymn, its rhythm soothing, and his body surrendered to it. Each word a tether, pulling him back from the brink.

He needed to find something to keep his mind from spiraling into the hell of his memories. It was too dark to see anything and so he closed his eyes and searched within. He seized the first image that came to him. It was Elsje's house with its bright colors, the sound of her voice, her bright smile as she opened the front door. She led him through the messy room with the many fabrics, down the hall, and into the kitchen. There was the chair he always sat in, the one facing the window. Sebastiaan paid close attention to the scene, noting every detail, for he could not allow his imagination to fill the spaces between his memories. If there were empty spaces, he feared the fever dream would return; that he would look through the window and see Elsje's three children hanging from the tree branch, their faces purple, their tongues swollen as the ropes around their necks cut into their tender skin.

"Stop!" he shouted, not caring that his voice bounced around the room. "Where is that blasted kitchen table?" he demanded. If there was another in the cell with him, his unexpected outburst of seemingly senseless words would scare seven shades of shit from the bastard and hopefully keep him in his corner.

Seeing himself as the imagined cellmate would, chained to a wall, growling and shouting at the top of his voice, brought a smile to his face. The absurdity widened it, then amusement bubble up from his stomach, and he burst out laughing. He tried to bend forward as the spasms of his mirth tightened his stomach muscles, but the chains kept him from moving, and so he threw his head back and laughed harder.

Reason eventually won out and his composure returned. Sebastiaan closed his eyes against the darkness and hung his head forward. He was exhausted.

It was a waiting game now.

Chapter 15

It was late afternoon when Orion left Mostert's farm. The wind lashed his face as he tore back to the settlement at breakneck speed. Each jolt of the horse's stride struck his arse like a fist as he collided with the saddle, his clumsy horsemanship the sole reason for the pounding. The saddle creaked under the strain, and he wondered how long it'd be before the beast hurled him off its back. Smothering the nagging voice of self-preservation, he urged the animal faster. There seemed to be fewer hours in this day than the ones that had come before, and Orion let the events flash through his mind.

This morning, he and Sebastiaan had loaded the cart and driven it into town. The memory felt old and far away, as if it had happened days ago.

When the soldiers pulled Sebastiaan from his horse, a red veil of rage had settled over Orion. He was fully prepared to spill an ungodly amount of blood. Had Gijs not stepped in and pulled him away, he would have turned that street, with its quaint white houses and neat little gardens, into something resembling a frenzied pagan ritual on a full moon.

"Think, Orion," Gijs had whispered in his ear as he'd pulled him deeper into the crowd and away from the eager soldiers. He had only released the iron grip on Orion's arm once they were safely hidden behind the grocer's store.

Orion's eyes had traveled from the hand on his arm to Gijs' face. "Let go," he had warned, but Gijs had ignored him and furthered his intention to subdue Orion by pushing him against the wall.

"I will not," Gijs had persisted. "You've already assaulted a soldier. That alone is enough for the captain to call for your arrest. Hear me well," Gijs urged in a low voice. "If you kill one of them, they will hang you without trial. Do you want Sebastiaan to witness that? It will break him. What good will you be to him if you are locked up or dead?"

He'd listened, but turning his back on Sebastiaan had threatened to tear his heart out. Nothing had ever been that hard. Nothing had ever made him feel as wretched as he had in that moment, his self-loathing barely surpassed by his raw anger. He wanted to gag and had to swallow hard to keep his stomach under control. Seeing Sebastiaan's blond hair splayed over the gray stones of the street had twisted something inside him. Why that image haunted him so, he couldn't understand.

He had struggled against Gijs' words but eventually conceded that twelve against one were unfavorable odds. Still, he'd never walked away from a fight. "Damn their chains," he growled under his breath, the sight of Sebastiaan hobbling with an uneven gait, feet bound by iron, burning a hole through his chest.

He then realized why he preferred life at sea to land. Raiding pirates was controlled chaos – every enemy unique, but the landscape was the same and the choice of weapons finite. But here, things were different. Laws reigned supreme, their restrictions crippling effective violence. One wrong move, one unlawful death, and the consequences were severe. He despised the murkiness of the law and its many interpretations, the shadowy power wielders with their hidden agendas, false promises, and empty declarations.

What should have been a straightforward matter of right and wrong, easily settled by blade and skill, had spun into a web of legal uncertainty. Loopholes and pitfalls appeared out of nowhere, and the outcome, detached from the larger truth, hinged only on the latest events. It was a morass of ambiguity that bordered on insanity.

His grumbling thoughts came to a gradual halt as the road ahead slowly revealed itself. Sebastiaan never spoke of his time as an Ottoman slave, but Orion had seen enough broken and tormented souls over the years to know what Sebastiaan had gone through. Orion knew that being chained and imprisoned would wreak havoc on Sebastiaan's mind, and though he was one of the strongest men he knew, such conditions could chip away at a man's sanity.

Sebastiaan needed to be freed before this day gave birth to another, and for that to happen, Orion needed information. He needed legal advice. Once he knew where he stood with the law, he could plan a successful strategy. If the law did not allow for a clear and straightforward way for Sebastiaan to be released immediately, then Orion had no intention of playing by the rules, but to break the law, one must first understand it.

It didn't take long for his mind to find its cold, calculating pulse again. Gijs' interference had served its purpose, the calm he so badly needed had found him, and with it had come a scourge across his pride for acting the fool.

Gijs' resonant voice was starting to grate on Orion. The man was annoyingly reasonable under adverse circumstances, and surprisingly robust against the threats Orion flung at him. "Negotiation is always better than confrontation," Gijs said calmly. Orion had paid little attention to what Gijs was saying, but that idiotic assertion was impossible to disregard.

"Gijs, enough," Orion hissed under his breath. He had endured all the words of wisdom and pleas for caution he could bear. "I'm not one of your errand boys."

The baker fell silent, but he kept his eyes locked on Orion, as if trying to judge the soundness of his mind and the permanency of his temper.

"I need to think, and your prattling is driving me to distraction. Take the horses and cart to your house. I will collect them later," Orion had ordered.

Gijs was apparently incapable of taking offense and Orion grudgingly felt a kernel of respect for the man. "Where are you going?" Gijs asked.

"I need to talk to Wouter Mostert," Orion answered. Having his movements questioned was a fresh experience and one he did not care for.

"And then?" Gijs pushed. Orion shot him a sharp warning look.

"And then we'll see. Let's move," he said and pointed to where the three horses and cart had been abandoned by the side of the now-empty street.

***

The wind had become bothersome, and Orion knew it would only increase as the evening turned into night. By the time he reached Mostert's farm, another displaced farmer and his family had arrived and were in the process of unloading their humble belongings from a cart. A handful of small children were running about in lively play, their shrill voices in sharp contrast to the tension written on the adults' faces. Women with bewildered eyes and thin lips and men with tight jaws and bunched shoulders were milling about, trying to create order.

Orion dismounted and tied his horse to a post near the brick kiln, then slowly made his way to where Mostert was talking to three men he recognized from the meeting a few weeks ago. He paused his advance well away from the group and waited, taking the time to study the unfolding humanitarian crisis.

Thick smoke was billowing in from the west. The attacks on the farms were escalating. The fort was sending a clear message: any dissension would exact a high price, and the rebels would feel the consequences of their actions for years to come. Orion inhaled deeply, filling his lungs with the bitter, pungent scent of destruction.

These people had nowhere else to turn for help but to Mostert. He was their most affluent ally, their voice, and their leader. Orion briefly wondered how safe the Mostert farm was. It seemed the fort was not planning on killing the farmers – yet. As such, their safety would lie in their numbers. If they stayed together, the soldiers might not attack.

Orion realized he'd made a mistake in coming here. He was only adding to the weight already resting on Mostert's shoulders. He wanted to turn back to his horse and ride away, but Mostert had caught sight of him. Excusing himself from the conversation, he made his way toward Orion.

"Good afternoon, Captain," Mostert greeted in his ever-polite, calm tone.

"Mister Mostert," Orion returned, but did not extend his hand. Touching others was not something he willingly subjected himself to.

Mostert looked over Orion's shoulder, expecting to see the cart loaded with wheat. A light frown tugged at his brows when he found the road empty. "You came alone? I thought– "

"Sebastiaan was arrested about two hours ago," Orion stated.

"Where?" Mostert asked as his face contorted with concern. "On what charge?"

"Murder," Orion answered, addressing the most important question first. "In town, on our way here."

"Oh God, have mercy," Mostert prayed, and the chill shooting down Orion's spine told him the words were spoken in earnest and not merely as an expression of alarm. "Could the charge possibly be true?" Sparks of panic darted across Mostert's eyes.

Orion shook his head. "I am not entirely sure."

"Let us talk inside." Mostert pointed toward the large house that also moonlighted as an inn, and as of right now a refugee shelter.

"No," Orion declined. "You have your hands full enough as it is, and I don't have much time. I needed legal advice, but …" The incomplete statement hung in the air as his voice trailed off.

"The timing is peculiar," Mostert noted, almost absentmindedly, ignoring Orion's refusal. "The farms are under attack, but it looks like a scare tactic only. No lives have been lost, only property. Putting Sebastiaan in chains sends a clear message. As for the murder charge," Mostert scrunched his face and sucked a breath of air through his teeth. "If it holds any truth, then there is very little we can do." At this, Orion's lips thinned and his fists balled for a moment before he caught himself and relaxed his hands. Mostert seemed not to notice. "I must go into town in the morning to report the events of today to the commander and see if we can come to some sort of agreement. I can ask about Sebastiaan then. If luck is on our side, they might let me talk to him. Once we have more information, we can start building a defense."

Orion nodded his understanding. He understood that the wide, well-trodden path of justice would not lead them to a favorable outcome. Time and circumstance were not on their side. Besides, his life had always led him down shady, often non-existent paths to whatever goal he pursued and it had worked just fine so far. There was no point changing course now, not with stakes this high. Begging for a meeting with some over-inflated arsehole and then having to patiently wait for the verdict, which could make or break a man's future, was not in the cards he'd been dealt at birth.

At best, a lengthy legal process stretched before them. At worst, Mostert would argue a stay of execution for life in prison or indentured service, which was a civilized term for slavery. Orion refrained from telling the man to shove his legal advice up his arse and instead had thanked him for his time, then mounted his horse.

He wished he could fight alongside his men, smiting the soldiers and defending the farms. But Niccolò was more than capable of handling the situation. Orion needed to return to the *Shack* and find Van Leyen. Perhaps Daka had returned from town. Between the three of them, they could spring Sebastiaan from prison.

Returning from Mostert's farm, Orion let several scenarios unfold in his mind. He could recall his men and leave the farmers to defend their own lands. What was the old saying? If you are too weak to defend it, you don't deserve to keep it? He dismissed the adage as cold-hearted cowardice. These folks were not fighters, they were farmers; honest, peaceful people who wanted nothing more than to carve a new life for themselves. Their role in society was not to fight, but to feed. Men like Orion and his mercenaries had an obligation to protect them.

He could bribe the new commander. Men of the cloth always have a weakness for coin. Enough gold, some groveling, and a lot of arse kissing could secure Sebastiaan's freedom. It was the *'could'* that drove that idea into the dust. Also, Orion had never groveled or kissed any part of another man before, and he sure as certain would not start tonight. Bribery was a more solid option, but if the man was insusceptible to the idea, then he'd have tipped his hand. No, that would not work. That strategy was pimpled with uncertainties.

He could threaten the commander. That notion held a significant amount of appeal, and he explored it further. Imagining his hand closing around the pastor's throat sent a jolt of pure bliss through him. He shook the fantasy from his mind and, with a detached eye, considered each possibility from every possible angle.

In the end, it came down to one – brute force. He was going to have to crack some skulls and bust Sebastiaan out of prison the old-fashioned way. The only glaring problem was that he was short on men, but then it occurred to him that so was the commander, for the soldiers were engaged in bothering the farmers.

First, he needed to see Sebastiaan, to reassure himself that he was all right and to share his plan. He also had to learn where he was being held and under what circumstances. If he wanted to break Sebastiaan out, he had to do it tonight while most of the soldiers were away from the *Castle*. He would not have another chance like this.

Chapter 16

The discomfort of not being able to sit down was still manageable. Shackled, Sebastiaan could only shift his feet farther apart, unable to draw them together, causing a slight ache in his hips and knees and a swelling in his lower legs. He closed his eyes and drew his mind away from the immediate, blocking the dark room from reaching the part of him that vividly remembered what it felt like to be chained to a bench and made to row for days on end without rest.

In moments of distress, he'd always called Danielle's face to mind – holding on to her image, reminding himself of his goal, of his purpose in life. She was his bedrock, the foundation on which everything was built. Had it not been for Davit filling a small portion of the void left by her absence, he would have been adrift. Since he'd learned of her death, he'd tried not to disturb her peace. He would see her soon enough. She would be standing on that threshold between the living and the dead, waiting to guide him home, and his lips curved into a grin. Out of habit rather than need, he gave his imagination the freedom to drift to her one last time.

The grinding of a key in the lock drew him from his daydream. In a way, he was grateful for the intrusion, for there was a moment of trepidation when he couldn't recall the details of her face and for the first time, he'd wondered if he ever could. Was she now just a collection of disconnected memories of the things she'd said, the way she'd laughed and sounded, her smell, the places they'd sat and gone together, the things they'd done? The recollections were like loose ribbons he'd found streaming in the wind. Over time, he bound them together and told himself that was what she looked like.

The door scraped and footsteps clipped across the stone floor. He smelled the fuel from the torch and the light caused a red haze over his closed eyes, giving him a strange, intimate view of his eyelids from the inside.

The visitor did not speak or move, and the haze remained constant. Sebastiaan tightened his core and the muscles in his face, knowing an attack was imminent; his open and vulnerable body would be too much of a temptation to resist. After long seconds passed without punches landing in his stomach or knuckles slamming into his jaw, Sebastiaan slowly opened his eyes, blinked rapidly and then squinted. The light would have been soft in any other location, but in the *Dark Hole*, it was harsh.

Refusing to take in the room at large, he focused solely on the man standing before him. Alain Du Bois stared back, cold hatred blazing in his black eyes.

Du Bois waited for De Vries to open his eyes. Suppressing his cold hatred for the man, he stepped closer until they were less than two feet apart, close enough to touch.

He studied the face before him: strong lines, sharp nose, expressionless eyes, a mouth neither tight with tension nor sneering but relaxed and lightly closed. Dustings of a day-old beard covered his cheeks. The disheveled blond hair, at some point cropped short but then forgotten, shone like antique gold in the flickering light. A vein pulsed at an even pace in his neck. The large sun-browned, scarred hands hung relaxed in their shackles. Not a single finger twitched to betray any internal conflict. Du Bois inhaled the man's scent, searching for information as it passed through his nose. He discovered an amalgamation of fresh sweat and hints of the ocean, but no fear. The man looked as docile as a kitten; however, Alain was not fooled. This was a cold-blooded killer.

"You murdered my son," he said, his voice smooth and melodic, like he was reading the charge from a poem.

De Vries remained silent, blinking lazily. He wore the bored expression of a man idling at a market stall.

"There is no need to admit or deny it," Alain said. "Last night, your man, Daka, confessed to your crimes." Once more he studied the prisoner and once more there was no reaction, not even a small nod or a slight frown to indicate the words had sparked at least a splinter of interest.

It mattered little, Alain told himself. He had not come here for conversation or debate. He came here to inform the man of both his immediate and distant future.

"Are you right or left-handed?" he asked, and the odd question unlocked a response.

De Vries' brows flickered before settling into place. He shrugged a shoulder, keeping his eyes locked on Du Bois at a languid downward angle that emphasized their difference in height. Not caring for the effect, Alain turned away and secured the torch in the single sconce on the wall, then stepped closer to Sebastiaan's right hand and unlocked the shackle. It was a minor concession, a gift that could be taken away.

There was every possibility that the hand would snap out and close around his throat, but he had a dagger hidden in the small of his back and would use it, but only far enough to secure his release and not to inflict serious harm. However, his concerns were unwarranted. De Vries slowly lowered his arm to his side and flexed his fingers. Alain stepped back, increasing the distance between them. The man was civil now, but that state was bound to change once the conversation fermented into its true form.

"I know what you are thinking," Alain said in a conversational tone. "You think I came here to gloat or torture." He looked at De Vries and had to admit he never, in all his years, met a face so persistently devoid of emotion. "But as you can see," he said, pointing to the arm he just freed, "I am not a monster."

Alain studied the shadowed eyes; it was like looking at a painting – whatever emotion you see was purely a trick of the light or a conviction of the imagination.

"I've learned something of late," Alain continued, as if they were old friends sharing confidences. "One does not stop being a father once your child dies. You are still a parent, still a person, albeit an empty one." He nodded at De Vries. "You and I shall soon share this knowledge." The cryptic statement elicited a minuscule twitch of the brows and Alain knew that a glimmer of understanding was dawning.

"You are a father." It was a statement and not a question. "Your child announced himself as such that fateful night in the tavern. I haven't seen the boy myself, but rumors are he favors you in looks. You must be proud."

A ghostly shadow passed over De Vries' face, causing a muscle to jump in his jaw and his nostrils to flare with a flicker. Even though De Vries' eyes were still locked on him, they seemed to have lost their focus, staring at a distant scene beyond the bounds of the room.

As if only just realizing the state of the cell, Du Bois looked around the morbid innards of the room.

"I will order some changes here. The shackles will be removed and replaced by a collar and chain long enough for you to lie down and use the bucket, which will be delivered shortly," he said and frowned at the apparent neglect. "You will also be provided with a cot and blankets, and your bedding and clothing will be laundered once a month. You will receive one meal per day and if you behave, a guard will lead you around the courtyard once a week. You will not be abused in any way whatsoever. I will check on you regularly to ensure these conditions are upheld." He paused to gauge De Vries' reaction. The faraway look had vanished from his eyes and had been replaced by something acute, but still no sound escaped his lips.

"There will be no trial, and you will not be hanged, shot or killed by any other means. You will live in this cell or one similar to it for the rest of your natural life, the length of which will depend on you, for no one will stand in your way, should you wish to put an early end to it." Alain paced the length of the small cell his hands clasped behind his back. He huffed a silent smile and continued. "Tonight will be the beginning of the rest of your new life. A life in which you will live every day henceforth like I have, knowing that another has killed your son."

Fire ignited in De Vries' eyes and Alain watched as raw fear and desperation snuffed out the indifference he'd been so carefully nurturing.

"Your boy will die tonight, by my hand, as justice for the life you took from me. *He* will pay the price for your crime."

"Just like yours paid the price for your crimes," De Vries said in a jagged voice, not bothering to preserve his silence any longer.

"I will not debate the matter with you. The life I've lived, the choices I've made are mine to contemplate, not yours to judge. I came here to inform you of my plans for your family and your future, both made vulnerable by your actions."

The meeting was over. Alain had delivered his message, and he reached for the torch. It was time to make good on his promises. He was aware that the crew from the De Vries ship was lurking about in the forest acting as some sort of vigilante protectors of the border and with the soldiers attacking the farms, they would have their hands full tonight. The situation created the perfect window to accomplish his task with minimal resistance.

Sebastiaan winced at the sharp rap of iron against stone as Du Bois lifted the torch from the sconce. He had always known his meddling with the farmers could land him in chains, but he'd wagered the lack of a clear cause would keep him free. Daka's confession had shattered that hope. Du Bois now knew he was responsible for the death of his son and the matter had turned chillingly personal. Du Bois craved revenge – an eye for an eye, a son for a son. Cold dread coiled in Sebastiaan's gut, twisting the life from him, warping his thoughts into jagged fragments. The sordid affair had tilted his world, shaking it to its core.

The threat to Davit's life gripped him with a suffocating force, like a hand seizing his neck and thrusting him beneath the water. Du Bois was leaving. Sebastiaan was drowning. He needed to keep Du Bois with him until he could get a grip on the situation, but try as he might, not a single thought seemed to stick. They all floated by like debris after a storm. Fear pulled at his stomach and the sinking feeling caused saliva to flood his mouth. It tasted foreign and bitter. He swallowed it away only for it to return, like digging a hole in the beach and scooping water from its base, only for more to seep through the sand. His lips felt cold and a burning desire to weep pulled at the edges of his face.

This was the most important battle of his life, and he needed a clear head. Every problem has a solution, he reminded himself, but to find it, he must distance himself from all emotions, memories, and perceived threats. Through sheer force of will, his mind sharpened into cold clarity, focusing solely on the reality before him. He discarded the irrelevant, homing in on what might prove advantageous. Instead of seeing defeat or disaster, he hunted for opportunities – ways to distract his opponent, to provoke a mistake, to divert him from his plans and ultimately, kill him.

Though chained to the wall, his options were limited, yet he had one free hand and the power of speech. As far as he could see, there were only two options available.

He could reveal to Du Bois that Davit was not his son, that he didn't father the boy, that Davit was Elias Coopman's child. It was a very tempting option; it had the potential to save Davit's life. But to betray Danielle in such a way was unthinkable. To hand her child over to the man who'd killed her father, to the half-brother of the man who'd violated and abused her? No, he could not do it. The only path left was to get Davit away from the Cape and out of Du Bois' reach.

"If you kill that boy, you will destroy what is left of your soul," Sebastiaan said as Du Bois reached the cell's door. He doubted his words would have any effect on a man whose soul had most likely shriveled up and died a long time ago, if ever he had one. To his surprise, Du Bois paused. A second passed as he contemplated the words and then he slowly turned and advanced on Sebastiaan.

A cold smile spread across Du Bois' face, his eyes dead as a demon's, the gray in his once-black hair gleaming like molten silver in the torchlight. The words, seemingly trivial, had struck a nerve.

A tenuous plan unfurled in Sebastiaan's mind. Du Bois would not have come here unarmed. No weapons caught his eye, but his instincts warned of a dagger nestled at his back, far easier to draw in a hurry than one tucked in his boot. If he could taunt Du Bois into losing control, lure him close, Sebastiaan could reach for the weapon and slit the snake's throat and to hell with the consequences. He would happily spend the rest of his life locked away in this dark hellhole if it meant ensuring Davit's safety.

"Don't lecture me, boy," Du Bois breathed. "Not when your own hands drip with blood." Every word pushed him closer to Sebastiaan. "Your actions have been far more diabolical than I could ever have managed." Sebastiaan saw the pulse throbbing at Du Bois' temples, and the battle between hatred and restraint raging behind his dark eyes.

Another half a step was all he needed.

"I doubt that," Sebastiaan said and allowed an arrogant smile to spread across his face. "Your decision to trade in human lives robbed your son of his." The need for violence was crackling in the air around Du Bois and Sebastiaan artfully tilted his head back, exposing his jaw, inviting the blow that would put his adversary in perfect proximity. Seeing the baiting gesture, Du Bois stilled, his body shaking with rage.

"You said you didn't come here to debate the matter and that I would not stand trial. I am beginning to understand why," Sebastiaan said.

"Yes?" Du Bois was still bristling with anger.

Sebastiaan didn't think Du Bois would rise to the ploy and was pleasantly surprised when he did.

"In here you may have the upper hand, but in court, you have no leg to stand on. You claimed Daka revealed the events that led to your son's demise, but where is he? You can't keep him locked up and then produce him as a witness, for that would drastically reduce his veracity. One could safely argue that he would admit to anything to secure his release. No, you either killed him or he fled, but be that as it may, there is no witness. Your claim is nothing but hearsay and idle gossip."

"You forget," Du Bois said, his eyes narrowed, but he stood dead still. "I don't have to produce your man, Daka. My word, coupled with another witness, would suffice. A sailor from the *Zuiderland* has escaped and returned to me. I am not afraid of taking this matter to court."

"You should be. Your so-called sailor arrived at the Cape months after the alleged incident, filling your ears and everyone else's with a fantastic tale of how a horde of men stormed their ship. How they killed, maimed and slaughtered without discrimination. How he had fought his way to freedom and practically crawled hundreds of miles through the African wilderness to bring you this news." Sebastiaan raised his brows at Du Bois. "A deaf, dumb and mute man will tell you that credibility is going to be an issue with that one. As for me? It is your word against mine, which brings us back to your problem of hearsay." Sebastiaan sighed and shook his head. "You don't have a case and you know it."

Du Bois stared at Sebastiaan for a few beats and then clapped his hands in applause. The loud, forceful smacks brimmed with suppressed frustration.

When the noise died down, Sebastiaan continued. "How long do you think you can keep me here without trial? How long before news reaches my uncle, Davit De Coninck? We both know he is not a man to underestimate, nor one you would want breathing down your neck. How long do you think you can survive in the bright light of day, when the shadows you hide in are being ripped away?"

"Why, Mister De Vries, you've missed your calling. You should have been an advocate. You can stand there all night listing the technicalities of the law. But, look at you, chained to a wall, while I am free. While most of what you say might be construed as the truth, none of it matters. Your son will still die tonight, regardless of what tomorrow might bring."

Du Bois tilted his head and touched his forehead in a cordial goodbye, then smiled and made to leave. Sebastiaan knew his time was running out. He had one move left to prevent his enemy from calling checkmate. It was time to play the King's Pawn and open a point of weakness.

"Do you want to know how your precious boy died?" Sebastiaan was playing a dangerous game, but all he needed was for Du Bois to advance another six inches. "Did Daka tell you?" The blood leached from Du Bois' face, but his feet remained unmoved. "No?" Sebastiaan mocked.

The war inside Du Bois was now plain to see. Sebastiaan knew that dagger was burning in his back, the need to drive it into Sebastiaan's heart was palpable, but the man valiantly held himself in check.

"He died with his intestines spilling from his hands as he tried to push them back into his gaping belly. All the while screaming for deliverance and begging for mercy. In the end, I gave him what he wanted and cut his throat."

The tortured growl that tore from Du Bois rang through the cell and the connecting hallways. Sebastiaan opened his mouth to speak again.

"Enough!" Du Bois shouted, spun on his heel and left the cell, leaving Sebastiaan to stare at the empty room and the open door.

Fuck!

The air was cold and in a state of shock with the sudden absence of sound, and Sebastiaan stared blindly at the empty doorway. The ghost of Du Bois' voice lingered, buzzing like a swarm of insects at dusk, only to be drowned by the deafening thrum of his heart pounding against the inside of his chest. A scream rushed over his tongue, but he pressed his lips together and bit down on his teeth until spikes of pain shot into his temples. The need to slam his head against the stone wall until it burst open was nearly overwhelming.

He had gambled from a poor position and lost. Failing to push Du Bois over the edge had only turned a disaster into a calamity. All he had accomplished was to motivate him further, leaving Davit more vulnerable than before. In Sebastiaan's youth, he'd learned that no matter how bad things were, they could always get worse – and they just did. He knew with stone cold certainty that Du Bois would not only kill Davit and be done with it, but he would also ensure Sebastiaan bore witness. He would gut his beautiful boy right here in the middle of this cell, recreating the scene that Sebastiaan had painted of his own son's demise. All because he had underestimated his opponent, a mistake he'd never made before, but did so now when the stakes were at their highest.

A guard was approaching the cell and Sebastiaan closed his eyes in anticipation of the darkness that would soon follow. The door was firmly shut, and locked once more. Sebastiaan teetered on the edge of despair, and then he fell. It was as if the darkness had become a sucking pit. The room spun as the abyss pulled him down. Had he been in the ocean, he would have fought against the suction, but as it was, he surrendered to the whirlpool. Vertigo set in and nausea pushed up, and he heaved, but his empty stomach produced nothing but air and a slight acid burn in the back of his throat. Abandoning the attempt, he dropped his chin to his chest. For the first time in his life, he could see no way out.

***

By sunset the wind had reached gale-force speeds. A waterfall that typically fell a perfect curtain from the top of Table Mountain into the forest below was now tossed and torn by the gusts. Half of it was blown back the way it had come, defying gravity, while the rest was scattered in all directions, causing a watery cloud around the severed area. Orion stood inside the double, metal spiked doors of the *Castle*. The doors seemed more decorative than functional, as there was no locking mechanism on the inside. It simply opened and closed without resistance. *How very foolish*, he thought and then thanked his stars for the folly as it was one less obstacle to overcome. He needed to see Sebastiaan and the pouch of golden ducats and silver guilders in his pocket, earmarked earlier for the milling, would secure his goal.

To his right, further down the colonnade, a weary-looking soldier stood guard, his back pressed against a closed door, his faithful rapier securely sheathed at his side. Orion silently counted the doors from the entrance to the guard. Sebastiaan was the only prisoner held in the *Castle,* and now he knew the exact location. He counted three more soldiers on patrol on top of the wall. Just then, another hurried across the empty courtyard, his pace faltering as he caught sight of Orion heading toward him.

"Where is the captain of the guard?" Orion injected a healthy dose of urgency into his voice, hoping the fool would not take it upon himself to conduct a preliminary interrogation with the usual nonsense: *Who are you? What business do you have with the captain? Is he expecting you?* Orion groaned inwardly at the imaginary scene.

The guard's eyes sharpened, his scowl deepened and his shoulders squared. Extracting his hand from his pocket, Orion skipped a silver guilder back and forth between his fingers. "Just point," he said and caught the coin between two fingers. The soldier could earn a week's wages simply by lifting his hand.

The gangly young man gave the coin a yearning look, his brows pinched high. Like a wet puppy, his face fell, then he shook his head. "He's not here."

"Where is he?" Orion bit back the sharp tone and deliberately softened the question. The soldiers left behind at the settlement were most likely the runt of the litter, being the youngest and most inexperienced and used to others barking and ribbing them.

"He went out with the soldiers." The boy gave the coin another covetous glance before adding. "But the commander is at the fort, should you wish to speak to him instead."

Orion exhaled heavily and closed his hand over the coin. The soldier's shoulders sagged but immediately perked up when Orion produced another silver coin from his pocket. His prudence in avoiding the village was paying off. The idiot standing before him clearly had no idea who he was. People came and went, new faces appeared and old ones disappeared with every ship docking and leaving the Cape of Good Hope.

"How many soldiers are on duty tonight at the *Castle*?" he asked. The young man hesitated, then shook his head.

"With much regret, sir. I cannot tell you that." The boy looked close to tears when Orion nodded with a soft, understanding smile and dropped the coins back in his pocket.

"I understand completely," he said, staring at the soldier in an assessing manner, while thinking of a different strategy. "You seem competent and I now understand why they tasked you with defending the *Castle* and the village. With the farmers' uprising at the border, I am sure you have a long night stretching before you, and I will detain you no further." The boy nodded, his large eyes swimming in disappointment when Orion took a step away. However, his expression perked when Orion paused.

"May I be so bold and ask one more question?" Orion raised his eyebrows prettily at the boy, silently asking for permission to continue. His humble tone, sinless request and diminished demeanor spurred the soldier to puff out his chest and tilt his chin with a freshly minted air of male pride and self importance.

Orion examined him for a touch longer. Then extracted two golden ducats from the small pouch. He faked a nervous swallow and fluttered his long eyelashes, while looking toward the mountain behind them. As he delicately laid his closed hand over his heart, he stifled a lip curl that threatened to protest his own spectacle.

"In this unfortunate time, and as a vulnerable and concerned resident, I was only wondering if our esteemed commander is safe in the fort. I would sleep so much better if I knew that he was well protected," he said in a snow-pure innocent, almost feminine tone.

The boy had failed to recognize the mischievous glint in Orion's eyes that belied every faux concern that dropped from his lips like pellets from a goat's rear end.

"Of course, sir," he said, smiling reassuringly. It wasn't every day that someone took the time to talk to him as if he were the only person worth the effort, let alone look to him for their safety. As long as the man did not direct his questions to his immediate post, there was no harm in laying his fears to rest. Besides, the captain had hounded him all week for the slightest missteps. If he was not supposed to put the settlers' minds at ease, the captain should have ordered him not to. "Our job is not just to keep the *Castle* and the commander safe, but also to instill confidence in the good people of the settlement. I would not want you to lose a moment's sleep and would therefore ensure you that five of our best men are guarding the commander, and that there is absolutely no need for concern."

Orion did a quick calculation. There were twelve soldiers at the arrest this morning. With the captain overseeing the raiding party, eleven remained; subtracting the boy and the guard at the door left nine unaccounted for. Five were stationed at the fort, leaving four to patrol the *Castle* walls.

"Thank you. I feel safer already." Orion said, extending his hand. He let it brush lightly over the soldier's, stifling a shiver at its clamminess, then eased away, leaving two golden ducats behind.

The young soldier did not look at the small fortune in his fist. Instead, his hand smoothly disappeared inside his jacket before straightening the garment. He executed a neat bow, mumbled his leave-taking, and continued in the direction he'd intended before Orion had accosted him. When his shadow passed the corner and Orion was sure he would not return, he lengthened his strides toward the guarded door.

Orion recognized the guard as one of the pair who'd dragged Sebastiaan from his horse and his gut clenched as his innate need for violence instantly set to simmer. The lout leaned against the door, and lazily turned his head toward Orion. Were the man under his command, he would taste boot leather for the rest of his days.

Controlling his growing annoyance at the disgusting lack of discipline, he said, "I have permission from Commander De Voogd to see the prisoner. Open the door." Orion was surprised at how eloquent his voice was, given that his hands were itching for a confrontation.

The man scoffed, then released a squirt of saliva that landed close to Orion's feet. He rolled his head back and stared straight ahead, doing a fine job of dismissing the visitor.

Orion reminded himself that Sebastiaan was less than ten yards from where he stood, and that it was unwise in the extreme to let this cretin, who'd have to look up to see the underside of a cockroach, distract him from his mission.

"Look, his trial is tomorrow, and I am his legal representative. It is imperative that I speak to him immediately," Orion explained with the humility befitting a clerk of the law, but stripped of the feminine charm he'd used on the young soldier.

"No one is to visit the prisoner," the guard drawled, stubbornly forgoing common sense for arrogance.

"By whose order?" Orion demanded, and by some stroke of divine intervention, he refrained from raising his voice.

"Mister Du Bois."

"I think the commander outranks Mister Du Bois," Orion said as he took the man's measure. They were of a similar height, but the brute was heavier in the shoulders, waist, and thighs. He would be slow in a fight, but savagely strong.

"I don't give half a fart for what you think. Show me the written permission," the guard ordered.

Orion shook his head in bewilderment. "I just need five minutes with my client." Then he uttered a word he despised and rarely, if ever, used. "Please," he implored.

The man returned his gaze to the empty courtyard, casting Orion from his sight. The gossamer thread that held Orion's civility in place snapped. He took a non-threatening sideways step and planted himself in front of the man. The guard peeled his head from the door, tilted it slightly to the left, cleaned his teeth with his tongue, and leveled an unimpressed look at Orion.

"Open the damn door or I'll cut your fucking throat," Orion growled.

The man had a simple face, with a scattering of dim features. Low brow, fleshy lips, and a jawline that came together in a round and unremarkable chin. Dull eyes betrayed a mind untouched by the spark of curiosity or the light of understanding, utterly content with the vast and empty wasteland that stretched between his ears.

The threat straightened the rest of him from the door and he quickly examined the length of Orion's body, from his face to his boots and back again. His thick lips parted in a cunning grin, revealing teeth similar in appearance to the stones of a forsaken graveyard.

"With what?" he goaded, having seen no significant weapons on Orion's person. He was not wrong. Orion had expected a pat down and therefore had left his daggers and saber with his horse, safely tucked away in Gijs' stable. With serpent-like speed Orion delivered an open-handed slap across the man's oily cheek, hard enough for spots of spittle to mark the black slate stone at their feet and with his left hand drew the rapier from the guard's side, took a step back and nudged it past the barrier of clothing to prick the man's vulnerable groin. It all unfolded in the fleeting space between one second and the next.

"I changed my mind," Orion said and looked downright cheery as the man's round eyes lowered to where the tip of his own rapier cut through the front of his breeches. "Listen carefully, this is important. I am going to start counting. When I reach four, the door will already be open. If it's not open by the time I reach five, your left nut will drop to the floor." The man hesitated, glancing at his companions on the western wall, their silhouettes shadowy in the distance. They were close enough to hear, should he scream for help, yet their attentions were directed outward, away from the courtyard and the danger currently threatening his manhood. "They won't be able to save you," Orion read his mind. "Two … three."

"Wait," the man said, patting himself down as he tried to remember in which pocket he'd dropped the key.

"Four." Orion pressed the blade deeper. The lock yielded and the door opened on dry hinges. The guard was somewhat out of breath and looked like a child proud of tying his first shoelace. "Nicely done," Orion praised. He retracted the weapon and pointed down the corridor. "Lead the way."

They walked down the narrow, whitewashed hallway that ended in a small vestibule with multiple doors studded in its walls. The guard opened the door to Sebastiaan's cell and stepped inside. It was the most horrible space Orion had ever seen. From the ugly domed ceiling, the wooden door, thick enough to block any sound produced by the tortured prisoner, to the bare, uneven stone walls.

Seeing Sebastiaan chained to the wall by three of his four limbs made Orion's anger explode. Channeling his rage into something useful, he hooked his foot around the guard's ankle the instant it lifted with his step. The foot, poised to touch firm ground, was unexpectedly checked. The mind worked in mysterious ways; all its power and focus were instantly drawn to a failure in procedure – a procedure that usually operated quite smoothly beyond the realm of awareness.

The guard tilted forward, his hands instinctively snapping out to catch himself, but everything unfolded differently than it should have. Orion took a firm hold of the man's dirty hair, pulled him up and slammed his forehead into the wall. The guard's body softened, but not sufficiently to indicate a loss of the senses. Orion yanked the man's head back and searched his unfocused eyes, frowned and repeated the assault.

"Very impressive," Sebastiaan spoke after Orion had slammed the man against the wall for the third time. "If death is your aim, then by all means, continue. Otherwise, I'd say he is thoroughly subdued."

Orion looked at his efforts. The skin was broken on the soldier's forehead, and a decent sized lump was forming near the hairline. He shoved the body aside and stepped closer to examine Sebastiaan. Except for being chained to the wall, there were no discernible signs of abuse.

"Are you all right?" he asked.

"Yes," Sebastiaan's voice was strong but hushed.

"We don't have much time," Orion said and reached to pull the key from the door and dropped it in his right pocket. "The others will notice his absence soon enough and come to investigate. Have you learned anything about the conditions of your arrest? Who is behind it? De Voogd?" He could still not understand how that man came to power. Yesterday he was just a corrupt pastor tupping his slaves and selling children to whorehouses, and today he was occupying the highest seat at the settlement.

"No, Alain Du Bois," Sebastiaan answered.

Orion's stomach turned sour. If ever a man needed to be rushed toward his demise, it was that bastard.

"Orion, listen to me," Sebastiaan said urgently. "You must make me a promise. Here and now."

"I will make all the promises you demand of me, but not here. This is just a quick reconnaissance visit. I am sorely tempted to break you free now but the risk of being caught is too high. I will return later, after dark, and we'll put a stop to this insanity."

Sebastiaan's free hand snapped out, and he pulled Orion close.

"There will not be a later, and you will not come back. So, listen to me now," Sebastiaan spoke in his ear. He could feel Orion's body go as rigid as a plank at his words.

"I don't understand," Orion said and pulled from Sebastiaan's grip. "I *will* come back. What is this nonsense? Do you think I would leave you here a second longer than necessary? The number of guards on patrol is low. After tonight, that will change. I will not waste this opportunity."

Sebastiaan shook his head in frustration and ignored Orion's words.

"Promise me that when you leave here, you'll go straight to the *Shack*. Gather your men as quickly as possible. Ready the ship and take Davit away. Take him to Batavia, to my uncle."

Orion's frown was deep enough to cast a shadow visible even in the poorly lit room.

"Watch over him," Sebastiaan pleaded.

"What the hell happened here?"

"Orion!" Sebastiaan's voice was low but fierce. "Forget about me and this place. Just promise you'll do as I ask."

Forget about him? Orion nearly laughed at the idea, but something had precipitated this urgency, this defeated attitude from an otherwise unflappable man. He could see that Sebastiaan was beside himself with worry and it would serve no purpose to argue with him at this point. Orion had grown up in the man's shadow. He knew when to push and when to retreat. Now was the time for the latter. There was an unfamiliar fragility to Sebastiaan, but he would be damned if he was to let a man chained to a wall dictate how he should proceed, especially when that man's life was hanging in the balance.

Orion knew he could be discovered at any moment. He crouched next to the unconscious guard and quickly searched his pockets. After finding what he was looking for, he straightened. It was time to go.

"Yes, I promise," Orion agreed. "But I don't understand why you are giving up so easily. Compared to all you've been through in your life, this is a walk in the park."

After seeing the layout of the *Castle* and knowing where Sebastiaan was held, he had all the angles he needed for an attack tonight, but for that, he needed Van Leyen.

"Earlier this year, during a raid on a slave ship, I killed Alain Du Bois' son, Lucien. He was the captain."

"Did you know who he was when you snuffed him?" Orion asked

callously. He had no softness in his heart for slave traders and even less for the captains of the ships who transported the poor souls.

"No, and it wouldn't have made a difference had I known. The fact remains that Du Bois is not planning on putting me on trial or executing me. He wants revenge. He plans to kill Davit tonight, while our men are engaged at the border. Do you understand what I am asking of you?"

"Yes, I do," Orion bit the words out. "However, I do not agree. This is a fixable problem, and the solution is not that difficult. I'll kill Du Bois. I'll do it tonight, before he gets the chance to lift a finger against any of us. Nothing is easier."

Sebastiaan was shaking his head long before Orion had finished speaking.

"Orion stop," Sebastiaan snapped. "Don't argue with me. I gave you an order. For once in your blasted life, follow it." It was rare for Sebastiaan to lose his temper with him, and Orion immediately understood his intent. He wanted Orion angry enough to abandon him. It was a desperate plan and bound to fail, for he would have to try a lot harder and for a lot longer and they simply did not have the time.

"Uncle, I will follow any order you give me," Orion extended a finger to mark the conditions of his submission, "granted that you are of sound mind and I understand what I'm doing. I've given many shit-and-drivel orders in my life, and understand well the anatomy of the deed." Orion paused for a moment to read Sebastiaan's expression. Something was dreadfully wrong. The light that normally shone so brightly from his eyes was gone. Although the tilt to his head and the strength in his shoulders remained, it all seemed forced, as if he might crumple the moment Orion turned his back. The sight was tearing at his heart. They were not bound by blood, but he'd loved this man almost like a father and to see him so broken was stirring Orion's bloodlust beyond what he feared he could control.

"You can't kill him," Sebastiaan said quietly.

"Why not?" Orion shouted, then winced as his voice bounced off the walls.

Sebastiaan took a deep breath, held it for several counts and then released it slowly through his nose. His lips tightened around the words that needed to be spoken, words that had been kept secret for over two decades.

"Tell me," Orion demanded impatiently. He feared the guards would storm the cell at any moment, and although he could undoubtedly deal with them effectively, he still didn't want to spill blood so soon, no matter how loudly his insides were screaming for it.

"You can't kill him because he is your father," Sebastiaan said, and locked Orion in a hard stare.

Orion felt the strength leave his knees, and he snapped his hand out to steady himself against the wall. "What?" he whispered. As the words slowly found their resting place in his mind, he knew it to be a lie – a dirty trick Sebastiaan was playing on him.

"I would never lie to you," Sebastiaan said, as if reading his thoughts.

Orion shook his head in disbelief. "No," he protested. "I was an orphan. Arent found me at a slave market. You know that is the truth."

"It is one half of the truth," Sebastiaan said. "Arent never wanted you to know. He wanted you to live free from the past and from your lineage, to carve a life of your own not defined by your father. But," Sebastiaan paused and swallowed thickly, "I cannot allow you to have his blood on your hands. I don't think a man's soul could survive such a thing." Sebastiaan's words were bathed in sympathy, for this was a hard truth to share.

"Then tell me the whole truth," Orion demanded.

Everything about Orion instantly appeared cold and hard, as if he'd turned to stone. His face grew tight as he steeled himself for what Sebastiaan was about to reveal. His shoulders relaxed, but his fists were balled. He no longer leaned against the wall, but stood with his feet planted firmly on the floor.

"I never knew your mother, but Arent did. That is to say, he met her briefly. Her name was Samira. She and her two-year-old child were chained to a pole in a slave market in Ribeira Grande."

"Me?"

"Yes," Sebastiaan said and continued with his telling. "Her miserable condition had drawn Arent's attention. He had approached her, asked her name, but she was extremely weak. You were both in a bad way, abused and starved, but she was dying. Many beatings had broken her body and spirit. Arent had seen to your most immediate needs, providing food and water. All the while prying information from her: where she was from, who owned her, why there was no seller auctioning her off, what price they wanted for her. He had already decided to free both of you. She'd told him she was Algerian and that her father had sold her to Alain Du Bois, who had over the tenure of her service fathered her child."

"It doesn't make sense," Orion said. "The Cape Verde islands are a Portuguese territory and at the time at war with Holland. Why would Du Bois visit it? More importantly, what were *you* doing there?" Leave it to Orion to, in a time like this, focus on the logistics first.

"We were running under a false flag gathering information for the navy. It was before De Coninck took command of the *Drommedaris*. When Arent discovered your mother, Du Bois was long gone, and the only explanation we had was that he'd left her there to die. If she'd lived long enough to tell her story, no one would know or care who he was."

Orion absorbed the revelations, wearing the look of a man who'd been doused with a bucket of cold water.

"Arent searched for Du Bois and when he couldn't find him, he went to the magistrate," Sebastiaan continued. "The magistrate did not want to get involved, for the implications that he'd harbored a Dutch ship in a Portuguese port would most certainly put him in an unfavorable position. When Arent could not make headway with the magistrate, he returned to our ship and told De Coninck everything, begging for his help. They knew they couldn't save Samira by buying her and so they went with men ready to free her by force. When they reached the slave market, everyone had gone home, and she was already dead. We buried her outside the city. That was the night you came into our lives." Sebastiaan fell silent then. Orion was staring at the floor, swaying like a tall tree in a firm breeze.

"That is the reason for the hatred between Du Bois and De Coninck," Orion said after many minutes had passed.

"It is the reason for the hatred between Du Bois and all of us," Sebastiaan replied.

"Does he know?" Orion asked.

"No."

"So, this Lucien Du Bois you offed?" Orion prodded further.

"He was your half-brother," Sebastiaan said, regret clouding his face.

"No," Orion said decisively. "He was not my anything. The same man who fathered me fathered him. That doesn't make him my brother, it makes him unfortunate."

"Forget about Du Bois," Sebastiaan insisted. "He will have his reckoning, but it must never be by your hand."

Orion's eyes snapped to Sebastiaan's, dancing with an unspoken storm of emotions.

"Remember your promise to me. Take Davit away from here and keep him safe." Sebastiaan fell silent for a moment. He knew he had to reveal Davit's identity to secure Orion's cooperation. It was a secret he did not want to disclose, but it seemed the only way to divert Orion from the path of vengeance he was set on.

"There is one more secret I must share with you."

Orion blankly stared back at him and then nodded slowly.

"You must keep Davit safe," Sebastiaan repeated.

"I've already given my word."

"Protect him, not just because I asked it, but because you share the same blood."

Orion's brows slammed together once more.

"He is your blood cousin."

"I know this seems to be my word of the day, but – what?" Orion asked.

"He is not my son, Du Bois' half-brother, Elias Coopman, now dead, fathered him. Danielle was forced into marrying him and Davit resulted from that wretched union."

Orion turned away from Sebastiaan, leaned his back against the wall and slowly sank to the floor, dangling his arms over his bent knees.

"Did you kill him?"

"No, he died while I was in captivity."

"Does Davit know?" he asked and tilted his head up to look at Sebastiaan.

"No. Danielle raised him in my name and he knew no other."

"How did you come by this knowledge?"

"It is not something I wish to talk about right now, but some day, ask John." Silence stretched between them as each worked through all that had been revealed in such a short time, and it was Sebastiaan who broke it by speaking first. "You can tell Davit, if you wish, but not now. Let him be mine for a little longer."

"He looks like you," Orion said incredulously.

"People see what they want to see. He has blond hair, but he mostly favors his mother. However, you share the same build, the same swing to the shoulders when you walk, and the same unyielding arrogance." The last was said with a smile. Voices were drifting from outside, softly intruding on their conversation.

"Orion, you have to go, but I must beg one last favor," Sebastiaan said, his voice husky and somewhat broken. Orion stood and nodded. "I need you to walk from this cell without a word or a backward glance. I cannot bear to bid you farewell. Grant me that small mercy."

The door to the cell was open and so was the one at the end of the hallway leading onto the open colonnade. The guard was still unconscious, but would recover soon enough. It was nearly dark outside. Orion avoided Sebastiaan's eyes, nodded silently, then wordlessly turned and left the cell.

Emerging onto the colonnade, he darted from shadow to shadow and made his way to the large double doors. His visit with Sebastiaan had left him badly shaken like someone had taken his body, pressed a thumb over the opening and shook it violently, mixing his insides and tearing apart things that should have been tied down. He feared the underpinnings of his life had been grievously injured.

His mother's name was Samira. As a young lad he'd often laid on the open deck of De Coninck's ship, staring at the stars, making up names for her. The names were never constant; usually those of a star or constellation. Often, he'd said a prayer for her, and in his prayers, she was just his mother, no name, no face, just the person who had given him life. Perhaps one day he'd have a daughter of his own. He would name her Samira. That unexpected thought brought him sharply back to his senses. Thinking of one day having a family of his own was all the evidence he needed to know that he was not himself. He gave his mind a firm shake. He could dwell on his mother, fret over his cousin, and plot his father's death later. Right now, he needed his head clear for what lay ahead. He had made many promises tonight and intended to keep every single one, but only after he'd freed Sebastiaan.

Chapter 17

The wind had intensified since this morning, finally yielding something worthy of its efforts. Layers of low-slung clouds raced in over the harbor, dotting the night sky as they bunched up and pushed deeper inland, releasing light bursts of rain along the way. Earlier, the moon had hung ripe and heavy above the horizon, and now only sporadic strips of light peeked through the clouds. If the clouds continued to gather, it would soon become a very dark and wet night. Orion wondered how his men were faring. Amidst all the extremes that had defined this day, the temperature had remained steadfastly neutral – neither too cold nor too hot. On any other day, it would have evoked a sense of cozy tranquility, but against the surrounding chaos, it failed to reach such lofty aspirations.

Everything was eerily quiet as he approached the *Shack*. The building, which usually glimmered a stark white in the bright light of day, now appeared a melancholy gray, its black door the only clearly defined feature. The seamless blend between the tall building and the wide pale beach infused the scene with a haunting softness, enhanced by the dark mass of the surrounding forest.

Normally, a fire would burn on the beach, either for cooking or for gathering, but tonight all appeared lifeless except for the thin yellow line glowing beneath the black door.

Orion did not need the stars to tell him that the night was still a good few hours west of midnight. His stomach was tight with urgency. He needed a fresh horse and, above all, he needed Van Leyen. Orion brought his horse to a halt near the *Shack*. The animal, agitated like its rider, pounded the sand in reaction to the hard pull on the reins. Sweat lathered its flanks and neck. He had pushed the animal hard, and it would need a thorough rubdown and a decent meal. However, any pampering would have to wait. He directed the sentiment at himself as much as at his horse, as the thought of food made his stomach growl.

The best he could do for the horse was to free it from the saddle and the rest of the tack and hope it would find its own way to the nearby stream.

Orion was still standing with his arms wrapped around the saddle and his hands tangled in the leather straps when the door burst open, bounced against the outside wall and swung back until Van Leyen's booted foot propelled it back to the wall again.

"Where have you been?" Van Leyen's eyes darted back and forth as he searched the beach and the road behind Orion. "And where is Sebastiaan?" he did not bother to hide his displeasure or his concern as he barked his questions in rapid succession, leaving no room for answering them individually.

Davit, who was following at Van Leyen's heels, paused in stunned silence, his hand frozen on the door latch. He'd never heard anyone dare to speak to Orion in such an aggressive tone, and he'd never seen Van Leyen lose his temper so thoroughly without warning.

"Sebastiaan was arrested in town shortly after midday. They are holding him in the *Dark Hole*." Orion delivered the news without prelude. "Du Bois had him arrested on the charge of murder," he explained, seeing the many wordless questions on the older man's face.

There was a fleeting moment when something very dangerous lit in Van Leyen's eyes, but it was just a flash, and Orion wondered if he had imagined it. The brief sight sparked a hint of alarm. He had fought many men, with varying degrees of skill but the idea of facing John in battle churned his gut. Shoving the unease aside, Orion relayed the day's events concisely. He omitted the emotional parts, including the secrets Sebastiaan had revealed, and focused only on the highlights.

Orion's words were still warm in their ears when Davit's explosive reaction erupted. "They pulled him from his horse like a common criminal?" he shouted. "How many men has that sack of shit Du Bois killed in his lifetime?"

The knowledge that Davit was referring to his blood uncle was such a ridiculously twisted thought that Orion fought the urge to burst out in hysterical laughter. With every passing second, his lineage was looking less like a well-tended family tree and more like a hazardous shrub, studded with large thorns.

"Why is he still free to walk this earth?" Davit continued. "He should have been hanged years ago. This is hypocrisy at its bloody finest." A faint silver spray of spittle flew from his lips. "It is nothing but horse shit thrown at an innocent man, an empty accusation designed as a distraction so that nobody can see the mess Du Bois has made with the farmers. He is pissed because they turned their backs on him, and he's too much of a coward to face them." Davit paused to draw breath, then continued, "If I find that son of a bitch, I will rip his beating heart from his chest and lick the blood from my hands. I'll give them a proper reason to charge someone with murder."

If Davit's voice could carry the fire that lit each word, the night would not be half as dark. Orion could not help but think that Davit's words held more than just youthful bravado. Recalling the night they'd liberated the *Vlieland*, he found the gruesome picture Davit just painted disturbingly easy to believe. He let the boy vent his anger, then held a finger in the air to signal for a pause in the bloodthirsty rant. It was time to bring matters back under control.

"The charge is not false. Your father told me so himself," Orion said. The inferno that was raging through Davit dropped a few degrees at Orion's cool admission. "However, it would never hold in court, but that is beside the point. The path of the law is a long and winding one, and we simply do not have the time for it."

Van Leyen stared at Orion with unblinking eyes as he absorbed the news, his hands clenching and relaxing by his sides. Davit's outburst had given him time to recover from his shock. He was listening to every word, and with each one, his bearing grew tighter.

"There were only three people who knew that Lucien Du Bois was the ill-fated captain of that slave ship: Sebastiaan, Daka, and me," he said slowly, opening three fingers one after the other.

"Has Daka returned from town yet?" Orion asked.

"No," Van Leyen answered, the simple word loaded with suspicion.

They both chewed on the implications of Daka's absence.

"Do you think he betrayed Sebastiaan?" Orion wondered. He had known Daka for many years, but had no particular attachment to him.

"It is a question for later. Right now, we need to work out a plan to free Sebastiaan," Van Leyen said. "We could use more men. The two of us might not be enough."

"The *two* of you?" Davit spat when he realized they were not including him in their discussion. "I am coming with you."

Orion's head snapped in Davit's direction, his eyes practically spitting fire. "No, you will stay here," he ordered. "And you can bag that temper of yours. It will not serve anybody tonight."

Davit's hold on his fury was tender at best. The only reason he was not tearing the world from its pillars was the knowledge that he would soon rescue his father. Now Orion was refusing him that right.

"We could use another man and he is not half bad with a blade in his hand," Van Leyen said.

Orion waved his hand as if clearing the air between them. "It's not an option." He saw the frowns on both faces and did not allow them time to pepper him with questions. "The situation is more complicated than just freeing Sebastiaan from prison, although that is our priority." Neither Van Leyen nor Davit asked the obvious, but they both leaned in as if that would bring them closer to the explanation.

"Du Bois is planning to use the disturbance at the border and Sebastiaan's arrest as an opportunity to capture and kill Davit tonight as revenge for his son's death." Orion exhaled and dragged a hand through his hair.

Van Leyen gnawed on his bottom lip and stared vaguely into the bleak night. Davit's reaction was less muted. He violently spat into the sand and tightened his fist around the dagger hanging at his side.

"Let him try," Davit sneered coldly, his face a study in defiance. "I'll be waiting for him."

"Davit," Van Leyen cautioned. "Don't call on the darkness." He shook his head when the lad readied himself for more taunts. "Give us a second to think. Aye?"

"The upside is," Orion said, ignoring his cousin for the moment, "that they suffer from the same impediments we do. They are short on men, just like us. But, they have the *Castle* to defend, a fort to protect, and a border to harass, whereas we only have to free Sebastiaan and keep Davit alive." Orion stared at Davit for a long moment as he contemplated the plan he'd put together on his way back from the *Castle*.

"You and I," Orion said pointing to Van Leyen, "will free Sebastiaan. It will not be too difficult. The guards are soft and there will only be five at the most. If we go in quickly and quietly, it should all be over in less than five minutes."

Van Leyen listened, but his eyes were slightly out of focus as his mind worked through the events that lay ahead of them, picturing the scene, visualizing a strategy and then pulling it apart, searching for weaknesses.

"What about the sailors on Du Bois' ship?" he asked.

Orion's frown was instant. "I haven't seen hide nor hair of them. I don't think he has engaged them in this at all."

"Let's hope it stays that way. If he deploys them, then we might not succeed. Also, should he decide to remove Sebastiaan from the *Dark Hole* and lock him in the hull of that slave ship, we would have very limited options." Van Leyen's voice trailed off.

Limited options was an optimistic view of that scenario, and Orion prayed they would be in time to prevent that possibility from unfolding.

"Let's focus on what we know. We can deal with hypotheticals later," he said, forcing the acid rising in his stomach back down. He was tired and the knots in his shoulders were tugging at his thoughts. For a fleeting moment, he wished he could start the day over – he would definitely have implemented some changes.

Davit's irritation at being excluded from their plans was reaching a tipping point. It was becoming increasingly difficult to swallow the patronizing behavior of his two companions. He cleared his throat loudly and was about to object.

"Shut up," Orion cut him off before he'd drawn breath to carry his words.

Sensing the beginnings of his protests, Van Leyen shot Davit a quelling glance, then turned to Orion. He shifted his weight on his feet and scratched the back of his neck. "I don't think it's wise to leave Davit here alone, especially knowing that Du Bois is out for his blood. I agree he should not come with us to the *Castle*. Sebastiaan tasked us with watching over him and putting him in harm's way goes against that. I propose we leave him with Gijs and Elsje instead."

Orion shook his head; he agreed that taking the boy along would be a mistake, but leaving him with Gijs and Elsje was not ideal. He did not want to involve Gijs' family on this night that had every potential for turning bloody.

"I am not a child," Davit's anger flared again, lending volume to his words. "And I am standing right here," he declared with a pointed finger. "So, you two can quit acting like my fucking keepers. I am coming along to free my father, and that is the end of it."

"I swear if I wasn't in such a hurry, nothing would give me greater pleasure than to haul your arse onto that ship, where I would find a quiet corner and beat the snot out of you in peace. Now watch your tongue. You've cussed and cursed enough for a lifetime." Orion speared Davit with a menacing stare, which the boy returned in equal measure, fury blazing from his green eyes.

"Lads, we don't have time for this," Van Leyen said when it became clear that neither Orion nor Davit was ready to back down.

Orion tilted his head at Davit and raised his brows in a silent question. Davit blinked and rolled his eyes beneath his lowered lids, then opened them slowly and stared past Orion at the black forest.

Finally tearing his gaze from Davit, Orion asked, "How close is Jiya?"

"Another messenger came with a request for reinforcements. Jiya left less than an hour ago," Van Leyen replied.

Orion stared at his ship where she bumped against the *Shack's* loading platform. A faint light was swinging on the upper deck. If Du Bois were to damage or destroy her, they'd have no means of escape. That crippling thought sent a shard of pain through his chest. The wind had whipped the cove into a bowl of choppy waves that stood like scales on a lizard's back, causing the ship to creak and groan against her moorings.

"How many men do we have here?"

"There are four onboard, including Harja," Van Leyen said.

Orion turned to Davit. "I need you to take the ship out into the cove."

Davit looked at Orion as if he were freshly relieved of his senses. However, the order had sufficiently doused his temper, enough to cause a race of emotions across his face – disbelief the clear winner by a long mile – leaving him to gawp at Orion.

"You want me to sail that ship into the cove with only four men?"

"Yes, I am placing my ship in your hands. Did you not proclaim it to be your greatest wish?" Orion asked. Looking into Davit's astonished face, he could not help but search for resemblances. From the very first moment, there had been something about Davit that had drawn him in, and now he understood why. Even his volatile fits of temper were not entirely unfamiliar.

"Push far enough from the shore to make for an uncomfortable swim. Once in position, drop the kedge," he directed, referring to the lightweight anchor used for short stays. "Then get up on the mainmast lookout and prime the falconet. Should Du Bois or his men be foolish enough to swim the distance, you blow them out of the water."

One of the first improvements Orion had made to the *Sword of Orion* was reinforcing the lookout platforms on all three masts, equipping them with swivel-mounted falconets for added firepower. Davit had proved early on that he could out-shoot most of the crew, except for her captain and Niccolò. The boy had a good eye and a steady hand. "I need you to stay on the ship until we return. That is an order. Do you understand?"

Davit nodded. Van Leyen had disappeared back into the *Shack.*

"Say the words, Davit," Orion demanded. "I don't want there to be any confusion or misunderstanding between us this night."

"I will take the ship into the cove, drop the little anchor and shoot Du Bois."

Orion closed his eyes and pinched the bridge of his nose. "Close enough," he said and looked up to see Van Leyen approaching, his twin blades strapped to his back and a bolt cutter the length of his arm clutched in his hand.

Van Leyen tilted his head toward the makeshift stables where the horses were housed. "Let's go."

***

The storm's bite gnawed at the night as they emerged from the forest's shadowed edge. Guiding their horses carefully to remain unnoticed, Van Leyen and Orion skirted the village streets making their way to the dockside buildings.

"I suggest we tie the horses behind the *Slaughterhouse*," Van Leyen said, heading for the drab building and its bedraggled storage shed at the back. The leaning wooden addition was cluttered with a jumble of buckets, wood scraps and a few broken chairs stacked high against the back wall of the tavern. It was the perfect place to hide their horses as it was close to the beach from which they had planned to approach the castle. The only drawback was its proximity to the harbor jetty and the Fresh River beyond, where Du Bois' ship *De Feniks* lay anchored.

"We will be in full view of that ship when we leave." Orion squinted against the wind in the direction of the slave ship, where not a single light shone.

"Aye, but it is dark, and the beach is littered with large boulders which will come in handy should things turn bad. Besides, everybody is more concerned about the entrance to the tavern than the storage area at the back. Also, from here it is a short and straight line out of the village and into the forest," Van Leyen countered and gestured toward the edge of the village where the forest was nothing more than a black mass hugged by the even darker mountain at its back.

At least the beach wasn't far from the *Slaughterhouse*, as shown by the small ripples of white sand scattered across the lean-to's floor.

Once on the beach they selected a cluster of boulders that put them in an ideal position to scout the rest of the way to the *Castle*. It was low tide, and the waterline had receded well beyond its usual level. They were crouching near a large black boulder, completely enshrouded by darkness. Intermittent bursts of rain came down at an angle, stinging the exposed skin of their faces.

"Shall we try to keep this as dry as possible?" Van Leyen asked, not referring to the weather. "I don't have the stomach for killing innocent boys."

"Absolutely," Orion agreed sotto voce as he searched the top of the forty-foot wall. "I'm all for new experiences."

Despite the foul weather and the late hour, a few scattered souls still braved the outdoors. They'd passed three drunken men leaving one dockside tavern for the next den of ill repute, not five minutes earlier.

"I see only one guard on the wall," Orion reported.

"And another two by the doors," Van Leyen added.

Orion peered at the double doors, and sure enough, a pair of nearly invisible guards stood against the dark stone wall.

"Is that usual for them to guard the doors at night?" Orion asked.

Van Leyen shook his head, a troubled frown decorating his forehead. "No, I've never seen it. The whole idea of the *Castle* is to offer protection for anyone seeking it. That is why they patrol the walls and keep the doors open. Posting guards at the door and not on the wall doesn't make sense."

"Ah," Orion noted, and Van Leyen slowly looked from the guarded *Castle* doors to his accomplice. "That means they've discovered the missing keys," Orion explained, widening his eyes in mock apology.

"What keys?" Van Leyen wanted to know.

"These keys," Orion said and held up two keys on either side of his face, making him look like a girl showing off her new earbobs. Van Leyen leaned in to get a better look.

"This one unlocks the door of the passage leading to the *Dark Hole*," Orion said, shaking his right hand. "And this one is the key to the *Dark Hole* itself," he added, shaking his left before dropping both back in his pockets.

"*Jesus,* Orion!" Van Leyen exclaimed in a harsh whisper. "You nicked the keys to the *Dark Hole?*"

"And the hallway beyond," Orion added.

"What were you thinking?" Van Leyen fumed. "You might as well have nailed a notice to the door that reads, *'Beware, we are planning a jailbreak.'*" Van Leyen lifted both hands and moved them through the air, as if he were the owner of a theater troupe promoting his latest production.

"Have you seen the door to the *Dark Hole?*" Orion asked, unfazed by the harsh criticism. "It is as thick as your thigh. Also, picking the lock would take time and it is mighty dark in there. I figured we could get to Sebastiaan faster with the keys at our disposal."

Van Leyen conceded the point with a loud exhale through his nose. There was no use getting upset over the theft. The keys had already been stolen, and their absence had undoubtedly been noticed.

"With the doors either unable to lock properly or locked with a spare key, it stands to reason that they would have doubled the guards at Sebastiaan's cell," Van Leyen deduced.

"It does indeed. Keep in mind that the moment the rest of the garrison return, security will be impossible to breach. I suggest we get a move on."

"Shall we disable the guards at the door to gain entry?" Van Leyen suggested.

"No," Orion said and pointed further down the structure to where the construction of the second bastion was underway. "If we do, we might alert the others to our presence. If we climb the scaffold, we'll go unnoticed."

"Exiting the *Castle* should not be difficult if we replace Sebastiaan with any guards we encounter," Van Leyen said. "We lock them in the *Dark Hole,* leaving none to raise the alarm."

Orion smiled at the uncomplicated brilliance of Van Leyen's exit strategy.

As one, they pushed from the boulder and headed for the unfinished bastion in a crouched run, hugging the shadows and avoiding stepping on anything that would signal their approach.

Though the wooden rungs of the scaffold were slick from the rain, they paled compared to the perils of a shifting ship's shroud amidst a storm at sea. Orion reached the top long before Van Leyen did. He silently slithered onto the wall, keeping his belly low, and then rose into a crouching position. It didn't take long for the patrolling guard to stroll past, completely oblivious to the danger lurking in the darkness behind him. The soldier stopped less than ten feet from Orion and leaned against the parapet to stare down at the two guarding the entrance. He mumbled something under his breath and shook his head, apparently displeased by what he saw.

Orion crept toward the guard, keeping his body below the parapet's edge. His left hand reached for the hilt of his dagger, and he smoothly drew it from the sheath under his right arm. When he was within striking distance, he rose to his full height, raised his hand, and brought the pommel down onto the unsuspecting guard's temple.

The man instantly went limp and Orion caught the body, laying it carefully against the parapet just as Van Leyen completed his climb and emerged onto the wall. Then sinking to his knees, Orion pushed the sides of the man's jacket away to unbutton the doublet underneath, before wrestling the garments from the unconscious body.

"Help me with this," he whispered to Van Leyen.

Van Leyen stepped over the prone form, grabbed the front of the man's shirt in his fists and roughly pulled him into a near sitting position. The guard's head lolled back and his mouth gaped open. Orion stripped the sleeveless jacket and the padded doublet from the man's shoulders and arms. Then motioned for Van Leyen to drop him back in the shadows.

"Put that on," he said and tossed the doublet to Van Leyen.

Van Leyen examined the doublet. It was far too small; he doubted he could even get his arm through the sleeve without tearing it, let alone get it to fit over his shoulders.

"It will never fit," he said. "You'll have to wear it."

Orion caught the garments as Van Leyen flung them back at him. Both pieces were damp from the rain, and they smelled stale and yeasty. Orion stared at the multiple sweat rings where the sleeve met the rest of the doublet. The thought of the moist armpits that had caused the damage sent several shudders through his body. The jacket was in no better condition. It had not seen a wash in many a month, and even in the diminished light, he could see the stains on the front. Covering himself in the vile things was unthinkable.

"I can't wear these," Orion said.

"This was your plan. Now, put them on and be quick about it." Van Leyen's words were stern, but the amusement shining from his eyes ruined the effect.

"Yes, my plan for you," Orion grumbled as he closed his eyes and forced his arms through the sleeves. The jacket was a touch too small for him as well, but unfortunately still wearable.

"Then you should have felled a larger guard."

Van Leyen watched Orion squirm and shook his head. "How you've lived this long is a miracle of nature herself."

Having finally won the battle with the doublet and jacket, Orion strapped the man's rapier to his side, rolled his shoulders, and swallowed thickly.

"If my assumption is correct, we are looking at five guards. Two outside the front doors, one down," he said, pointing to the unconscious body at his feet, "leaving us with two more. They are probably standing guard outside Sebastiaan's cell, seeing as it can't lock." He glanced at Van Leyen, who was trying his best to stay in the shadows while searching the walls stretching at a slight angle to the left and right of them. "Ten minutes at the most. Then we need to be out of here. I don't know when the soldiers will return from the border."

"Let's double the number of guards we're expecting to find inside, just in case they've called in help from the fort," Van Leyen said.

"I doubt they would have. Losing the keys and being unable to secure the prisoner paints a somewhat embarrassing picture. They will, most likely, hold off until morning to inform the captain of their predicament."

"Aye, but being a pessimist by nature, I'll either be right or pleasantly surprised," Van Leyen said softly.

Finding no other guards patrolling the wall they stepped from the shadows and headed toward a brick staircase paved in the same black slate as the top of the wall and the floor of the colonnade below. Orion looked down the black cavern of the staircase. By his estimation, they would emerge roughly above the *Dark Hole* and the small hallway leading to it. The stairs descended steeply, ending in a neat square landing from where it continued at a precise ninety-degree angle before opening onto the colonnade.

"When we exit the stairwell," Orion whispered, "turn right. Assuming there are two guards by the passage door, I'll leave the first for you and take the second."

"Lead the way, soldier," Van Leyen said and gestured to the stairs.

Orion did not bother to quiet his approach. Instead, he maintained an even, lazy tread. The guard patrolling the wall would not have bothered to hide his presence and so when he reached the second leg of the stairs, he coughed loudly, masking any sound Van Leyen's strides might make. He stepped onto the colonnade, looked down and fumbled with the buttons of the jacket, hiding his face from the two guards flanking the door to the hallway less than ten feet to his right.

They were locked in what appeared to be a serious conversation and only spared him a cursory glance, mistaking him for the watchman from the wall.

Orion kept his head down and slightly tilted away from the men. He passed both and then spun back, as if he'd forgotten something. He approached the second guard, looking as if he wanted to speak to him. The ruse worked, and none of the men reacted to his proximity, not even when his fist connected with the underside of the guard's jaw. The man's head snapped back, hitting the stone wall, and the body slumped instantly.

Van Leyen did not waste any time. The moment Orion's fist slammed into the guard's jaw, his bolt cutter connected with the side of the other's head. He pulled the swing at the last moment, hoping not to kill him.

Orion dragged his victim into a sitting position and then hoisted him over his shoulder. He bounced him a few times until he was comfortable, then opened the door to the narrow hallway. Van Leyen threw the body of the other guard over his shoulder as if he weighed nothing at all. Once the door closed behind them, the darkness was complete, and they felt their way down the passage until it made a sharp turn to the right.

"We should have brought a torch," Van Leyen said.

"No time. Keep going, we're almost there," Orion said in a low voice.

"I can't see my hand in front of my face."

"Don't bother, you know what your hand looks like. Keep it against the wall to guide you," Orion said and smiled at the curse Van Leyen slung at him. "Making a right turn," Orion navigated. "I'm at the door," he whispered and waited until he felt Van Leyen behind him before pushing against the heavy obstacle.

"Sebastiaan?" Orion called, keeping his voice low and trying to see through the blackness that felt thick enough to chew.

"Orion?" Sebastiaan's voice sounded tired, but the anger in his reply was unmistakable. "Did I not tell you to leave?"

"Yes, you did, and we will as soon as you are free. John is with me."

A dull thud sounded as Van Leyen dropped his cargo. "This place is as dark as a witch's heart. Keep talking, so I can find you," Van Leyen said.

"John," Sebastiaan replied. "How could you let this child talk you into this madness?"

Sebastiaan fell silent, waiting for Van Leyen's answer.

"Keep talking," Van Leyen said somewhere to his right.

"Did he tell you that Du Bois is coming for Davit tonight?" Sebastiaan asked.

"Yes, he did," Van Leyen said and touched Sebastiaan's shoulder. His hand traveled down his right arm as he searched for the shackle and the chain.

"Other arm and both feet," Sebastiaan supplied.

Van Leyen dropped to the floor and found the shackle around Sebastiaan's booted ankle.

"Good thing you still have your boots on," he said as he guided the bolt cutter into place. The iron was thick but flattened, which aided the process of cutting it much more than if it had been rounded.

Orion dropped his soldier and took up position outside the cell door. He could see absolutely nothing, but that would change the moment someone opened the door at the end of the hall.

Sebastiaan kept deadly still as Van Leyen worked on the shackles around his ankles.

"We put the boy on the ship and sent him out into the cove. He is safe for now," Van Leyen assured his friend.

"You shouldn't have come here, you're wasting time," Sebastiaan argued.

"Aye, and you should know better than to think we would leave you chained to a wall. Best to stop berating us and tell me where you are injured. Getting in was easy, but things might get hairy when we leave."

"No injuries," Sebastiaan said.

Earlier, the guard, having recovered from his involuntary nap – courtesy of Orion repeatedly slamming his head against the wall – was understandably a touch upset. He'd landed a few punches on Sebastiaan's stomach, none hard enough to cause harm, but stopped when fear of Du Bois' wrath for the unsanctioned act overrode his urge to soothe his bruised ego.

"Glad to see you finally found a use for your bolt cutter," Sebastiaan said as John rose to free his left hand. The relief of being able to move his legs together was instant and Sebastiaan pumped each a few times, forcing the blood to flow properly again.

"Indeed, a good thing the blacksmith did not have coin at the time he lost that bet, otherwise we would be up shit creek tonight with no paddle," Van Leyen replied. "Hold still, before I cut more than just iron." Sebastiaan stilled as he waited for Van Leyen to gnaw through the last restraint.

"Daka betrayed us?" Van Leyen asked.

"It would appear so," Sebastiaan said, but there was not a trace of anger in his voice. "However, I think he was coerced. There are some things Du Bois does not know, which makes me think Daka revealed only as much as he needed to."

"You give him a lot of credit," Van Leyen said, not caring for the betrayal and not bothering to soften his words.

"I think Du Bois used the woman as bait. We would have done the same had we been in his shoes." Sebastiaan caught the unyielding edge in Van Leyen's voice.

"She wasn't his wife," Van Leyen retorted, not ready to forgive their friend so quickly. "And what do you mean, Du Bois doesn't know everything?"

"He knew we killed his son, but he doesn't know who Davit really is."

"So," Van Leyen drew the word out as he analyzed the information. "Daka weighed his options and gave him what he wanted."

Sebastiaan nodded in the dark even though Van Leyen could not see the motion. "Yes, I think he was trying to protect Davit by exposing us. It's twisted, but it makes sense."

"Do you think Du Bois killed him?"

"No," Sebastiaan answered with certainty. "If he did, he would have dragged Daka's body here just to torment me."

"You know we'll have to leave here tonight and we can't wait for him." Van Leyen dropped the last shackle to the floor.

"Daka's no fool. He would not return to the *Shack* and he would not linger; he's gone." Sebastiaan rubbed his freed wrist.

"Are you two about done in there?" Orion asked from the door.

"Aye, we're good to go," Van Leyen returned.

Sebastiaan felt weak from standing for nearly twelve hours, but as soon as he started moving the fatigue faded.

"Here." Van Leyen pushed one of his sabers into Sebastiaan's hand.

"God, I miss my own." Sebastiaan adjusted his grip and rolled his wrist.

"There is no time to search for it," Van Leyen said, closing the door behind him.

Orion locked the two soldiers they'd deposited inside the cell, then pocketed the key before sprinting down the hall to catch up with Sebastiaan and Van Leyen.

Stepping onto the colonnade, all three exhaled in relief as they stared out at the courtyard stretching before them. It was a dark night by all considerations, with the low clouds completely obscuring the moon and the stars, but a welcome change from the torture chamber. Van Leyen scanned the top of the wall but could see no patrolling guard.

"There are two guards outside the main doors," Orion stated.

"The doors open to the inside," Sebastiaan offered. "It should not be too hard to dispatch them. Do we have any news on the rest of the garrison?"

"They are not back yet," Van Leyen answered. "But their whereabouts are unknown."

With that, the three hurried down the colonnade toward the entrance. Sebastiaan and Van Leyen flung the doors wide and Orion stepped through. He stood in the middle of the opening, feet braced apart and one hand resting on the hilt of the stolen rapier. The two soldiers spun around to face the unexpected disturbance behind them. Both faces wore similar expressions of surprise, which slowly morphed into confusion when they noted the familiar uniform on the unfamiliar person.

Only when Sebastiaan and Van Leyen stepped from the shadows, sabers at the ready to flank Orion, did the guards scrabble for their weapons.

"Leave it," Orion commanded, and the authority in his voice was enough to cause a moment of hesitation. They recovered soon enough and drew their rapiers.

"Boys," Orion cautioned and held out one hand to calm their rising unrest. "This is a fight you will lose and you will lose badly. We did not come here to take your lives, but persist down this ill-advised path and you will leave us no other option."

One guard was barely past boyhood and his stance faltered. However, his older companion remained steadfast, which emboldened the younger to some extent, but not enough to steady his rattled nerves.

Sebastiaan studied the two faces before him, recognizing one as his erstwhile tormentor by the sizable lump on his forehead. The man was a long way south of sober and was, without a doubt, sporting a monstrous headache. He could smell the alcohol on him as he stepped closer and knew this was going to be one of the easiest kills of his life.

"Uncle," Orion cautioned. "Don't give them any more reason to hang us than they already have." Van Leyen chose that moment to advance on the young soldier, causing the boy to completely abandon his quest for valor.

"Drop your blades," Sebastiaan snarled and slid the saber under the drunk guard's chin, leaving a thin blood trail in its wake. Feeling the burn of the cut, the man opened his hand and dropped his weapon to the ground. The younger soldier relaxed his grip on the rapier and extended his hand toward Van Leyen, the blade dangling from his fingers. Van Leyen grabbed the weapon and cast it aside.

"Here is how this is going to play out," Sebastiaan pinned the two guards with his stare, his blade still perilously close to the vein pulsing in the drunk's neck. "We can kill you." The younger one inhaled sharply and Sebastiaan smiled, his teeth glimmering in the faint light. "Or," he reasoned calmly, "you can march your arses straight to the *Dark Hole*, where you will spend the night in mild discomfort but with your lives intact."

This time, the young soldier did not wait for guidance from his companion. He took careful steps around the gleaming tip of Van Leyen's saber and all but leaped through the double doors.

"Not so fast, sweetling," Van Leyen called. The boy halted. "Turn around." The boy turned to stare at him, his eyes stretched large and round with confusion and uncertainty. "You will walk backwards. Did no one ever teach you not to turn your back on your enemy?"

Sebastiaan shot a questioning glance at his captive, doubting the fool could take three steps without falling flat on his backside. His suspicions were promptly confirmed. The man's left foot hooked behind his right and he hit the deck on his first attempt.

It had taken them almost as long to get the two soldiers to the hallway as it had approaching, breaching and escaping the *Castle*.

"This was perhaps the worst Tuesday I've ever lived through," Orion grumbled as they jogged toward the *Slaughterhouse* where their two horses were waiting. Van Leyen had split from their group moments earlier to collect Sebastiaan's horse from Gijs' house.

There had been many Tuesdays in Sebastiaan's past a lot worse than this one, but the sentiment held merit and so he huffed a crooked smile and kept his thoughts to himself.

Chapter 18

Jiya stood in the deep shadows, the forest wrapping around him like a heavy cloak. His ears sifted through the stream's gentle susurrus, alert for any sound, movement, or hint of danger lurking in the dark. The narrow stream flowed not far from the *Shack* and served as their main source of fresh water, which it carried from the crags of Table Mountain behind them to the Atlantic Ocean below.

The night was dark and warm, with moist heat drifting up from the thick carpet of decaying leaves covering the forest floor. He breathed in the rich, musty smell, searching for traces of scents that did not belong, but the mixture of smells emanating from his own body hindered the effort. The low sky and the thick canopy of trees had reduced visibility to less than twenty feet. He blinked hard to clear his vision and to dispel the dull headache pulsing behind his eyes. All evening and most of the night, the rain had fallen in annoying gusts and bursts rather than a consistent downpour. The showers lacked the intensity to stop the soldiers from setting fires to the farms, but they kept the fires from leaping into the forest. The dead weight of the body draped across his shoulders was growing heavier with each passing moment. Jiya's side, from his waist down to his knee, was slick with the man's blood.

A crimson moon had risen and the night had lived up to the omen it foretold. Early on, the groups of soldiers gathered near the deserted border farms had taken to destroying the humble buildings and fields with boyish enthusiasm, hooting and hollering as flames licked high into the black sky from the thatched roofs. The farms had fallen one after another in quick succession, leaving the soldiers with an unquenched lust for violence, no more targets, and plenty of time to spare.

It had taken only one of those groups to stretch the interpretation of their orders and encircle a still-occupied farm in hopes of provoking the mysterious band of mercenaries lurking in the surrounding forest to reveal themselves. Their strategy had proven effective, leading to pockets of heavy fighting as the soldiers hacked at Niccolò and his men with zealous fervor.

For Niccolò, the odds were not ideal, they were outnumbered three to one, but the terrain was in his favor. In the dense forest, the crew's exceptional discipline, training, and experience as mercenaries had carried them through. They had suffered losses, but not nearly as much as the young and inexperienced soldiers.

One of Niccolò's men had returned to the *Shack* with the news of the slaughter and the request for more reinforcements, which had prompted Jiya to set out with a small band just after dark to join Niccolò, leaving the disgruntled newsbearer behind with strict orders to rest and replenish himself. However, they had been caught in an ambush, leaving only three to press on to their destination.

In the dark of the night, they had assumed the attackers were soldiers who had wandered off course. But once they came face-to-face with their assailants, they detected the distinct stench of a slave ship on the men. No matter how far removed from the source, there was nothing on this earth that could wash that smell away. Unlike the inexperienced soldiers, these were hard men, comfortable with violence. The clash was quick and bloody, and their victory had come at a high price. One of Jiya's men had died when a dagger pierced his heart, and another was severely wounded when a blade cut deeply into his thigh. Jiya had dispatched the last of their attackers before sinking to his knees next to his fallen friend. The metallic tang of blood was unmistakable, and it had not taken him long to locate the source. The wound was ugly, squirting thick gusts of blood with every spasm of his heart. Pieter Van Dyck was a decent gunner and average sailor but an absolute menace with a cutlass, who lived by the thrill of the blade.

"Don't bother," he'd protested when Jiya had tied a strip of cotton torn from his shirt around the wound to stem the bleeding. "I've caused many such wounds. There's no stopping it."

"Save your breath," Jiya replied.

"Just help me to that tree and leave me with a blade in my hand," Pieter demanded.

"What, leave you here to die so your hairy soul can traipse through these woods, tormenting its peaceful creatures for eternity? I don't think so," Jiya said, rejecting Pieter's dying wish. He refused to let this friend bleed out alone while he and the rest of them moved on. "And if you plan to talk shit for the rest of the night, you might as well shut up now," he threatened.

"Jiya, listen," Pieter urged, but his voice was faltering already. "You don't know how many more are hiding in the forest. You'll need to move fast if you want to survive. I will only slow you down. You must leave me behind."

"All right, keep talking if it will make you feel better," Jiya grunted as he took Pieter's arm, slung it over his shoulders, and hoisted him to his feet. Jiya ordered the remaining three men to make their way to Niccolò while he took Pieter back to the *Shack*. The bleeding had slowed but hadn't stopped, and if Jiya didn't get him patched up soon, he might not make it through the night. Pieter hobbled along as far as he could before collapsing from blood loss.

Even though the area around the stream seemed quiet, Jiya still regarded it with suspicion. The surest way to meet a quick end was to trust the stillness. He moved forward with caution, keeping his senses sharp and his free hand wrapped firmly around the handle of his cutlass. The soft bed of damp leaves cushioned his steps as Jiya silently headed for a spot where the shrubbery reached all the way to the water's edge, their leaves dancing in the passing stream. Staying low, he approached the spot, laid Pieter on his back and immediately assessed the state of the wound on his thigh. Jiya was pleased to find no blood pulsing from the gash.

"I told you it would be fine, you stubborn goat," he murmured and then chuckled softly. Pieter wisely remained silent. Jiya approached the stream and filled his water bladder, but when he turned to offer Pieter a sip, he found his friend staring blankly into the night, his eyes dull and lifeless. He slowly lowered the bladder, secured the stopper, and leaned in to press his fingers to Pieter's neck, searching for a pulse he knew he would not find. The skin beneath his touch was clammy and cold.

Jiya wondered why everything felt dead. Why did the skin feel like thick leather where only an hour earlier it was supple and soft? Why did the eyes lose their shine when he was sure they were still moist? Even when sick, the eyes still shine, but the moment the soul leaves the body, that light dies. He believed that a person's soul resides in his eyes and not the heart, like the clergy claimed, or the mind like the scholars professed. It was not the first time Jiya had seen a corpse, but somehow Pieter's death reached a place inside him that was still untouched by such a morbid sight. Exhaling deeply, he laid a heavy hand over Pieter's eyes and lowered the lids. *I don't want to die like this. In some nameless place for some godless reason.* Everything in this moment felt wrong, and he shook his head at the maudlin thought.

"Find peace, brother," he whispered.

Jiya dragged Pieter's body away from the stream and laid him under the waterlogged boughs of a nearby willow. He needed to take care of himself. There was a deep cut to his right upper arm, not life threatening but still oozing blood.

With his wound washed and bandaged and his thirst slaked, Jiya made his way to the edge of the forest, north of the *Shack*, where it ended abruptly at a cliff that plunged to the beach below. He'd stood there many times before, for it provided the perfect place to study the beach, the cove, the surrounding forest, and the road leading to the *Shack*.

Jiya knew it was impossible for anyone to see him, but he remained in the shadows. The scene below was lifeless. The *Shack* stood like a lone sentinel, quiet and dark, with not a shard of light and, more alarmingly, no ship tied to the jetty. A frown formed at the odd occurrence. His eyes snapped to the cove, searching the troubled water, and found the ghostly outline of the *Sword of Orion* riding her anchor in the middle of the cove.

Even from a distance, Jiya could see the droops of her sloppily furled sails. His confusion deepened at the puzzling sight. Orion was clearly worried for her safety and had taken her out into the cove, but there did not exist a world in which his fastidious nature would allow for untidy ship handling no matter how hurried, short on hands, or drunk he was.

The feeling that something was not right touched his cheek like a cold kiss and he absently rubbed the spot. He returned his attention to the still beach. A dark line of dead seaweed and driftwood marked the high-water line, with foot and hoof prints dotting the sand beyond. In contrast, the wet sand was completely smooth and unmarked, leaving him to think that no one had been to the *Shack* in hours. Jiya looked to the ramshackle stable at the edge of the forest and found it empty. Nothing was making any sense.

His sense of foreboding rooted him to the ledge for a while longer. Finally, he turned around, wanting to collect Pieter's body and take him down to the *Shack* for a decent burial in the morning. Before melting back into the forest, he gave the ship another glance. His eyes swept the water one last time – habit more than expectation – and snagged on something. Jiya stepped closer to the outcrop's edge, trying to get a better view. The waters of the cove were still troubled as the wind had not settled, but amidst the low white caps, he saw a swimmer cutting a straight line toward the *Shack*. Judging by the pace and strength of the powerful strokes, he knew instantly that it was Davit.

Jiya stared at the unfolding scene, trying to piece together a scenario that seemed logical. Van Leyen and Davit had spent most of the day in the forest, but whether Orion and Sebastiaan were onboard the ship was unknown. The empty stable nagged at the edge of his mind. He simply did not have enough information to draw any conclusion other than what he could detect from a distance. Davit was no fool and Jiya knew he would not abandon the ship without good reason.

Movement on the beach drew his attention. He narrowed his eyes as he watched five men emerge from the tree line. Squinting harder, he tried to identify who they were, but the dim light offered little help and he abandoned the effort. His puzzlement only grew when he watched them spread out, moving with deliberate caution like they were expecting danger at any moment.

The men investigated the stable and the small rings of long-dead cooking fires spread along the beach and the underside of the jetty. Four were clearly sailors, looking similar to those that had attacked his party earlier. They were heavily armed with cutlasses, rapiers, and daggers. An older, more distinguished-looking man among them was dressed entirely in black, from his shirt and leather vest to his breeches and boots. A pair of dueling pistols bracketed his hips, their ivory grips incongruous against the all black attire.

The pieces were falling into place. The picture twisted Jiya's stomach as he looked back at the fast-approaching swimmer. Davit must have spotted the approaching party from the ship's lookout platform, likely seeing them long before they reached the beach, and assumed trouble was afoot. Given the men's appearances and the threat of violence hanging over them, his suspicion was hardly unfounded. Jiya would place even money on the notion that Davit thought the *Shack* might be in danger of sabotage and had set out to protect it.

If these men were from the same crew as those they'd encountered in the woods, then the odds were hopelessly against Davit. Five hardened fighters, one carrying two pistols, versus one cocky boy armed with nothing but his dagger and a healthy dose of arrogance and courage. An ear-blistering oath escaped Jiya as all but two of the men disappeared into the *Shack*, and the full deathtrap Davit was swimming into became clear.

Jiya's body was already moving toward the unfolding disaster long before his mind decided that it was the only option left. He swiftly stepped back into the forest and sprinted down the narrow footpath they'd cut to and from the stream in the months since their arrival. His feet pounded the ground with inexorable force, mindless of mud puddles, loose gravel and low-growing shrubs. At one point, he slipped on a patch of loose dirt, his hands instinctively snapping out to break his fall. His fingertips grazed the ground before he righted himself in time to slap aside a branch heavy with precipitation before skidding the rest of the way to the soft sand of the beach. He did not break stride and continued to the jetty at a dead run. There was no time to concoct a plan or strategy, and stealth was a long-forgotten luxury. His only goal was to get to the *Shack* and keep Davit alive.

The brown shirt and black breeches he'd hastily donned earlier to blend into the darkness of the forest were of little protection now that he was sprinting across the beach. As soon as he burst into the open, the two sentries at the door locked their eyes on him.

There was not enough time for them to do much about the rapidly approaching threat. Jiya was by no standard a small man. He was agile and athletic and moved with grace, sure of where to put his feet and what to do with his hands. The sentry brought his cutlass up into a guard position while his other hand drew a dagger from his waist. The other man turned to open the door, perhaps to warn his companions or call for help, but his intent never ripened to action.

As soon as Jiya's booted foot drummed the first dull echo on the wooden jetty, his hand found the hilt of his dagger. He drew it in a smooth, seamless motion from the sheath strapped to his thigh, swung his arm up, and sent the weapon flying in a straight line, aiming at a spot just left of the man's spine. With lethal precision, the blade found its mark, piercing the heart from behind as its target's hand still clutched the door latch.

The survivor did not dare take his eyes off the fast-approaching dark figure. The loss of his friend went unlamented, for the man's face showed no signs of distress or shock, instead he bared his teeth in a cold sneer. He had but a fraction of a second to move his feet to provide a solid base to counter the imminent assault. The sentry was no stranger to hand-to-hand combat, and wisely did not rush his would-be attacker. Instead, he rolled his shoulders and lifted his blade with calm efficiency.

Only four steps remained between Jiya and the sentry. He was living in a nightmare. The urgency of the situation maintained its speed, but Jiya's movements felt sluggish and hampered. He could hear the dull thud of his foot landing on the jetty, and this muscles rippled with the impact. The other foot was still airborne, and he waited for it to move forward and down to the wooden planks. He pulled the cutlass from his left side.

The sentry straightened his arm, aiming his blade at Jiya's unprotected belly. He could not fault the man's thinking and would have perhaps done the same had he been in a position with no room for retreat and a fast-advancing enemy. Jiya swung his cutlass low and parried the blade out to the side. His eye caught the dull flash of a dagger, and he quickly stepped back to avoid the blade that flicked past his neck. The failed attack left his opponent momentarily off balance. With no obstacles in his way, Jiya turned his body sideways, opened his cutlass arm wide and then swung with all his might, using the extra momentum of the half turn to add power to the swing. His cutlass entered the left side of the man's torso, just below the bottom rib, pushing through soft tissue, organs, and intestines, severing everything in its path. The attack was so sudden that the man's brain had not yet registered the catastrophic damage, and his legs still held him upright as dark blood spilled over his lower body. The putrid smell of rot and decay slammed into Jiya's face as the sentry's exposed gut released its contents. Only when the tip of his blade found resistance against the bones of the spine did Jiya yank it free, leaving the nearly severed corpse to fall to the jetty.

From within the *Shack*, a sudden explosion roared into the night, its brilliant light sliced through the gaps around the closed door and the narrow slits between the wooden slats of the walls. An orange glow enveloped the *Shack* as light and searing air burst from its two glassless windows, billowing the leather coverings outward to hover like eyelashes.

Someone was pushing at the door, frantically trying to escape the nascent inferno inside, but the dead body outside was blocking it. Muffled voices became audible, but the unyielding barrier smothered the words. Rough pounding, as if someone was using his shoulder against the door, made the upper corner push out a few inches with every charge. It would make a lot more sense for them to exit through the double doors at the other end of the *Shack*, and Jiya could only think of two reasons they didn't. Either that part of the *Shack* was completely engulfed or someone was blocking the exit. The last of his deductions turned his blood cold. He had hoped with all his heart that Davit had not made it to the *Shack* yet.

"Please, *Allah*, grant me this favor, and slow him down. Keep him away from here," he prayed, but he knew the prayer was too late. Davit was the reason the men could not use the other exit.

Not a second after the first explosion, another hissed with a rush of air as one more brandy barrel caught fire. Then, the unmistakable report of a gunshot rang out, and all went deathly still. The blood rushing through Jiya's veins made goosebumps rise on his skin and the frantic hammering of his heart reverberated inside his ribcage.

Jiya turned away and pulled his dagger from his first victim's back, then grabbed his body by the vest, hoisted him up, and threw him on top of the other. With nothing barring the door, it burst open, and two men rushed wildly into the night. The brightly lit interior they'd fled had ruined their night sight, and they stumbled down the jetty, unaware of the bloody scene inches from their pounding feet.

The sudden rush of air that entered the building as the men exited, fueled and spurred the flames to dance higher. Jiya raised his arm and pressed his mouth to the inside of his elbow, trying to avoid breathing in the hot air. A conflagration consumed the *Shack's* interior, devouring all but a narrow path between the bales and sheaves of wheat, which glimmered white against the orange haze that engulfed the rest.

It was a symphony of destruction. Clusters of burning wheat spewed sparks, like clouds of freshly disturbed fireflies in a summer garden, toward the underside of the tarred thatch roof. Brandy barrels burst open one after another, releasing their contents. The fire skipping on the fast-spreading alcohol created golden rivulets of fire that connected the wheat islands. The usually dimly lit interior was now ablaze, with all the energy of some hellish carnival.

Jiya noted the lack of shadows. Everything was brightly lit, but nothing was casting a shadow, and the oddness of the occurrence captured his attention for a stunned moment. He could not help but stare at the devastation. Then he remembered the discharge of a pistol before he'd entered this hell.

"Davit!" he called, and his throat burned as he inhaled the scorching air. A small barrel of tar succumbed to the inferno and the smoke was both blinding and suffocating. The thick tar flowed slowly to where the wall met the floor, and the flames took to it like bees to nectar. Soon after construction, Van Leyen had tarred the lower half of the walls to keep out insects and moisture. The fire reached the wall, devouring the tar coating, and within seconds, a bright skirt of glaring heat engulfed the inside perimeter.

Flames were now licking at the underside of the roof. Jiya raised his arm higher to protect the side of his face and head against the fresh influx of heat. He called Davit's name again as he tried to wade deeper into the *Shack*. Blinded by heat and smoke, Jiya turned to go outside wanting to dunk his shirt in the water and wrap it around his head to continue his search. But the door frame was completely ablaze, long tongues of fire flicked at each other across the opening. Taking hold of the back of his shirt, he pulled it over his head and wrapped it around his face covering his mouth and nose. The fabric offered immediate relief from the smoke and air.

"Davit!" he called once more as he kicked a burning sheaf to the side, and then he saw the hazy outline of a figure moving near the back doors. Despite his voice being burned and hoarse from calling, Jiya kept repeating Davit's name over and over, like a plea shouted to the heavens, hoping for an answer. The shape turned toward him; it raised an arm. Jiya realized it was the older man he'd seen on the beach earlier. The man seemed oblivious to the hell he stood in. His eyes were gleaming and his teeth shone white in his open mouth as he shouted something, but the roaring chaos swallowed his words. Another sharp clap pulsed through the thick air, and Jiya knew the man had fired his second pistol. Then a warm pain seared his belly and wrapped around him like barbed wire, but he ignored it. He needed to find Davit. With every step he took, his feet struck flames. His breeches were on fire, sticking to his skin in icy cold patches. For a fleeting moment, he wondered why he felt no heat, or whether his mind was playing tricks. He kept moving forward. He'd discarded his cutlass when he'd pulled his shirt off, but his hand searched for it nonetheless.

The man removed his leather coat and flipped it over his head, leaving only a small slit for his eyes and then he rushed past Jiya before leaping through the flame-covered opening. There was no time to spare, and Jiya suppressed the need to chase after the vague form. Davit was here somewhere, and he needed to find him before the roof caved in. His search turned frantic when he remembered the small keg of gunpowder he'd left near the back door that morning, intending to take it to the *Sword* at the earliest opportunity, but he had never gotten around to it.

The flames had reached one of the back corners of the *Shack*; the opposite was still clear and Jiya felt a measure of relief for the barrel of gunpowder was still untouched by the fire. He knew the heat was not an immediate threat to it, for the double barrel would lend it a bit of extra protection. Then came a deep moan and the sound of cracking wood as a crossbeam splintered away from its moorings, sending a cloud of smoke and glowing splinters over him as it crashed to the floor.

"Jiya!" Davit's voice reached him through the tumult of the blaze. The room was breathing like a man on his deathbed, sucking in air and releasing it with loud raspy expulsions. Jiya dropped to his knees as he tried to get below the smoke. Flames covered the floor, but he did not notice the sharp burns that pricked his hands and lower arms. Violently shoving burning piles of wheat aside, he saw Davit sitting against one of the support pillars pinned in place by the cross beam resting heavily across his thighs. His eyes were wide with terror, and he was gasping for breath, his legs trapped and useless. The flames were licking at his breeches as if they were testing him for taste before committing to the meal. A large red stain was spreading from the left side of his chest.

"I see you! Hold on, I'm coming!" Jiya shouted, but his voice emerged as a dry scraping sound, like sandpaper on a glass pane, and it hurt. He crawled to the end of the beam. Wrapping his hands around it, he rose to his feet, suppressing the groan that would tear at his throat, hoisted the heavy beam, and threw it to the side. Then he rushed to Davit's side. The boy's breathing was shallow and his head had dropped forward with his chin resting on his chest.

The burning sensation in Jiya's stomach intensified, and his breeches were now completely stuck to his body. He hastily unwrapped the shirt from his head and roughly covered Davit's face with it before lifting the unconscious boy in his arms. For a moment, he stood motionless as he weighed his options. The double back doors were closed. To open them, he would have to set Davit down again. He glanced at the powder keg and saw the flames licking at the barrel.

Disregarding the fire now raging higher than his head, he turned toward the front door without another thought, hoping with every stride that his legs would hold long enough to deliver Sebastiaan's son to safety.

***

A scant hour had passed since Sebastiaan stepped from the *Dark Hole*. They had hastily mounted their horses and thundered out of the village, racing to reach the *Shack* before Du Bois did. The air was bitter with smoke and the farther they rode, the thicker it grew.

They sped into the night in silence, each man consumed by his own thoughts and fears. Sebastiaan had lost all sense of time and tried to knit the events into a workable timeline. He had left the *Shack* late that morning, reached town, and been arrested shortly after midday. After that, things became hazy as his distraught state of mind had twisted and warped the hours. When they'd left the castle, it was already dark and overcast with no visible stars to judge the depth of the night.

All his thoughts stilled in one endless moment when he realized that the smoke that had been gradually coating the inside of his lungs was coming from the wrong direction. The wind was blowing in from the Atlantic and by all accounts should have pushed the acrid smell inland, away from the settlement, but it didn't. Instead, heavy billows of smoke were coming from the direction of the *Shack*. *Please God, no!* With a loud and sudden "Ha!" he leaned further forward, urging his horse to go faster leaving Orion and Van Leyen behind.

There was an unmistakable heat in the wind that rushed past his ears. They were too late. Du Bois had already attacked the *Shack*. He remembered John's assurances that Davit was on the ship and safely out of reach. Maybe Du Bois had reached the *Shack*, found it empty, and burned it out of spite and frustration. Sebastiaan was a religious man and prayer had always come easily, but tonight his mind could not form the words of entreaty. His thighs were aching, and the discomfort anchored him. His horse showed no signs of exhaustion. She'd been with him for almost five years and was loyal and smart. She would carry him home to the best of her ample ability. Even though they were racing at a blistering pace, the road seemed longer than usual, as if the devil had taken hold of the end and was stretching it out. Van Leyen and Orion were close behind; he could hear their horses' snorting breaths and pounding hooves.

They rounded the last bend without slowing down, sending clumps of mud flying into the saplings and ferns by the roadside. The road bled seamlessly into the beach of the cove. The sand sparkled like gold dust in the wash of light coming from the *Shack*. Sebastiaan snapped a look over his shoulder and saw his own shock reflected on the two faces behind him.

He pulled on the reins, slid from the horse, and ran to the edge of the jetty. The *Shack* was burning voraciously from its floor to its roof. The wooden walls were glowing bright orange as the firestorm ravaged them from the inside and at the back, clumps of the roof were falling in, causing plumes of smoke to rise from the newly created openings. Tall flames leaped from the two windows and the partially open door.

Two dead bodies were flanking the door, blocking it from opening fully.

"They are not mine," Orion answered the unspoken question.

"How can you tell?" Sebastiaan asked.

"My men don't die like that," Orion spoke with true conviction. "When they fall, the ground is already littered with enemy bodies."

"Du Bois' then?" Van Leyen asked. "If so, somebody tried to stop them."

Sebastiaan narrowed his eyes against the surge of hot air washing over them as he searched for the *Sword of Orion* beyond the burning building. It was difficult to see past the bright glare. Orion must have been searching for the ship too, because when Sebastiaan looked at him, he saw a small hopeful smile on his face.

"She's not here," Orion confirmed, and relief hit Sebastiaan with enough force to nearly send him to his knees.

"*Jesus*," Van Leyen appraised the flaming building, "there's nothing to be done for it. We'll have to let it burn itself out."

It was a devastating loss as – apart from one small wagonload of wheat – last season's entire harvest, together with three hundred barrels of brandy, tools, tar, and whale oil were all stored in the shed. At least they had moved the oak logs into the forest. The jetty was still undamaged and would most likely remain so, but it mattered little; they would not use it again.

The complete destruction and their inability to do anything more than just watch had spun a solemn web around them, and they continued to stare. It had been their home, the beginning of a new life, and to see it destroyed was gut-wrenching.

"Did you see that?" Van Leyen asked, his eyes focusing sharply on the door.

"What?" Sebastiaan asked and then tried to see what had drawn Van Leyen's attention. Sebastiaan had learned to trust John's instincts with blind faith. The man could sense danger and opportunity in equal measure. Searching beyond the white and orange blaze, he tried to see inside the building. Flames were swirling around the doorframe, flicking across the opening like pugilists exchanging jabs and crosses.

Sebastiaan did not know how long he'd been staring at that flaming aperture when he saw the ghostly outline of something moving within. In the next moment, he was running for the jetty and the burning *Shack* beyond. Orion and Van Leyen were shouting at him, but he was heedless of their warnings.

The shape moved again then filled the doorway where it hovered before stepping onto the jetty. Jiya's hunched form turned sideways to allow for the body in his arms to pass through without further injury. He'd taken only a few steps when Sebastiaan reached him. Jiya's breeches were on fire and Sebastiaan could smell his burning flesh.

"Jiya!" Sebastiaan shouted and violently tried to rid himself of his coat to cover Jiya. Sparks glinted in Jiya's tightly curled black hair; in places, his scalp shone pink where the hair had burned away. With his face contorted by determination and pain, he kneeled before Sebastiaan and carefully laid Davit on the rough timbers of the jetty. A large, fast-spreading red stain covered most of the front of Davit's once-white linen shirt.

Ice-cold fingers of dread wrapped around Sebastiaan's heart.

"Jiya, what happened?" Sebastiaan asked, but when he looked at Jiya, he froze in place. Not a single patch of skin on his face was intact. The heat had eaten away at the soft parts first. Jiya's eyes were swollen, and his eyebrows and eyelashes were completely burnt away. The skin of his eyelids looked like clumps of freshly peeled dragonfruit; large blisters bubbled at his temples. The flames had eaten away at the cartilage of his nose and ears, causing them to melt from his face and the side of his head. What was left of his lips had turned a deep purple and they were cracked and blistered.

Sebastiaan flung his coat over Jiya, then grabbed hold of his forearms to pull him away from the burning building at his back. The skin was wet and came away like molten wax as the blisters burst open at his touch, leaving raw, painful flesh to gleam pink in the firelight. Sebastiaan's eyes ran over his friend's bare chest. The only parts where the skin was still visible were the parts covered by Davit's body as he had cradled the boy against him. Large open wounds ringed with charred skin stretched across his abdomen and sides. Sebastiaan immediately wanted to rip the coat away from where it was laying across Jiya's body, knowing his back would be worse than his front. The fire had turned Jiya's skin into a wet mosaic of purple, pink, and pale yellow. The shirt, which was supposed to protect him, was wrapped around Davit's head covering his face.

Jiya was trying to speak, but the words were faint and nearly lost in the surrounding noise. Sebastiaan sank to his knees and took hold of his coat's leather lapels to pull Jiya close. Their joining upper bodies formed a triangle over Davit's unconscious form at their knees. Jiya spoke again, the words shredding the remaining pieces of Sebastiaan's broken heart.

"He's alive," Jiya whispered in a labored wheeze. "My debt to you is paid, Effendi."

Jiya's words left his charred lips, and he slumped against Sebastiaan, raggedly releasing his last breath.

"There's no debt," Sebastiaan's voice choked. "Jiya, listen to me. There never was. *Jesus*, don't die. Hold on. We'll fix this. Just don't die. Not yet." Sebastiaan knew his words were useless, yet he persisted, speaking in Jiya's native Arabic, knowing his soul could still hear him. He berated the lad's foolishness, praised his bravery, begged for him to stay, and pleaded for a miracle.

"Let go, Sebastiaan!" Van Leyen shouted above the din of the roaring fire behind them. Van Leyen was prying Sebastiaan's hands away from Jiya. "We have to get away," his voice was tight with urgency. "There is a barrel of gunpowder near the back wall. It is going to blow!" When Sebastiaan did not move fast enough for his liking, Van Leyen pushed him out of the way and hoisted Jiya over his shoulder.

"I'll take him," Sebastiaan said when Orion stooped to lift Davit from the jetty. "See to Jiya." Then he pushed his hands beneath his son and raised him to his chest.

Sebastiaan rushed down the jetty to where Van Leyen and Orion were crouching over Jiya. He carefully lowered Davit to the sand. Fearing for what he might find, he paused for just a breath and then reached to pull the shirt away. Cold relief washed over him when he saw the boy's beautiful face, skin red and swollen, hair singed but otherwise undamaged.

A thunderous roar split the night as the powder keg finally detonated, hurling the remnants of the Shack skyward in a pillar of flame and splintered timber. Sebastiaan threw himself over Davit, his body shielding the boy's chest and head, as burning shards and debris rained down around them. Most hissed into the cove, extinguishing in the dark water. Only when the last ember fell did he cautiously raise himself, ears ringing, heart pounding, and check that Davit still breathed beneath him.

Davit tried to take a deep breath, but his chest felt heavy, as if someone were sitting on it. The best he could muster was a small gasp. His head rolled to the side, and he wondered where Jiya was. A strange ringing filled his ears, his eyes were scratchy and unfocused, and a chill crept into his bones. He blinked hard, and his vision cleared. A few feet away, people huddled over something. One turned, and he recognized John. Then Davit saw what they crouched over; Jiya, staring back at him. He tried to call out to him, but his voice would not work. Something was very wrong with Jiya and he wondered if his mother could help him. Perhaps she could talk to the gods and ask them to give him back.

The large red stain on Davit's shirt was spreading steadily, and Sebastiaan knew that if he didn't stem the flow, there was a very real chance he could bleed to death right before his eyes. His mind raced, working at a frantic pace as he took inventory of what he had at hand to treat whatever injuries lay hidden beneath the boy's clothing. He reached for the front of Davit's shirt and tore it open. The golden sun-browned skin was undamaged, untouched by the fire's fury, except for a neat round hole where a bullet had entered the left side of his chest.

A calculating calm descended on Sebastiaan as he stared at the gunshot wound. The boy was conscious but not lucid. He called to him, but he received no response. Turning Davit onto his side, he searched for the bullet's egress. They usually travel in straight lines, leaving small entry holes and larger exits. The spot where it should have torn through was whole. *Oh dear God, no.* That meant the bullet was still lodged inside Davit's chest. It would need to be removed, along with the small piece of fabric it took with it. The delicate, time-consuming procedure would have to wait until they were aboard the ship. Blood loss and the bullet weren't the only threats to his son's life, and Sebastiaan fought against his rising fear. Even if they removed it and he survived that long, the fever to come might succeed where the bullet had failed.

Orion's Hindu surgeon had passed away a little over a year ago, and Harja, the cook, had taken his place. While not as skilled, the crew's shadow occupation had exposed him to a wide variety of wounds and injuries, giving him ample opportunity to hone his craft, and leaving him with more men saved than lost.

Harja was aboard the *Sword*. It would be a while before Davit could be treated. In the meantime, Sebastiaan must staunch the bleeding. He tore a narrow length of cotton from Jiya's shirt, wrapped one end around his pointer finger, took a deep fortifying breath, dreading what he must do, and stuck it deep inside the bullet hole, following the path of the bullet until he met resistance. Then he started feeding the rest of the strip of cotton into the wound, working his finger back and forth. The treatment was excruciating, and he knew he was tearing the wound, but simply applying pressure on the surface would not stop the bleeding. He needed to pack the wound from the inside, pushing as much of the thin bandage into the cavity as possible to absorb the blood and allow it to clot.

The searing pain pulled Davit from the depths of the black pit he'd sunk into. He surfaced with a roar, trying to escape the source of his discomfort.

"Hold still," Sebastiaan said, wonderfully relieved to hear the boy's voice. Davit's eyes were wild with pain. "You were shot. Now, hold still. It will all be over soon. You'll be just fine." Sebastiaan repeated the phrases over and over, offering the timbre of his voice as a lifeline for Davit's abused senses. "I've got you. You will be all right. Listen to my voice." However, the pain was too much and Davit roared and fought to get away.

"John," Sebastiaan called.

Van Leyen appeared and immediately took hold of Davit's arms and pinned them down.

"How is Jiya?" Sebastiaan asked, and his breath caught when Van Leyen only shook his head.

Sebastiaan nodded his understanding, not trusting himself to reply and instead focused on the wound beneath his fingers. Soon after, Davit fainted, his head dropped back onto the sand and Van Leyen let go of his arms. Sebastiaan hastened his efforts, making good use of Davit's loss of consciousness, praying all the while for the boy to wake up again.

The wound was tightly packed with only an inch of fabric left that he couldn't fit into the hole. The top of the cotton strip was already turning dark as it soaked the blood from the walls of the wound. Davit's eyelids fluttered, then opened, his gaze locking straight on Sebastiaan.

"It's all done," Sebastiaan soothed, knowing the worst was yet to come. "We just need to wrap you up nice and tight."

"Jiya saved me," Davit said quietly as tears streamed down the sides of his face.

"I know. Hush now," Sebastiaan said and continued his work. He tore another strip and deftly folded it into a thick wad, which he placed over the injury. Taking Davit's limp left hand, he laid it over the neatly folded wad. "Push down," he ordered. Even if the boy could not obey the command, giving him a task would focus his mind.

"I'm sorry." Davit's voice was a mixture of sound and dry air.

"You have nothing to be sorry about," Sebastiaan's voice was steady but tight. "Keep pressure on that wound." Tearing the rest of the shirt into long strips, he layered them to create a bandage that, if he was lucky, might be long enough to wrap around Davit's chest twice.

"Take me to my mother." Davit spoke the words in a near whisper, but Sebastiaan heard them.

"Stop it," he barked. "You're not dying. I will not allow it."

"She's not dead."

Sebastiaan's hand stilled as he stared into Davit's face. The boy's eyes were shining with moisture, his face twisted in pain.

"What did you just say?" Each word fell from Sebastiaan's lips like strangers in a line, measured, stiff, and disconnected from one another.

"I lied. She's alive."

Chapter 19

Sebastiaan climbed the shrouds with agility and speed born from years spent on board his uncle's merchant ship. His hands and feet moved in perfect unison – fearless and sure. Reaching the first lookout platform encircling the mainmast, he stepped onto the yardarm and walked to its far end, which extended high above the deep blue waters of the cove. It had been seventeen years since he'd walked a spar, but his feet easily found their place on the thick wooden beam. The morning sun warmed his back as he crouched to inspect the rigging, testing the tension of the lines. The ship was flawlessly maintained. Even so, he let his fingers run over the taut cords as he ensured there were no frays or twists. As a young man, he'd reveled in these tasks – being up there alone with his thoughts, the sun on his skin and the wind in his hair. In those moments, he had felt truly free. Today, that long-forgotten feeling returned as a fleeting comfort to his battered soul.

The wind was still coming in from the ocean, but the angry gusts and gales had softened into a gentle breeze. He turned his face into it, inhaling the sweet, clean smell of the ocean. Tufts of clouds fleeced across the sky. They would eventually clear, leaving behind a ceilingless and unblemished pale blue canopy – an ideal day for sailing.

The *Sword of Orion* was not a large ship compared to the rest of her merchant cousins in Sebastiaan's fleet, but she was fully rigged with three proud masts equipped with a complex sail plan that would, in ideal circumstances, require a minimum of twenty men to handle her. However, she was short on hands, and while at least six men would normally traverse the yardarms, today there was only him.

The wind tugged at Sebastiaan's shirt and his bare toes spontaneously tightened on the spar. Everything was in order, and he rose, ready to walk across to the other yardarm to continue his inspection of its twin, but the sparkling white sand of the familiar beach caught his eye. There was no time to spare, for they were soon to set sail, but he could not look away. A slow melancholy weighed on his thoughts as he stared at the empty beach. It was hard to believe that twenty-four hours ago he'd stood on that same strip of sand and the only concern occupying his mind was how to best fit the wheat onto the wagon. The events felt as if they belonged to a different world, as if he'd read about them in a book. He shook his head in disbelief at the lifetime that had transpired between this morning and the one before.

Beyond the beach, in a hidden clearing by the stream, lay nine fresh graves, unmarked, never to be visited again. When Orion's mercenaries had emerged from the forest, carrying their fallen comrades, the men had dug the graves, and all had gathered for the funerals of their brothers. Five wounded, nine dead, including Jiya. Sebastiaan swallowed hard, clearing his throat against the painful knot gathering there. Jiya's death was a raw, gaping wound he was not ready to examine. He gave the beach a last look of farewell, let his eyes rest on the burned-out husk of the *Shack* and then willfully turned his back on the scene.

Sebastiaan's thoughts drifted to earlier that morning. The sun was already four fingers above the horizon when they'd secured Davit in a harness and hoisted him up the side of the ship. It was a careful journey that had ended when Harja reached out and pulled him onto the upper deck. With the help of the four sailors onboard, they'd whisked him into the cavern of the forecastle. Sebastiaan followed close behind, and as he ducked his head to step through the low door, Davit was already lying on the table with Harja hovering over him, armed with a cautery knife, rolls of bandages and a large brown bottle of laudanum.

The chef had made good use of his time while they kept the ship out of reach in the middle of the cove. He'd scrubbed the forecastle down, moved all the spare sails, rigging, and water barrels to the side, and with the help of the few men at his disposal, had carried one of the long tables from the mess to set up a makeshift sickbay and operating area in anticipation of the wounded men returning from the settlement's border. Sebastiaan had always liked Orion's chef, but seeing him standing there with a clean apron and a steadfast expression had served as a buttress against the wave of fear that threatened to crush him.

Davit had regained consciousness once during Harja's examination of his injury, but it had lasted mere seconds before he'd slumped back into darkness, causing Harja to reach for the bottle of laudanum, then carefully set it aside again.

When the last of the crew had cleared the railing, Orion called all hands on deck, signaling their departure. Only twelve of the twenty-one crew had survived the night, and some were still bleeding from their wounds. One was cradling a broken forearm. The order was still wet on Orion's lips when Harja had stepped from the forecastle, hurried across the upper deck and planted his squat form in front of his captain, looked him in the eye and, for the first time in his life, gainsaid his commands.

"Captain," Harja entreated, his eyes sharp with concern. "We cannot set sail yet."

"Why not?" Orion barked, ready to push his chef out of the way to see his orders carried out and to take his place at the whipstaff, not trusting anyone but himself to steer them through the narrow mouth of the cove.

Harja laid a beseeching hand on Orion's arm, drawing his cold gaze. Orion's eyebrows rose to half-mast as he slowly tilted his head toward the offense. Harja yanked his hand back and retreated a step before he spoke.

"The bullet is in a precarious position. How it didn't strike the heart is a miracle, but it nicked the lung and is stuck to the side, in the muscle that covers it."

Orion's scowl had only intensified, but he'd remained silent, which emboldened Harja to further his plea. "I need to remove the ball without doing further damage to the lung. My hands need to be sure. I fear I cannot undertake the procedure on a moving deck." Seeing Orion narrowing his eyes as he searched the forest beyond the beach for danger, Harja pushed an advantage he did not have.

"In fact," he continued. "It would be best to do it on the beach."

"Out of the question," Orion snapped. "No one is going anywhere near that beach. We will stay in the cove where the waters are calm, but as soon as you rid him of that bullet we are leaving. I trust the rest of the procedure does not require a steady deck?" Harja had been with his captain long enough to recognize the signs of his tightly held temper: the vein throbbing in the middle of his forehead, the white line around his lips and the hard light glinting through his eyes.

"Aye, Captain," Harja replied, hurriedly saluted Orion and rushed back to where Davit was waiting.

Having so brazenly questioned the captain's orders had nearly depleted Harja's resolve. Seeing Sebastiaan standing over the boy like a golden guardian angel, arms crossed, feet planted firmly apart, threatened to drain the last few drops he needed to save the boy's life.

"He will live, boss," Harja assured Sebastiaan. "But it might be best if you don't watch."

"You think me new to the sight of blood?" Sebastiaan scoffed.

Harja shook his head. "Best for me," he clarified with a soft, deprecating smile.

Sebastiaan bit back the rebuke he wanted to fling at the chef and headed for the open deck, stripping his coat and boots as he went. The deck was an ants' nest of activity. Every member of the crew was doing the work of two. He'd made his way to the boatswain, requested a task and was promptly pointed to the yardarms. Rasmus Konstantin Mirosław, Miro for short, gave him a shrewd, assessing look. A fresh cut across his left cheek was still oozing blood and there were traces of mud in the wrinkles of his wide neck. The boatswain was a good head shorter than Sebastiaan, but what he lacked in height, he made up for in solid slabs of muscle and brute strength. His stocky build, permanent glower, bald head always covered by a red kerchief, deep-set eyes, and bulbous nose lent him the look of a dangerous wild boar. The daring glint in the boatswain's eyes momentarily dowsed Sebastiaan's dread surrounding Davit's condition. It was a common challenge to send new crewmen up the shrouds to test their mettle. He gave the man a crisp salute, suppressed a knowing smile, and took to the shrouds.

Now, with his task successfully completed, he jumped the last distance and firmly landed on the deck. The ship was prepared, and the men were waiting at their stations, ready for their captain's orders to release the sails. Sebastiaan took a spot at the nearest line, which lay rolled in a neat pile at his feet. He did not dare look at the door to the forecastle and deliberately faced in the opposite direction, where Orion was standing by the whipstaff, locked in deep discussion with his helmsman. Sebastiaan quickly snapped his eyes away. The picture was all wrong, for usually it would be Orion and Jiya standing there discussing the voyage ahead. The deck was unusually somber, and he could feel the heaviness of Jiya's absence in the men around him.

A loud call burst from the forecastle, and then the sailor with the broken forearm cleared the doorway.

"Bullet's out!" he shouted, lifting his working hand to show the small lead ball pinched between thumb and forefinger as evidence of his announcement.

The men were hungry for a bit of good news, and a raucous cheer rose from the deck.

"All hands!" Orion roared, calling his men to their tasks.

Hearing their captain's call unified them and even Sebastiaan reveled in the power of Orion's voice. Everything happened at once in a solid burst of activity. Lines were released, sails unfurled, hands snapped out to secure the ends, and the deck shuddered beneath their feet. The sailors divided into groups, taking hold of the halyards to set the sails at a precise angle to the wind that would guide them out of the cove. When the first deep notes of the boatswain's baritone voice, singing a bawdy shanty, rolled over them, they joined in, using the steady rhythm of the song to coordinate their efforts. The men were dirty, bloody and bone-tired, but they worked with the spirit of a fresh crew, all eager to return to their familiar life at sea.

Occupied by the complicated task of adjusting the sails, Sebastiaan was too busy to give the receding shoreline another look. The boatswain's voice never faltered and the men's hands remained sure as they steered the *Sword of Orion* through the cove's entrance. Orders were shouted and relayed, adjustments were made, and then the noise of the waves slapping against the hull and the sharp wind drove all from his mind as they reached the open ocean.

Away from the protection of the cove, the canvases instantly bulged in the strong wind.

"Let fly, Miro," Orion called, and the boatswain relayed the order for the top gallants to unfurl, followed by the royals. He had the ship at a slight angle, white spray bursting from her bow as she cleaved through the waves.

The men secured the lines, exchanged backslaps, and inspected the deck to ensure that all hatches, braziers, and barrels were fastened, just as the boatswain called them to order.

"Right lads, listen up," Miro shouted over the buffeting of the wind and the slapping of the waves as he read the names of the men who'd take the first shift. The boatswain's short stature disappeared amidst the surrounding sailors, but his voice rang crystal clear. Sebastiaan thought it would serve them all better if they could secure the man a crate to stand on, but kept the thought to himself as he pushed his way to the front of the group. His name was not on the list and he was about to protest the omission when Van Leyen spoke close behind him.

"The boy is awake and asking for you."

Sebastiaan entered the forecastle followed by Van Leyen. Bloody bandages littered the floor. Harja's apron was smeared with blood from wiping his hands multiple times. Davit was lying on the table, his head tilted to the side and his eyes closed. He was deathly pale and the veins on the side of his jaw stood in stark green and purple relief. A crisp white bandage stretched tightly around his chest. With Davit's animated face relaxed in sleep, the whispers of Danielle's features, in the shape of his brow, the tilt of his lips, and the angle of his jaw, became louder.

"I didn't cauterize the wound," Harja reported tiredly. "It can sometimes sour the wound, especially if the patient is not moving much." He looked from Van Leyen to Sebastiaan and then to his patient as he readied himself to deliver the rest of the news.

"Go on," Sebastiaan ordered, and the sound of his voice made Davit's unfocused green eyes flicker open.

"He is weak, lost a lot of blood," Harja continued. "I gave him laudanum for the pain. The ball was deep, but it came away nicely, bringing with it the piece of cloth from the shirt."

Sebastiaan's stance portrayed a man ready to do battle, but he spared Davit a reassuring smile.

"Father," Davit whispered and the wheeze in the word instantly ignited Sebastiaan's simmering fears.

"Don't speak," he cautioned. "All will be well."

"What else, Harja?" Sebastiaan prodded the chef, not wanting to give Davit the opportunity to speak again.

"The lung is damaged," Harja said with trepidation. He was never completely at ease in Sebastiaan's presence, as he sensed something feral and dangerous crawling beneath the too-thin, polite exterior. "That is why there is a wheeze in his breathing, and he will have to remain abed until fully healed. We must guard against fever. I will clean the wound regularly and brew an herbal remedy, but it is not a guaranteed solution. The pain will be with him for some time, until the lung heals, but I don't know if it will heal completely. Some suffer from shortness of breath for years, but he's young and strong and might fare better than most," Harja concluded with a nervous shrug when he saw Sebastiaan's face screwed up into something fierce.

"Thank you, Harja," Sebastiaan said.

They carefully lifted Davit onto a wooden stretcher. Orion had ordered three cabins to be readied for Sebastiaan, Van Leyen, and Davit. Van Leyen had thanked him for the consideration but declined the luxury stating that he preferred to stay with the rest of the crew since he'd be working shifts with them.

The laudanum and the pain of being transported from the table in the forecastle to the narrow cot in his cabin had sent Davit back into peaceful oblivion. Sebastiaan and Van Leyen settled Davit into his bed, with Harja anxiously directing their movements – though they would have managed better without him underfoot. It didn't take long for Van Leyen to put an end to the chef's prattling, succinctly reminding him that if he did not start on the dinner preparations soon, Van Leyen would personally lead the crew to help themselves to the barrels of cheese, cured meat and dried fruit stored in the hull.

Harja fled the cabin, narrowly missing Orion, who quickly stepped back to avoid being trampled.

"What did you do to Harja?" he demanded as he stepped over the sill.

"Reminded him of his duties," Van Leyen grumbled and adjusted a pillow under Davit's head. Orion glanced at Sebastiaan, but his uncle's dark mood meant he hid all emotion behind an inscrutable stone mask.

"His color is not good," Orion remarked once the two men stepped away, affording him his first look at his cousin since they'd hoisted him onboard this morning.

"Aye, Harja did what he could, and it is good enough for now, but he'll need the care of a proper physician soon, that is for sure," Van Leyen said and scratched his raspy chin. "There is a half-competent physician at the Cape, but we can't return there, for we are all fugitives and would be lucky if they only arrest us when we set foot on land again. With us out of the way, Du Bois will come for him again."

Orion nodded; John had an unusual knack for effectively summarizing unpleasant realities. Harja was good enough for simple cuts, breaks and the odd bothersome tooth, but not for complex injuries. The need for a well-trained physician once more pushed to the forefront of his mind.

"Perhaps there's one in Mauritius?" Van Leyen ventured.

Orion shook his head. "None that I'm aware of. Unless we want some quack from the village. No, he'll have to hold until we reach Batavia."

Sebastiaan was leaning against the far wall of the cabin next to a narrow stern window, his arms once more folded across his chest. There was no doubt in his mind that if a fever set in, Davit would not reach Batavia, and a wound like that would sour, of that he was certain. He'd seen stronger, tougher men succumb to far less. But, perhaps their salvation lay closer at hand.

If Danielle was alive, if he could believe Davit, then there was hope for more than just her son. Sebastiaan tried to subdue the faint throbbing of an old dream drumming in his heart. He did not want to believe that it was true. Davit had spoken in pain and despair, but there was a certainty in the boy's eyes when he'd professed that his mother was still alive that Sebastiaan could not scrub from his memory. He stared at his bare feet, lost in thought, until Orion's voice calling his name broke through. Slowly raising his head, he met the guarded expressions of the two faces before him. They knew the boy would not last until Batavia. Chewing the inside of his cheek, he wondered how much, if any, he should reveal to them. Then his eyes drifted to Davit's still form and the faint wheezing from his injured lung pushed the words over Sebastiaan's lips before he could think better of it.

"Danielle is alive," he blurted out.

The admission, hearing the words in his own voice, sent a spark down his spine. Orion's eyes instantly narrowed in speculation. All expression left Van Leyen's face and Sebastiaan knew the news had hit him hard. They had spent the last seventeen years searching for her and before that, he was the only other man who never lost hope she might still be alive.

"Davit confessed last night," Sebastiaan revealed. "He said he lied when he told me she'd died."

"Why though?" Orion asked. "Why would he keep that from you?" Orion's questions remained unanswered for some time, leaving the unspoken accusation to drift through the small cabin.

"He was protecting his mother," Van Leyen's deep voice cut through the silence and Sebastiaan released the breath he held.

"Maybe so," Orion said, "but the question is: do you believe him?"

"I don't know," Sebastiaan replied. "If I choose not to believe him, and we leave here …" His words faded as his mind worked through the impossible scenario. He would never leave Africa knowing she might still be here. Then again, he knew he could not abandon Davit by sending him to Batavia with Orion while he stayed behind, searching for Danielle. He was stuck between two impossible decisions. Leaving was not an option, and staying was impossible. Then Orion opened his mouth and spoke the words that had eluded Sebastiaan for nearly two decades.

"I think I know where she is, and if the wind is in our favor, we could reach her in less than a week."

***

The *Sword of Orion* embodied a striking paradox. On the one hand, she was fast, battle hardened and armed to the teeth. On the other, she was pampered and primped like the only daughter of a rich man. She was meticulously maintained and enjoyed the reverence of her crew and the devotion of her captain.

Her stern cabins were tastefully furnished with an eclectic collection of pieces pilfered from wealthy prey and foreign markets. Thick oriental rugs sprawled on the floors, paintings contradicting everything else adorned the walls, and works of art were carved into her wooden panels and balustrades. She walked the thin line between gaudy and interesting, with the confidence of a seasoned courtesan. However, beneath the beautiful, polished façade, beat the heart of an assassin. Stepping from the debonair cabins onto her decks, the panorama transformed into one of deadly menace. Demi-culverins ringed her upper and lower decks, some out in the open, others hidden behind silent gun ports. Falconets and crossbows adorned every lookout platform and discreetly placed crates filled with cutlasses and daggers hid in dark corners. She was the most alluring predator Sebastiaan had ever encountered, but now, with Davit's life hanging by a thread, he scarcely noticed her beauty.

He was sitting by Davit's bunk, a damp rag hanging from his fingers. The day had turned to night, and a candle was burning on the nightstand.

Staring at the steady flame, he tried to remember performing the small task of lighting it. He'd lost count of the hours; had hardly noticed the change between day and night. Davit's fever had set in late Wednesday evening, the day they'd left the Cape. After that, his every moment was consumed by watching over him. Sometimes he would wake from an unintentional nap with a headache caused by the unnatural position he'd slumped into. He held Davit's hand when the demons seized control of his mind, filling him with fear and making him speak in a mixture of Dutch and what seemed to be his native childhood tongue, calling for his mother one moment and begging his father's forgiveness in the next. Some words made sense, others were just a jumble of sounds. The wheezing intensified and breathing became more laborious as the inflammation grew stronger. Sebastiaan dropped the rag in the bowl of water by his feet.

A soft knock on the cabin door drew his attention and moments later Harja's shiny bald head appeared.

"Sir, I've laid out fresh garments in your cabin, along with warm water for washing and your dinner," he said in a soft tone, holding the door open in his none-too-subtle attempt at dismissing Sebastiaan.

"Thank you, Harja, but I'm not hungry," Sebastiaan said, as he remained seated.

"It's been nearly three days, boss," Harja persisted. "You have not had a decent meal in all that time and you have been wearing the same shirt since Tuesday morning."

"What day is it?" Sebastiaan asked. He looked down at his shirt, still caked with Davit's dried blood, and wrinkled his nose when he detected the rank scent of his unwashed body.

"It is Friday, sir," Harja answered. "I need to wash the boy and tend to his wound, and it would be better for him if I do it while he is asleep." Davit's wet hair lay plastered against his skin, and the sheets were soaked through with sweat and water from when Sebastiaan had sluiced him down. The once white bandage was bloody and sweat stained. Sebastiaan nodded and rose from his seat.

"Eat first," Harja ordered as he closed the door behind Sebastiaan.

Sebastiaan ignored Harja's advice and stripped the filthy clothes from his body as he entered his cabin. A bowl of warm water and a cake of soap stood on a small table by the foot of his bed. He reached for the soap and scrubbed days of grime from his skin. When he'd sufficiently taken care of his personal hygiene, he hastily dressed and headed for the door, but it flew open before he reached it and Van Leyen entered.

"Fantastic," his friend exclaimed. "You're clean. Let's eat."

"John," Sebastiaan protested as he tried to sidestep Van Leyen, whose large form diminished the available space of the small enclosure even further. "I'm not hungry, and I need to be with Davit."

"I've just been. Harja is still with him. Now, sit down. I am starving." It was only then that Sebastiaan noted the second plate of food on the small desk. "According to Orion, we are two days away from the inlet where he'd encountered Davit the first time. Do you want to face your woman, after all these years, looking and smelling like a half-dead gutter rat?"

"I just washed," Sebastiaan defended, but lowered his head to smell under his arms all the same.

"Yes, it is a vast improvement. Now, eat," Van Leyen spoke around a large serving of cheese he shoved into his mouth.

Sebastiaan remembered Orion visiting him in Davit's room to provide updates on their progress. At one point, Harja had discussed the state of the hull and the provisions for the journey, while Van Leyen had come and gone at irregular intervals, always wearing a disapproving scowl and delivering harsh admonitions to Sebastiaan, which had softened when his attention turned to Davit. The events had no beginning and no end as they faded into the fog of the past few days.

The smell of buttered venison made him turn his head away as he lifted the silver dome from his platter.

"Here," Van Leyen pushed a glass of red wine in front of him. "No one can eat on an empty stomach. Start with that. It will break the spell."

Sebastiaan raised the glass to his nose, inhaled deeply, but then promptly forgot to analyze or appreciate the bouquet. He took a sip and let the velvety richness line the inside of his stomach. However, his thoughts were not with his meal and once he'd absently placed a piece of bread he'd coated with the sauce from the meat in his mouth, the next followed without objection. Van Leyen had the good sense to let the meal pass in silence. Either that, or he was simply too ravenous to interrupt the event with conversation.

Sebastiaan stared at his friend. The years had carved deep grooves into his face, mapping the man he was: wise, intelligent, and courageous.

"What if she's not there?" Sebastiaan spoke the fear that had been gnawing at him since he'd learned of Danielle's possible whereabouts.

"She'll be there," Van Leyen said with absolute certainty. He wiped his mouth and leaned back in his chair when he saw the frown on Sebastiaan's face. "This is not the time for doubt. If you do, the boy will sense it and it might end him. He needs your strength and faith now more than ever. Besides, do you want to be the one to tell that fire-breathing, green-eyed hellion that her son died?" Van Leyen asked, but he did not wait for a response to his reasoning. "Women like that don't mellow with age. They hunker down, and don't you go making the mistake of thinking Danielle is any different from the rest of her kind." He took a formidable bite of his dinner and left Sebastiaan to mull over his words as he set about to chew the mouthful of venison.

"You make her sound like a witch." Sebastiaan's words carried resigned amusement, but no heat.

"I'm not entirely convinced she isn't. If not in deed and skill, then certainly in temperament." Van Leyen huffed a crooked smile. "You should have seen her at the settlement all those years ago. So feisty, filled with anger and fire. Ripping into the governor and fighting for those who couldn't do so for themselves. She was a sight to behold." Van Leyen's entire being softened with something close to paternal pride as the memories flooded back. "I was harsh on her then. Filled with my own anger at the injustice and unfairness of the time." He fell silent again, playing with the candlelight on the crystal of his wineglass.

"I have grown wary of hope," Sebastiaan said after a while. Van Leyen only stared at him, wordlessly urging him to continue, to let out the poison of his doubts. It reminded Sebastiaan of the many campfires they'd shared, talking about their pasts and their futures, their philosophies on life or just mundane nonsense to pass the hours. There was no judgment between them, only deep understanding and unquestionable loyalty. Neither of them had spoken about Jiya and he knew it was a pain they both carried. "This life exacts a high price for the small flickers of joy we are allowed. I get to *maybe* have Danielle back, but in return I had to give Jiya up? I would give anything to have her in my life. Hell, I would give everything just for the mere *possibility*. But this? Jiya? It feels like a sacrifice."

Van Leyen took a long time to digest the words. When he finally spoke, his voice was soft and dreamy, as if he'd just woken from a long, peaceful sleep.

"Jiya was a good man. We are all in agreement on that, but he was not yours to keep or give. I believe we come into this world with a path already determined, and I don't think we have much of a say in it, not while we're here, anyway. We just do the best we can with what lies before us at any given moment. Sometimes the *why* of it becomes clear when we complete our tasks and other times, we remain ignorant, like fools fumbling through the dark." He stilled the glass and placed it back on the table, then looked at Sebastiaan. "It is a frightening prospect but here's the thing: Jiya's death was set in the stars long before he was born. His death was not your fault. It happened the way it was supposed to happen. And you, my friend, were just a player on his stage. We are all just actors in each other's worlds."

"You're telling me I have no control over my life?"

"Does it seem like you do?"

Sebastiaan bit his lower lip, then pensively shook his head.

Van Leyen's words carried the quiet weight of acceptance when he spoke again. "We do what is in front of us, and we do it well. Our control lies not in the *why* or the *who,* but in *how* we choose to go through this life."

Chapter 20

The *Sword of Orion* was tacking an easterly course and pushing an easy six knots. Not exactly flying across the ocean, but rather walking at a hasty pace, like someone in a hurry prohibited from running by the bounds of decorum or some wardrobe restriction. They were less than a handful of hours away from the lagoon where Orion had first encountered Davit almost a year ago.

Warm air from the continent washed in over their port side, and at exactly four bells, a shout from the masthead slammed into the decks below.

"Sails, ahoy! Two points off the port quarter!"

"Coming or going?" Orion shouted back. They'd seen a set of sails a few days past, sticking to the horizon as it made its way from the East to the Cape of Good Hope to replenish their stores before continuing to Europe.

"Coming – fast!"

Orion reached for his telescope and strode calmly to the aft railing. With no adjustment to his position, he immediately located the growing speck of white on the hazy powder-blue horizon. The shape clarified, and he watched it intently. Slowly, the ship came into focus. He knew it was the *Feniks* long before her sail plan confirmed her identity. Her masts were canting over sharply as she ran before the wind. Alain Du Bois, no doubt, was standing on the bow, his own telescope pressed to his eye. If they were any closer, they would stare straight at each other.

The *Feniks* was a fluyt – a Dutch merchant vessel with homely curves, designed for carrying cargo and, in her unfortunate current occupation, slave hauling. The *Sword*, in contrast, was fast and dangerous, built for mischief and exploration. But the advantage meant little with her depleted crew. If locked in a fight, which seemed more likely with every passing minute, the outcome would be a draw at best. There were simply not enough hands to make her dance this time. She would have to brawl like the rest of them – punch for punch with her feet tied together. Damn shame, that was. She deserved better.

A flock of birds passed overhead in a crisp V, the stern-faced leader setting a determined pace for his squadron as they raced over the endless ocean. The day was flawless and distilled sunlight reflected on the water's surface. Orion slammed the telescope shut and, with a cold smile, turned his back on his father.

"Miro, get Niccolò up here, if you please," he ordered, just as Miro, the first shift's boatswain, barreled up the quarterdeck companionway. After assessing Van Leyen's skill at carpentry and finding it adequate, Niccolò had taken over the role of boatswain of the second watch, leaving the care and constant maintenance of the ship in Van Leyen's hands.

The *Sword of Orion* had no first officer, as Orion could not bring himself to appoint anyone in Jiya's position just yet. In time he would, but with his small crew there was no pressing need.

"It's the *Feniks*?" Miro asked when he and Niccolò stood before their captain.

"Indeed," Orion nodded. "She is either kindly escorting us to Batavia or looking for an arse whipping."

"I would bet my last *stuiver* it is the latter," Miro muttered.

Niccolò, true to his nature, remained silent. His narrowed eyes flicked over the *Sword's* sails and the small swivel cannons mounted on each mast's lookout, before cutting down to the sparsely populated decks calculating scenarios and outcomes.

"Miro," Orion said, "I want you above decks." Miro nodded eagerly. The sparks in his blood kindled brightly in his eyes.

"Niccolò." His carpenter uncrossed his arms and tilted his head. "The gun deck is yours." Niccolò acknowledged his responsibility with a crooked smile and then his tongue flicked out to wet his bottom lip.

"Any concerns?" Orion asked. The men looked at each other, shrugged their shoulders and shook their heads.

"None, Captain," Miro needlessly relayed their silent conversation.

"Good, then get me all hands on deck," he ordered.

"I'll wake up my team," Niccolò said, and left the quarterdeck to shake his men from their hammocks.

"Slow us down, Miro," Orion said. "Give her a chance to catch up. We'll make our stand here. I don't want to carry trouble into the lagoon."

"You are spoiling for a fight, Captain?" Miro prodded.

"We'll have to deal with her sooner or later. Sooner is always better."

"They will no doubt outnumber us." Miro voiced his half-hearted concern with an indulgent smile.

"Aye, if we're lucky," Orion replied, which drew a deep chuckle from his boatswain.

The crew gathered at the ship's waist. Some dropped from the shrouds like ripe fruit, and others squinted sleepily against the harsh morning glare. The upper deck was clean and tidy. The hatches were closed but not covered, allowing checkered sunlight and fresh air to enter the gun deck below. Black demi-culverins, resting on wooden blocks, lined the sides at precise intervals with coils of rope nesting piles of iron cannonballs at each side. Shadows from the shrouds, along with the array of lines running from the side of the ship to the sails, cast sharp shadows across the gleaming planks of the open decks. Barrels and crates were lashed to the masts, tight as pearls on a stout woman's throat.

The men murmured among themselves. Those recently woken from sleep craned their necks to catch sight of the approaching ship. Orion leaped onto a weapons crate by the mainmast, and the hum of the surrounding voices died down. He looked each man in the eye. Gone were their breeches, fancy shirts, boots, and coats. They faced him, ragged and barefoot, in tattered slops and dirty kerchiefs. The sound of water clapping against the side, the creaking of the lines, and the thrumming of the wind in the sails filled the space between their voices and his.

"Lads, as you can see from the growing sails, we're expecting company within the next two hours. It is the *Feniks* under Du Bois' command." Anger replaced the crew's initial equanimity. Their eyes sharpened, stances widened, and hands lifted to rest on the handles of the cutlasses strapped to their waists. "Du Bois and his men have dipped their hands in our brothers' blood, leaving us with a score to settle. However, we are short on hands and therefore cannot sail and shoot as we normally would. That does not leave us without options, though." He waited until he had their full attention once more before continuing. "We can run. We are faster and will lose her at some point." The men dropped their heads and shifted their feet. Their distaste for that option hung among them like a bad odor. "But I'm not one for running," Orion said after a loaded pause. An approving hum rose from their ranks. "So," he twirled his finger and grinned, "we lift our skirts and spread our legs."

Warm laughter rumbled.

"The *Sword* is a rich prize, one that would ill serve them from the bottom of the ocean. My guess is they won't sink us. We'll make a stand here and when they are close enough, we shoot to kill. Bear in mind, when they board us – and they will – we will be outnumbered. We will give them no quarter. They set foot on our decks without invitation, and we will slaughter them. Whether they choose to die on their feet fighting or on their knees begging makes no difference. We will slaughter them all the same." The war cry that never failed to raise goosebumps on his skin tore through the morning air. "One last thing," Orion said when they quieted down again, "spare a slave should he surrender, for we are not murderers."

He then turned to Miro and Niccolò.

"Miro, ready the ship. I want top sails only, reef all others. Wet anything that can burn and see that everyone is armed and armored. Get a lad on the port-piece and one on each falconet up top and load the guns on the open decks." Orion pointed to the dainty swivel cannons mounted on the sides of the ship and on the lookout platforms as he spoke.

Then, to Niccolò, "Load the guns below deck, but don't run them out just yet, and conceal our caches of weapons. Make sure the men know where they are. Once the ports are open, the gun deck is yours. Fire at your discretion. Help Miro hang the boarding nets. The *Feniks* will come up on our starboard side, so leave a gap there." He saw the confusion on both men's faces. Boarding nets were designed to prevent the enemy from boarding the ship; leaving a gap defeated this purpose. "It will create a nice shooting alley for us," he explained. "They'll not turn themselves into pincushions for our arrows cutting the nets when a wide-open gap beckons."

His boatswains left to see his orders carried out. Orion gave the deck a quick glance. Braziers were lit and sand barrels were at the ready as a standard precaution. Longbows and buckets of arrows lined the inside of the bulwark but would only be used once the cannons stopped firing, as there were not enough men to do both.

"Beat to quarters," he roared, and the rest of the crew ran to their stations.

Those on Miro's watch split into small groups to load the starboard guns, while Niccolò's men disappeared below decks. Orion exhaled deeply. He needed to speak to Sebastiaan, and he hastened across the deck toward the narrow stairs leading to the stern cabins. After collecting the chest containing a small arsenal of weapons from Sebastiaan's cabin, he made his way to his cousin's, softly scratched on the door, and then slowly pushed it open.

The small cabin was recently cleaned. There were fresh linens on the bed, a new candle in the holder, a full jug of water, and a clean earthen mug. A platter of bread and cheese was laid out on the bedside table. Orion took care not to bump into the small cabinet as he closed the door with his foot. Even though the cabin was sparingly furnished, it was luxurious in its comforts. The furniture and bedding were of fine quality, and a thick rug covered most of the floor. Fresh air streamed from the open window at the back wall, ruffling the tassels of the drawn velvet curtains, yet it did little to shift the lingering scent of stale sweat.

Sebastiaan was sitting in a chair next to Davit's bed, his face lined with concern. The boy was doing poorly by frightening degrees. Orion had never seen a fever take hold so fast, and a tight knot of dread settled in his stomach. At this rate, he would be gone before they even reached Madagascar, let alone Batavia.

"How's he doing?" he asked and shuffled between the chair and the wall to carefully lower the chest of weapons to the floor.

"Worse." Sebastiaan sounded tired.

"We are two to three hours from the lagoon." Hope flared in Sebastiaan's eyes, but the worry on Orion's face doused it instantly.

"What is troubling you?" he asked.

"The *Feniks* is on the horizon and approaching fast. With the crew so heavily reduced, we have but two options: face her or run." Orion had made up his mind earlier as to which course to take, but he wanted to hear Sebastiaan's opinion.

"We can't lead them to the lagoon," Sebastiaan said and stood from the chair to pace the small cabin.

"I agree," Orion nodded. "It will also take days to outrun her, and then returning for Danielle is uncertain. The way Davit is slipping, I fear running is out of the question." Orion brushed the back of his fingers across Davit's forehead. The boy was burning up. He stared at the deathly pale face. Davit's eyes moved beneath the closed lids, as he fought the monsters in his dreams. This was *his* cousin, *his* flesh and blood. Orion had never known want, as far back as he could remember. Cherished as a child, he had never truly felt the sting of being an orphan. Yet, the quiet sense of isolation – that gnawing feeling that he was alone in the world – had always lingered in the shadows of his mind. Everyone else had someone, and now, for the first time, he did too. But for how long?

"Running is never a good strategy, not with an enemy like Du Bois." Sebastiaan pulled him back to the conversation.

"If I were him, I would have put spies in the forest surrounding the *Shack* that night. And if he did, he will know that Davit is alive, that he'd failed to kill him and failed to capture you," Orion reasoned. Sebastiaan dragged a hand through his hair.

"He will follow us to the ends of the earth to avenge his son," Sebastiaan concluded. "Best make a stand and pray for succor from the Almighty.

Now, Captain, tell me where you need me."

Orion pointed to the chest. "I need you to stay below decks. There is only one set of stairs leading to the cabins. I need you to guard them. It won't be easy. You will have to go it alone with no help to come. Du Bois will flood our decks, but his principal goal is to capture you and Davit. Whoever slips past us upstairs will find their way here."

"Orion," Sebastiaan's warning voice was whisper-soft yet vibrating with menace. He thought Orion was keeping him below decks, out of sight and out of danger when, in fact, the opposite was far more accurate. Sebastiaan was his last line of defense; the only person he trusted not to die.

"Uncle." Orion winced at how tight his voice stretched over his apprehensions. He made a point of burying his true fears and rawest emotions under layers of arrogance and indifference. This was a side of him he never showed to the world. He hardly allowed himself a glimpse. Sebastiaan had heard it too, because he swallowed the rest of his protest.

"I trust my men with my life, but I trust you with my family. Keep yourself and Davit alive. If Du Bois takes you, he won't repeat his mistake. He'll kill you slowly, but too fast for us to do anything about it." Orion's jaw tensed in impotent frustration and he looked off to the side. "I can't …" he swallowed, exhaled, then shook his head. "I can't lose you."

"Du Bois will not be your enemy on this day," Sebastiaan said. When Orion remained silent, he continued. "Fear will."

Orion opened his mouth to protest the bullseye hit.

"No, listen to me," Sebastiaan urged. "You have fought many battles in the past, some close to hopeless, and you've triumphed because you had nothing to lose. Yes, you care for your crew, and you love your ship, but family weighs differently on a man's sensibilities. If you want to survive this day, be the man you were before, forget about Davit and me and everyone else. Turn cold. Kill every emotion other than the one you need to win. This is not about protecting your family; this is about winning. That's all."

"It sounds shallow," Orion said.

"Winning often is, but it is practical. You get hung up on blood and family and you lose your edge, that special thing inside you that few have, the thing that filters out that which is not needed in the moment. All that matters is that you kill more of theirs than they do of ours." Orion looked toward the window and the beautiful day outside, but Sebastiaan had more to say.

"You think this boy is all you have?" he said, pointing to Davit. "You're forgetting those you have chosen, and who have chosen you. Blood's not the only tie that binds us. Often, the bonds we pick run deeper and hold dearer." Sebastiaan turned his head and stared at Davit, and Orion could see the love shining through his eyes. The image was so powerful that it halted his breathing. It was the same look he'd seen on Arent and De Coninck's faces throughout his boyhood. He had bratishly accepted it as the way of life, not recognizing it for what it truly was.

"Do what you have to do today. Then come and see me when it is done." Sebastiaan said and waved his hand toward the door, effectively shooing him from the room.

"Orion," Sebastiaan called when Orion was already in the hallway. "Don't forget you are Du Bois' son."

That statement ignited the inferno Orion had tried so hard to control since seeing the sails on the horizon.

"Do not insult me," he growled.

"It's not an insult," Sebastiaan countered calmly. "You are a fool and therefore doomed if you can't see your enemy's strengths as well as his weaknesses. For all his faults, I have never seen anybody as tenacious as Alain Du Bois. You have inherited nothing of him except that."

✳✳✳

The first round hit them precisely at noon, with the sun beating down on their crowns where the only shadow was the one beneath their feet. The shot didn't fall short or overshoot its mark. It gut-punched them right in the hull, sending wood splinters the size of a man's arm shooting in all directions and leaving a torso-sized hole in the *Sword of Orion's* starboard side.

They'd seen the red-orange flash from the deck of the *Feniks.* A dull boom had followed within the stretch of the same second before the air screeched as the projectile tore through it and crashed into its target. The impact threw everyone off their feet. One cannon came loose from its moorings, rushed across the deck on creaking wheels and slammed into the opposite railing. Orion clambered to his feet and shook his hair from his eyes. He wondered if Du Bois was holding an hourglass in one hand and a burning match in the other, waiting for the last grain of sand to settle before firing the shot. The flagrant melodrama was nauseating.

The *Feniks* bore down fast, spilling wind from her sails to slow as she closed the final distance. Armed sailors, soldiers, and slaves crowded her decks, dancing and shouting as they celebrated the hit. Orion could only hope their poor discipline would not desert them as the battle wore on. He glanced around, assessing the damage on deck. His men were uninjured and already securing the stray cannon.

"Miro?" Orion called for a damage report.

"No complaints, Captain. Just got a bit of sense knocked into us, but that is the extent of the damage."

"Niccolò?" Orion shouted down the latticed latch into the gun deck below. The space was uncomfortable with a low ceiling, forcing those occupying it to hunch over when walking. It was claustrophobic, stuffy and with lots of clutter, especially during battle. That was another difference between the *Feniks* and the *Sword.* Unlike the *Sword,* which had gun ports studded along her sides, the *Feniks* featured an unblemished hull. In place of a gun deck, it had slave bunks. She only carried what she could fit on her open decks, and presently eight heavy cannons were pointing at the *Sword of Orion.*

"All good, Captain. A few scrapes, one damaged cannon, but I daresay the airflow down here is much improved." Orion shook his head at the report. Niccolò sounded downright cheery, and he could well understand why – the man was surrounded by mercenaries and a room full of artillery.

"Open your ports, roll out your guns," Orion shouted down.

"Your will, Captain," Niccolò called back.

A muffled sound drifted up as the men below knocked the wedges out of the ports. The starboard side of the *Sword of Orion* looked like she'd just blinked, all her gun ports lifting at once like the lids over many small eyes. A dull rumble drifted up through the hatches as the men below pushed the guns forward on their blocks and soon, long black barrels protruded from each aperture.

A tense silence hung over the deck. All had seen the number of men on the *Feniks* and, by a rough and generous estimation, they were outnumbered three to one. Orion looked up to the three marksmen on the lookout platforms, one on each mast, crouching over their falconets as they lined up their sights. It was an easy enough cannon to load, but it took time. By his calculation, they would be lucky if they got three shots off before abandoning the cannons and reaching for their bows and arrows. The *Feniks* was within hailing distance, and Orion heard urgent shouts from her decks as her gunners rushed to load their next rounds.

"Marksmen," Orion called to the men high above his head. "Find your targets, first shots to her masts. After that, even the odds for us a little, if you please. Fire at will!"

Three 'ayes' drifted down. The men blew on their slow matches, then calmly lowered the flames to the small cannons' pans. The powder flared, and the cannons roared simultaneously.

Orion and his men were crouching below the bulwark, flanking the gap in the boarding nets and well hidden from sight, waiting for the cannons to finish tenderizing their prey before they laid into them with their arrows. Wolfish grins spread across their faces at the sound of their guns delivering their first punch of the fight. Then the deck shuddered beneath their feet, as the cannons fired their rounds in quick succession, perforating the *Feniks* in a neat line. Niccolò did not fire his cannons before the falconets. Smoke from the discharge would blind the marksmen. But he had timed his shots to perfection and barely a heartbeat had passed between the barrage of the falconets and the deafening release of the cannons on the gun deck.

The ship heeled in the aftermath, then composed herself. A cloud of smoke enshrouded them. Orion's ears were ringing at a screaming pitch, and he yawned to restore his hearing. The sharp tang of sulfur and burned charcoal coated the back of their tongues. Miro spat to the side – not to rid himself of the taste, but to articulate the sentiment on deck. Shouts and screams of agony were drifting from the *Feniks,* and Orion's men nocked their arrows.

Fresh white smoke matured to a dirty gray. Through it, his men rose as one, ghostly and ominous, as they raised their bows and released the first volley. The swarm of arrows screamed across the short distance between the two ships, felling a respectable number of the enemy. They did not aim at specific targets, as the smoke had obscured much of their vision, but most of the *Feniks'* men were unused to the hazards and expectations of battles at sea and were standing in a tight group, making them difficult to miss. After the first volley, the survivors were much more inclined and motivated to spread out and find cover.

Sweat was running in a steady, narrow rivulet down Orion's back and the hair at his nape was slick with moisture. The sun was beating down on them, and apart from the advantage of stealth, he now understood yet another reason most naval skirmishes occurred in or around the fringes of darkness.

Water rolled in disturbed swells between the two ships, undulating back and forth, slapping against the sides and making the deck pitch and fall at unpredictable intervals. The *Feniks* and the *Sword* exchanged cannon fire like a handball game, ripping each other to shreds. In the moments between barrages, Orion's men would unleash a cloud of arrows at the enemy, who scrambled desperately to avoid being hit. Those unaffected would try to load their muskets with shaking hands then rise to return fire, producing not so much as a hurt feeling as the weapon was unreliable at best and utterly useless at worst. Orion's crew were expert marksmen, and only the odd arrow flew wide. The *Feniks* crew would have to board the *Sword* soon, or there might not be enough men left to do so at all.

Orion watched as the *Feniks'* cannons discharged, their shots aimed with intent. The volley struck hard. One shot slammed into the *Sword's* stern, and the ship's motion shifted, sluggish and uneven. Orion knew the rudder had taken damage before his helmsman's shout from the quarterdeck confirmed it. Another shot landed closer to the bow, but no reports of damage followed, leaving him to hope the harm was minimal. When the *Feniks* fired again, only five of her eight cannons bellowed smoke and flame, the others silent, having misfired. It was a common enough occurrence, and even more so when the guns were not regularly cleaned and tested.

Without her rudder the *Sword* was reduced to a floating bucket at the mercy of the ocean. She was barely moving and by the second hour of the afternoon, the first of the *Feniks'* grappling lines dug into the *Sword's* railing.

Below decks, Niccolò's team had ceased firing their cannons and were hastening to the upper deck, doubling over to keep below the bulwark and taking position with their crew-mates.

"The guns are too hot to fire, sir," Niccolò reported. "We reckon you might have something to keep us busy while we wait for them to cool down."

Orion slapped him loudly on the back. Niccolò was usually a man of few words until the excitement of a battle loosened his tongue. "Get two men on the port-piece. They are preparing to board," Orion said and pointed to the small cannon mounted on the starboard-side bulwark near the stern. Another was mounted on the other side of the ship. They were the pure essence of anti-arsehole guns, the sort of thing used at close range or not at all, but worth every hard-stolen florin when repelling boarders.

Both port-pieces were loaded with grapeshot, but only one was aimed at the tangle of grappling lines where Du Bois' men hung like laundry on a wash day. The other was on the other side of the ship and impotently staring out at the calm ocean. Amidst all the lines, sails, rigging and general on-deck clutter, the small cannon was easy to overlook. However, after her first shot had cleared the lines of men, the element of surprise was no longer on the *Sword's* side and as soon as a man stepped up to load and fire the cannon, he was downed. The *Sword of Orion* simply did not have enough crew to sacrifice, and so the port-piece was abandoned.

Orion's men hacked at the grappling lines, and many fell away, sending those hanging from them screaming into the water between the two ships. However, they were not fast enough to stop the inevitable. Men from the *Feniks* boiled over their ship's side, like porridge from a forgotten pot, spilling onto the deck. The *Sword's* crew were firing a steady volley of arrows, but nothing could stem the flow.

The first man to clear the bulwark successfully made it a full six paces before a crossbow bolt pinned him to the inside of the wooden barrier where he stuck like a freshly published 'wanted' notice. That shot marked the last clean crossbow strike that afternoon.

Soon, fighting men crowded the decks. Du Bois was one of the last to cross the grappling lines. Age slowed his hand over hand movements. Where the younger men moved with primate agility and coordination, Du Bois' movements were slower as if he had to think about each before committing to the act. His arms were straight and his body hung heavy from the sagging rope, offering a buffet of options to land an arrow. A serpentine emotion coiled and hissed in Orion's heart. He nocked an arrow and raised his bow. He had his father dead in his sights; he would have preferred to kill him with his bare hands, staring into his eyes until his body went slack.

Drawing the bow, he felt his arm muscles stretch under the strain. The arrow was perfectly aimed at Du Bois' throat and Orion was a hair's breadth away from opening his fingers and releasing the arrow when someone slammed into his back, causing the projectile to fly from the bow and strike the inside of the bulwark.

"Whoreson!" Orion shouted, flung the bow aside as he turned and drew his dagger and cutlass from his belt. He was locked in a lopsided duel with two *Feniks* sailors and soon the familiar swing of his arms and rhythm of his feet drove all but the blades flashing before him from his mind.

The cannon fire had ceased as all hands were locked in combat. A few musket shots were ringing out from somewhere, but they soon died down too and then the only sounds were the scraping of blades and clanging of steel. Once during the melee, Orion caught sight of Van Leyen on the bows, swinging his twin blades in an arc of liquid silver, leaving behind a trail of destruction as he moved to his next group of targets.

Orion parried an advancing cutlass to the side, lowered his body and thrust his own with a sucking sound into the man before him. The strike was instinctive and precise, and he did not stop to assess the damage. A wet gurgle, then a dull thump as the body hit the deck, concluded their brief encounter. The deck was thick with struggling bodies. The *Sword's* crew was heavily outnumbered and for the first time in his life, Orion could not taste victory. An alarming number of his men were dead or dying, and that was only as far as he could see. He sank his blade deep into the chest of a soldier who seemed to have appeared out of nowhere, and then the world stopped spinning. All sounds died away and Orion's vision cleared.

Du Bois was running across the quarterdeck, ducking blades and side-stepping pockets of fighting as he made his way to the stateroom. It took Orion less than ten strides to reach the companionway, cutting the throats of two men and gutting another as he went. His feet touched the narrow steps only once before he bounded onto the quarterdeck.

Cut the head off the snake and the body dies. He needed to end this battle and hoped the theory would hold, for he was running out of time and men.

***

Alain Du Bois swung his legs over the bulwark of the *Sword of Orion* and landed heavily on the deck. His booted feet slipped in a puddle of blood and his hand tightened around the hilt of his cutlass. The dagger in the small of his back pressed uncomfortably against his skin, and he yanked it free. The deck before him was a mess of swinging blades, curses, and death grunts. In his youth, he had lived for moments like these, but with age had come wisdom and the need for a battle of a more refined nature. Manipulation, blackmail, and control had become his weapons of choice.

The rewards were infinitely larger, and the satisfaction of his victories lasted long after his opponent had perished.

Nearby, two men were locked in a duel. He could easily sink his blade into the back of one of them, but he held back. He needed to savor his vengeance, allow it to ripen and intensify. In killing, Du Bois was a purist. Slashing throats and gutting bellies were a brute's business. He reveled in the power that came with the slow release of desperation and fear, and in the warmth of his enemies' life force as they silently bled to death, having long realized that screaming and begging would not save them. His only goal was to find Sebastiaan and his son. They would both die by his hand on this day.

Du Bois pushed his way up the companionway to the quarterdeck where the fighting was less dense and finally, he made it to the stateroom door without spilling a droplet of blood either of his own or that of another.

The door was unlocked, and he stepped inside, then, almost as an afterthought, closed it softly behind him. There was a short wood-paneled hallway of about four feet leading to the main cabin. Intricate carvings decorated the panels, and he ran his fingers over the swirls before stepping forward into the captain's main quarters. His feet carried him to the center of the cabin, where he stopped to take in the room. It was unoccupied, and he sheathed his weapons. Rarely did he find himself at a loss for words. The tasteful opulence of the room was unexpected. Thick oriental rugs overlapped to cover the floor from wall to wall, leaving only the barest glimpses of the polished floorboards beneath. Carved bookshelves, filled with leather volumes and cloth-covered tomes, held in place by a thin brass rod, covered the left wall from floor to ceiling and end to end.

Toward the back of the cabin, center with the bank of windows and facing the door, stood a large, ornate, dark wooden desk topped with charts, ledgers, sheet music, and navigational instruments. A violin rested on top of the clutter, as if left there in haste. Several brass candleholders with fresh candles and a Turkish lamp vied for space on the busy desk. A cushioned chair of similar wood stood at an angle behind it.

The room felt bright and airy, with light streaming through the bank of windows. A few were left open, allowing the breeze to stir the thin, gauze-like curtains.

To his right, a meticulously made bed with its accompanying side table and a sea chest at its end stood against the wall. That was the extent of the furniture in the room, but each piece was a work of art and demanded admiration. This was not a space where others were regularly welcomed, as there was only one uncomfortable-looking chair facing the desk. This was the haven of a solitary man.

A clean scent of bergamot and beeswax clung to the air. The serenity and comforts of the captain's quarters stood in violent contrast to the chaos outside. He had not seen Sebastiaan on deck and was certain he would find the coward hiding in the stateroom, but the only sign of life was an unholy growl followed by a sodden hiss. Du Bois looked around the room searching for the source of the unnatural sounds. His eyes landed on a gray cat of mediocre proportions hiding under the desk. He tried to shoo the fiend away but merely enraged it further, for it snapped out a puny paw studded with needle-like claws and opened its mouth, displaying a perfect set of small fangs. He briefly wondered if the thing would do him the favor and die of vexation when the small hairs on the back of his neck rose in warning.

Orion entered the stateroom on silent feet, his wet blades still clutched in his hands, soon realizing that his stealth was entirely unnecessary, for Gamora was raising a tempest that drowned all other sounds. He had seen Du Bois slip into his cabin moments earlier and had fought his way up the stairs of the quarterdeck. Du Bois was standing by the desk with his back turned to Orion. His posture was proud and regal.

"Found what you were looking for?" Orion asked in an easy low voice as he stepped from the dark passage and leaned his shoulder against the bookshelf.

Du Bois snapped around, sending the ends of his black jerkin flying with the suddenness of his movement. Orion tucked his cutlass back in his wide leather belt, and pushed the dagger back into the sheath on his forearm, hidden beneath the sleeve of his once-white shirt. The two men took each other's measure in a moment of silent appraisal, sparking the air between them with static energy.

Silver currents flowed through Du Bois' coal-black hair. He was dressed in black, from his neckcloth to the tips of his boots. Orion figured it suited his equally colorless soul perfectly. This was his father, he thought as he stared into the unfamiliar face, searching for anything that would resemble a feeling of kinship. Regrettably, he found none. The only feeling swirling through his heart and mind was the need for justice. Justice for the faceless woman who had given him life, in whose womb he had grown, and whose breast and hands had fed and nurtured him, who had kept him safe and with her dying breath had begged for his life. Samira, the mother he could not remember, but whom he would avenge if it was the last thing he did. Winter crept into the space where his heart used to be and the longer he stared at the tall slender form before him, the further its tendrils reached.

Alain Du Bois' eyes narrowed as he stared at the man who was undoubtedly the mysterious captain of this ship. He was younger than Alain had expected, and utterly captivating. There was something about the man's calm, confident demeanor, standing in his quarters as if he had nowhere else to be while a battle raged just outside the door, making it impossible to look away from him.

"I assume you are the captain of this ship," Du Bois said. His words were met with a tight nod. "Quite a little setup you have here. Such a pity something so beautiful is about to be lost." He shook his head in false remorse.

"What do you want?" Orion asked.

Du Bois closed his eyes and exhaled loudly. "Give me Sebastiaan De Vries and his son and we will cease all hostilities and leave your ship immediately."

Orion cast him a lazy smile. "You labor under a misconception, thinking you are in a position to bargain. Let me remedy it. You boarded my ship with boys and slaves who are being massacred as we speak, while you hide in my sleeping quarters."

"I'm not the one in labor here," Du Bois drawled. "We both know the battle is lost. You simply do not have the men needed to win it. By the glint in your eyes, I am assuming you're a smart lad. My guess is that you've never been in a situation quite as dire as this and now you are at a loss for how to proceed." Alain waited for the young captain to respond, but he was met with cold, almost black eyes that showed not a single speck of emotion. They reminded him of Lucien's - similarly cold and equally dark. Shaking the untimely memory from his mind, he continued, "You can still save the last of your men and your ship. For no matter how beautiful she is, I will send her to the bottom of the ocean without a moment's hesitation." The only reaction he got was the captain crossing his arms over his chest and looking as bored as he'd previously sounded. "Give me what I want, and we will call an end to the destruction. I will even gift you men to fill your numbers sufficiently to continue your journey. Satisfy my demands and you have my word that I will let you go in peace. I will neither follow nor search for you, and I will turn a blind eye, should our paths ever cross in the future."

"Now that sounds familiar, doesn't it?" Orion sneered. "At least you're consistent. I'll give you that much." Uncrossing his arms, he toyed with the spines of a couple of books, ensuring they were perfectly aligned with their neighbors. Then he ran his fingers over the inch of exposed shelf, testing for dust, finding none.

"What is your meaning?" Du Bois asked as he contemplated the odd statement.

Orion wished he could remember his mother. Wished that the unexpected whiff of flowers would remind him of her scent, or the celebratory clink of wine glasses would have made him think of her laughter. But there was nothing. Where her memories were supposed to live was only the burning need for vengeance sprinkled liberally with flecks of hatred.

Orion ignored Du Bois' question and instead posed one of his own.

"Tell me, what kind of man chains his two-year-old son and his child's mother to a pole in the middle of a Portuguese slave market, then turns and walks away without so much as a backward glance?"

The blood drained so fast from Alain Du Bois' face, that Orion was worried the man would die of a brain malfunction before he had the chance to kill him. Du Bois sank back against the edge of Orion's desk, his knuckles white as they gripped the solid wooden surface. He was clearly having trouble remaining upright without assistance, but soon recovered. Years of deceit and condescension had armed him with enough composure for his walls to not crumble at the first direct hit.

"I am a tall tree, son. I catch a lot of wind. Rumors, like all debris, love to gather at its base, hoping to draw its attention. You should not lend your ear to gossip, as it makes a fool of its master."

"And yet, here you are, ashen-faced, clinging to my desk, and feeling the need to warrant this supposed rumor with a response," Orion said with a slow smile of true amusement. He would love nothing better than a verbal game of cat and mouse, but the sounds of battle permeated the silence between them. "I am willing to discuss the terms of your departure." That was enough to lift Du Bois off the desk. Color returned to his cheeks and a vulpine light lit in his eyes. "On one condition," Orion added, and Du Bois silently raised his eyebrows in anticipation. "I want to hear you say her name."

"For the love of–" Du Bois threw his hands in the air. "Let the past stay as it lies, boy. You have no idea what you are talking about."

"Say her name," Orion demanded. "Say my mother's name and we'll talk about your demands."

Orion watched as the meaning of his words drove their way home. The cunning light left Du Bois' eyes, and their actions were momentarily disconnected from his intentions as they widened in surprise. His lips parted and once more he tilted backward, reaching again for the solid support of the desk.

"Your mother?" he breathed in disbelief.

"Say her name." Orion's voice carried no traces of doubt and disbelief. Instead, his whisper carried the weight of a warning.

Du Bois' shoulders sagged. He closed his eyes and dropped his chin to his chest as if in prayer. Orion wanted to slap the man into action. While they were standing here exchanging nonsense, his men were dying outside. He refused to think about what was happening below decks, and his frustrations almost made him scream. Instead, he bit down on his teeth so hard it felt as if he were clamping down on a lightning bolt as pain shot in streaks over his skull. Still, Du Bois remained motionless.

"Say it!" Orion shouted, and Du Bois' head rose as if drawn by a string from an old man's hands. He stared at Orion with clouded eyes and something that resembled resignation. "I am your son," Orion continued, his voice bouncing off the walls, drowning the clash of steel outside. "The one you left for dead. Show me at least that courtesy."

Du Bois' composure finally caved and what was left revealed a man ravaged by sadness and regret.

"Samira," Du Bois breathed the name, and it floated through the cabin like warm dust on a dry day. Orion felt the rays of victory, like the sun breaking through a thick bank of clouds.

"Explain it to me," Orion said, not caring that the man standing before him looked ready to collapse.

"That was not our agreement," Du Bois said in a feeble attempt at control of the situation.

"Make me understand," Orion urged, and deliberately gentled his tone. "I am a man, not a child. I know the way of the world, but I need to hear this from your mouth. Do it and I will hand over De Vries and his son, and let you have your revenge for the murder of my brother."

Du Bois remained silent, staring at Orion and after what felt like a lifetime he finally spoke, sounding tired and suddenly very old. Orion swallowed the sigh that threatened to reveal his relief.

"Her father, an Ottoman merchant – I can't remember his name," Du Bois said and waved his hand as if to clear his memory, "sold her to me when she was eighteen years old. She was the most beautiful woman I'd ever seen, but she was unruly, headstrong, and stubborn, with an uncanny ability to drive me to the edge of my sanity. Yet, despite it all, I couldn't resist her. When she became pregnant, I knew the child was mine and when the babe was born, she had threatened to expose me if I did not claim him as my own." Du Bois shrugged, but it was more a gesture of hopelessness rather than lack of care. "Of course I couldn't. Claiming a bastard child would have ruined me and my family. In return, I offered her freedom and money, the chance to make a life of her own. But, she refused."

"And so you beat her and left her to die," Orion said when Du Bois' words died away.

"She haunted my dreams for years after I'd left the two of you, at that godforsaken market." He shook his head. "It would have been well within my rights to kill her. But I couldn't. And now I understand why." His throat worked as he tried to contain his emotions while staring at Orion. "You are my son. It is written on your face – clear as day. You are the spitting image of every Du Bois of the last fourteen generations, save for the color of your skin. That is a gift from your mother."

Orion's insides revolted against the knowledge, but he kept his mouth shut and his face impassive. Du Bois studied him the way a man might a prize horse he never knew he owned –hungry, possessive, suddenly certain of the bloodline.

"You have done well for yourself," Du Bois said after a weighted pause. "Not only have you survived, but you've thrived." He frowned as if the circumstance was difficult to believe, and perhaps, for him, it was. "What is your name?" he croaked, his voice laden with emotion.

"Orion."

Du Bois nodded, ruminating over the discovery of a son. He had lost the only child he'd ever known, yet fate had returned another – one that was strong, courageous and resilient. "Orion Phillipe Alain Du Bois. That is your name," Du Bois finished the half introduction. "My son." Pride was giving his words strength, and he straightened himself once more.

"Yes," Orion said. A soft smile leaped onto his face, and he fought to keep it in place. It would be a bitterly cold day in hell with the devil and all his disciples wearing snowy white robes singing *Hallelujah,* before he would ever claim that name as his own, but for the sake of expedience he was willing to overlook the stain on his identity.

"My blood," Du Bois said and pushed away from the desk and stepped toward Orion, opening his arms to gather his son in their first embrace.

Orion could swear there was moisture in the man's eyes as he approached him. This was the moment he'd been dreaming of for as long as he had thoughts worth remembering. His skin broke out in gooseflesh.

"Father," Orion said, and took a step to meet Du Bois. He felt boneless, amazed he could still stand. He was about to claim his birthright, not as Du Bois' son, but as his own man. The blood spilled today would be his baptism. Today, he would balance the scales.

As Orion moved toward Du Bois the thin blade slipped from the sheath on his forearm, and the cold steel dropped quietly into his hand. His heart hammered against his breastbone, and his lungs felt tight, causing him to inhale sharply through his nose.

Orion wrapped one arm around Du Bois in a tight embrace, and with his other hand, drove the dagger deep into his father's heart. Du Bois stiffened, a gasp rushed involuntarily from his mouth, then he slumped against Orion.

Orion pushed his hand into Du Bois' hair, his scalp warm under his fingers, and mercilessly yanked his head back.

"This is for my mother. May you rot in hell, you vile son of a bitch," he spoke in Du Bois' ear as he held him close. Pulling back, he saw the words register in his father's wide, stunned eyes before the light faded from them. Orion pulled the blade free. Du Bois' arm fell from his shoulders and he let the lifeless body sink to the floor.

***

The first man to make it halfway down the stairs was a boy no older than Davit. He took immediate panic at the sight of Sebastiaan waiting in the dark hallway, blades drawn and ready. The boy paused, staring straight into the eyes of the man, who seemed to have never encountered a threat serious enough to ruffle his calm.

"Come on, boy, I don't have all day," Sebastiaan invited. The boy's neck and shoulder muscles were so tightly bunched with fright, he could barely shake his head.

"Then go back to where you came from," Sebastiaan suggested. The boy climbed a step backward, but then remembered the bloodbath he'd just escaped and froze to the spot.

"Sir, please." His voice came out all wrong. "I remember you from the castle."

Sebastiaan tilted his head and frowned lightly as he tried to place the face. It was dark the night Orion and Van Leyen had sprung him from the castle, and he'd not paid particular attention to the faces they'd encountered on his way out.

"And still you boarded this ship? Knowing what dangers lurk below her deck?" he teased.

"I …," the boy drained his mouth of the saliva that threatened to drown him and his large round eyes shone wet in the dimly lit corridor. "We have no choice; we are under orders."

"Ah, a soldier's conundrum," Sebastiaan said, sighing but not lowering his cutlass. "Well, my boy, you can return, hope to survive, and jump overboard." Sebastiaan raised his eyebrows when the boy made no effort to move. "Or you can lay down your weapons, come over here and let me tie you up. Unless, of course, you want to fight me and let the gods decide your fate. What's it to be?"

The boy bent down slowly and laid his weapons on the stairs, creating an unintentional and unexpected obstacle for those who would come down the steps next, then hesitantly approached Sebastiaan.

"Bring that rope with you," Sebastiaan ordered and pointed to the dark corner where a length of rope used for tying loose cargo lay in a neat coil. The moment the boy turned his back to do as instructed, Sebastiaan moved forward, raised his cutlass and slammed the hilt down on the back of the young soldier's head, rendering him unconscious, but not dead. He tied his ankles, then his wrists, hoisted him over his shoulder and dumped his limp form in the empty cabin that was initially set aside for Van Leyen. He had just closed the door behind him when two soldiers and a sailor came down the stairs. They were bloodstained and one was nursing his side where a wound was leaking through his fingers. The first tripped on the boy's weapons and slid the rest of the way, offering his jugular at the altar of Sebastiaan's blade. Sebastiaan moved with practiced precision toward the remaining two. He brought his cutlass down on the sailor's wrist severing the hand, still curled around the cutlass, from the rest of his arm. Before the weapon could clatter to the floor, he'd spun the shocked man around to use him as a shield as he approached the soldier. The witless creature took the bait and neatly stepped into the trap Sebastiaan was laying for him.

Not caring so much as a sparrow's fart for the sailor facing him, the soldier extended his rapier and rammed it into the man's belly, throwing all his weight behind the thrust. He correctly calculated that the force of the strike would drive the blade straight through the meat shield and into the man hiding behind it. Sebastiaan read the brute's thoughts as clearly as if they were carved into his forehead. When the blade struck the sailor, he twisted to the side, removing himself from the equation and let the duo rush past him. Momentum brought the sailor within striking distance and Sebastiaan sank his dagger into the back of his exposed neck.

He had deliberately chosen the hallway as his battleground. The corridor was narrow and dark. Most soldiers were carrying rapiers, which were impossible to wield in tight spaces. Sailors carried daggers and cutlasses, which were much more suitable, but they would suffer momentary blindness coming from the sunlit deck into the darkness of the hallway, giving Sebastiaan the advantage for a few seconds. That small window was all he needed.

What had started as a trickle soon grew into a steady stream of opportunity for Sebastiaan to brush up on his combat skills and weapons proficiency, which he had sorely neglected over the last few months of peaceful living at the Cape. It did, however, tell him that the *Sword* was losing the battle.

Chapter 21

Orion stared at the body at his feet. Death was an undignified affair. Muscles were rendered slack as the brain ceased to guide or command, leaving the jaw to gape and the unblinking eyes to stare into eternity, forever defined by the last unguarded emotion. Du Bois lay on the thick Oriental rug in front of the desk, coat panels splayed wide. For a few steady heartbeats, Orion fixated on the poison-green of the lining. The color and its placement suited the wearer – sophisticated, dark and hidden from view. He refused to think of Du Bois as his father, but he was not a barbarian either and so he crouched next to the body and closed the eyes with a perfunctory sweep of his hand.

"It is done, Mother. May your soul find peace."

His voice coursed through the warm silence of the room. Outside, the battle was still raging. A chorus of death grunts and clashing steel rang muted through the thick wooden walls. This cabin was his sanctuary. A place he shared with no other and Du Bois' presence, alive or otherwise, was a violation. Orion was about to hoist the body onto his shoulders and carry him from the cabin when the roar of a discharging cannon, the likes of which he'd never heard before, tore through the air. A sharp cracking sound followed, like a tree snapping through its last fibers before toppling to the forest floor. Orion ran for the door, the corpse forgotten in his haste.

Bursting through the stateroom, he cut to the quarterdeck rail, squinting hard against the glaring sunlight and collecting information as he went. The pulsing ocean gave the deck a soft roll beneath his bare feet and he knew that the deafening cracking of wood had not come from the *Sword*. The men he'd killed on his way to his cabin earlier were where he'd left them, their blood still wet and glistening, and he wondered how long he'd been in the cabin with Du Bois. It felt like days, but could not have been more than a quarter of an hour at most. Sniffing loudly, he searched for the stench of sulfur that usually clung to the air after cannon fire, but found none. The gray smoke from their earlier exchanges had vanished on the breeze.

Orion could identify most naval cannons by their sound alone, but the thundering he'd just heard was something he'd never encountered before. He looked at the *Feniks*. She was in trouble. There was a large hole in her hull, and it was sucking seawater at an alarming rate, causing her stern to sag, creating the illusion that she was sailing uphill. The last of her crew were leaping into the ocean and swimming for the assumed safety of the *Sword*. He contemplated reaching for a bow, then dismissed the thought – better to conserve arrows and energy for whatever had just blown a hole in her hull.

Whatever had spat the first shot now released another, shaking the air with its ungodly power. Orion threw himself onto the deck and covered his head with both arms as he braced for the hit. Once more, a resounding crack – louder and more fatal than the first – echoed, but the *Sword* did not shatter or keel over. She merely trembled like a boiling kettle. He slowly lifted his head, and the rest of him followed cautiously. Everyone, friends and foes alike, had thrown themselves down as well. Some were slow to rise, while others stayed flattened. Apart from pools of blood, the dead and wounded littering every available surface on the upper deck and bow, the *Sword* appeared intact.

The second cannonball had struck the *Feniks* above the waterline in center of her stern, capitalizing on the destruction of the first. Orion silently admired the gunner's aim. Both shots had passed right through the vessel, leaving devastating entry and exit wounds. The one he could see was large enough for a man to walk through without touching the fanged splinters and broken timbers. Shards of timber rained down on and around them. Planks on her quarterdeck stood like hair on an angry dog's back. The hull was completely submerged and gleamed darkly beneath the surface. Faint snapping of glass sounded as her stern windows shattered under the pressure. The great slave hauler was folding in on herself. Orion had sunk a fair number of ships in his time, but he had never been this close to the event before. Disturbingly, guttural sounds emanated from the distressed ship as it growled and groaned. Sheets of water rained from the *Feniks'* decks as her bowsprit and prow rose to an unnatural, near-vertical position. The mizzenmast was nearly horizontal and its sails were already heavy where they dipped into the water. So bizarre was the sight that it took Orion a moment to fully comprehend what he was seeing. Within minutes, she sank. Air gushed from hopeful cavities and her hull screeched like a wounded animal. When she finally broke apart, the ocean heartlessly swallowed the morsel in a single, gluttonous whirlpool.

Whoever had sunk the *Feniks* had done so in a spectacular display of naval dominance and Orion was not arrogant or stupid enough to think the *Sword* was immune to a similar fate. The ensuing battle would be a foregone conclusion. The *Sword* was a lame duck with no rudder, a dwindling crew and leaking badly. Even had she been in her prime and fully operational he knew there was nothing onboard that could defend against such an attack, and his breathing grew shallow as he waited for another explosion to herald the beginning of their journey to the bottom of the ocean. That his precious *Sword* would die alongside the likes of the *Feniks* rankled. It was an unbecoming end, and if there was anything he could do to prevent it, he would.

"I am sorry, my darling," he muttered and closed his hand over the narrow top of the quarterdeck railing.

On the upper deck, the *Sword's* men were cheering as their nemesis vanished, while the enemy combatants looked on in despair. However, none of the men had the presence of mind to search for the source of the destruction. Instead, all suffered a pointless fascination with the debris drifting and bobbing on the uneasy waters caused by the disturbance.

The armistice was short-lived as the *Feniks* men collectively came to the same conclusion: a battered and broken ship was better than no ship at all. What started as a battle for dominance quickly became one of annihilation. They no longer fought for Du Bois' goals, and the promise of a reward. They needed the *Sword*.

Renewed violence erupted with the suddenness of an alcohol-fueled fire. The men were putting blade to bone with vicious intent. Honor and humanity had sunk with their ship, and Orion watched as two more of his men fell. He needed to put an end to the frenzy that was fast turning into a bloodbath.

"Stand down!" he shouted. But he might as well have whispered the words into the wind. No one paid him any mind as the slaughter reached a fever pitch. He saw Miro on all fours crawling toward a prone body and driving his blade down into the man's back, then using the pinned cutlass as a crutch to push himself upright before being set upon by three men. One *Feniks* soldier, in the grips of blind hysteria, was repeatedly stabbing another, long after the man had died, his broken mind confusing ally for rival.

"Cease!" Orion shouted again, and the result of his second command was no more impressive than the first.

Looking around the deck, he searched for something that could cause a distraction long enough for his voice to penetrate the battle craze. He reached for the ship's bell beside him, gripped the knotted rope and slammed the hammer persistently against the copper dome. It felt like he'd rung the damn thing for hours, during which he vowed to install a much larger one at the first opportunity. But eventually, what started as a faint interruption to the chaos became louder, as the pealing sound pierced the thick, black fog of madness that had descended over the deck.

"Cease!" he shouted. "Stand down!"

Orion's ears were ringing, and he realized he was still striking the bell. It took more effort than he thought necessary to get his hand to quit the back-and-forth motion. Movement caught his eye, and he threw a quick glance over his shoulder. Where hours earlier there had been nothing but open ocean, the horizon, and water were now obscured by a behemoth of sails, rigging, and teak-brown hull topped with decks crowded with fresh, hard-looking fighters. The figurehead of an intricately carved mermaid, arms flung back, spine arched, and hair streaming as if in flight, elegantly glided past, in a slow and controlled advance. The newcomer dwarfed the *Sword of Orion.* Orion's knees nearly gave way as he read the single word painted on the hull, revealing itself by increments. *Danielle.*

Closing his eyes, Orion shook his head violently, hoping with all his heart that he was not dreaming. He briefly wondered if he'd taken a knock to the head. The day had been busy enough that such a blow could have gone unnoticed in the heat of the moment. The therapy seemed to work. His mind snapped to attention and his feet remembered their calling and swiftly carried him down the stairs of the companionway and onto the upper deck.

The situation had just taken a drastic turn for the better. Sebastiaan had messaged his uncle Davit De Coninck months earlier, requesting the *Danielle* to be sent to the Cape with provisions, and more importantly, money. Amid the upheaval of late, her imminent arrival had completely slipped their minds as more pressing matters had arisen.

"*Feniks,* lay your weapons down and surrender," Orion bellowed as he ran. "Heed my words and no more blood will be spilled." As soon as the words left Orion's lips, he wished he could recall them. He should have stayed the order and kept fighting, killing every one of the *Feniks* scum who'd dared to think they could take the *Sword.* Weapons clattered to the deck as the men glanced at the looming ship, then one by one raised their empty hands.

The *Danielle* and her decks, brimming with armed, bloodthirsty men eager for battle, were now in full view of all. A collective groan of disappointment echoed through their ranks as they watched their prey surrender. There was no sport in slaughtering an unwilling enemy.

Davit De Coninck was standing on the *Danielle's* bow with the breeze in his silver-and-gold hair and a brilliant smile sparkling on his face.

"Ahoy there. And not a moment too soon it would seem," he called down in a booming voice.

Orion ducked his head to hide the explosion of emotion that threatened to stream down his face at the sight of his grandfather. Relief dragged like fine silk over his raw senses. When he was certain his voice would not break, he shouted back, "You sure know how to make an entrance. Magnificent calling card."

That Orion or any of his men had failed to notice the *Danielle* approaching was testament to how dire the fight really was. Du Bois' death might not have been enough to end it and despite his bloodlust of mere seconds ago, he knew they would not have survived a moment longer. De Coninck had just saved their lives.

"Could you not have put an end to this sooner, lad? Or are you partial to painting your decks with blood these days?" De Coninck was leaning over the railing to get a better look at the carnage below. The *Danielle* was coming to a gradual halt, a bell was ringing at intervals marking her position with men's voices shouting and confirming orders as they took great care not to collide with the drifting pinnace.

The *Danielle* dwarfed the *Sword* with her massive displacement. Her bow and stern stretched far beyond the smaller ship's, and with her decks and masts towering overhead, she looked ready to topple onto them. De Coninck had planned the angle of their approach with precision, long before Orion had even noticed their presence, and effortlessly came to a controlled stop. What was supposed to be a cumbersome event turned into an elegant display of seamanship. Fresh orders were shouted and anchoring lines flew from the *Danielle* to the *Sword*, tying the two ships together.

"There really was no need to sink every ship in the vicinity just to draw my attention. I graciously grant you permission to come aboard," Orion called across the small distance and spread his arms wide. His insolence elicited a booming laugh from De Coninck. With that, Orion turned to face the battlefield that was his upper deck.

"All *Sword's* men on your feet," he ordered.

Only four leaped to their feet. Orion surveyed them grimly. Miro was completely covered in blood, from his head to the puddle he stood in. Niccolò sported a nasty slash across his thigh, but the bleeding was controlled and he looked unconcerned. Samuel was clutching his left hand. Three fingers were missing and then there was Harja. His chef was blood-splattered and wide-eyed, but apart from being badly shaken, he seemed uninjured. Orion prayed for more survivors that were just too wounded or deafened by the explosions to obey his command.

"Everyone not belonging to the *Sword of Orion*, get on your knees, and put your hands behind your backs," Orion barked and several men kneeled. "Now plant your foreheads to the deck planks and point your arses to the sun." The men obeyed and several round bottoms rose like mushrooms. Orion nodded his approval and looked to the many still forms, either dead, dying or pretending to be. "Anyone found hiding behind an injury or playing dead will face immediate execution." Four more mushrooms sprouted. One man was spluttering blood and clutching his gaping belly. His eyes were glassy and his body convulsing. "Those who wish to die of their own accord, feel free to do so now or raise a hand if you need assistance." The gurgling stopped, and the man exhaled his last breath. Two raised their hands. Miro and Niccolò approached them, whispered brief prayers in their native tongues, and then administered the mercy. There was a moment of silence, as no one took death lightly, but the subdued mood quickly vanished when a heavy boarding plank slammed down on the *Sword's* gunwale. She was about to be boarded for the second time this day.

***

"What's all this then?" De Coninck asked as he released Orion from an embrace that had squeezed warmth deep into his bones and infused him with an instant sense of peace. Orion had thought adulthood would have robbed him of the sensation. Just as Arent's presence brought a promise of safety, De Coninck's was marked by order and control.

The tinge of familiar teasing slowly faded from De Coninck's eyes, and a perplexed frown grew on his forehead as he took inventory of the surrounding carnage, his hand drifting to the hilt of his blade.

"What happened here today? Did you overestimate the size of your stomach and bite off more than you could chew?" he asked, concern weighing his words down into a low, measured growl.

"We were short on hands when we left the Cape, but trouble came faster than we could run." Orion's worn and tired tone did not go unnoticed.

"You look like hell," De Coninck said and avidly studied Orion from the hollows in his eyes, the effort with which he held his shoulders, to his bloodied clothes and boots. "Where's the rest of your crew?"

Orion looked over the deck that usually teemed with his bloodied but victorious men. Only four had survived, and they stood watch over the kneeling prisoners, cutlasses in hand. Seeing their miserably reduced number drove the reality of what had transpired home with a sickening drop of his stomach. Dread tightened around his heart. How could one man have held against so many?

"Dead," he said flatly. If he looked as tired as he sounded, he could well understand De Coninck's sentiment. "Those four are all that remain."

De Coninck drew his hand down his face. "I recognized Alain Du Bois' ship. She's been making a thorough nuisance of herself over the last few years. Why would she come after you? Or was it your hunting expedition that turned bad?"

Orion shook his head. "No, we were not hunting her, and she didn't come after me. She came for Sebastiaan and his son."

The thoughtless admission made Orion shut his eyes tightly. He wished he had kept his mouth shut, but the words had skipped over his lips before he could think better of it. De Coninck had no idea the boy even existed. Sebastiaan's letters had never mentioned a child.

He opened his eyes and saw how De Coninck turned stone-cold still. During Sebastiaan's search for Danielle, Orion had been the link between him and De Coninck, delivering letters back and forth. He knew Sebastiaan did not mention a child – he had no idea of the boy's existence. Knowing his careless words had landed him in a hole De Coninck would not ignore, Orion opened his mouth and began digging deeper.

"I'm sorry," he began, seeing De Coninck's pale blue eyes slowly iced over like a winter lake. "I, umm," he swallowed, and once more tried to shake the day's fog from his mind. The change from high combat to relative tranquility had come too fast and his muscles were still vibrating with unspent battle fever while his head was sending messages of a different nature. The dissonance was jarring, and it tangled his tongue. "It's new."

Crafting a concise yet comprehensive explanation of the last eleven months at the Cape required the verbal skills of a *notaire*. Conveying the events of the last week alone would require a stiff drink and comfortable seating – Du Bois, his cousin, Sebastiaan, Danielle, Jiya – oh, *Christ* – Jiya. He was not in the habit of indulging in a profligacy of emotion, but the thought of Jiya pushed him closer to the edge of the abyss that had been beckoning for his attention since he first saw De Coninck standing on the deck of the *Danielle*.

He craved solitude. Time and silence to sift through and organize the mess of the recent past. There were few people capable of stripping away his armor of indifference. De Coninck, unfortunately, was one of them and he knew it was an exercise in futility to salvage the situation. Since he was unable to find a foothold in the conversation, he abandoned the effort. Instead, he stared blankly at De Coninck. He knew the calculated equanimity decorating the older man's features was but a mask habitually worn to hide the strong emotions underneath.

The news about Sebastiaan and its blunt delivery had landed harder than Orion had intended. Silence, which should have been filled with his voice, hung between them. De Coninck's intent stare never wavered from Orion and then he slowly nodded, as if the narrowing of his eyes had brought everything into focus.

"Where is Sebastiaan?" he asked. There was a dangerous edge to De Coninck's voice, one that only surfaced when Sebastiaan's welfare was in question.

Fear for Sebastiaan was burning Orion's gut. "I haven't seen him since the battle started. He was below decks." Orion inhaled to say more, but De Coninck held his hand up, silencing him like he did when Orion was a young boy. The effect was the same, and he obediently shut his mouth.

"I have enough men to crew two ships," De Coninck said. "Look them over and select a temporary crew. Frans Heems will assist you." With that, he gently but firmly pushed Orion aside, and with clipped, powerful strides that put to lie the notion that age ruined all, strode toward the companionway leading to the cabins below.

Orion was about to ask who Frans Heems was when an impossibly large man stepped off the gangplank and stopped in front of him, forcing him to take an involuntary step in retreat and tilt his head upward to look the man in the eye. Images of the Colossus of Rhodes, which he'd seen in one of De Coninck's books as a lad, came to mind. Sharp eyes, narrowed by an overdrawn smile amid a thicket of bushy beard, stared back at him. A scar ran from the bridge of his nose across his cheekbone and into his beard; others crisscrossed his hands and arms, the marks of a man long familiar with violence. De Coninck had a reputation for recruiting skilled fighters and this man was obviously not hired for his amiable nature.

"I am Frans Heems," the giant rumbled, and Orion could tell by the movement of his cheeks that his smile had deepened. "Chief mate on the *Danielle.*"

"Orion Van Jeveren," he introduced himself, his voice carrying a clarity of conviction he'd never known until that moment. Something that had always been out of step had just fallen perfectly into place. For the first time, Orion felt sure of the man he was. "Well met," he said, extending his hand in greeting.

Heems accepted the courtesy with a crushing grip, which he good-naturedly gentled lest his newest acquaintance come away with broken fingers.

"And you, Captain," he said. "Pardon the query, but might you need a hand in securing your deck?" Frans asked in a tranquil baritone, honed by years of careful restraint to avoid provoking anxiety or untimely intimidation.

Normally Orion would take quick offense to any meddling in his affairs, no matter how dire they were, but lacked the strength to be affronted.

"Aye, let's get a move on. We need a few more men to wrap the dead and transport the wounded."

Frans turned toward the *Danielle* where she lazily played with the small waves pushing and receding against her hull and released an ear-splitting whistle. A sailor appeared at the railing. Frans flicked his fingers, the gesture was acknowledged and then the man disappeared again. Orders were shouted and moments later a stream of sailors carrying bundles of sailcloth crossed the connecting gangplank.

***

The instant the world shook with the thunderous discharge of that colossal cannon, Sebastiaan knew victory was theirs despite the increasing flow of *Feniks* men from the decks above. He'd only ever heard the *Danielle's* cannon roar once before, but that single time was enough to recognize it across the span of almost two decades. No matter how desperate the battle was on deck, the arrival of his ship would decisively tip the scales in the *Sword's* favor. Orion's call for surrender confirmed his supposition minutes later. Sebastiaan remained hidden in the shadows, awaiting any stragglers finding their way into the passageway, but there were none. When he was certain the situation was under control, he entered Van Leyen's cabin.

His prisoner was sitting on the floor against the back wall, feet and hands tied, exactly where he'd left him earlier. The boy's nerves were crackling around him. Having heard Orion's commands, the boy knew the *Feniks* had lost the battle and, understandably, was assuming the worst of fates now awaited him.

With shallow breaths and large, frightened eyes he tracked Sebastiaan's every movement. "My father was a sailmaker," he blurted nervously, then violently flinched when Sebastiaan crouched next to him.

"My felicitations." Sebastiaan gave him a quick frown and reached for his ankles to remove the restraints.

"I mean," he bravely persisted after clearing his tight throat. "He taught me the skill from a young age. I can be of service." The boy spoke rapidly and in a high-pitched voice. He'd make a terrible salesman, Sebastiaan thought. He wisely kept his career advice to himself as understanding dawned. The poor fool was trying to stay his presumed doom.

"So why did you become a soldier and not a sailmaker, like your sire, then?" he asked, more out of the need to prevent the boy from pissing himself than interest.

A scarlet blush rose from beneath the soldier's collar, and raced across his face and into his hairline.

"There was this girl," he said, and then a sad look of resignation gradually tempered the flood of color. Sebastiaan did not care enough about the young soldier's mooncalf notions to explore the matter, but the story emerged regardless of his disinterest.

"I came to the Cape as a sailmaker, but then I met Paulina. She is beautiful." His voice trailed off, and his eyes glazed over as he lost himself in his imaginings. "Her eyes–,"

And there it is, Sebastiaan thought caustically. "Yes, yes," he interrupted the all-too-predictable lament. "Eyes that rivaled the stars, lips as sweet as honey, dewy-fresh, rose-petal-soft skin and a body that could set a saint on fire." Sebastiaan's voice rattled with the repetitive tone of an anatomist listing the anomalies in a cadaver.

The boy stared at him in defeated wonder.

"So, you know her then?"

By the lovestruck mug's doused expression Sebastiaan got the feeling the lad had often found himself facing unwanted competition where Paulina was concerned. He released a heavy sigh and shook his head.

"No, I don't," he said curtly.

Several emotions, none of them good, warred for control of the boy's features. In the end suspicion won out, but Sebastiaan ignored it and tossed the bonds aside. He hoped his former captive would celebrate freedom and forego the rest of the story, but his wish died quickly.

"In any event," the young soldier continued. "She is an innocent and in need of guidance and protection. I can't do any of that if I'm away at sea and so I enlisted to serve in the guard at the settlement to be close to her."

"And yet, not two seconds ago, you were angling for a position as a sailmaker again. Did your love and devotion drown between here and the Cape?"

"No," he said, and looked like he was fighting to hold back tears. "She doesn't want me; never did. She chose another, my friend, over me," the boy replied, and then lowered his eyes to stare at his bound wrists.

"I see," Sebastiaan murmured with deep understanding, feeling almost sorry for him. "Women have a way of complicating matters and infiltrating wise decisions. Be that as it may, you gravely overestimate my authority on this sieve. Much as I see the merit of your expertise, I have no power over the direction of your future." Sebastiaan had no desire to offer advice or console the jilted idiot. "Now," he said, hardening his voice. "I presume you will behave yourself civilly if I untie your hands?"

"I vow it." The lad's eyes snapped to Sebastiaan's and his words shook with the vigorous nodding of his head. Sebastiaan untied his wrists and pointed to the open door as he took a precautionary step backward.

"Run along now," he prodded when the boy hesitated. "Find Captain Orion. Plead your case and pray he is in a peaceable mood." Sebastiaan resisted the urge to kick the young soldier under his bottom as he rushed past him and out the cabin that had served as his cell, and most likely saved his life, during the battle.

"Avast!" a harsh voice rang out from the passageway, and the soldier's footsteps stuttered to a halt.

"Not so fast, poppet. Where do you think you're going?" The unmistakable voice lowered ominously, and it drew a warm smile from Sebastiaan. Nearly two decades had passed since the last time he'd heard the familiar timbre of his uncle's voice. He burned to rush from the cabin but held himself in check, waiting for the minor crisis in the hallway to play itself out.

"Sir," the soldier pleaded. "I am unarmed and swear on my mother's life that I mean you no harm. I was sent to find the captain."

The soldier's sincere words elicited a hearty laughter from De Coninck. "Boy, I doubt you could harm a week-old corpse were you armed to the teeth and screaming like a Viking."

A loud slap and a sharp yelp followed the observation as the flat of De Coninck's cutlass blade landed on the boy's passing backside.

Davit De Coninck waited for the soldier to leap into the sunlight of the upper deck and then turned to survey the mess before him. He counted twelve dead bodies neatly lined up against the wall of the passageway, creating a death alley for anyone following in their wake. Blood slickened the floor, and he carefully stepped over the thickest pools.

"Sebastiaan!" De Coninck hollered and his heart leaped as his nephew emerged from one of the stern cabins.

He sheathed his blade just in time to slam his arms around Sebastiaan's shoulders. They collided with enough force to drive the breath from their lungs. There was not a scrap of softness in the body in his arms. Sebastiaan somehow felt taller and larger than he remembered and smelled of fresh sweat, ocean air and dried blood. De Coninck's shirt stretched as Sebastiaan fisted the fabric at his back, gathering it tightly. He realized he was doing the same, laughed and gripped his nephew harder.

They stood for a long while simply holding each other, wordlessly allowing their souls to reconnect, grateful for the privilege. Then De Coninck slowly released Sebastiaan. He took hold of his shoulders and held him at arm's length for a thorough assessment. They regarded each other with watery eyes and trembling smiles.

Years of hard living had left their mark on his nephew's face, but had not weathered him. Instead, he seemed to wear the alteration with a quiet elegance that spoke of a tempered and purified character, of indomitable integrity and ruthless confidence. His body was honed like a seasoned warrior. The brute force of his youth had been wrought into a quiet strength that shone from his eyes.

De Coninck fought to keep the surge of emotion, building like a storm in his chest from breaking loose and turning him into a snottering old woman. There were a million questions he needed to ask, but one pushed to the surface.

"Are you done?" They both knew what he was referring to, and no further explanation was needed, but the answer surprised him all the same.

"Almost," Sebastiaan said and pulled his uncle back into his arms. "God, it's good to see you," he spoke into his hair. The hug was short and fierce, ending with them pounding each other on the back.

"Are you well?" Sebastiaan asked. Age had settled around De Coninck like a fur cloak, yet the light in his eyes and the strength in his body belied his years. He was still lean and muscular, a testament to a life of discipline and an aversion to idleness. His blond hair, that once had shone like spun gold at high noon, was now shot through with silver. The lines on his face told of a life well-lived, but concern and hints of sadness had left their own marks – emotions Sebastiaan knew he was responsible for. He could read an amalgamation of wisdom, mischief, and longing in his uncle's eyes.

"I would be better if I knew what in the name of Hades transpired here," De Coninck said, clearing his throat and looking at the bodies against the wall.

"Sebastiaan," Orion called from the top of the stairs. There was an edge to his voice and a look in his eyes that sent a chill down Sebastiaan's spine. De Coninck must have noticed it too, for he tensed visibly. Their conversation was immediately suspended.

"Thank God you are alright." Orion leaned forward and peered into the dimly lit corridor. "*Are* you alright?" he asked, ignoring the dead bodies and focusing on the bloodstain at Sebastiaan's side.

"Just a scratch. What is the matter?" Sebastiaan dismissed his worry.

De Coninck followed the path of Orion's concern, then frowned at the newly discovered wound.

"You are needed on deck." Orion couldn't look him in the eye. Instead, he winced and stared at his feet.

"I can't leave Davit," Sebastiaan said.

"I'll find someone to sit with him, but you need to come with me," Orion persisted.

De Coninck looked from Orion to Sebastiaan. "Who is Davit and why does he need constant minding?"

Sebastiaan stared at his uncle, momentarily at a loss for words. It was not a quick explanation, albeit a simple one.

"He is my son. He was shot five days ago and developed a fever, but I will explain everything later."

De Coninck noted the shadows of despair as they passed over Sebastiaan's face. There was a tale here, and one he was most eager to hear, but he would bide his time. "Point me to his cabin and I will stay with him," he offered. "Orion, please ask Frans to send our surgeon to me at once." They were all powerful men in their own right, yet an unspoken, primal hierarchy obliged them to obey De Coninck without question.

Walking down the quiet passageway, De Coninck studied the corpses. Sebastiaan had always possessed a talent for violence, but the lethal efficiency with which these men had been dispatched was a source of both disturbing pride and rising concern. The latter was deftly suffocated before it could take another breath of fresh reasoning. He would have done the same, and far worse, to protect those he loved.

Sebastiaan and Orion emerged onto the *Sword's* upper deck. What was, by any measure, a beautiful day had matured into a breathtaking evening. A gentle dry breeze from the continent brushed the ocean, perfuming the air with notes of sweet grasses and rich soil. The water had turned a deep shade of indigo as the last of the sun's rays set the sky ablaze before dipping beneath a horizon of molten gold.

However, Sebastiaan missed the day's grand finale. Instead, his strides faded to a halt. Orion and a mountain of a man were locked in a brief exchange, but Sebastiaan ignored it. His attention was captured by the sight before him. The *Danielle* was lying like a sentinel at the *Sword of Orion's* starboard side. Several gangplanks extended between the two vessels, prohibiting them from touching but also stabilizing the wounded *Sword*. The *Danielle* was as beautiful as he remembered. Though signs of long journeys and hard work showed everywhere in delicate blemishes, the rigging was in perfect condition, as was the paint on her hull, hiding the dents and scrapes that came with countless voyages. Barnacle buildup suggested that if she had visited her home in Batavia, it was only for a brief layover before she was put to sail again.

Years ago, Sebastiaan had commissioned the sixteen-foot, twenty-ton cannon in her hull. It had required a special gunport and a custom pulley-and-crank system to maneuver it into place. The large black cannon was now safely lowered again into the hull, hidden from view.

Sebastiaan let his eyes drift over the name painted on the side. An old ache flared, kicking hard against his ribs. Where there had once been only the faintest glimmer of hope, there was now a growing certainty. *I will find you*, he vowed silently.

"Uncle." Orion's urgent words pulled him from his thoughts. "This way, please."

"Yes, of course," Sebastiaan said and followed Orion.

Small mounds of canvas-wrapped bodies painted a morbid picture as they lay scattered across the deck. The deck was stained with the evidence of the harsh battle. Here and there, men were sluicing the planks with buckets of seawater.

"Where's John?" he asked. Orion didn't answer and started up the ladder leading to the bow. Sebastiaan gave the decks a quick scan, but did not see his friend. If John was not on deck, he was below, helping Niccolò patch the hull. The *Sword* was leaking badly and the carpenter would need all the help he could get to keep them afloat.

The evening air was rapidly cooling, and the breeze tugged at his shirt. Up here the dead were still uncovered, showing that the clean-up had only just begun and had not reached this far yet. Most were lying on their sides and backs. Sebastiaan didn't recognize any of them and he released a long pent-up sigh. Orion crouched near the starboard railing, alongside Miro, Niccolò, and a sailor whose name he did not remember. The tiny hairs on his neck pricked in warning and he deliberately slowed his step. They were crowding around a body and when Orion twisted sideways, Sebastiaan turned cold from the crown of his head to the soles of his feet.

John lay on his back, a saber in each fist, his clothes splattered with blood. Sebastiaan stepped closer and then sank to his knees. A chilling stillness enveloped Van Leyen, one that did not belong to the living. Driven by slivers of hope and denial, Sebastiaan extended his hand. There was a light tremor to his fingers as he pressed them against his friend's neck, searching for a heartbeat he knew he would not find. The perfect round hole between Van Leyen's eyes ruled the verdict supreme and yet, beneath his touch, the faintest warmth still lingered.

Sebastiaan stared at the face he'd seen every day for nearly two decades and a surge of unreasonable anger welled inside him. *Your fucking bullet finally found him.* The thought thundered through his mind as he remembered the old injustice against Van Leyen when Jan Van Riebeeck had ordered his execution by musket shot. The governor had, at the last moment, changed his mind and ordered the shot to pass over his head instead. Sebastiaan bit down on his teeth and clenched his fists until his jaw ached and his nails dug into the palms of his hands. This had nothing to do with Van Riebeeck, but his rational mind was slow to douse the fire of resentment. He knew that once the anger faded, the impact of John's death would rip his heart apart. There was not a single memory for nearly half of his life that did not include John.

They had fought countless battles side by side, lived through each other's deepest fears and highest hopes, forging an unbreakable bond. John had been unwavering in his belief that Danielle was still alive, and at times when Sebastiaan had given up hope, it was his friend who'd pushed him on.

John's eyes were closed as if shielding him in a deep, peaceful sleep. He looked to be lost in a glorious dream, as the corners of his mouth were tilted in a soft, private smile – the kind reserved only for one's wife. Sebastiaan did not fight the soundless tears that trickled down his face, nor did he bother to compose himself as his shoulders shook under the weight of his loss. He did not see the other men leave with bowed heads and heavy strides, and he did not feel Orion's hand on his shoulder.

John Van Leyen's death was quick and merciful and, above all, without suffering. There was peace to be found in the knowledge. Sebastiaan had lived long enough to know how ugly and cruel death could be.

"Heavenly Father, please accept his soul. He was too good for this world,"

Sebastiaan prayed softly as he laid his hand over his friend's still heart.

Orion stayed at Sebastiaan's side. His own face wet with tears he did not understand. This was a day of extremes, and his emotions were badly out of sorts.

"Find peace, my brother," Sebastiaan said at last, then leaned forward and placed a kiss above the mortal wound on John's forehead. He slowly pushed to his feet. The sun had set, and the evening descended in a dull haze. Sebastiaan needed to retreat to a quiet place where he could be alone with his thoughts and memories, but it was not to be. There was too much to do, and he knew his own company was perhaps the worst thing he could wish for. He didn't realize how heavily he'd come to rely on John's counsel. It was in moments like these that his calm presence had soothed the world, like a steady hand settling an upset glass. Now, there was just the emptiness of his absence.

"I am sorry for your loss," Orion said. "He was the only one up here. I saw him right before I followed Du Bois into the stateroom. He was fighting like a lion."

Sebastiaan looked at the bodies scattered across the deck.

"Where's Du Bois?" he asked.

"In my cabin – dead," Orion said and held Sebastiaan's stare, feeling the strength from deep within himself pushing to the surface. "He died by my hand, and far too quickly," he finished in a low but finite voice.

Sebastiaan's nerves were frayed and perhaps it made him see things he normally would not. Orion was nearing his third decade, battle-hardened, blatantly arrogant and deadly intelligent, but beneath all that lurked the innocent child who'd grown up under Arent and De Coninck's wings. There was still a golden nugget of goodness in his heart, although he was determined to bury it under a heavy strata of indifference and irreverence. Orion's dark brutality when facing an enemy was perfectly balanced by his loyalty to those close to him. But killing one's father, righteousness aside, was an act that had the power to reach deep enough to shatter that something that used to be untouched by the ugliness of the world. Looking at Orion now, Sebastiaan could almost hear that small child scream in the face of such a reality and it twisted his heart.

"I am sorry for your loss, too," he said after a while.

"There was none."

"I don't mean Alain Du Bois. I will not pass judgment on his soul, for that is a sin in itself. But what you've done has taken a bit of yours."

Orion shook his head and tightened his lips as he stared beyond the decks and into the oncoming darkness.

"Alain Du Bois had whored upon this earth for far too long. He was eminently devious and had spread misery with every step he took. His life was marked by corruption and evil deeds. He will not be missed."

Orion bit out the last of his declaration in clipped words, his loathing clearly conveyed by the curl of his upper lip and the cold, flatness in his eyes. He wanted this day over and dealt with. It had brought too much loss and destruction. Sailors were superstitious by nature and entering the night with so many dead uncared for was not to be done.

"I want them all buried before nightfall," Orion said, choosing practical matters over dissecting his confused emotions.

A group of men led by Niccolò was heading to the bow with bundles of canvas in their arms.

"John will not be buried at sea," Sebastiaan said, and took a protective step closer to where his friend's body lay.

"He will not keep even in this mild weather," Orion protested. Burial at sea was not something anybody wanted. Spending eternity in the very waters they fought to avoid with no marker to stake one's final claim was a cruel end, and he could well understand Sebastiaan's apprehension.

"I will not commit him to the ocean." Sebastiaan's words held an edge that brooked no argument. "He will be buried on land at a place of my choosing. And that is final." A dangerous light had lit in his normally warm eyes. His sorrow at Van Leyen's loss was masking itself as anger and it was hammering at his control.

"Then we will double wrap him and transfer him to the *Danielle*," Orion yielded.

"I will take care of John," Sebastiaan said as Niccolò unfolded a large piece of canvas. "And when I'm done here, I will do the same for Du Bois. He will have a proper Christian burial along with all the others."

"He does not deserve one," Orion said.

"Nonetheless, what we do here this evening will not reflect on him but on us. Now, go find the surgeon to tend to your arm," Sebastiaan ordered.

"My arm?" Orion asked, his face wrinkled in perplexity as he looked down at his left arm. Sebastiaan waited patiently for Orion to remember that he had another. There was a laceration across his right arm just below the shoulder joint.

The cut was deep and needed cleaning and most likely stitches, but Orion would rather scrub the decks with his fingernails than let someone stick a needle in his skin. "You will need help here," Orion protested, trying to delay his impending treatment.

"No," Sebastiaan countered with a sad smile and gently shook his head. "I need a few moments alone with him."

Chapter 22

15 November 1671

The *Danielle* leaned into the breeze as her navigator wrung every droplet of wind from the air, pushing her toward the mysterious inlet Orion had described. Sebastiaan was standing on the bow, relishing the feel of the breeze brushing against the small triangle of exposed skin on his chest where his linen shirt fell open. By society's standards, he was only half dressed and quite scandalous at that, with his sleeves rolled past his forearms and only a pair of fawn breeches and black leather boots to cover his modesty and preserve his dignity. He scoffed at the petty notions of propriety and loathed the idea of joining civilization again. All the pomp and fuss that came with his status, bought with wealth he had not lifted a finger to create, keep or expand, vexed him.

His mind was in a tumult of conflicting thoughts. So, he had sought the isolation of the bow, as he'd done in his youth, to find clarity. With every passing second, Davit slipped deeper into unconsciousness, inching ever closer to death. He couldn't dream of shaping the boy's future if he failed to save his life. Yet that future weighed heavily. As sole heir to the De Vries fortune Davit would need to live among his own people, learn the rules of society and one day find a wife among them. Letting him run wild across Africa, half-tamed, would not serve that end. Nor could Sebastiaan imagine leaving Africa without Danielle.

Torn between the two worlds, he turned his attention to the activity on deck. Shouts drifted from the chief mate to the men in the shrouds and back. The rigging creaked as the sails shifted, and he felt a surge of speed when the ship obeyed the command of the small adjustment.

Sebastiaan had been awake for nearly thirty-six hours, with one day seamlessly bleeding into the next, and he could feel the lack of sleep tugging at the edges of his strength. His eyes were gritty, and his shoulder and back muscles ached. Three tolls from the bell on the quarterdeck marked the ninth hour of the morning, and Sebastiaan huffed a wry smile. It was precisely a week ago, almost to the hour, that he had stood on the beach of the cove, loading the wagon to take the first load of wheat to Mostert for milling. A lifetime had passed since that lazy, sunny morning. He had been imprisoned; the *Shack* had burned down, and he had lost Jiya and John. If they did not find help soon, he would lose Davit as well.

Davit had briefly opened his eyes as they'd carried him from the *Sword* to the *Danielle*; they were unfocused and glassy and then he'd slipped into a coma. Death was hovering over his son like a dark cloud. He did not know what was keeping it at bay, but the feeling that John Van Leyen had not yet left him was hard to shake.

They had departed from the *Sword of Orion* in the early hours of the morning, leaving behind enough men and supplies to sustain her. The *Danielle* would return as soon as possible to tow her into the cove where she would be beached for repairs.

Upon seeing Davit's condition, Orion had willingly parted with Harja in exchange for De Coninck's cook. Since leaving the *Sword*, Sebastiaan and his uncle had secluded themselves in the stateroom, locked in deep conversation. Sebastiaan had recounted all that had transpired since they last saw each other. It was a difficult telling, one not even their customary glass of French brandy could soften. De Coninck had silently listened as the details of the last eighteen years were revealed in startling detail. Sebastiaan had left nothing unsaid, and by the end, they were both exhausted. De Coninck had left to check on Davit and Sebastiaan had climbed the ladder to the bow.

Sebastiaan sensed his uncle's presence before he saw him. De Coninck joined him at the railing, and together they stood in silence, each lost in thought as they stared at the approaching coastline.

The land ended abruptly, as if a part of it was torn away like the other half of a loaf of bread, leaving sheer, black cliffs plummeting over a hundred feet to the ocean below. Lush, vibrant green vegetation blanketed the plateau, stretching as far as the eye could see. Sebastiaan surveyed the area carefully, yet he could not spot the entrance to the inlet. Nonetheless, he placed his trust in Orion's coordinates, surrendering his doubts to the hope that it was simply hidden among the dark crags. There was something vaguely familiar about the landscape. If he could venture a guess, he would estimate they were about an hour's ride on horseback, southwest from where he'd killed Du Bois' son earlier this year. A sharp breath left him at the thought of how close they had been to Danielle back then.

"How is he?" Sebastiaan asked, knowing his uncle had just come from Davit's cabin.

"He is still breathing." The concern in De Coninck's voice touched Sebastiaan.

"At first glance, that boy looks just like you," De Coninck said without looking at Sebastiaan. "There are hints of his mother, and if I stare long enough, I swear I can see your father in his features too." He shook his head in bewilderment. "But it is not possible."

"I think we see what we wish was there. The color of his hair plays a neat trick. But I can see only his mother, with occasional glimpses of Orion," Sebastiaan remarked. A melancholy smile touched his lips as he recalled the two of them walking toward him, carefree and full of life. "They look like cousins, same aristocratic noses and indomitable arrogance." He spoke the last with a gentleness that took the sting from the words.

"Who would have imagined that both my grandsons would carry Du Bois' blood?" De Coninck exhaled heavily, his chin dropping to his chest as he shook his head in mock defeat. The light moment evaporated as he locked eyes with Sebastiaan in an uncompromising stare.

"Do you love this boy?" he asked.

"Like he is my own," Sebastiaan replied without hesitation.

"And are you going to tell him the truth of his paternity?"

Sebastiaan winced and turned his back on the lively water to lean against the railing.

"The truth would break his heart," he confessed. "But I cannot live with such a lie." He gnawed at the inside of his cheek as he thought on how to proceed. This was a fear that had lurked in the back of his mind since that night he'd first met Davit in the tavern. "It makes no difference to me who fathered him."

"I know what it means to raise another's child and to love him as your own. It is a profound and unexpected gift," De Coninck said with a contemplative nod.

"Thank you," Sebastiaan's voice was rough as he spoke around the knot in his throat. "But you and I always had the truth between us. We chose each other. With Davit, I fear the truth might drive him away."

De Coninck pondered the situation, turning it over in his mind for a long while. "Time will tell. You must grant him the opportunity to choose for himself. It will not work any other way. And if he decides to walk away, you must let him, but *never* stop fighting to bring him back. However, that is not your most immediate problem," he added.

"What then?" Sebastiaan's expression darkened as he glanced sharply at his uncle, the cryptic remark still hanging between them.

"Sebastiaan," De Coninck started. Time had not eroded the bond they shared, and Sebastiaan was deeply grateful for it, but he sensed the shift in the conversation would not be to his liking. "She might not–"

"She will be," he interrupted. He was not in a mood to tolerate negative postulates.

There was a steel in Sebastiaan's voice De Coninck had heard countless times before, and he wisely held back the rest of his worry until he could formulate a diplomatic warning. However, Sebastiaan spoke before he could find the right words.

"For years, I have fought against injustice, driven by vengeance and anger. Even during these few months at the Cape, I've tried to correct the wrongs inflicted upon the innocent and the powerless." The words were slow and measured. "I believed it was what I wanted." He met his uncle's wintry gaze, searching for the light of understanding. "I sought to define myself. There was a perverse pride in combating injustice, particularly when the cause was bolstered by brute force and unlimited wealth. But it was an empty, blood-soaked existence – one I do not wish to pass to my child." He fell silent as he re-evaluated the events of the past, studying each thread of the complex tapestry. His uncle made no attempt to fill the void. "It was not until Davit's arrival that I realized my folly. He brought clarity, stripped away the notions I held dear for so long. All I had accomplished seemed insignificant compared to the pride I felt as a father."

De Coninck did not respond, but instead, his face softened into a gentle, knowing smile. He could sense a quietude beginning to settle in Sebastiaan, one he hoped with all his heart was genuine and not just a figment of his imagination. Perhaps the boy was enough. If – God forbid – Danielle was no longer with the tribe, or lost to him through death, perhaps her son could be enough to calm the storm that had raged inside his nephew for so long.

"I am done fighting for others," Sebastiaan declared, shaking his head, oblivious to the fears and hopes swirling behind his uncle's composed expression. "From now on, I fight for my family and for myself. I don't regret my past; my only regret is the worry I have caused you." He looked at his uncle, but there was no scorn or reprimand in his eyes. Yet, he felt the need to explain; to purge himself. "If I hadn't walked this path, I never would have found Davit. I would never have come this close to finding Danielle."

"There are no guarantees, Sebastiaan," De Coninck could no longer hold his tongue against the warning he must speak. "Eighteen years is a long time. She believed you died. What if she …" *is dead*, he wanted to say.

"What if she …?" Sebastiaan prodded.

"She could be dead," De Coninck said, softening his voice as much as he could. He knew how violently Sebastiaan had reacted to such a possibility in the past, and no matter how much time had passed since, he doubted that instinct had changed.

By all appearances, Sebastiaan had become the man De Coninck had always prayed he would be. He just hoped the years had not quieted the heart of the young lion he once was. It would be a crying shame to dim that brilliant spirit. All he had to do was scratch at the carefully manufactured polished veneer and remind his nephew who he was. True maturity, after all, lies in harmonizing the vitality of youth with the wisdom of age, without sacrificing one for the other.

De Coninck's words hit the bull's eye of their intended mark. Instantly, a fire lit in Sebastiaan's eyes. His nostrils flared and his mouth thinned, but he kept a firm hold on his temper and his uncle suppressed a satisfied smile.

"She's not dead." The sharp, unyielding tone betrayed the effort with which he was controlling himself. "She is out there." Sebastiaan made the simple statement sound like a threat and De Coninck found himself hoping for Danielle's sake that she was, as he followed Sebastiaan's outstretched finger stabbing the air between them and the growing continent. This sudden display of defiance was a welcome sight indeed, but perhaps a small nudge would solidify it.

"She might reject you," De Coninck said, knowing he was rushing in where others feared to tread. "If she'd survived all this time in the African wilderness, I cannot imagine that she would be any less willful than she was all those years ago. Women like that don't change into the opposite."

Even though Sebastiaan could hear the echoes of Van Leyen's words, his temper broke free from its moorings.

"Reject me!" The first word exploded from him; the second dropped to a fierce whisper as he glanced over the deck to see if there were any other witnesses to his outburst.

"I will not stand for it," he said with finality. "The woman is stubborn, not stupid." Too late did he see the mischievous glint in his uncle's eyes and he violently cursed under his breath, knowing De Coninck was baiting him on purpose, preparing him for what lay ahead.

"You are very sure of yourself," De Coninck said, his words dripping with satisfaction.

"No, uncle. I'm scared out of my mind. But it is a risk I must take."

"You know, all of this started with a stowaway on my ship. One I was not particularly fond of," De Coninck admitted, thinking back to when they'd first discovered Danielle hiding on his ship, running from Du Bois.

"And now?" Sebastiaan asked.

"After your mother died, your father lost his grip on this world. He never found it again. I feared the same for you." He gave Sebastiaan a meaningful look. "If she brings you peace, I will kiss her feet."

***

The sound of children's laughter drew Danielle from a short but deep sleep. The fur-covered straw of her sleeping pallet crunched as she sat up groggily. Craning her neck, she looked beyond the opening of her cave to judge how far the day was gone. The sun was already well above the horizon and she fought the pull of her bed. There was too much to do. The tribe was leaving today. They had been preparing for the past two weeks for their annual trek up the east coast, where the summer grazing was better. They alternated between the two locations, staying as long as there were adequate grasses to support their livestock. When that began to dwindle, they would return, giving the land time to recover.

The summer location was pleasant enough, but it was nearly a two-week walk. They had to skirt the ancient forest that lay between them and their destination. The forest was beautiful but treacherous, known for its disorienting, dense vegetation and roaming elephants. Before she'd come to live with the tribe, they had made their way westward to the Cape to trade with other tribes, but they no longer did that. Keeping Danielle safe from the European settlement had permanently altered their way of life.

Of the two sites, this one was her favorite. Here she had her cave, and it felt like home, solid and safe. This was where Davit was born. Thoughts of her son were never far from her mind and her heart, and were always accompanied by a dull pain. Pushing the ache aside, she focused on everything she needed to pack. There would be no time to visit her small herb garden near the inlet today, but there was no need. She'd been there the day before on her way to the cliffs. Most of the healing herbs she needed grew in the soil between the saltwater of the lagoon and the freshwater of the river. After Davit left, she'd started a small garden there, cultivating some of the rarer plants. The garden was her way of binding their hearts together, nurturing life in the place where he had played as a boy and the last place his feet had touched before he'd left to start his new life.

To her bitter annoyance, her shrine was often destroyed by rabbits and other furry opportunists drawn to the luxury of the abundance created by the sweat of her brow. Even the low-growing thorny shrubs she'd planted as a hedge had not kept nature's little poachers away.

Kai found her efforts amusing and showed no sympathy for her plight. "Keep feeding the rabbits, Little Flower," he'd teased. "They taste all the better for it."

"Yes, well, we'll see how much good tasty rabbit does you when you are sick and in need of those herbs," she'd shot back, but he'd only laughed. She was a strange woman in his eyes, but one he valued above all.

After rolling her furs into a tight bundle and securing it with a plaited length of twine, she dropped it near the collection of leather pouches and bags by the entrance. The young boys would soon come to gather her belongings and secure them on the back of her ox. She straightened and worked the kinks from her back. Spending the night on the edge of the cliff with the cool wind at her back had stiffened her muscles. She usually went there on the first moon of summer, lighting a fire to mark what she had calculated as early November – the date Sebastiaan had perished at sea nearly twenty years ago. She would spend the night imagining him sitting by her side, talking through the dark hours until the first light of dawn. However, the constant rain of the last two weeks had forced her to delay her requiem for practical reasons.

Standing in the middle of her normally cluttered cave, now empty and lifeless, she stared at the neatly stacked clay pots and woven baskets against the back wall, chewing her bottom lip and wondering if she should take a couple of pots as well. They were hardened over many fires and making new ones was a painfully tedious process. In the end, she abandoned the idea. Kai was already complaining that each year her bundle grew larger, and she did not want to provide fodder for his grumbling.

Their small peaceful village was anything but this morning, with everyone scurrying about to ready themselves and their families for the journey. Her task was much lighter than the other women's since she didn't have a husband and small children to contend with. Looking about, she spotted Maheena. Her friend was standing by the entrance to her large round hut, leather pouches and rolled bundles scattered around her. Danielle shouted a greeting and pointed to the river. The other woman acknowledged her message and Danielle quietly slipped away.

There was a bend in the river, surrounded by dense shrubs, where she regularly went to take her bath and wash her hair. The tribe did not subscribe to her cleansing routine, as they believed that washing the thick layer of animal fat from their skins would hurry their deaths. In the beginning, they had feverishly tried to rid her of her suicidal tendencies.

Reaching the secluded spot, she untied the leather strips of her covering, letting it fall to the ground. On impulse, she slipped the small pouch of casting bones from around her neck, and poured its contents into her hand. How strange her life was, she thought as she stared at the yellow bones. Yet, she would not wish it any other way. Living with the tribe had brought clarity she would not have found otherwise. It had given her time and space to make peace with the loss of her father and Sebastiaan – to some extent, at least. The memories of her father were still vivid, but time had washed them of the violence and bitterness surrounding his death. She was free to remember him with a quiet smile, and to call on him for guidance when she treated the sick. Sebastiaan was a different matter altogether. Although she had made peace with his loss, the wound did not seem capable of healing permanently. Every now and then, she would remember something that cut into her heart, leaving another scar. There were days when she'd isolated herself from everyone, when the pain was simply too much and she felt weak and in no shape to care for anyone, least of all herself. The tribe had sheltered her during those moments, never judging or interfering, just quietly allowing her to fall apart and eventually put herself back together again.

They had become her family. It was a place where her strengths were celebrated to the point of exploitation, and her impatience, short temper, and inability to accept any form of authority were accepted and tolerated through mockery and teasing. However, Kai was less forgiving of her flaws and often asserted his dominance through high-handed and overbearing means, publicly forcing her to bend to his will. In private, he would allow her to challenge him, though he rarely understood her perspectives or motivations, attributing her complexities to the differences between them.

She often challenged and baited him to consider broader ideas. Her father had raised her to question everything from the sacred teachings of religion to the fundamentals of politics and philosophy. There were, however, topics that she could not move Kai on. For instance, once she questioned the role of the women in the tribe, arguing and campaigning for them to have more freedom, especially when airing their grievances and opinions. He had argued that women did not have grievances or opinions, and that they were merely at the mercy of their emotions. To her mind, men were equally, if not more, victims of their emotions, especially when taking to violence. He'd promptly dismissed that notion, informing her that anger is not an emotion but a weapon, and therefore, it could not possibly rule them.

He had taken instant offense at her suggestion that the women were treated with anything less than reverence. Thinking of the men's domineering and often dismissive attitudes, she found his bruised feelings to be of little value.

"Everything we do, we do for our women," he'd argued. "Don't you understand that?" She had shaken her head quietly. "We don't need the large herd of cattle and sheep," he'd explained. "We can hunt for our food when we feel the need, but the women can't. They can't run for days tracking the antelope like we can, and so they will starve without the herd. We don't need any shelter as we can sleep under the stars at night and work in the sun day after day. We build our huts for the comfort and safety of our women. A woman cannot have a child without a man making it so.

Without children there would be no tribe, nobody to care for them when they are old, nobody to protect them and help them through life." It was a very one-sided view of society, and she was about to challenge that when he continued.

"Just look at you," he'd said, pointing a calloused finger in her direction.

"What about me?" she had asked defensively. The tribe revered her healing skills, and she thought this had secured her place among his people.

"You live in a cave," he'd said.

"I like my cave."

"Yes, but if you had a husband, he would have built you a hut. Now you have to rely on the gods to give you shelter and when we move to the summer fields that task falls to me. I have to build two huts, one for my wife and another for you." She had gasped sharply at that unwelcome bit of truth.

"Well," she'd snapped. "I am sorry to be such a burden." He'd stared at her, his face warped with perplexity. It was clear he could not understand her flare of irritation. The need to slap the confused look from his face was overwhelming, but she'd suppressed the urge with an ungodly amount of self-control.

"Who said anything about being a burden? I am trying to explain how important you are to us."

"You made it sound like it is a hardship, raising my hut. Like I was a nuisance and an inconvenience," she'd fired back. He had looked at her as if she had freshly lost her mind. His explanation and her understanding were obviously too far removed from each other and, as a response, he'd thrown his hands in the air in helpless surrender.

"Woman, did I say those words?"

"No," she'd said, vigorously snuffing the sparks of self-awareness about her own silliness.

"Then where did you get them from?"

But she was not ready to let the matter go so easily.

"Did you do the same for Koba?"

"Of course."

"Did you complain?"

"No! I didn't complain then, and I am not complaining now!" Slamming his mouth shut, he abruptly ended his shouting and advanced on her with narrowed eyes. "Do you know you are the first woman I have ever gotten angry with?" Even though he was still seething and his lips were tight as he snarled at her, she knew he would not do her physical violence. It was not their way.

"Hmm-hm," she purred, enjoying his frustration. "But anger is not an emotion?"

"How is that you always find a way to end a conversation at the exact same place where it started?" He had not waited for an answer and had stalked from her cave, refusing to speak to her for an entire week.

She shook her head at the memory. Life with the tribe was a soulful but simple experience, one where inference, sarcasm and conflicting ideas did not exist. If something couldn't be touched, seen, smelled, or heard, they considered it the business of the gods and therefore beyond their concern. Sometimes she craved the complexity of her culture and even though she had a place here, the simplicity made her feel like an observer.

She usually took her bath quickly and efficiently. There was always a chore that needed doing or someone with some ache or complaint to tend or listen to. Today she lingered. There would be no visitors and once they left, there would not be another opportunity to indulge in such idleness. Stepping into the cool water of the river until it reached her chest, she lifted her feet and tilted her head back, allowing herself to float lazily on her back, enjoying the feel of the sunlight on her skin. What she would not give for a cake of rose scented soap.

***

They had reached the inlet in two small rowboats, leaving the *Danielle*, with most of her crew, anchored a safe distance from the shattering cliffs but close enough for an easy row into the lagoon. Each skiff carried six men, with Sebastiaan commanding one and De Coninck the other.

The waters of the lagoon were a calm, clear blue as they reflected the empty sky above. The air was heavy with the smell of damp soil. Every now and again, bird calls pierced the constant high-pitched insect chorus. They rowed past a large island in the middle of the lagoon, their presence temporarily silencing the small critters as they took note of the strange intruders. The rowers moved as if locked in a race, sweat streaming down their faces and bare upper bodies.

Davit was lying on a wooden board supported by the skiff's horizontal benches. A thin sheet covered his fever-racked body from head to toe. Sebastiaan wished he could pull the sheet from Davit's face; lying covered like that made him look like a corpse, and the sight made him feel sick. The men knew they were racing against time; every passing minute was a minute closer to the boy's end. Sebastiaan could read their thoughts plainly enough in their eyes. These were not green lads, they knew what it looked like when death was close. He could not afford any doubts or distractions. Gripping the oar tightly, he rowed with renewed strength, calling the beat for the others to follow. The skiff skimmed over the calm water, its bow parting it into a large smooth V-shaped wake that rippled outward in soft waves. They were rowing at a bruising pace, their perfectly attuned rhythm reflecting in a single splash as six oars touched the water at precisely the same moment.

Following close behind them was the second craft carrying John Van Leyen's body, with De Coninck at the helm. Sebastiaan could hear his uncle's voice, commanding his crew to adjust their pace to keep up with the leading boat. The scene was a study in contradiction: the perfectly calm lagoon and peaceful morning against the two speeding rowboats.

What had initially appeared as a mere crescent of sand, much like the tip of a nail at the end of a thumb, was now rapidly growing into a beautiful white beach surrounded by thick shrubs and tall trees. When they were a few yards from the beach Sebastiaan called for the rowers to lift and stow their oars. As one, they leaped over the side and guided the boat at a near run onto the dry sand. In silent unison, they smoothly lifted Davit's wooden stretcher, and carried it into the cool shade of a nearby tree, their movements careful to avoid jostling their fragile charge. Lowering him gently onto the sand, the men lingered, waiting for further instructions.

Sebastiaan stared back at them, his mind wrestling with indecision. The need to search for Danielle was pulling against the duty he felt toward Van Leyen.

"Go find her." His uncle's voice unexpectedly sounded from behind him. De Coninck's men were already moving Van Leyen's body to a separate shaded area, away from where Davit lay, as if they feared the corpse's condition would somehow transfer to Davit.

"Here," De Coninck said. He handed Sebastiaan two sabers tightly wrapped in their scabbards. Sebastiaan stared at the blades, then slowly reached out to take them, stroking the straps that wrapped in neat crisscross patterns. The leather was soft, a testament to years of wearing, darker in places where it had absorbed the sweat from Van Leyen's chest.

"If they were mine, I wouldn't want them rusting away in the ground," his uncle said.

"I need to bury John first," Sebastiaan sounded as strangled as he felt. Davit was running out of time, but John deserved this last respect.

"I will see to your friend." De Coninck placed a heavy, comforting hand on Sebastiaan's shoulder. "I owe him much for what he's done for you. Let me bury him. Find Danielle and save your son's life. You can visit his grave when you return."

"Thank you, uncle."

Sebastiaan strapped the sabers to his back. It was a small token, but it felt good to have something of John with him, and then his focus sharpened on the surrounding terrain. A narrow but strong-flowing river fed the lagoon. Logic suggested the tribe would have settled near a water source.

"They cannot be far," he said as his eyes followed the gleaming strip of water inland until it disappeared among the trees.

"They'd better not be," De Coninck concurred. "Go now, as I am not digging another grave."

Sebastiaan loathed the idea of leaving Davit's side, but his uncle's words had the intended effect and he left without a backward glance. He followed the river at a steady jog. In places, the soil was too muddy, and he had to veer into the surrounding thicket, losing sight of the stream but finding it again soon enough. He knew the tribe was close. There were traces of human existence everywhere; he'd seen footprints along the muddy banks, and earlier he'd passed a small, freshly tended herb garden. There were also faint traces of smoke from cooking fires in the air, and the further he ran, the stronger the scent grew.

Gauging the distance he'd traveled from the small beach was difficult since he had often had to detour around obstacles before returning to the river, but he estimated he'd been running for about a quarter of an hour. Up ahead, there was an eastward bend in the river, forming an elbow enveloped by a dense tangle of shrubs. There was no need to hug the bank here, so Sebastiaan decided to cut directly through to where the river would reemerge from the thicket. As he moved further from the water's edge, the terrain gradually became easier to navigate. Making good use of the few open spaces, he broke into a dead run, vaulting over fallen, moss-covered tree stumps and ducking beneath branches. He ran blindly until he came to a large copse of saplings. The young trees, just tall enough to obstruct his view, momentarily blocked his path, but the sound of the river cascading over boulders and swirling in eddies around obstacles, served as his guide.

Chest burning, Sebastiaan paused to orient himself, a chill prickling the nape of his neck. Instinctively, his hand snapped to the dagger hilt at his back. His senses sharpened as he searched the surroundings, but found only silence and a faint footpath, previously unnoticed, winding toward the river. Hope flared to life, but he tamped it down and moved deeper into the shadows of the young trees.

Fighting to get his breathing under control, he kept his eyes locked on the footpath, every muscle taut with anticipation. Years of living dangerously had honed his senses to a fine edge. Taking slow, deep breaths, he coaxed his racing heart into its normal rhythm. Someone was there – close by. He could almost taste it, but for now, the footpath remained empty. A sharp snap of a twig and the rustling of branches made his fist tighten around the dagger's hilt, but then came the sound of a woman's voice humming a soft, tuneless melody, and his grip eased. Taking a step backward, he flattened his body against a narrow trunk, hoping she would pass by without noticing him. If he could remain unseen and follow quietly, she would lead him to the tribe. Her voice stopped abruptly and then there was just the sound of his heart hammering in his chest.

Danielle had sat on a patch of soft grass by the river's edge, allowing the sun to dry her skin as she methodically worked the knots from her hair with a bone comb Davit had carved for her when he was a boy. She was in no rush to conclude her moment of indulgence, wanting to savor the solitude, but a persistent, niggling sense of guilt stirred her to reach for her clothing. With care, she wrapped her clean feet in thick leather socks, which she secured with leather thongs around her ankles to stop them from slipping off. Kai had ordered Maheena to fashion the leather foot coverings for her when her boots had worn out, arguing that her feet would never become as hard as theirs even if she lived to be an old woman. Now fully dressed and with her hair still wet, she made her way back to the village, her steps light and soundless, humming a gentle, made-up tune.

As she brushed aside the branches of the protective shrubs and stepped onto the footpath, a primitive instinct froze her in place. Something was not as it should be. Her breath shallowed, and her stomach knotted in alarm. She knew with absolute certainty that she was no longer alone. The footpath lay empty before her, and as she peered into the patch of young trees, she searched for any sign of movement but there was none. Only an oppressive, deafening silence surrounded her, the chorus of birdsong and insect buzz conspicuously absent.

"Maheena?" she called out in a tentative voice, thinking that perhaps her friend had come to fetch her. Swallowing, she tried to moisten her raspy throat, chastising herself for the flush of panic. "Are you there?"

From behind the tree Sebastiaan listened to the woman's voice ringing sweetly through the morning air, speaking in a language he did not understand. Thin shards of tension underscored the unfamiliar sounds. Well-hidden from the footpath, he was concealed but blind to the scene, so he moved on silent feet for a better view. Slowly parting a branch, he turned toward the sound.

The moment would carve itself indelibly into his memory. Years later, he would still vividly recall what it had felt like to die – to feel his own heart stutter to a halt, to hear his blood slosh in his veins, and his soul leave his body in a brilliant flash. How he managed to remain upright would be a question to which there would forever be no answer. All sense had fled from his mind, as he stood transfixed, staring at the woman standing at the edge of the thicket. Long dark hair cascaded down her slender back, a few wet strands fell over her shoulder, creating a large wet stain on her leather dress. Her skin glowed like mountain honey and he knew without a trace of doubt that her eyes shone like emeralds even though he was too far away to discern their color.

Danielle.

Chapter 23

Standing stock-still, Danielle's body was rigid; only her eyes darted around, searching for what had spooked her. There was nothing, just the pregnant void. Spurred by the unseen threat and the uncommon silence, she dashed down the footpath, her legs churning as fast as her leather dress's limited width would allow. It felt as if something was reaching from the shadows, trying to touch her, and she could have sworn she heard her name floating on the wind, like a whisper from a ghost. But there was no wind, not even a breeze, and the leaves hung motionless from the trees. Goosebumps erupted on her skin.

"Danielle!"

This time it was not her imagination. The voice rang clear from close by and she shrieked and skidded to a halt. Or rather, her mutinous feet ceased to obey the urgent command from her brain to keep moving, preferably a little faster than before.

"Stop. Please."

Something in the rich, deep voice made unbidden tears shoot to her eyes. The sound pierced her memory like a thousand needles, sending painful ripples over her already sensitive skin. She tried to scream again, but her mighty intentions shrank to a puff of body-warm air as her mouth gaped silently. A man materialized from the shadows and stepped onto the footpath. He was broad-shouldered and tall, with golden blond hair. She tried to blink the moisture from her eyes and then fought to remain upright — *Sebastiaan.*

No, it cannot be, she reasoned. Her mind, frayed from a long night of imagining him, was playing her the fool. The voice was too deep, too raspy. Sebastiaan had spoken in a smooth, youthful tone, and it was only her ears that twisted the notes into something vaguely familiar. At first, she'd mistaken him for Davit De Coninck, but he'd be an old man now, if not long dead. No, this was merely a man who resembled Sebastiaan, her exhaustion twisting his features to soothe the old ache in her heart.

Squinting against the bright sunlight striking her face, she studied him. His breeches and shirt were clean, and his recently shined boots were lightly coated with fresh grime from the day's demands. He did not appear lost, nor like he'd just survived a shipwreck. This left one inescapable conclusion – he was here on purpose. He knew her name. The last of her deductions fell into place like a boulder dropping from a great height. He was here for her.

"No," she breathed, the word barely a whisper, but her voice soon strengthened. He was blocking the narrow footpath. She could dart around him, but she doubted she would get very far. Best to confront him head-on and hopefully buy herself some time. Somebody from the village would soon come to look for her. All she needed to do until then was master her fear. She had not seen another European since the day she'd fled the Cape, and this one's presence did not bode well.

"Who are you? Who sent you? How did you find this place?" Not giving him time to answer any of her questions, she fired the next. "Was it Van Riebeeck? Did he send you after me?"

A look of confusion scuttled across the man's face, his brow furrowed and his eyes narrowed. He seemed to search for the correct response, and she used his pause to take several steps in retreat.

"Gods in heaven, but the bastard can hold a grudge," she mumbled quietly as she edged farther away from him. "After all these years, and he is still searching for me."

She was nearly at the edge of the shrubs by the river. To her consternation, the man was following her at a sedate pace, each of his calm and deliberate steps shrinking the distance between them. His presence felt like a slowly closing noose.

"Tell him you couldn't find me." Her words tumbled out in a frantic rush. "I am worthless to him. Tell him I died."

The clattering of her heart, the blood rushing through her veins, and the heaving of her breath were creating a symphony of chaos. She felt as though a large wave was crushing over her. The man was speaking; she could see his lips moving, but the words bled into each other and faded away as the noise drowned them out. Gasping, she fought for her next breath.

This was not Sebastiaan, she upbraided herself sharply. It was impossible. People don't rise from the dead. They had told her he was dead, with eyewitnesses to swear it. This man simply looked like him, nothing more. She stubbornly clung to the only logical explanation — that she was fast losing her mind.

"You don't have to do this," her voice trembled with her plea. Tears were streaming down her face, but as much as her weakness infuriated her, she could not stop the flow. Her worst nightmare was coming true – they had been found her. He would drag her back to the settlement and straight to the gallows, where she would hang for the murder of Elias Coopman. She had lost. The last seventeen years had been a taunt, a diversion to trick her into believing she was safe. Unknowingly, she'd been living on borrowed time, stolen moments in the governor's relentless pursuit. Her freedom was nothing but an illusion. *Oh God*, she would never see her child again. For an insane moment she wished it *was* Sebastiaan, if it were she would be safe.

Sebastiaan felt a sharp pain with every word that fell from her lips. She looked like a rabbit caught in a snare. Her eyes were large and dark with panic. The healthy golden glow had drained from her skin, leaving it ashen. It broke his heart to see her so trapped and terrified. Her mind was consumed by fear and he knew his words were falling on deaf ears, yet he kept talking to her in a gentle voice, much like Van Leyen had when soothing a skittish horse.

If she was anything like her former self, this wave of fright would soon pass, her senses would sharpen and then anger would take its rightful place on the throne over her emotions. At the moment, she was a sad sight to behold, yet still manageable. Once that magnificent temper of hers ignited, he knew he'd have his hands full. Sebastiaan found himself wishing for that hellion to surface, anything to remove the dreadful look from her face. He gained ground with each step, stealthily navigating her toward a large tree. Her pleading stopped the instant her back hit the solid trunk.

"Easy," he said, and continued to step closer. "I will not hurt you."

There was a fleeting glimmer of recognition when she'd first heard his voice, but her rising panic had quickly drowned it. Her misery was too much to bear. He reached out, cradling her face in his hands, using the pads of his thumbs to brush away some of her tears. Her response was immediate. She flinched and tried to pull her head away, her fingers closing around his wrists. He couldn't bring himself to let go and kept his hands on her face in a firm but tender hold, anchoring her to him, soothing the turmoil in both of them.

"Danielle, please," he entreated. "It's me – Sebastiaan."

She stilled. Her face relaxed into a deceptive mask of calmness, looking almost serene. Almost – had it not been for the green fire igniting in her narrowed eyes.

"It's Sebastiaan," he repeated, knowing that his name might be the only way to reach her.

"Don't you dare," she hissed through her teeth, her lips thin and hard. There was no trace of her erstwhile fear.

"Don't speak that name. That name belongs to the man who owned it and *me*." She stabbed her finger against her chest on the last word. "Let go," she demanded, trying to pry his hands from her face.

"No," he refused. She attempted to slap him, but his arms were in her way.

"This is a dirty trick, even for Van Riebeeck, sending you here with your blond hair and your green eyes and that name on your lips. What were you hoping to achieve?" Apparently, the answer for which she'd left little room did not come fast enough. "Answer me, you half-dried pile of shit!"

The more she spoke, the angrier she became. The years had not only fed her imagination, but had also honed her tongue to a fine, lethal edge. She was flinging insults at him and the settlement's former governor that broadened even his already expansive sailor's vernacular. Unfortunately, he could only understand about half of what she was saying, as the more interesting-sounding words were spoken in the tribe's language.

She was delivering the most delectable earful he'd ever received, every word a little morsel of scorn. What had seconds earlier been pleas were now transformed into stinging affronts and biting threats. He fought to suppress the laughter that threatened to reveal the rush of joy swelling inside him, barely able to wait for her to recover from her shock so he could pull her into his arms.

"Nobody sent me," he rushed, seizing the moment when she paused to catch her breath. "Van Riebeeck is not the governor at the Cape any longer. He hasn't been for ten years." He let go of her face and grabbed hold of her shoulders, giving them a light shake. Her head tilted up, and with the back of her hand, she tried to wipe the moisture from her eyes. "Nobody is looking for you. They all believe you died seventeen years ago."

Her chest was rising and falling sharply with the rush of her breathing. She was slowly gaining control of her emotions. Sebastiaan tried to pull her closer. She stiffened. He halted.

"Look at me," he urged softly. "Look into my face, into my eyes. Listen to my voice." She complied with his peremptory commands, but the haunted shadows still clung to her eyes. "Who do you see?" Giving her time to think would be a mistake, she would only drive herself to all the wrong conclusions. "Stop fighting," he whispered, when he felt her muscles tighten under his hands. "Who do you see?"

Danielle fought against the restraining hands on her arms, but the heat from his palms seeped into her numb skin calming her ragged nerves. Her mouth opened and closed as she tried to continue her protests, hopelessly clutching at the remnants of her fury, but they slipped through her fingers and slithered away. The tumult of her emotions was quieting down, allowing her some clarity of vision and hearing. His voice that earlier had sounded distant and muted was becoming clearer.

She'd always thought smell the most powerful of all the senses, capable of resurrecting the deepest memories with the slightest hint, but she had underestimated the visceral power of sound. There was a familiar timbre in his voice, and it pulled her back to a young man and woman, standing on a beach bidding their farewells. He, begging her to go with him; she, pleading with him to understand why she couldn't. Danielle closed her eyes, trying to block out the flashback, wishing he would stop speaking. Scent and sound might wield the greatest sensory power, but hope was the most dangerous of all. She shook her head against the faint voice calling from the depths of her past.

A jolt of recognition had nearly cut her in half the moment he'd stepped onto the footpath. Years had worn Sebastiaan's image thin in her mind; some details lost; others blurred. This man was older, and yet *everything* about him tugged at her memory, sharpening the old contours until they flared back to life. But it couldn't be. It was impossible – a cruel mirage.

He repeated his name, and she tried to close her ears against the soft battering of his words. Feeling once again the sun on her face, hearing the voices of the people on the beach shouting to load the ships. Van Riebeeck standing with his wife in his arms, begging her to help him.

"No," she exhaled, her throat constricting as fresh, heavy tears leaked from her closed eyes. How she wished for this to be true. Opening her eyes, she stared at the face before her. Soft, moss green eyes, filled with understanding and … uncertainty. "No, it cannot be." There was a tremor in his arms and she felt his hands shaking against her skin.

"Sebastiaan De Vries died years ago at sea," she delivered the verbal tombstone with cold finality.

She looked so fragile, Sebastiaan feared that at any moment she would shatter into a million small pieces. The denial was spoken with such deep sorrow that it summoned a bitter sob, and then, no longer able to carry the burden of her grief, her knees buckled.

Unable to keep his distance, he pulled her tightly against his chest, pushing her head to rest against his shoulder. She did not fight him, but cried with wretched, uncontrollable gasps, releasing the heartbreak that had been buried for years. The warmth of her tears seeped through his shirt, and he held her closer as he absorbed her pain. Her fingers dug into him, clutching and clawing as if she feared he would vanish.

"Shh," he soothed, stroking her sun-warm but still damp hair. "I'm here and I won't leave you again."

Time passed on silent feet as they stood in the shade of the old tree. But however long it was, it was not long enough when she finally pushed away from him. She had no intention of fleeing, rather she stood back to study him.

"Explain it to me then," she said in a skeptical and almost mocking tone, daring him to spin a lie thick enough for her to believe.

"I came back for you, just as I had promised. But not long after we departed from Batavia, Ottoman pirates attacked our convoy. They sank two ships, including the one I was on. A third managed to escape. I was captured and taken as a slave. I spent months in captivity, and when I finally made my way back to the Cape, you were gone. They told me you had died, but I refused to believe it. I have spent the last seventeen years searching for you."

She listened impassively to his heavily redacted version of the past, then slowly turned her head away to stare sightlessly at the untamed expanse around them.

He couldn't stop himself from touching her. His hand reached for hers, profoundly grateful when she did not pull away.

When she spoke again, she sounded hollow, as if she'd viewed the past and found it extremely tiresome. "I don't believe you." Wrapped in sad hopelessness, she gave his hand a consoling squeeze.

He had not for a second expected that victory would come easily, and so promptly dismissed her declaration, knowing full well that she was simply trying to come to terms with the whirlwind of the morning's revelations.

"Yes, you do," he said unequivocally.

Danielle heard the undercurrent of arrogance in his words and the slow wink that followed his rebuttal gave her stomach a brutal twist. As a young man, Sebastiaan was intelligent and charismatic, but it was that unadulterated cockiness that had snared her.

"No, I don't." Her voice gained strength, and she petulantly tried to pull her hand free; to no avail, as he tightened his grip.

"You thought you could waltz in here, declare yourself to be my long-lost husband, and I would run into your arms and everything would be settled?"

Her words were wondrously telling, and this time, his triumphant smile could not be controlled.

"I didn't declare myself to be your husband, but that is an error we will rectify soon enough."

She groaned at the slip of her tongue, but it was the self-assured smile and the way it creased the corner of his left eye that thawed the layer of ice she'd so carefully constructed around her heart. That damn smile. It had always been his most effective weapon; one she was powerless against. Something – a stern voice in her head rose to the front demanding attention – an imposter could not fake. Everything inside her screamed that this beautiful creature before her was Sebastiaan, but she could not allow herself to believe it.

Sebastiaan saw the longing and the doubt waging war within her, pulling her in opposing directions.

"I can prove my claim," he said. "Would you let me do that?"

She shook her head in denial, but said the opposite. "Yes."

He pulled the dagger he had taken from Davit from the small of his back. She followed his movements and when he presented her with the hilt of the weapon, she snatched it from his hands and a split second later, the tip was pressed firmly against his throat.

"Where did you get this?" she seethed, her eyes cold and menacing. "Think fast and speak plainly, for I will end you right here if you lie to me."

She was magnificent.

"It belongs to Davit – *our son*. He found me at the Cape."

"Where is he now?" she asked, her tone harsh and unfeeling.

Sebastiaan swallowed and tried to lower the blade with a nudge of his finger, but she leaned in closer. He would have to tell her the truth and risk her cutting his throat. However, the words he needed to explain the situation seemed to have found urgent business elsewhere, for he could not find a single one to fill the silence between them.

"Speak," she demanded, and he felt his skin yield under the dagger's tip. A thick, warm drop of blood was slowly running down his neck.

"I brought him with me. He is on the beach by the lagoon."

"Oh, ply me with bullshit and see if it sticks," she bit out. "Do you think I would believe for a second, that Davit is at the beach? Doing what? Twiddling his thumbs, waiting to see if you can find his mother, when he knows perfectly well where I live."

The pressure on his neck increased and Sebastiaan clamped his hand around her wrist and firmly pulled the blade away.

"Listen to me," he said, all softness fled his face and voice and her eyes widened with fear. "I am not lying to you, but you must prepare yourself." Her features sharpened, and her brow knitted. "He is in a bad way."

"What does that mean?" she asked, concerned but still fearful.

"He was shot a week ago." She drew a sharp breath, and Sebastiaan softened his grip on her arm but did not let go. "We've treated the wound as best we could, but he developed a fever, and he is asking for you."

The last of his words were spoken with so much tenderness that Danielle nearly believed him.

"Then bring him to me," she said callously. "I'll wait right here."

He shook his head. "You don't believe me. I can see it in your eyes. If I leave, you will disappear and I will never find you again."

You're bloody right about that, Danielle thought but kept her mouth shut.

"Danielle, think," he said urgently. "How did I get the dagger?"

"You killed him!" she shouted, her accusing words pelted him like rocks.

"No," he breathed and shook his head. "What would it take for you to believe me?" Helpless frustration was clawing at him. "I pulled you from the *Drommedaris'* hull, sat with you while you lay unconscious. I took your beating when you'd slapped De Coninck and then teased you about it afterward. I asked you to marry me, and you said yes. I have never lied to you and never will." He stared into her eyes, searching for a way to reach her but finding none. "Damn it," he muttered, releasing her wrist as he dropped to his knees before her. "Take Mary and cut my throat if you don't believe me. But when you're done, go to the beach – your son needs you."

"Mary," Danielle whispered as she looked at the dagger in her hand and then at his upturned face. He could easily have disarmed her, but he didn't.

"Yes," he said. "Do you remember the day in the forest? I told you I named her Bloody Mary, and you laughed at me."

She was no longer pale, frightened, or angry, but calculatingly calm as her mind worked to absorb the meaning of his words.

"Who else would know that? We were alone that day."

Her heart screamed for her to believe him, but her mind was still reluctant. Traces of the young man from her memory lingered in his face, hidden beneath the years. The eyes were still the soft moss-green, but where once alight with mischief, they now shone with frustration and flecks of desperation. A short line dented his left cheek where once a dimple had been. Her eyes dropped to his hands. The fingers were long and elegant, his hands wide and strong, freckled now from years in the sun. A thin white scar traced the top of his right hand, stretching from the first knuckle to the base of his thumb, a relic of a childhood injury, when a shard of ice from an iron railing had cut the top of his hand.

"How did you get that scar on your hand?" she asked.

"I got it when I was young. I reached through the iron fence at our house for a cat on the other side. The fence was coated in frost; a broken piece cut my hand when I pushed it through."

"Sebastiaan?" she spoke the name carefully, afraid to connect it to the man kneeling before her.

Hearing her say his name after all these years filled him with an incomparable, unsurpassed joy, and he sank onto his heels, exhaled forcefully and dropped his head forward.

"You, sir, have much to explain," she said, her tone crisp but brittle, like a blade honed too thin. Her hand shook as she reached out, offering to pull him to his feet. He took it, his calloused palm warm against hers, and rose slowly, his eyes never leaving her face.

For a moment, they stood there, hands clasped, the weight of the years pressing between them. Danielle's chest ached with questions she burned to ask. But her child's crisis rose above the tumult of emotions raging inside her. She pulled her hand free, the dagger still clutched in her other fist.

"Take me to Davit," she said, her voice low but steady, carrying a quiet urgency.

Sebastiaan's nod was slow, his face softening with something Danielle couldn't name –yearning, perhaps, or torment. He gestured toward the path, and as they stepped from the tree's shade, she felt as if she were walking in a fugue, dazed with shock and tenuous hope. The past and present tangled like vines around her ankles, making each step falter as her mind wrestled with what her heart dared to believe.

***

They reached the beach quicker than it had taken him to find her. Danielle led Sebastiaan down a steep path hugging the hillside, shaving off much of the distance he had covered earlier in his frantic run. Throughout the journey she had relentlessly questioned him about Davit's condition – pressing him for details about the nature of the wound, how it was sustained, the exact location, the treatment, and the symptoms that had followed.

When they arrived, his uncle was standing by the boy's side, his expression one of restrained frustration at his own neutered power to save him. The instant he saw Danielle, his composure slipped, leaving him to attempt his most convincing impression of a wooden stage puppet with a broken jaw string. Sebastiaan had never seen Davit De Coninck at a loss for words before. All the years that had passed fell away and his uncle wordlessly drew Danielle into a long, fatherly embrace before allowing her to turn her attention to Davit.

Sebastiaan watched Danielle bend over her son. The viscous layer of fear that had congealed around him the past five days was slowly pulling apart, allowing him to breathe deeper. There was no frantic panic in her movements, no trace of the hysteria one might expect from a mother in such a situation. Instead, she was calm and composed, her hand steady when she reached to touch his forehead, her brow creasing in faint displeasure at the heat radiating from his skin. Then she leaned in, pressing her ear to his chest and closing her eyes to listen to his breathing and assess the lung damage, piecing together all the information available to her.

After her brief examination, she'd concluded there was nothing she could do for him there. They needed to get him out of the elements, and she needed her medicines.

"Careful," Danielle cautioned, as De Coninck and Sebastiaan hoisted Davit's stretcher to follow her to the village.

"We've gotten him thus far, my dear. I am sure we won't drop him on the last stretch," De Coninck replied. Apparently, nothing had changed between them, Sebastiaan thought when he noted the flash of heat in her eyes at his uncle's brusque tone.

It was shortly after midday when Sebastiaan unstrapped his weapons and laid them against the wall of the cave where Danielle had lived for the past seventeen years.

The two young scout boys who had met them halfway to the village clung to Danielle's side like burrs, unsure of what to do since she would not let them run off to raise the alarm about the strange men accompanying her. They gripped her hands with white-knuckled strength, their large brown eyes darting between the men before falling to Davit's form lying limp on the wooden stretcher. The weight of their sadness pulled at their narrow shoulders, folding them inward as they stared at him.

"They will soon return with my bedding and then we'll settle him more comfortably," Danielle said after she'd dismissed the boys, ordering them to remove her belongings from her ox and return them, as fast as possible, to her cave.

Danielle knew the children feared her more than their chief. His temper was wild and dangerous, but they believed she could summon the gods' wrath if they disobeyed her. It was a power she rarely wielded, but today was a day of exceptions. She had sternly forbidden them to speak of the men accompanying her, warning that the gods would not look kindly on those who ignored her command. Kai would find out about their presence soon enough, and she did not want every warrior in the tribe to storm her cave, weapons at the ready, and blood in their eyes.

Sebastiaan sensed a moment of indecision where there was too much to do and too little to do it with. The cave was bare, with only a few neatly stacked pieces of crockery at the back wall, and he wondered at the obvious lack of comfort she had suffered. It was his uncle who broke the tense silence.

"If you two are quite settled," he said, skewering Sebastiaan and Danielle with a meaningful glare as he flung a leather satchel from his shoulder and placed it next to Sebastiaan's weapons. "I am off to rescue Orion, then." He was standing with his hands firmly clasped behind his back, his elegant shape in sharp contrast to the rugged environment. "I will return in three days. At that time, I expect to find my grandson alive, and the two of you right here where I left you. Should you become missing, lost or dead, I will find you, and when I do, I will take my sweet time to skin you, alive or otherwise. After which, I will feed your remains to the nearest shark." He enunciated each word with lethal precision. "Am I making myself perfectly clear?" He was actually expecting replies and stared them down until he was satisfied with their understanding and compliance.

"Thank you, uncle. We'll be here waiting for you," Sebastiaan said. The best Danielle could manage was a tense nod.

"Keeping this family together is like plucking eggs from a *fucking* apple tree," De Coninck muttered under his breath as he walked away.

Moments stretched into what felt like hours as Sebastiaan and Danielle stood in silence, both battling to put the surfeit of their emotions into words. They inhaled at intervals, poised on the brink of speech, only to close their mouths against the poverty of their intended words. There was so much that needed to be said, so much that needed to be explained, but with concern for Davit overshadowing everything else, finding a starting point seemed impossible. Neither was ready for such an intimate, unexpected moment of privacy.

They were jolted from their impasse by a sudden clamor of voices. Sebastiaan did not have to be a linguist to know that the loudest was that of a man in high temper. His only regret was that the specifics of the fiery rant were once again slipping through the cracks of his comprehension.

Danielle seemed unimpressed and utterly indifferent to the growing noise. She merely rolled her eyes in a slow blink, released a long-suffering breath and cast a quick glance at Davit. His condition was stable, but critical. The depth of his sleep was a concern. Not once during the journey to the cave had he shown any sign of life beyond the faint, wheezy whisper of his breath. She moved to stand in the entrance, much like De Coninck had earlier, hands on her hips, shielding Sebastiaan from view, ready to confront the oncoming storm.

"Why in the name of all the gods are you unloading your ox?" Kai bellowed from a distance, his voice carrying clearly up the narrow, winding path. "We are moments away from leaving. Everyone is packed and ready to go. Yet, you disappeared this morning without a word, only to return with half the day gone, setting us all behind, demanding your belongings – which," he paused, and she knew, without needing to see him, that he was waving his finger in the air. "I've secured with the utmost care, since the last time you lost a godforsaken pot, you threatened to wrap my balls in a shrinking curse should that ever happen again. Why?" he demanded as he came to a halt before her, his legs covered in dust and his shrewd black eyes dancing with annoyance. A line of young boys laden with leather bags and pouches containing her herbs, sleeping furs, and an assortment of clay pots and bowls, stood like toy soldiers behind him.

Sebastiaan silently stepped from the shadows, snaked his arm around Danielle's waist, pulled her behind him and drew the dagger from his back. He had always been acutely sensitive to anyone taking a less-than-conciliatory tone with Danielle, and it became blindingly obvious that this facet of his personality had not dulled with time.

"No!" Danielle exclaimed, her hands closing around his upper arm, feeling the tense vibration of the muscle beneath her touch.

If Kai was shocked or surprised by the large white man, he did not show it. Instead, he narrowed his eyes, bared his teeth, and drew his club and spear from the leather harness on his back in one fluid motion. The men always carried their weapons, and the sight had become so commonplace to Danielle that she barely noticed it – until now, when it was pointed at Sebastiaan.

Danielle tried to push past Sebastiaan, but he held her in place. The line of boys scrambled backward, creating room for Kai to move should this budding confrontation take a more animated turn. Danielle could just see how her much needed supplies might be moments away from disaster.

"Kai, stop!" she demanded from behind Sebastiaan. "I need my things or Kwala will die," she spoke in Khoekhoe and hastily repeated the statement in Dutch, bringing the men to their senses.

"Kwala is here? What happened to him?" Kai asked, concern written plainly on his face, the weapons in his hands momentarily forgotten.

"Yes," Danielle said, pointing to where her son lay.

Sebastiaan was unceremoniously shouldered aside as the chief leaped into the cave. He lowered his dagger, his attention instantly drawn to the silver scar cutting through the walnut-brown skin of the man's thigh. Could this be the arrogant young chief from the waterhole years ago, the one Danielle had treated? Van Leyen had always been of a mind that Danielle had escaped the settlement on the day she'd killed her husband, with the help of another. Could this have been the man who'd come to her rescue?

Kai rushed to Davit's side, mumbling soft words that sounded like a prayer. He kneeled beside the stretcher and ran his hand over the boy's golden hair. The line of boys filed into the cave, marching like dutiful ants, and with extreme care, they laid Danielle's belongings against the back wall. Then, one by one, they drifted toward Davit. It was a difficult sight to comprehend him so strangely garbed and gravely ill, set against the memory of the vibrant, fearless and seemingly invincible older brother they once knew. This was not the Kwala of their memories, the one who had laughed in the face of danger and introduced them to countless adventures. Their fascination was quickly curbed when the chief barked something at them over his shoulder, and they scampered out of the cave.

"Tell me, Little Flower," Kai said as he stroked Davit's hair. "Will he live?"

Danielle remained silent as she rummaged through her bags, retrieving a bundle of fresh leaves, a handful of dried herbs, a large brown bulb, and a piece of sharpened flint she used for cutting and scraping. With her medicines spread around her, a tightness formed in her belly. Kneeling next to Davit, she placed the bulb between her knees and began to scrape thin slivers from it into a bowl, then stilled when Sebastiaan laid his hand over hers.

"Here," he said and handed her the dagger. "Use this."

"Thank you." Her hand closed around the familiar grip and she continued her scraping.

"Is he the man who brought Kwala to you?" Kai asked.

"He is," she said, knowing that there were many more questions to follow.

"You seem comfortable with him. Do you know him?" Kai kept his voice deliberately even.

She glanced up from her work. "Kai, I do not have time for this right now," she said, scowling at him for his poor timing.

"Do you think so little of me that I would leave you with a stranger? One who might do you harm?" he replied in a soft growl, partly not to disturb Davit and partly not to stir the large man leaning docilely against the cave wall. He had not forgotten the speed with which the man had moved earlier, and he did not wish for a repeat performance.

Danielle knew that once he dug his heels in, nothing short of an earthquake would move him from a topic he wished to discuss. Social inconveniences, such as timing or propriety, were ruthlessly ignored. As her protector and friend, her safety was his principal responsibility, a duty he would never shirk, even at the risk of his own.

"Do you believe he would do me harm?"

Kai frowned, but refrained from answering. "Answer me properly," he demanded.

"Very well," she said. "He is the man I've loved all my life, the one in whose image I've raised my child." She did not translate their conversation for Sebastiaan's benefit, but could feel the heat of his stare on her back.

"The one you light the fires for?"

"Yes."

"You have summoned him?"

"Not exactly," she murmured, keeping her eyes on Davit. The conversation was unnerving her, and she wished it would end. The day's events had unfolded too fast, they were too fantastical to accept so readily. She needed time to come to terms with them. Explaining it now, with Davit needing her full attention, was too much for her to bear. Kai seemed to sense her discomfort.

"I think I recognize him," he said, and slowly rose from Davit's side. "I saw him once near the settlement at the Cape. The day I first met you."

That day had nearly ended in disaster as Kai and Governor Van Riebeeck, through sheer stubbornness on both sides, failed to reach a trade agreement. During the standoff, Danielle had noticed a wound on Kai's leg. For some inexplicable reason, he had allowed her to tend to it. As a result, he had offered the governor the requested number of cattle, not as part of the trade negotiation, but as payment for her care. However, Sebastiaan had left early that morning to go hunting and so was not present that day.

"He was not there," she said, certain that Kai was mistaken.

"He was not at the settlement, but I met him afterward by the waterhole near the large tree, the one you were so fond of. Remember?"

Danielle had not felt like fainting in many years, but the sensation sent a chill over her skin and she shuddered.

Sebastiaan listened to the conversation flowing between Danielle and the chief. There was an ease and familiarity between them that skewered him with an unexpected, and most unjust stab of bitter jealousy. Their voices wrapped around euphonious words, interspersed with sharp clicking sounds, none of which made any sense to him. Unwilling to abase himself, he sought something to do.

A neat pile of firewood was stacked near a ring of stones encircling a blackened patch on the cave floor – evidence of many fires. She might need boiling water to steep her medicines; he remembered her always steeping some or other concoction when she had treated the sailors at the Cape. Grateful for the diversion, he set to build the fire.

"We will not leave today," Kai said. "I will send Xhitha and Maheena to assist you, if that is your wish."

"Thank you, Kai," Danielle stood and touched his arm. His face was stark and unreadable, and she pulled her hand back. There was something cold and distant in Kai when he touched his forehead to hers, and the feeling of loss lingered in the air long after he was gone.

Once she'd scraped enough flesh from the bulb, she took a handful and closed it in her fist. Squeezing the pulp, she dripped a few drops of the thick, white liquid into Davit's mouth. Lifting his head to prevent him from choking, she guided the medicine to slowly trickle down his throat. She continued feeding him the milky sap, a few droplets at a time, until he swallowed by himself. The milk would fortify his liver, giving him the strength to fight the fever. No other medicine could be administered until it had worked its way through his stomach, leaving her with time to complete the rest of her preparations.

During the afternoon Maheena had made several visits bringing armloads of grasses she'd cut for bedding, while Xhitha had brought another freshly dug bulb and a bowl of milk. Both women had quietly cast worried glances at Davit, ignored Sebastiaan, and softly cried when they hugged Danielle good night.

She took comfort in their support and thoughtfulness, but her mind was occupied with Davit's needs. With Sebastiaan's help, she made a bed for Davit and, together, they lifted him onto it. He was resting in a near-sitting position, his back and head propped up by several rolls of fur.

"It doesn't look very comfortable," Sebastiaan said, as they finally settled him.

"It will keep the pressure off his lung," Danielle explained. Stepping around Sebastiaan, she began creating a poultice for the wound and an infusion to combat the fever. It would be another long night.

Sebastiaan had slipped out earlier with a large clay pot, and a sharp fear had gripped Danielle. What if this day had just been a dream, and he was merely a fabrication of her imagination? Looking around the cave, she saw the unfamiliar weapons and the satchel his uncle had left behind. It was real. He would return. And then he did, appearing in the entrance, a soft smile playing on his mouth and a pot brimming with fresh water in his hands.

Sebastiaan saw Danielle's shoulders sag in relief. She was tired and her nerves were torn and frayed. Her hands fidgeted together as if she meant to wash them – a nervous tell she didn't have before. She narrowed her eyes at him and reached for the water. After setting the pot aside, she scooped some of the water into a smaller bowl, then emptied several small pouches of herbs into it before placing it among the glowing coals to steep.

"Sebastiaan," she said, her hands paused and her gaze fixed on the glowing embers, as she tried not to look at him. "There are things you need to know. About me, about Davit. But I can't …" She shook her head in despair, unable to voice the rest of her troublesome thoughts.

"Let it be for now," he said, reaching over and tucking a stray lock of hair behind her ear. "Focus on Davit. There is nothing that needs to be said so urgently that it can't wait for the morning." If only she knew that there was nothing to confess – that he'd long since uncovered her past and that she had nothing to fear. But he kept these thoughts to himself, knowing it would only serve to distract her.

"I am more and more convinced that you are not real," she said with a relieved smile, trying to lighten the mood.

"Would a ghost bring you water and light a fire?" he teased.

"Don't speak of ghosts just yet," she warned, her smile fading. "Death is hanging over Davit. I can feel it. When I am near him, the air is cold and hostile."

"We'll fight it together," he said, reaching for her, but she stepped back, her eyes wide with fear as she frantically shook her head.

"No." The word burst from her, and she chased down the bile rising in her throat with a quick swallow. "No, you stay away from it." Sebastiaan had come too close to death before, and she would not allow him near it a second time.

Sebastiaan stared into her haunted eyes. Her voice was thin and taut, and it slid down his spine like a frosty, wet finger, making him shudder involuntarily.

"There is something I must do," she continued. "Something the tribe believes fends off the darkness. Perhaps it would be better if you were to wait outside."

Sebastiaan took instant offense at being coddled like some tender innocent. Satan's balls would no sooner freeze to his throne than he'd leave her to face this alone. Sure, he might be as useful as a lace teapot in a situation involving phantoms, presences, and dark spirits, but he would stand guard; he would watch over her.

"Wish for something else, sweetheart," he said stubbornly. "I am not leaving you. Now, do what you need to save his life. And do it quickly."

Sebastiaan stepped back, allowing her the space she needed to think and work. He busied himself with the task of fashioning a bed, putting to use the thick layer of reeds the women had brought earlier. The sun had long since disappeared below the horizon, and night had settled over them, alive with the sounds of nocturnal critters. A soft breeze stirred the air, bringing with it a blend of ocean brine and lagoon mud.

Danielle scooped coals from the fire to build four smaller ones, adding kindling to each. She placed the first at Davit's feet; waited until the flames grew strong, then sprinkled dried sage onto the open flame. It flared bright orange, and a thick stream of blue-white smoke curled toward the ceiling. Closing her eyes, she spoke the prayer she always did at the beginning of every procedure, beseeching the Almighty for protection and guidance and a cleansing of her soul.

She placed the second fire to Davit's right, calling on her father to guard over her son. The next was kindled at his left; in a language Koba had taught her, she invoked the old witch to stand by her side and augment her power. The last fire took to life near his head; it was once meant to call on Sebastiaan's spirit, but now she made an offering of gratitude.

As the smoke coiled in thick, serpentine swirls against the ceiling, Danielle began to circle Davit's bed. Her voice, smooth and resonant, vibrated with the weight of the ancient prayer of banishment and purification. She closed her mind to all around her, allowing her eyes to see beyond the veil separating the living from the dead, and let the words flow from her lips like water from a brook. Over and over, she chanted as she circled her child's bed.

Time took on a different rhythm, no longer matching that of the stars. The darkness hovering over Davit sensed the gathering forces against it and intensified. It reached down with long, black talons to scratch and claw at his pale skin but the crescendo of Danielle's voice pushed it back. She reached for another bowl of leaves and cast them into the flames. When the sharp, pungent scent of burned wormwood rose, the darkness recoiled. It coagulated above her, priming itself for a second attack, and her voice rose further. Then it streaked toward the mouth of the cave, where it melted into the night. The air instantly felt lighter, and soon afterward, the smoke drifted away on the night breeze.

Sebastiaan watched as she walked in the penumbra between the living and the dead, the liminal space where shadows and light mixed to create a narrow strip of no-man's-land, and the passing made their final choice or voice their last plea. Her eyes were opaque and dull, shrouded beneath a milky sheen. But he knew on the other side of that veil they were blazing with green fire, for he had seen them too.

She had kept him tethered to this world when he had ventured too close to that desolate place. In those moments, there was not a single scrap of softness or understanding about her. She was formidable and stern, scorning him for giving up. He knew she was fierce enough to turn away the reaper's touch.

Poor boy, he thought as he looked at Davit with a sympathetic, fatherly smile. *He won't get to die tonight.*

Exhausted to her very core, Danielle forced Davit to swallow some of the infusion she had brewed earlier, then bent down to lay a soft kiss against his forehead. The fever's heat was already fading from his skin. With heavy feet, she walked to where Sebastiaan was lounging against the wall on a large fur covered pallet.

"Are you hungry?" he asked.

She shook her head, needing nothing but the feel of his arms around her.

Chapter 24

avit had been plunged into a disorienting realm of strange, vivid dreams where colors and shapes were distorted and events jumped erratically between one scene and the next. At times, his father's voice echoed faintly, calling from a great distance. Hands touched him, each contact searing his skin like a devil's caress. He had drifted between worlds where time either rushed past or stood still, incessantly shifting in unpredictable surges.

Once more he was drifting, but this time it felt controlled. Davit felt himself rising slowly from the bog of confusion toward the surface, toward the light. It was a peculiar sensation, like returning home after a long absence. Everything seemed familiar, yet slightly askew. His soul felt older, scarred and weathered by countless veiled experiences.

The closer he moved toward the light, the more physically uncomfortable he became. Every muscle ached. It hurt to breathe, and his head pulsed. He tried to pinpoint the source of his misery, but complaints flared from every corner of his body, pulsing like stars on a cloudless night. There were areas in distress he had not actively thought about in years. With a deep, measured breath, he tried to ease the discomfort, but a brilliant shard of pain speared through his chest, forcing him to immediately adjust his breathing.

He wondered what the hell had happened to his memories, for he sure as shit could not find a single one bright enough to shed light on the recent past. The few that were too stupid or too slow to have fled with the others were nursing a hangover, spewing jumbled images at irregular intervals.

And then, he wished he'd never wondered, because in an instant, it all came back.

He remembered being inside the burning *Shack*. A man dressed in black was holding a pistol and purposefully advancing on him, but the rising flames slowed him down. A shot rang out. Then a sharp burn flared in his side, and he crumpled. Jiya was there, lifting him and carrying him away. *All will be well.* Davit relaxed. When he next opened his eyes, the air was cool and fresh against his skin, and his father was with him. Then his heart dropped.

He had lied to his father. The last thing he remembered before the darkness had swallowed him was Jiya's sightless eyes and the devastating shock in Sebastiaan's.

He searched the dregs of his memories for what came next, but there was nothing, just a sucking void that expanded the longer he searched. Desperate to free himself from the oppressive darkness, he snapped his eyes open and then instantly closed them against the harsh light. He tried to listen for familiar sounds, but there was only birdsong, the kind he hadn't heard since leaving home. He missed his mother. Memories of her were always with him, quiet and distant, content to rest on a shelf in the back of his mind. For the first time in almost a year, he was homesick. Warm tears leaked from the corners of his eyes. He tried to wipe them away, but his arm was too heavy to lift.

Davit shifted his attention back to his aching muscles, thankful for their posturing, as it gave him something tangible to latch onto. He tried opening his eyes again, putting the lesson learned earlier to good use and letting the light in by small degrees until he was staring at the familiar, dark stone ceiling of their cave. He was home, which meant Sebastiaan had found his mother.

"I'm sorry," he tried to say, but his voice failed. Where was Sebastiaan? He tried to call out, but all he could muster was a dry cough that scraped and stabbed at his chest. His father would *never* forgive him for lying about his mother.

Davit slowly turned his head to the side, and then his eyes shot wide.

There, against the far wall of the cave, in a golden glow of morning light, sat his parents – *together* – lost in sleep. He could see their peaceful faces and, for a moment, his troubles and pains were forgotten.

They both looked decades younger; the lines that usually marked their thoughts, even in sleep, were gone. Sebastiaan's arm draped loosely over his mother's shoulders, while her head rested against his chest, rising and falling with his steady breaths. They'd fallen asleep watching over him. The moment, though entirely chaste, was profoundly intimate, and he felt like a thief.

"Now there is a sight I never thought I'd live to see." Davit's weak voice scraped from across the cave.

Sebastiaan knew the exact moment Danielle awoke; she jolted and then her head snapped up. He tightened his arm around her, holding her close when she tried to scramble away.

"Are you alive then?" Sebastiaan called back. The relief he felt at hearing the lad's voice threatened to swallow him whole.

"Parts of me are," Davit paused for dramatic effect and released a slow theatrical groan. "But I would be better if I could have something to eat. Perhaps berries," then after a brief pause, "with honey." He sent his father a lopsided smile, only because he did not have the strength to lift the other side of his mouth.

"Davit?" Sebastiaan had a way of dipping the first part of his name and lifting the last when he was about to tease or scold him.

"Yes, Father?" he answered sweetly.

"Kindly shut up and go back to sleep, if you please."

"Sebastiaan," Danielle objected, stabbing her sharp elbow into his ribs as punishment for his reckless words, and renewed her efforts to escape him.

"But I am so thirsty," Davit mewled from his cot.

"Good thing you're not hungry anymore," Sebastiaan said.

The boy was still weak, but he was alive, and in good humor. The morning was perfect and Sebastiaan threw his head back and laughed, pulling Danielle tighter against him and then burying his face in her sleep-messed hair. However, his laughter was not loud enough to drown Davit's next innocent jest.

"You are a cruel man," he teased. "I clearly take after my kind and gentle mother."

Danielle's body tightened like a bowstring. Sebastiaan ran a calming hand down her arm, but the moment was irrevocably shattered.

***

Sebastiaan emptied the satchel his uncle had left the previous day. Inside, he found a roll of cheese, a loaf of bread, and a small flask of French brandy. He stoked the fire, and watched the flaring heat ripple the air like poorly poured glass. Setting the food on a flat earthen dish, he crouched next to Davit's sleeping form. Shadows still clung to the hollows under the boy's eyes, but color was seeping back into his cheeks and his old arrogance was almost back to full, annoying capacity. He had woken that morning demanding attention, and had kept up a steady effort, purposefully breaking the awkwardness that had settled among them. After assuring himself that all was well, Sebastiaan stepped outside to take care of his personal needs, giving Danielle the opportunity to fret and fuss over Davit in private.

Sebastiaan walked a wide circle around the cave, familiarizing himself with the terrain, evaluating its defenses and vulnerabilities, intuitively searching for hiding places and escape routes. There was no need to be on edge, but old habits die hard and with his family so close, he needed the deranged little voice in his head, screaming for caution, assuaged. He came across a cluster of huts built in a circle around a large fire pit. The place was deserted, not a soul in sight. Fresh footprints dotted the dirt between the dwellings, weaving around the remnants of cooking fires, now nothing more than cold ash, before trailing off. He ducked through the low entrance of a hut, it was bare, empty of life and belongings.

Leaving the small hut village, he approached a bramble enclosure large enough to have once contained hundreds of cattle. Now it was home to only five: a cow leisurely chewing fresh grass from a large pile, her calf energetically enjoying his breakfast courtesy of his mother's udder, and three stout yearlings, standing off to the side waiting their turn at the pile of greenery. Tilting his head to the side, Sebastiaan listened for any sound of the tribe, detecting nothing.

Leaving the deserted village, Sebastiaan trudged toward the river under a merciless morning sun. Its banks, lined with dense trees, scattered boulders, and soft grass, stretched cool and inviting. He disrobed slowly, placing his saber atop the pile of clothes within easy reach, then waded into the shaded waters. In the river's depths, he sank beneath the surface, until it closed over his head.

***

Danielle looked into her son's face, cataloging the many subtle changes. His hair had grown longer, nearly brushing his shoulders, and his hands were work-worn and rough. But it was the internal shifts that caught her attention. He no longer resembled the carefree, restless boy; a stillness had settled within him.

"Welcome back," she said, and brushed a golden lock from his forehead. He didn't reply, instead he closed his eyes, took her hand and brought the back of her fingers to his fever-cracked lips.

"What is the matter?" she asked softly.

"I'm just happy to see you," he said, producing a weak cough.

Not fooled for a moment, she gently freed her hand and reached for an earthen mug and raised it to his lips. He drank greedily, then pulled a face.

"That was not water," he protested.

"You should have known better." A sly light danced in her eyes. "But don't worry, it is the last of the medicine. Now, tell me what is bothering you and don't try to hide behind a fake cough, you'll only hurt your lung."

"My lung?" he asked.

"Yes, you've been shot, as you very well know. The bullet grazed the side of your lung. It will heal, given time and plenty of rest. So, stop wasting your strength on questions and instead use your limited supply to answer mine."

Davit's head rested heavily against the fur rolls, and he closed his eyes as his mother's fingers sifted through his hair. Long moments unrolled in which he did not speak, and Danielle thought he'd fallen asleep.

"I have broken my promise to you and I have lied to him," he finally said in a weak voice.

"Do you want to explain that? Or shall I draw my own conclusions?" She sounded deceptively soothing, but Davit recognized that tone all too well. It was like a sharp blade hidden beneath a soft blanket.

The exhaustion from their brief exchange was pulling at Davit, drawing him toward the blissful oblivion of sleep, compelling him to ration every word.

"I spoke your name on the night I was shot. I told Sebastiaan you're alive after lying to him for months, making him believe the opposite."

"Why did you tell him I was dead?" she asked. "He would have kept our secret."

"I'm sorry," Davit said and turned his head away from her, but her hand cupped his sunken cheek and she turned his head back toward her.

"I'm not scolding you. You were cautious, but I need to understand why."

"I needed to know the kind of man he was before leading him to you. But then," he swallowed, and she reached for the cup. He shook his head. "He was heartbroken when I told him you were dead, and I was too damn scared to fix it."

"Scared of what?"

"Scared of losing him."

"And now?"

"I don't think he'll ever forgive me for what I've done."

"Then, my love, you don't know him at all," she said as she stared into his troubled face.

"And you do?" Davit asked with the last of his strength. Danielle offered no reply. Instead, she waited until his breathing was deep and even, then silently slipped from the cave. At the entrance, she paused, finding two bowls, one filled with nuts and the other with berries, and gathered them up.

It was the unfamiliar absence of children's chatter and adult voices that made her head snap toward the village. The area, always bursting with activity, now lay silent and uninhabited; the tribe had left. Danielle inhaled sharply, held her breath and then slowly let it flow from her nose. Kai had decided for her – the arrogant, high-handed, self-righteous *bastard*.

The people she'd known and loved for almost two decades were gone. Blind rage flashed bright red across her vision; the need to scream burned in her throat, but she swallowed it down, and staunchly fought back the tears that threatened to spill. Her grip tightened around the bowls, thoughtful farewell gifts they might be, and she contemplated throwing them at the empty huts. She would not give in to her emotions this way. Instead, she turned back slowly and placed the food near Sebastiaan's satchel. He had prepared a platter of cheese and bread. A small flask was balanced against the plate. She uncorked it and lifted it to her nose, groaning appreciatively at the elegant notes of oak and spice. Raising it to her lips, she swallowed deeply. After years without tasting so much as a drop of alcohol, she'd forgotten how potent it was and spluttered as it blazed a trail from her tongue to her stomach.

Danielle glanced quickly at Davit, hoping her unexpected reaction had not woken him, but he was still asleep. Reassured, she took another sip, rolling the brandy in her mouth before letting it slide down her throat. This time, she savored the soothing burn. Reaching for the plate of bread and cheese, refusing to even look at the nuts and berries, she went in search of Sebastiaan. With determined strides, she made her way to the river, knowing she would find him there; waiting for her. The Spirits help him if he wasn't, for she was not in the mood for another disappointment. They needed to talk. She couldn't predict how he would react once she laid everything bare, but it would be better to wake from this dream now than to dance around the past, fearful of what the future might hold.

Sebastiaan sat sprawled against the trunk of a large tree, enjoying the cool shade as he waited for Danielle. She would be deeply upset, feeling abandoned and betrayed when she discovered the missing tribe. As he watched her step from the footpath, he knew he wasn't wrong. Her eyes flashed a bright ocean green, her lips pressed into a thin line, her eyebrows drawn tight, and two large dark pink blotches stained her cheeks. There was only a small falter in her stride when she spotted him, but she continued until she stood before him, food in one hand, flask in the other.

"It is better this way," he said lazily, not bothering to stand. He knew his offhanded remark and casual attitude would instantly light her fire; the sooner she boiled over, the sooner she would settle down again.

She heard the provoking words and knew exactly what he was doing, but seeing him relaxing in the shade, his shirt hanging loosely over his pants and his long legs stretched out and crossed at the ankles, robbed her of her anger. Saints above; if her heart had eyes, it would stop to stare.

Realizing that she had nearly tripped over her own feet at the sight of him, Danielle gave herself a firm mental slap. She was not a blushing, easily distracted, doe-eyed, young girl anymore, and she hastily raked the embers of her annoyance back into place.

"Better for who?" she snapped.

"Better for you," he drawled.

"That is for me to decide; *not* Kai, or you, or that child lying in the cave, who only just sprouted hair on his ba–," she paused to search for a more appropriate anatomical feature, found one, and continued. "Chest – and thinks he can get wise with me."

Sebastiaan bit down on the inside of his cheek, and snapped his eyes to his lap. She was damn adorable when her hackles were up; always had been.

"Danielle," he began, when he was certain he could address this serious matter without smiling, "they did not abandon you. They saved themselves, and you, the heartache of saying farewell." He let her chew on his words. "Nothing is set in stone," he continued, "except for how I feel about you. Everything else can be undone or rearranged." He remained seated, even though the need to reach for her burned inside him. The next move belonged to her and he would not rob her of it.

Finding Danielle had dug a deep well of peace inside him, slowly leaking its elixir into his bloodstream. He understood that their reunion had come as a shock to her; unlike him, she had not had days of anticipation and preparation. One moment she had been walking along a lonely footpath, and the next she had been confronted with a man she'd thought dead and a son gravely wounded. Her emotions had been cruelly abused, leaving her raw-nerved and unsettled. Previous experiences had taught him that leaving her alone with her troubles was a mistake; she had a knack for ensnaring herself in a web of worries, like a spider getting caught in its own trap. But this was not one of those times. She deserved a moment to gather herself.

Sebastiaan's declaration settled like warm milk in Danielle's stomach. But he had spoken prematurely. He did not know the things she'd done. She had woven lies around him, without his knowledge, lies that now lay the responsibility of fatherhood at his feet. He had an absolute right to understand why she had done it, but she feared his reaction.

"How can you be certain of what you feel for me?" she asked.

His eyes stretched wide in astonishment, and his mouth opened to answer, but she silenced him with a raised hand.

"Wait, I didn't mean it like that."

A deep furrow dipped between his brows, but his silent outrage was momentarily curtailed.

"You might want to revise your opinion once I've said what I came here to say." Her breath wobbled as she inhaled nervously. This was the deciding moment for both. She would reveal everything that had transpired since she last saw him. Once the entire sordid truth was laid bare, he might change his mind. She had married another, then had murdered her husband and lied about the paternity of her child.

Even if he forgave her for all that, he would still not be able to take her back to Batavia with him. Living with a native tribe for nearly two decades had dulled her sense of society's standards. She would become his greatest embarrassment, and if he didn't turn away from her today, he would someday.

Here in the African wilderness, all was well, but once they returned to civilization, she would be utterly clueless about what was expected of her. Worse, she feared she would never care enough to conform. Society often judged worth by shallow measures – fine clothes or polished words – over true character. Having lived with people who owned nothing, who shared what little they scraped from the barren earth, had taught her the value of kindness, generosity, compassion, and acceptance. Those qualities defined greatness, and that could not be faked by a beautiful dress or well-rounded, educated eloquence.

Danielle gnawed at her bottom lip. Where to start digging one's own grave? It was a difficult conversation to start, and Sebastiaan made no attempt to help her.

"You know as well as I that Davit is not your son," she said, deciding that the best way forward was with blunt force trauma. Once the most important point was addressed, the other concerns would follow at their own pace.

"I think I would have remembered making him," Sebastiaan said flatly. The crude remark found its mark, causing her to blush deeply and easing some of her tension. He took the plate of food and gestured for her to sit. She stubbornly remained standing. Keeping his expression relaxed and his eyes pinned on her face, he snapped his hand out, caught hers, and pulled her down next to him.

"Careful sweetheart, don't trip," he said, when she fell against him. Using the moment to his advantage, he tipped her head back and kissed her. She admirably resisted his high-handed methods for about half a heartbeat and then relaxed and kissed him back until Sebastiaan was in serious danger of forgetting which continent he was sitting on. Unfortunately, she ended their interlude as abruptly as he'd started it.

"No," she protested, and tried to move away. "I need to think clearly."

"You can think just as clearly when sitting down," he said, slinging his arm around her shoulders and keeping her pressed against him.

"Not when I'm this close to you."

A wolfish grin spread across his face at her beautiful objection.

"You'll get used to it," he said. "Now, I suspect, you are about to tell me that Davit was fathered by a man named Elias Coopman. May his soul burn in hell," he added in a low growl. All amusement blew away like dried leaves on an autumn gust, as the conversation instantly turned serious. "And that you've raised him in my name since birth, believing I had died at sea. Which would lead me to question why you'd married him when you promised to wait for me. Then, I believe you would assume, incorrectly if I may say so, that I'd be deeply offended at carrying the unexpected burden of another man's child." She tried to pull away. "Hold," he commanded softly and tightened his arm around her. "To which I would say that I know the circumstances of your wedding. And that I wish you hadn't killed him."

She stilled completely; the fight had gone from her body but her shoulders were tight as she held her breath. Her hand unconsciously fisted in his shirt.

"I wish he was still alive," he spoke softly, "so I could slowly kill him myself for what he did to you."

She did not speak, but relaxed by slow degrees and then they sat quietly, simply holding each other. They listened to the river gurgling over rocks, the birds calling and answering in the trees overhead, and a rustle in the underbrush that stilled after a moment.

"How did you know?" she finally asked, lifting her face to look into his eyes.

The memory of that cold, gray house flashed through his mind. For years, her screams echoing within its walls had filled his nightmares. "Hand us that flask, will you?"

She did, and he took a fortifying sip.

"I arrived at the Cape about six months after your wedding and went to the house." He wanted to say that he had stood in her bedroom, that he found her clothes neatly folded in the chest at the foot of the bed, that he had discovered her picture and kept it with him, but somehow the memories could not find words with which to paint themselves.

"Is it still there?" she asked.

"The house? No, Elsje told me they burned it down."

"Elsje?"

"Yes, Mrs. Boom's daughter. Do you remember her?"

Danielle nodded.

"She is still at the Cape. Married with three boys."

"How is she?" Danielle asked, thinking back to her beautiful friend, who was as close to her as a sister.

"Loud," Sebastiaan offered and then fell silent.

"When I woke the morning after my wedding," Danielle said as she picked up the painful story, "I was in shock, alone, and with no idea what to do. I was too embarrassed to seek help from any of my friends. I couldn't go to Van Riebeeck. My actions in the months after the news of your death had ruined my relationship with him. Besides, Elias was his most trusted friend and advisor."

Sebastiaan listened to the smooth texture of her voice. Had the words been any different, it would have been soothing. Now, in the full light of day and this close, he saw the faint white line running across the delicate bridge of her nose; a permanent testament to where it had once been broken. A wave of violence swept over him and his hand tightened around her shoulder, relaxing only when she brushed her fingers against it.

"I'm sorry," he said, and tenderly tried to rub at the marks he had left on her skin.

"There was a man named Blanx, who used to be a patient of mine. He had come to check on me that morning. I must have been a sight, because when Elias returned, Blanx attacked him. Elias killed him, right there on the front step," she spoke in toneless words, her mind trapped in the scene. "That's when I ran from the house, blind with fear. Elias chased me, but I was fast. I was running for my life, and it gave me strength; I practically flew up the side of the mountain." The memory made her tremble, and Sebastiaan pulled her onto his lap, wrapping both arms around her, trying to shield her from the ugly past.

"Go on," he urged when she grew quiet. "We'll speak of this now and then bury it." She nodded faintly.

"We ended on a ledge, high above the forest. You must understand, Elias had been conspiring against Van Riebeeck, and I uncovered evidence of his betrayal. He was furious, threatening to push me off the ledge, and I believe he would have. When he came for me, I stabbed him in the heart with your dagger. Soon after, Kai found me. He led me off the mountain, took me to the tribe, and helped me escape." She took several deep breaths, as if cleansing herself from the inside out. "When I discovered I was pregnant, I vowed my child would never know his real father's name, that he or she would grow up in the memory of a good man. I murdered my husband the day after my wedding, and I have no remorse. I have never once prayed for his soul or sought forgiveness for what I have done, and I raised my child in a lie. How can you want somebody like that?" she asked, sadness and acceptance pulling at her eyes and her mouth.

Not wanting to hear his reply, Danielle pushed away from Sebastiaan, and went to the river's edge. There, she kneeled and scooped up water to wash her face and arms.

"Danielle," Sebastiaan said, straightening into a more rigid pose when she sat down beside him again. "Every morning, for a fleeting moment, my world would fall apart. When I opened my eyes, knowing I was about to embark on another day without you." He smiled when she frowned. "From the first moment I saw you unconscious in the hull of my uncle's ship until now, you were my first thought of every new day and the last before sleep robbed me of your face. It seemed all I've been doing is losing you. But now I've found you." His words ran dry, and he simply looked at her. "I loved you then, and I love you now, and every heartbeat between. There is *nothing* in your past that could erase that. What you've endured and how you survived only make me love you more."

She shook her head in disbelief, wanting to deny his words.

"But I'm no longer the boy you once knew," he continued. "You deserve to know who and what I've become."

Sebastiaan was a far cry from the optimistic young man, with innocent aspirations and bright dreams for the future she had met all those years ago. He sincerely doubted she would so readily entrust her life and that of her child to him once she knew the details of how he had lived. She was worried about his reaction to her killing a man in self-defense, he could only imagine her reaction when she realized his hands were dripping with enough blood to tint the ocean pink.

She frowned, as if puzzling over a truth yet to take shape. However, she held back, asking nothing, offering no reassurance. She simply gazed at him, her eyes brimming with wisdom and faint traces of concern.

Sebastiaan began recounting the events of his past, starting at the night the Ottoman pirates had attacked the convoy, and taken him as a slave. He spoke with the ease of a man who'd told this tale a million times before, his voice dark but even as it rolled over the callouses and scars of past traumas. Often, he would glance at her, noting her pale face, seeing shock, anger, and sadness in her eyes – sometimes an amalgamation of all three – then he would look away again and continue, relentlessly bludgeoning her with the unfiltered truth of his life.

More than once her hand moved to wipe her cheeks. She did not cry when she had recited her past, but she was weeping for his. He took perverse comfort in her tears, knowing they would soon dry and be replaced with disgust.

He recounted meeting Van Leyen, his voice tracing the heavy years that followed. Her questions flowed softly, searching, warm with empathy and he met each with unflinching honesty. In return she filled the empty spaces Van Leyen had refused to speak about, adding color to his friend's black and white line drawing of what had happened to him at the Cape.

Too late did Sebastiaan realize what she was doing.

She'd woven herself into his narrative, tempering the harshness of the conversation, denying him the scourge with which to flay himself. They shared a few understanding smiles and resigned sighs as he spoke of Davit – how the boy had become his anchor after the news of her supposed death. In return, she offered fragments of his childhood, like pieces torn from a large canvas, each one painting a vivid picture of the boy Sebastiaan had come to know and love.

There was no telling how long they'd sat by the river. Danielle listened as Sebastiaan brought the past to life, rushing through some parts, like the battle that had claimed John's life only a few days ago, and lingering on others, particularly when it came to Davit and Orion. For the most part, he kept his voice drumming at a steady, detached beat until it faded into silence when he'd reached the end.

"Alain Du Bois is dead," she spoke the words carefully, as if saying them out loud would make her believe them faster. Sebastiaan nodded. "Orion was his son? Did you know this all along?"

"Yes, but Arent never wanted him to know. I guess, like you, he didn't want the boy's paternity to influence his future."

"Does Orion know the truth now?" her voice was small, almost dreamlike as she considered the weight of what he had done. It was difficult to imagine that sweet little boy with the large brown eyes and curly black hair as a grown man capable of killing another.

"I told him right before we fled the Cape, but it meant nothing to him. He never considered Du Bois his father."

She digested the revelations in silence. The parallels between Orion and Davit were impossible to ignore.

"Orion and Davit are cousins," she realized with a pained expression, "and they don't know. Oh, my God." She dropped her head in her hands. "What have I done?"

"Orion knows about Davit," Sebastiaan said, and tilted her head up with a finger beneath her chin. "I have sworn him to secrecy. In the end, it was only Orion, Van Leyen, and I who knew your secret."

"I have to tell Davit. There is no other way. He has a right to know. But," she paused, a troubled look casting deep shadows on her face, "I can't predict how he will react. He has a volatile streak a mile wide." That was the part he'd inherited from Elias; the part she'd always tried to temper.

"He is also loyal, a trait he got from you," Sebastiaan said, as if he could read her troubled thoughts. "You won't lose him."

Lose Davit? No, she supposed she wouldn't, but the truth would have a profound impact on him. At the time, it had been an easy lie to tell, and soon enough, it had become their way of life. She had woven a backstory for him with no apparent consequences and no one to challenge its falsehood. The problem was too large to confront right now, so she deliberately pushed it aside. He was still weak and needed time to recover. She had a few days at least to prepare herself and find the right words to put to him.

Her mind drifted back to everything Sebastiaan had shared about his past. Although she did not doubt his words, she sensed that much remained unsaid, hidden in the shadows. He was consciously revealing only the dark parts, like a bat showing off his cold, black cave where he spends his days, keeping his good deeds, done in the dead of night, well hidden. The life he described tore her heart to pieces, and she stared at him, wondering what horrors were carved into the skin beneath his shirt. The love and pride he felt for Davit was obvious; his face relaxed and his eyes wrinkled at the corners when he spoke of him. She was amazed that he'd kept such a large part of his heart soft enough to still hold that much affection for another.

The thought of him as a slave, tore at her – picturing that proud young man shackled, degraded and stripped of worth twisted her heart, and she fought back fresh tears. Had she known of the years Sebastiaan spent hunting his tormentors, Danielle would have been sick with worry, yet those deeds troubled her little now. He was here, alive, the answer to her every wish and prayer. Her fears of inadequacy faded before such a magnificent gift. If the path ahead demanded transformation, she'd embrace it, molding herself into what he needed.

"Your silence is neither unexpected, nor even a disappointment," Sebastiaan said with a wry, self-mocking smile that caught Danielle off guard. "I can well imagine what your answer will be, but I still need to hear it." He had spoken at length, and she had listened to every word. Yet as his voice fell silent, she sifted through his revelations, sorting them into a quiet, tentative order, and in doing so she had missed the question he had asked her.

She was about to clarify the matter when his next words did it for her.

"I know I'm no longer the man you fell in love with," Sebastiaan declared. "You deserve the chance to choose your own future without being coerced or chased into any direction. If you wish to remain with the tribe, I will take you to them; they could not have gone far, not with such a large group. Alternatively, if you wish to return to Holland, I will make the necessary arrangements and ensure that you are comfortable and never want for anything."

Danielle waited patiently for him to conclude his offer, laying out her options. The more he spoke, the more convinced she became of her choice.

"Is that it? No other choices?" she asked when he reached the end of his suggestions.

"There are a thousand choices. I just can't think of them right now. You can have whatever you want, live wherever you choose. Just tell me where you want to go from here," he said, looking so defeated she had to fight the need to wrap him in her arms and keep him safe.

"None of it," she said with a stubborn tone and a cold-eyed look.

"Then what is it you want?" he asked, unable to hide his exasperation.

"You," she said without leaving room for even a breath to pass between his question and her answer. "I want you."

Sebastiaan stared at her as if she'd abandoned her wits. His mouth was slack and his eyes narrowed at her as he tried to gauge the depths of her loss. She held her ground, not withering an inch under his scrutiny.

"Are you … have you …," he tried several times to speak, but somehow his words could not find the right lines to stand in and kept milling about. "Have you not listened to a word I said?"

"I did," she said calmly. "I can't claim to know you now better than I did before, not after the years we've spent apart. But from what I've seen thus far, you have not changed all that much. Everything you do is either coldly calculated or forged by passion. Which leads me to believe you've intentionally highlighted the darker aspects of your past, deliberately leaving the parts about bravery, justice, and virtue unsaid, an omission I am willing to overlook for now, but not for long."

"What do you want from me?" It was a rhetorical question because he did not allow her to answer. "I will not sit here and paint a heroic picture aimed at deceiving you."

"I understand," she said. "But know this: everything that had happened to you resulted from a decision I made. I chose to stay behind at the Cape when you left for Batavia. If I had gone with you, none of this would have happened. You would not have suffered the way you did. But none of that mattered to you, because here you are after years of searching for me, driven by nothing more than wisps of hope."

"None of this was your fault," he said fiercely, his eyes sharpening and his mouth drawing into a hard line.

"All of it is," she persisted. "I had driven Van Riebeeck to a point where he had no other choice than to marry me off to Elias."

"That," Sebastiaan stopped her with a pointed finger, "falls squarely under the category of horseshit. There was a myriad of different ways to deal with that situation. Marrying you to that snake was just the easiest option, and he took it. Fate pushed us down paths that turned us into the people we are now. There is no telling how our lives would have been, had we made different choices," he forged on. "But none of it matters, for I will not have you beholden to me. You owe me nothing." His heart screamed that it was reason enough; his pride would not allow it.

Danielle was near boiling point, listening to the words spilling from his mouth.

"I am not beholden to you," she nearly shouted in frustration. "I love you. I don't know when it happened, only that it did, and Lord knows I've tried for years to convince myself otherwise. It didn't work. Whether you take me back to the tribe or ship me off to Europe, it changes nothing. I'll just keep loving you from a different place."

Her words were pushing effervescent light into his blood, and it was making him dizzy, but he could not accept them. Not until he was certain she understood what she was agreeing to. "Danielle, I've spent seventeen years lost in a constant haze of violence and bloodshed. I was chasing revenge – vengeance – anything to numb the pain. I wanted to settle the score, right the wrongs that had been perpetrated against you and against me. I've murdered men in their sleep, many of them, assuming they were guilty of some crime or another. If I had the luxury of self-control, I never would have touched you with these hands." Then he simply stopped speaking as if his words had suddenly dried up. There was nothing left to say. He had said all that he could, and the rest was now up to her.

They were sitting close but not touching. Sebastiaan's skin prickled with unspoken tension; all his nerves were standing at silent attention, but outwardly he remained calm, waiting for the hammer to fall.

"Oh, stop being so dramatic," she snapped. "You're not the first man to live a life of violence when the circumstances demanded it, and you won't be the last." She waved her hand dismissively. "We all have a darkness inside us. It is not something we can eradicate; it is part of who we are. If there was no devil, no one would need a god. It is the darkness that reveals the light's true value. We choose who we aspire to be, share the parts we wish others to see, and to quietly walk beside what we keep private. The question for us is, can we live with each other's demons? I look at yours and I see how dangerous they can be, but I also know that they are not a threat to me."

"I was so certain before, that I would not allow you to turn away from me, that I would make you understand, but the reality of the situation is a touch more – ," he searched for a way to complete his thought, "*real*, than I thought."

"I see the monster you're trying to paint, and I am not intimidated, disgusted, or scared."

"It was not my intent to do any of those things to you, least of all scare you."

"Then what was your intent?"

He shrugged with one shoulder, a gesture carried from boyhood. "Informing you for one, making you see who and what I've become, and also, I thought if I laid the dark parts out in the light, perhaps they might bleach a bit."

"Sebastiaan, it is not my acceptance or even forgiveness you seek, though you have both, but your own. Keep bleaching until you see yourself through the darkness. I can see you clear as day." She cast him a sly smile as she remembered his long-ago words to her: "If only you could see yourself through my eyes, you would be unstoppable."

"Those were my words," he said, remembering the harsh conversation they had after Maria Van Riebeeck's baby died.

"I know, and they saved me." She gave him a soft smile.

He could not look away from her; instead, he studied her face, noting every new line and freckle. She had been beautiful when she was a young woman, but the years had carved her with a thin, sharp blade. Where once the soft innocence had rounded her cheeks, they were now slightly sunken, leaving her cheekbones high and pronounced. Her lips, still full, bore the straightened edges of sorrow, hardship, and disillusion, but determination and sheer stubbornness kept them from drooping. Her eyes were as vivid as when she was a girl, but the groove, between her brows, spoke of relentless thought or swift temper – likely both, he mused. Fine lines fanned from their corners, a quiet comfort to him, proof of her frequent laughter. The blatant beauty she carried now could only be sculpted by time, and it was powerful enough to steal his breath.

"Are you listening to me?" she asked, and that line between her eyes deepened.

"Yes," he replied immediately.

"Liar," she laughed. "Do you want me to repeat what I said?"

He nodded guiltily.

"If we met now, as strangers," she said softly, "we'd still be drawn to each other. You might court me, and in time, we'd share pieces of our past – just the ones that matter – leaving the rest buried. Over time we would evolve into new versions of ourselves. Why can't the same be true for us now?"

Sebastiaan knew he'd missed more of the conversation than she realized, but the sentiment rang true enough, and he understood what she was trying to explain.

"So, do you want me to court you then?" he teased.

She pinned him with an annoyed stare, pressed her lips together and huffed through her nose.

"No," she said, as if trying to explain to a small child that round things roll, "what I am trying to say is that the past doesn't matter as much as you believe it does. We did what we had to do to survive."

"You don't want me to court you?"

"What?" Her confusion was etched into every line on her face, and she burst into laughter born from sheer hopelessness, which grew into relief and then into release. Her outburst ended with a few hiccups as she fought to regain a measure of composure. The weight of their conversation that had been pressing down on them lifted, leaving the air clear and light. They had reached a point where turning away from each other was no longer an option. Acceptance had been hesitantly sought and generously granted.

"You are an unrepentant arse!" she said and then giggled when she saw the shadows clear from his eyes, only to be replaced by something predatory.

"Sebastiaan," she squealed in alarm, and tried to squirm away, but he grabbed her ankle and pulled her back.

"Are you certain this is what you want?" he asked, and she laughed at the disbelief that still clung in small patches to his features.

"I've been certain from the moment I said 'yes'." That statement instantly brought a frown to his face, and he looked at her with a dumbfounded expression.

"When have you ever agreed to anything?"

"When you asked me to marry you."

"Then we are done talking," he said and his breathing roughened despite the pains he took to control it.

Danielle had underestimated her reaction to the sudden intimacy of the moment. Panic rose swiftly from her belly, pushing its poison through her limbs, paralyzing her.

"Sebastiaan, wait." She stayed him with a hand on his chest, surprised by how easily he yielded. Dread and shame coiled through her, tightening with every turn and making it nearly impossible to voice her trepidation.

Sebastiaan watched as the color drained from her face, the earlier merriment evaporating, her eyes darkening with fear. Understanding dawned and took a firm stand against his own desire and disappointment, offering her a solid wall of protection.

"Do you want to go back to the cave?" he asked and withdrew his hands from her. No matter how difficult it would be, or how badly he wanted the opposite, he would wait until she was ready.

"No, I want to stay here with you," she murmured, her gaze fused to the soft grasses as if searching for a lost trinket. She took a deep breath through her nose. "I just," she paused, cleared her throat then tried again. "I just don't have any experience beyond my wedding night." Abandoning her search of the grass, she lifted her eyes to stare at a point over his shoulder.

Sebastiaan nearly wept with relief. He stood up and helped her to her feet before stepping back, giving her the distance and freedom to walk away if she so chooses.

"First," he said, seeing she had no intention of leaving, "your wedding night has nothing to do with this. That was rape, and being his wife does not change that it was an attack. We can talk about it as much as you need, or never again if that is your wish, but I am not afraid of it, and neither should you be." He silenced her when she wanted to respond.

"Second," he continued, reaching to touch her cheek but pulling back midway, closing his hand. "I am somewhat grateful for your lack of experience, because I have not done this since I was Davit's age."

"In all this time, you've never been with another woman?" she asked disbelievingly.

He shook his head and tried to hide his heightened color. "The last time I was with a woman was the night before we left Amsterdam for the Cape. Then I met you and that was it."

Scorchingly drawn-out moments, each shaving years off Sebastiaan's life, passed in which he scarcely dared to breathe. She stared at him with the blank expression of someone trying to solve a very complex mathematical phenomenon. Then she slammed her mouth shut, blinked several times, squared her shoulders.

"Fine," she said, her voice firm, as if she'd weighed a decision and landed on it. She stepped forward, not quite closing the distance he'd left, but near enough for him to feel the shift in the air between them. "I'm done with talking too."

Sebastiaan exhaled, a faint smile breaking through his tension. He nodded once, his hand twitching at his side but staying put. For the first time in years, the world felt steady beneath his feet.

Chapter 25

Danielle was still asleep when Davit rose from his pallet and, with one hand against the cave wall to steady and guide him, stumbled outside, listing like a poorly ballasted ship caught in rough seas, hell-bent on his morning constitutional.

"There is nothing I would like more than to take a piss by my own hand again," he protested when Sebastiaan tried to drag him back to his bed.

"It is still dark outside," Sebastiaan argued in a whisper. "Can you not hold it?"

"I'm not holding a damn drop. I plan to toast the dawn, if it is the last thing I do. All that stands between me and that noble goal is this infernal weakness in my legs. So, please, just help me to the nearest shrub." There was a familiar mulish glint in Davit's eyes, the sight warmed Sebastiaan's insides, and soundly lost him the battle.

Sebastiaan steadied Davit with a firm arm wrapped around his waist, mindful to avoid the wound on his side. Davit leaned heavily against him, draping his arm loosely over Sebastiaan's shoulders. Sebastiaan clasped Davit's limp hand where it hung, gripping it tightly to anchor him, and together they hobbled from the cave, appearing very drunk for two stone-cold sober men. The going was slow, and it wasn't until they reached the river that Davit finally nodded at a suitable shrub. From there, Sebastiaan had to practically drag him the last few yards to a flat rock jutting into the river.

After a brief respite, during which Sebastiaan watched him like a hawk for any signs of fainting, Davit wrangled the long undershirt over his head, tossed it heedlessly to the side and lowered himself into the river, clad only in the white bandage wrapping around his torso.

Now, with the sun cresting the horizon, Davit was back on the black stone slab with his damp linen shirt tied haphazardly around his waist. He was shivering like a newborn as cold water streamed off him in shimmering golden rivulets.

"Your mother is going to murder us both when she finds out that you took a bath," Sebastiaan muttered ruefully and grimaced at Davit's sodden bandage.

Davit leaned back on his hands, opening his chest, lifted his chin, and tried to deepen his breathing, though he could only manage what felt like a quarter cup of air at most. It was still a victory over the previous day's shallow, gasping breaths. He was home, and yet it didn't feel like home anymore. He'd noticed the tribe was gone when they'd left the cave, but it was more than just the silence that bothered him. Something had shifted inside him. This spot by the river had been his favorite childhood playground. He'd waged countless battles along these muddy banks, defending the flat rock, his stronghold, with sticks and stones. It was here he'd made his first blood oath and where his mother had taught him to swim. Everything was familiar, with a memory hanging from nearly every branch, but nothing was the same. Today it felt just like any other place.

How many times had he sat on this rock, imagining his father beside him, their conversations stretching long and deep, filled with the important matters of life? He'd listened to that phantom voice, sharing the wisdom every father passes to his son. Yet, in all those imagined moments, he'd never pictured himself apologizing, never felt the crushing weight of his own callous deceit. He feared his lies were sharp enough to sever their newly woven bond. How bitter the irony that the moment he'd dreamed of would be the very one where he would lose all he'd ever wanted. If he had the strength, he would have cried like a babe.

"Your thoughts are loud enough to knock the birds from the trees," Sebastiaan said as he shifted for a better seat. The rock was a damn uncomfortable resting place. Tilting his head, he cast Davit a sideways look. The boy was staring into the depths of the river, barely blinking, his face a study in sorrow.

Davit dropped his chin to his chest. He wished he could sigh, or scream, anything to unravel the knot of guilt twisting inside him. He had deliberately led them to this place so he could confess and apologize to his father, but with the moment upon him, he wished he had stayed in his bed.

"Father," he said after a weighted silence, the word more plea than acknowledgment. "I lied to you. I don't know how to –"

"Don't," Sebastiaan cut in. It was a reflex, and he sounded harsher than he'd intended, halting the words he knew were coming. The boy was about to apologize, and if taken in isolation, the notion would have held merit. But it was Davit who deserved an explanation and an apology, not the other way around. Sebastiaan had been lying to the boy from the moment they'd met.

At first, he'd soothed his conscience with the excuse that he'd withheld the truth because it was what Danielle would have wanted. *She was dead*, a small voice whispered in the back of his mind, trying to ease his guilt. He raised a fist and rubbed it against his breastbone. Dead or alive, it mattered little. The truth would have been the same, but he was greedy, desperate to have something of Danielle, to look into the boy's eyes and see his mother. Later he'd convinced himself that concealing Davit's identity was a bid to keep him safe, and perhaps there was truth to that, but it still rang hollow. No, he had used the truth as currency for his selfishness, gambling with Davit's trust.

This was not the father he wished to be, one who would disregard the needs of his child to satisfy his own desires. He'd been in dark places in the past, yet his integrity, his sense of right and wrong, and his honor had always seen him through, but that was back when he had nothing to lose.

Sebastiaan turned his head away from Davit, ashamed at his own weakness, which had only multiplied since he'd found Danielle again. The last two days had been perfect, and he wished he could keep the world at bay, make time stand still, just for a few hours longer. She had accepted his past, wrapped him in her understanding, given him a family, and he was not ready to give it up and have this fragile dream shattered. He had never known that fatherhood would heal him, never realized that responsibility would stitch together his torn and stained soul. The thought of losing it was unbearable.

He could manipulate almost any situation to his advantage, twist and wring blood from stone on an average day, but for this, his staunch moral compass was incapable of finding north. If only he could float above it all, give himself distance and time to study the situation, he would be able to salvage it, but he was both too close and too late.

The gentle morning breeze rolled in from the ocean, heavy with brine. Where he once would have filled his lungs with its freshness, this morning it abraded his skin like sand carried by a desert storm.

"Father, please," Davit pleaded.

"Don't call me that," Sebastiaan said softly. He was not worthy of the word. Davit flinched as if narrowly avoiding a slap to the face, his already pale face draining further as the few drops of blood still in his veins beat a fast retreat away from the skin. Sebastiaan closed his eyes and swore under his breath at the sight of the physical toll his words exacted on the boy.

The words tore through Davit like a second gunshot. What he had feared most had come to pass. The lie, coupled with Jiya's death, was too large to forgive. He had never lost a person before, not until Jiya, but even his death seemed to take a step back against the loss of his father. Perhaps if he'd been stronger, he would have been angry, would have fought to be heard, but now, all he could feel was the crushing weight of sadness dragging him down.

Sebastiaan wished he could rip his tongue from its roots the moment the callous words flew from his mouth. Of course, Davit would misunderstand his meaning. There was no context to guide him otherwise. Everything was spiraling beyond his control; with each thought that spilled into words he caused more harm. What had been a glorious morning now lay in ruins, torched by the truth that was screaming to be revealed. *Enough,* he scolded himself quietly. This had gone too far. It was time. He would rather lose him to the truth than let him believe he did not want him as a son.

"Davit," Sebastiaan rasped, his voice raw with regret, "no, you misunderstand. I am not worthy of being called 'father' – not when it was I who had been lying to you. I can't let you apologize for protecting your mother."

Davit clamped his eyes shut, his father's voice a distant drone bleeding into the background, his words melting into a meaningless slurry. His breathing thinned to shallow gasps, the air was thick enough to swallow, and he felt the blackness gathering at the edges of his mind. The world stilled, the morning rays nothing more than a cold smear. Jiya's death was a wound that would, over time, harden into a scar. The ache would eventually fade. But losing his father was unlike any pain he'd ever known. It burned, eating the flesh around it, burrowing deep. He knew if he opened his eyes, his stomach would turn inside out, as he could feel the ground tilting beneath him.

Sebastiaan closed a hand around Davit's arm just as the boy tipped sideways. He was deathly pale and struggling to remain upright.

"Come on," he said and gently pulled Davit to his feet. "It is time to head back. You nearly fell into the water again."

Sebastiaan tugged the shirt from Davit's waist and pulled it over his head, dressing him as if he were a small child. Their conversation would have to wait until Davit was rested. The morning's outing had been a mistake in more ways than one.

***

When Sebastiaan and Davit returned from the river Danielle knew instinctively that something was wrong. The cave instantly felt crowded, and so she resigned herself to the position of quiet observer.

Davit's complexion held a sickly color, and he seemed weaker than she would have expected. Perhaps he was not ready to be up and about just yet. Still, the sooner he started moving, the faster he would heal. It was

449

always so with those who had a close brush with death; they needed to be up and moving long before they felt they were ready. She would give him a few hours' rest and nudge him toward some small task to get his blood pumping again.

Sebastiaan was a greater concern. She'd woken with a feeling of wellbeing. They'd slept entangled in each other's arms. After their intimate afternoon by the river her muscles were wonderfully sore, and it drew a secretive smile to her face. But in the quiet of the morning, alone for a fleeting moment, a flicker of self-doubt crept in, wondering how they would face each other now, fearing the awkwardness would create tension when all she wanted was to breathe and enjoy the euphoria of having him back in her life. It was as if she was slowly waking to reality. The first day was a blur of emotions, too many and too confusing to unravel. The day before shimmered like a dream, and today everything was beginning to feel real. She could still remember the smell of his skin, the low resonance of his voice, and the warm touch of his hand. Then he returned from the river and Sebastiaan was a stranger – distant, closed off behind the high walls he'd erected somewhere during their brief time apart. Danielle refused to attach meaning to his behavior, determined to wait for a chance to speak with him alone. If she'd learned one thing about herself, it was that she had a talent for improvised misconstruction, and it was a deuced inconvenience.

Sebastiaan had guided Davit to his bed. Then, without meeting her eye, murmured that the cow needed milking and left the cave with determined strides.

"Is everything alright, darling?" she asked Davit when they were alone.

He nodded and leaned his head back against the roll of fur.

"Just a bit tired," he replied. "I'll feel better in a moment. Don't fret."

Danielle frowned; it was unlike him to pass up a chance to coax even a trickle of sympathy from her. With a faint sigh and a small shake of her head, she turned to her scant belongings, splitting them into two piles: things to leave behind and things to take with her. She'd begun the task earlier, and with each pass, the 'leave behind' pile grew larger.

True to his word, Captain De Coninck arrived around mid-morning, whistling a jaunty tune to announce his approach to the cave. Sebastiaan had returned moments earlier, and De Coninck strode in, carrying a basket of freshly cooked flatbread dusted with speckles of char from the bakestone. He clapped Sebastiaan firmly on the back and delivered a quick kiss to Danielle's cheek, then studied them both with a knowing look. Mercifully, he kept his thoughts to himself and turned to Davit's bedside instead.

Danielle watched as De Coninck gently eased Davit back down when he struggled to rise. Their introduction was softly spoken, meant for their ears only, and she battled against the emotion pressing behind her eyes. De Coninck was doing this for her, a silent message of acceptance, a promise that all would be well without having to persuade her. With his generous heart, he had built a fierce and devoted family, and now she and her child were drawn into that exclusive circle. She stood among men who did not know how to surrender or fail, who would rip the world apart to shield their own. Sensing the weight of her thoughts, Sebastiaan's hand sought hers, his fingers closing around it in a steady, comforting grip.

"I don't deserve this," she sighed.

"None of us do," he said, glancing at his uncle. "He has a way of fixing everything."

With De Coninck's arrival, Sebastiaan's mood seemed to shift. The heaviness lifted from the air, leaving it lighter, easier to breathe. When his eyes caught hers, the warmth in them flickered back to life. Danielle swallowed the urge to pry into his dark mood from earlier; perhaps it was best to leave it alone for now.

The conversation between De Coninck and Davit drifted languidly, as if they had all the time in the world, their hushed tones occasionally interspersed with laughter.

The smell of the flatbread was too much to resist. Danielle sank down next to the basket, handing one to Sebastiaan before tearing into hers with unapologetic enthusiasm, barely able to suppress the satisfied groan that followed the first bite. Her bliss, however, was short-lived, as Sebastiaan reached over and pried the bread from her fingers.

"You'll choke if you eat it so fast," he cautioned.

"I haven't tasted bread in nigh on two decades. If I die now, it'll be with a smile on my face. Now, give it back," she demanded, thrusting out her hand, only partly faking her aggression.

"Let me make this better for you," Sebastiaan said, then took his time slathering the flatbread with honey. Crumbling hard cheese between his fingers, he dusted it over the glistening surface before passing it back to her. The sweet-savory mix flooded her mouth, and she leaned in to kiss him right then and there in front of their small audience, before quickly dipping her head to hide her flushing face.

When De Coninck joined them, his eyes were sparkling with amusement. The force of his gaze landed on Danielle, noting the deep blush that covered her face, before steering the conversation to practical matters – tasks to be done, plans to be set – dulling the spark that had flared between her and Sebastiaan.

Danielle considered the weight of her decision, her thoughts growing more troubled as the minutes wore on. She was about to leave her life behind again. This time, it was of her own choosing. No one pursued or threatened her; she wasn't running for her life; she was simply leaving, like an insect morphing into another form, leaving behind the skeleton of its old existence. Closing her eyes, she fought against the rising tide of fear.

She and Sebastiaan had scarcely known each other when they'd parted years ago, both so young and naïve. A lifetime had passed since then, during which they had lived separately, and now they were about to start a life together. What if they no longer fit as they once thought? What if they woke one morning, not far from now, realizing that they have been chasing ghosts, memories of people that no longer existed, and that reality is far from their youthful imaginings? They would be stuck; he was too honorable to leave her, and she was too selfish to let him go. Not leaving with him today was unthinkable, and yet the alternative was terrifying. Today demanded her to take a leap of faith, placing her fate in the hands of another.

From above the fray, her mind silently judged the situation, finding it fraught with obvious dangers and pervasive uncertainty. But, for the first time in her life, the war-drum beat of her heart overpowered her thoughts, drowning out reason's persistent cautions. Dreams were born from the heart, pure and free of doubt and dispute. Those were the burdens of the mind. Now, her longing surged past her logic, wild and unyielding. This was what she'd craved for as long as her memory held, a family to call her own, people belonging to her and she to them. It was not just her vision but that of Sebastiaan and Davit too, their hopes and needs woven into hers.

She looked at her son, and the last of her doubts lifted. He was her blood, her steadfast anchor. Together, they would navigate the unknown. This time she was not alone.

Sebastiaan must have sensed her mounting trepidation, as his body tensed and the lines on his face deepened.

"The cattle are yours, Danielle. What do you want to do with them?" he asked, his voice emotionless, bordering on cold.

She had missed most of what had passed between him and his uncle, and it took her a moment to gather her wits.

"Kai left them as a gift to you," she said. "They are not mine."

"It is a generous gift," De Coninck stated. "I am not sure how I can repay it."

"We can't," she said with a sad smile. "There is nothing we have that they need."

Inhaling deeply, she tried to push through the weight of grief that had unexpectedly settled over her. The *Cochoqua* were not her people, but they had opened their hearts and their home to her when she had nowhere to go and no one to turn to. With them, she had found safety and purpose. Sebastiaan and De Coninck planned on returning to Batavia in less than a week. How could she just walk away from this life and leave everything familiar behind?

"I would like to visit John's grave," Sebastiaan said, pulling Danielle back to the conversation. "And then, I want to sleep on my own ship tonight."

"I thought as much," De Coninck replied. "I had the stateroom readied for you."

"Thank you, uncle, but no. You will captain us home. We'll stay in the guest cabins below."

Davit remained on his pallet, unsure and uncharacteristically shy upon meeting the man after whom he was named. He stared at his grandfather with a mixture of awe and wonder, matching similarities between De Coninck and Sebastiaan and those he knew of himself. He drank in every movement and gesture De Coninck made. Time stilled, and the world shrunk to a single moment where the mythical creature of his mother's stories took on a living, breathing form, close enough to touch, sitting with his parents and sharing food. Davit was too afraid to move, scared that he would wake and the picture would vanish.

He did, however, wake when his father ordered him onto the stretcher for the journey back to the beach. There was an unfamiliar edge to his voice.

"Father," the word slipped out before Davit could stop himself. "I am not riding that plank like some shipwrecked pirate," he protested. De Coninck's laughter rang out, cracking the tension between Sebastiaan and Davit like sunlight over a frozen lake.

"Do you prefer I carry you on my back instead?" Sebastiaan asked with a heavy frown, clearly unimpressed by Davit's untimely attack of pride.

"No," he said, and his breath caught painfully in his chest. "I prefer to walk."

"And I prefer to get to the beach before sundown. You can't even speak without losing your breath. Now, get on the damn stretcher." Sebastiaan countered. His gaze was sharp and his tone cutting, brokering no further arguments.

Defeated and embarrassed, Davit rose from his bed and slowly lowered himself onto the wooden stretcher.

"May I make a suggestion," De Coninck spoke from Danielle's side, and when father and son looked at him with identical expressions of exasperation, he had to employ an unusual amount of self-restraint to contain the rest of his amusement. "Why don't we carry the lad until near the beach and then let him walk the last few yards, for appearance's sake?"

Davit was not fool enough to defy his father, not with this hard glint in his eye and not after the morning they'd shared, but when he caught his father's terse nod he sighed in relief. He would rather not have appeared weak in front of his grandfather. However, maintaining his dignity in front of Orion and the crew was his next best option.

"Thank you, grandfather," he said.

Something broke behind De Coninck's eyes at the boy's words, and he quickly turned to help Danielle pack the last of her herbs into a large leather satchel.

"Why don't the three of you go ahead," Danielle said. "I will follow soon."

She needed a moment alone. The last few days had been a whirlwind of change and upheaval, and her emotions stretched in every direction. She was standing on a precipice and needed a moment of stillness to collect herself, to bid farewell to a significant part of her life, to be alone with her thoughts and memories before embarking on her new life.

Sebastiaan rounded on her with such speed that she involuntarily took a step back. His fingers clamped around her upper arm in a firm grip as he hauled her from the cave. Danielle had to quicken her steps to keep up, lest she wanted to be dragged behind him.

They marched down the narrow path until they were well out of earshot of Davit and De Coninck. Then he spun her to face him. He was upset, his lips pressed into a thin, harsh line that sliced through his features. He looked every bit the warrior going into battle. For a fleeting instant, Danielle thought he might burst into a thousand flaming shards. He didn't try to hide his fury from her; rather, he seemed ready to incinerate her with it. He was a far cry from the easy-tempered, slow-to-anger young man of her youth.

"Don't do this, Danielle," he spoke in her face, his breath scorching and his eyes burning with anger and panic. He gentled his grip, but he did not let go of her. "Don't you dare turn your back on me again. I know what is going on in that mind of yours, and will not stand for it this time."

Danielle's first reaction was complete amazement. She opened her mouth to defend herself against his bitter words, but understanding sank in and she swallowed her retort. This was what he had feared every day for seventeen years – that she might not want him anymore, that he had been living on the thinnest thread of hope, only for it all to unravel. This was Sebastiaan De Vries, laid bare in his most vulnerable form. She doubted anyone had ever seen him like this. This moment, this rawness, was meant for her alone, an unwitting show of trust and with that the uncertainty that smoldered in her belly died a silent, honest death.

Whatever he saw in her face led him down the wrong path.

"Damn you, Danielle," he breathed, his voice low and rough as he pressed a bruising kiss to her lips. "You are leaving here with me. If I have to tie you up and carry you to the ship, then so be it. Do not test me on this, sweetheart." His words hissed from between clenched teeth, his eyes flashing, and the muscles and veins in his neck bulged.

Danielle knew he was moments away from delivering on his promise and still he could not hold back the endearment, although it sounded more like a threat than affection. Those heated words shattered her doubts. He wanted her, and he was prepared to wage war to keep her. The relief flooding her was as fierce as his panic. The feeling was so liberating she burst out laughing.

Regaining control of herself, she said, "I will not leave you," then had to look away from him for fear of forgetting herself again when she saw the stunned confusion on his face. "I simply need a moment alone to say goodbye. I've fled Holland, and I've fled the settlement. This time I want to leave in peace." Her voice softened as she added, "This cave and that little village have been my home. Please allow me to do that."

Sebastiaan ran his hand through his hair and then down his face. The red haze of his temper was receding, leaving him shaking in the aftermath. His visceral reaction to the hesitation he'd sensed in her had shocked him.

"Forgive me," he murmured, shaking his head as if trying to clear away the last tendrils of anger. "Take all the time you need, but please, be as quick as you can."

Danielle lingered outside, watching Sebastiaan and De Coninck carry Davit slowly down the narrow footpath on the wooden litter. Only when they disappeared around the bend did she step into the shadows of her cave.

Standing in the open space, she took in the familiar surroundings. The sleeping furs, now tightly rolled into bundles, resting against the far wall next to the neatly stacked bowls. The fire was extinguished, the ashes still warm but lifeless. She traced her hand across the ancient paintings on the wall, remembering the night that Davit was born, when the fire had brought the primitive figures to life. She had drawn strength from them; they had endured, and so would she.

She closed her hand around the small leather pouch containing her casting bones and lifted it over her head. They didn't belong to her; they belonged to the tribe and their next healer. She brought the pouch to her lips, whispered a protective prayer over them, then tucked them deep inside the roll of furs.

Never look back. Kai's words drifted to her. With that, she straightened, stepped out of the cave, and into the sunlight.

***

Any trace of tranquility that once reigned over the small crescent beach was a long-forgotten memory pushed into obscurity by the clamor of fifty men consumed with ship repair.

Orion stood just one layer shy of being naked, but compared to the throng around him, he qualified as overdressed. The day had baked itself into a fine state of intolerability, forcing him to allocate two men to the endless task of hauling fresh drinking water from the river.

They had arrived the day before, towed by every skiff from the *Danielle* and the *Sword* to this ribbon of scorching sand. Guiding the *Sword* past the jagged rocks of the lagoon's mouth was a nerve-racking ordeal, that demanded stout hearts and flint-hard nerves, but a chorus of grunts and curses, honest prayers, and earnest pleas to long-dead kin, had seen them through.

A grueling day had bled into a relentless night without rest, during which they'd stripped the ship of anything not bolted down. They had also dismantled the three masts and set them carefully along the beach's edge, well clear of the fray and beyond the tide's reach. At dawn, Orion tasked ten men with raising two rows of tents with exact specifications as to the distance between them and their alignment. Just because they were on land did not mean they should live like savages. Order and precision were next to godliness, with cleanliness a close third, he added to appease the voice of his childhood governess still ringing from the far corners of his memory.

Now his beloved ship was lying on her side, secured and stabilized by hawser lines tied to trees and poles driven deep into the sand, looking like an insect caught in a gigantic spider web.

The two crews were split into three teams, one working on the ship, another securing timber and food, and the third sleeping. No loitering was tolerated and Orion prowled between the men in an endless cycle of inspection, his eyes catching every detail, change, and improvement. Pausing by a newly patched part of the hull, he ran his hand along the fresh caulking, testing its evenness, his disapproving frown already in place. A nervous-looking sailor stood next to him as he continued his inspection. These men were seasoned sailors, on loan from his grandfather. Even though De Coninck hired only the best, Orion didn't trust them on reputation alone.

"Tighter on the seam here," he said when his fingers stilled over a barely perceivable gap. He scanned the beach as the man stammered an apology. Signs of strain were beginning to show.

"Everyone, take a water break – now," Orion ordered. The men laid down their tools and muttered their thanks as they shuffled past him.

The lone measured tap of a hammer drew Orion's attention. He walked around the stern, hunting for the obstinate or deaf sailor. He found Niccolò hunched over the rudder, dressed in a long white tunic brushing his ankles and a wide-brimmed hat with one side slightly turned up. It was unclear whether this effect was due to poor storage or some fleeting stab at style. He looked like some Bedouin trying his hand at obscurity and failing spectacularly.

"Capitano," Niccolò said before Orion could call to him, and well before he thought his carpenter could hear his near-soundless approach. Niccolò straightened, arched his back, and winced.

"What's with the dress?" Orion asked.

"It is a *thobe,* not a dress," Niccolò corrected him pointedly. "Good for air flow, *capisce?*" He added and waved his hand in the direction of his groin.

"Yes, unfortunately I understand," Orion replied. "I'm sorry I asked. When was the last time you had a break?"

Niccolò looked like he'd just been woken from a deep sleep. Scratching the back of his head and squinting one eye half-shut, he calculated backward, thumbing through his memory as he tried to find the correct answer to his captain's question.

"Never mind," Orion said and punched out a sigh. He was about to put an end to Niccolò's shift when his eye caught the protrusion at the back of his ship.

"What is that?"

Niccolò never spoke more than five words consecutively, unless he was talking about his work or preparing for action.

"During the battle, I was surprised that the rudder was damaged. The way we were positioned made such a shot nearly impossible."

Orion studied the dismantled instrument that laid neatly spread out on a clean stretch of canvas, like the fossilized skeleton of some unknown beast.

"Turns out the rudder is fine, but the sternpost got hit."

The sternpost was a vertical piece of timber extending from the keel, providing the attachment point for the rudder. What used to resemble a thick vein running along the ship's spine now looked like an oversized dorsal fin.

"I've reinforced it with thicker timber and additional bracing," Niccolò continued. "To better absorb or even deflect a cannon shot in the future."

It was an unusual solution, but an ingenious one.

"It might also stabilize the rudder, keep it functional even after suffering a hit," Orion mused. "Good work, Niccolò."

The carpenter beamed at his captain's rare nod of approval. Orion did not toss praise around lightly; his crew took a dodged tongue lashing as proof of their competence.

"If the rudder was undamaged, pray, why must the entire thing be torn apart?" Orion asked skeptically.

"Aye, well, I want to replace all her fittings and grease them properly before mounting it again. Also, with your leave." Orion rolled his eyes at the belated request for permission. "I want to add some planking around the rudder area, for extra protection," Niccolò said, gesturing over the scattered parts with his finger.

The hum of the men's laughter and chatter abruptly died, and Orion spun around to determine the source of the interruption. There, at the edge of the beach, almost exactly where he and Jiya had encountered Davit nearly a year ago, stood a woman flanked by De Coninck, Sebastiaan, and a frail-looking Davit.

"Do as you see fit, Niccolò," Orion said absentmindedly. "Just remember, we are not staying until Christmas. We are leaving within the next few days, rudder or not." It was an empty threat and his carpenter knew it, but the sentiment was clear enough. He was not staying on this godforsaken continent any longer than absolutely necessary. Orion raised his eyes to the gathering bank of dark clouds slowly rolling in from the north, promising a wet evening that would most likely carry into the night. Cursing softly, he strode toward the newly arrived group.

The woman was clad in what might generously be called a leather dress. It was nothing more than a large strip of soft animal skin wrapped around her body and cinched at one side with a tangle of leather strings and knotted roughly over her shoulder. The covering would cause both men and women to faint, but for wildly different reasons. Though it covered her entire body from shoulder to mid-calf, it would be considered the height of indecency by civilized standards. She wore leather footwraps, bound tightly with a wide leather strip wound around her feet and ankles. Despite her primitive clothing, she stood as regal as a queen, her chin tilted and her shoulders loose, utterly at peace with herself and her surroundings.

Orion was quick to blame his shortness of breath on the brisk walk he'd just endured through the loose, hot sand, and snapped his attention to his cousin.

"Good to see you found your pulse again, cousin," Orion said, wrapping his arms around Davit and lifting him clean off his feet in a boisterous embrace. "You're just skin and bone. How am I to kick your arse when there's nothing left to aim at? Go over to Harja and find something to eat." He set Davit back on his feet and rounded on Sebastiaan.

"Hell uncle, with that blush on your cheeks, a swift wedding is not just a suggestion but a requirement. Good to see you."

"Good to see you too, you insolent whelp," Sebastiaan said as they clasped forearms. "Orion," Sebastiaan sobered and turned to Danielle. "This is–"

"Danielle," Orion rasped, his eyes fixed on the woman by Sebastiaan's side. Seeing his cousin alive and well enough to stand on his own two feet had caused the black cloud that had been hanging over him since Jiya's death to lift, but the sight of Danielle up close drove all merriment from his mind.

She was undeniably appealing. Orion checked himself; *appealing* was too tame, flat, like tepid tea, adequate to describe most women of his acquaintance, fleeting, forgettable, boring. This woman was stunning. Her beauty was not the kind to turn every head, inspire syrupy poems or pretty pictures. It was the sort meant for portraits that adorn gallery walls – timeless, arresting, indelible. She was one of those unassuming women who quietly judged you as you walked past until you glanced back to find yourself rooted to the spot because she wouldn't let you go. Her green eyes sparkled with intelligence, impatience, and humor. This was the type of woman for whom men went to battle and after whom ships were named. She could be dressed in anything from the finest gown to a simple wheat sack and it would do little to temper the effect – her makeshift leather dress, a case in point.

"Mistress De Vries," Orion coughed lightly and bent over her hand to place a reverent kiss on her skin.

Sebastiaan was momentarily stunned by Orion's rare display of chivalry. "Not yet, but soon," he growled and snatched Danielle's hand from Orion's grip.

"Orion," Danielle said and gave him a soft maternal smile. "The little boy I once spent a night under the stars with so long ago. You probably would not remember, but you taught me the names of the constellations, and in return, I taught you to play the violin. It feels like another lifetime, doesn't it?"

"I don't remember the night under the stars, more's the pity, but I do remember the violin lessons."

"Do you still play?"

"I do." He gave her his most radiant smile and turned to Davit, who had won himself a large piece of cheese from Harja's bleeding heart.

As Orion's scattered thoughts regrouped, he became aware of a peculiar tension that seemed to persist beyond his amateurish attempts at levity. The past fortnight had tested them all, and he chalked it up to sheer exhaustion, coupled with the emotional plunge Sebastiaan faced now that he'd finally found Danielle after nearly two decades of searching.

Still, lingering here, staring at his uncle's soon-to-be wife and waking to the epiphany of why every other woman he'd ever crossed paths with had been a dull misstep – they were all young, simpering, and foolish – wouldn't do a bloody thing to get his ship fixed faster, and the day was drawing to a quick end. It was Sebastiaan who finally ended their small gathering when he turned to De Coninck and asked, in a hallowed voice, to see John's grave.

Davit shot Orion a questioning glance. At first, Orion wondered if he'd imagined the strained atmosphere, but one look at Davit confirmed his observation. The lad looked nervous and unsure of himself.

"Why don't you go ahead? Cousin, let's take a walk," Orion suggested, nudging Davit's shoulder. To his surprise, Davit nodded instantly, almost eager to leave. The small group parted ways – De Coninck leading Sebastiaan and Danielle in one direction, while Orion and Davit turned toward the beached ship.

As they neared the *Sword*, Davit's strides faded to a halt. "Oh no," he breathed, the two words thick with sorrow. "She's torn to shreds." He paused to assess the damage and to collect what little scraps his memory offered. "I remember flashes of fighting. But I had many confusing dreams, and I had hoped the cannon fire was part of them."

"It's not as bad as it looks," Orion said. "She has a double hull. Most of the damage was confined to the outer skin."

"And John died." Davit said as if Orion had not spoken at all. Orion narrowed his eyes at his cousin, wondering at the boy's disconnected observations, but indulging him. Something was most definitely not as it should be. This demurred, almost defeated attitude was very much in opposition to the lad's normal bluster and swagger.

"He died during the battle, five days after we left the Cape. Your father insisted he be buried on land." Davit's face twisted further into a knot of confusion.

"The days won't stitch together," he said, and pressed the pad of his thumb between his gathering brows as if to push the events into place. Orion let out a weary sigh, then pointed to a large tree a few yards off the beach, far enough to offer privacy for their impending conversation, near enough for him to keep an eye on the activity of the sailors.

"Davit," Orion said, once they were seated, his voice low and steady, drawing his cousin's full attention. He wasn't sure how much more Davit could bear in his fragile state, but he pressed on all the same. "Jiya's gone. He died the night of the fire – the night you were shot."

"I remember," Davit said quietly, and shuddered visibly. "I saw him lying next to me on the beach." He remembered Jiya's burned body, his ravaged face. Jiya had used the last of his strength to turn his head toward him. It was a sight that would haunt him to his last day. Jiya had made the ultimate sacrifice to save his life. Davit turned his head away, swiped his hand across his face, surprised when it came away wet with tears.

"He died saving me," Davit said, his grief susurrating through his words. "It is a debt I can never repay." He shook his head, and when he spoke again, his eyes were dark and his lips twisted into a bitter curl. "He left that weight for me to carry."

"What? You'd rather he'd left you there to die?" Orion's temper flared, but he ruthlessly held it in check.

"How the *fuck* am I supposed to live with that?" Davit's voice burned with anger.

Pinching the bridge of his nose, Orion reminded himself that it was an exceedingly bad idea to strangle his last living relative.

"One grateful day at a time. Listen to me," Orion's voice held the same stern notes as De Coninck's when Orion's runaway emotions had pushed him down some steep and slippery slope. "Self-pity is unbecoming, so stop it right now. Yes, he died saving you and we are all humbled by it, but any one of us would have done the same in his place. You would have done that for him. It is who we are. Your duty now is to live a life worthy of his sacrifice."

"And besides," Orion went on, "this is not about you." Davit shot him a look of stark bewilderment. "It is about Jiya," Orion explained, faint bitterness edging his calm tone. "He reached the ultimate goal."

"What is that?" Davit asked.

"To die with honor."

A heavy silence unfurled. Neither wished to disturb it. Davit slumped against the tree at his back with his eyes closed, listening to the rise and fall of the men's voices. Orion leaned forward, arms draped over his knees, lost in a rare moment of reflection.

Harja arrived, bringing much needed distraction in the form of two trenchers of roasted fish and a modest stack of flatbread. Orion reached for the food and gave his chef a terse nod.

"Eat something," Orion said. "It will make you feel better."

"Food will not fix this."

"Nothing will fix this, but if you don't eat, you will not regain your strength and continue to waste away. Then all of this was for nothing." Orion knew the black spiral Davit was caught in and it was pulling him into a dark and dangerous place. His callous words had their intended effect. Davit jolted upright, then groaned in pain as the wound in his side protested the sudden movement.

"You can't really be this cynical," he said and pushed the food away.

"It's not cynicism. It is a way forward."

"I am going to kill him," Davit vowed.

"If you mean Alain Du Bois." Davit nodded, his green eyes sparkling menacingly in his pale face. "You are too late; he is already dead. Eat," Orion said, and pointed to the food between them. "It was Du Bois who gave us this beating."

"How was that possible? The *Sword* is fast. She can outrun most anything," Davit spoke around the food in his mouth.

"We lost a lot of men that night." Orion was referring to the night the crew protected the farmers from the fort's soldiers. "The *Sword's* fast if she's got hands on her sails, but we were cut down to a scant few, which made it easy for Du Bois to catch us. Outrunning him was not an option, so we decided to fight. We traded cannon fire back and forth and then they boarded us." His eyes were fixed on his ship, his flat, detached recounting painted the battle in stark black and white lines with hints of gray where the events bled into each other, but on the whole, it was untouched by any hue of emotion.

"You see," Orion paused as he carefully arranged the words in his mind. "I wanted to kill Du Bois the night we freed Sebastiaan from the *Dark Hole*."

"Why didn't you?" Davit asked.

"Well, for one, there was no time, and for another Sebastiaan was dead set against it."

"Why?"

"Du Bois was my father." Orion saw how the shock of the statement widened Davit's eyes. "Sebastiaan thought it would be a scar against my soul if I were to do such a thing." He shook his head. "It wasn't. I found him in my cabin, and I killed him."

"Did he know you were his son?"

"I told him right before I pierced his rotten heart." Orion's face was hard and cold. "It was a blood debt for what he did to my mother, to Jiya, and to you."

"I understand about your mother and Jiya, but what am I to you?" Davit asked.

Orion stared at his cousin. Of all the people in his life, Davit was the one he wished he could speak to without the barrier of secrets between them. The lad was his blood, something he never had before and never knew how much he would treasure. He opened his mouth to speak but quickly slammed it shut again. He had sworn an oath to Sebastiaan, and he would keep it.

"I don't know how the battle would have ended," he said, deciding to ignore Davit's question, "had our grandfather not ended it for us with that almighty cannon hidden in the *Danielle's* belly. Through it all, your father refused to leave your side. He was the only one below decks, and afterward, we had to practically climb a small hill of dead bodies to get to you."

"Where was John?"

"We found his body on the upper deck. He had been shot." A frown had worked itself between Orion's eyes. "I would never have thought it possible for a stray shot to slip through the chaos to strike true, but one found him, nonetheless. He died instantly." Orion fell silent, lost for a moment in the memory of that day. "He was a formidable son of a bitch with those twin blades in his hands."

"I am sorry about Jiya," Davit said, wishing he had more than just those few inadequate words to offer Orion.

"We all are," Orion returned.

"But Jiya was like a brother to you," Davit persisted, driven by a need to pierce Orion's guarded front.

"He was, and I will deal with that loss in my own time, and in my own way," Orion warned. "Leave it be."

Davit nodded stubbornly, refusing to bow to the barricades Orion was raising around himself. "I see," he said, narrowing his eyes. "What was that you said about self-pity?" He raised his chin to study the tops of the surrounding trees. "Oh right, I remember now – unbecoming, was that it?"

Orion could not swallow the wan smile quick enough, but he twisted it into a snarl at the last moment.

"Has anyone ever told you what a magnificent specimen of an arse ulcer you are?" Orion taunted, grateful for the break in the solemn conversation, but then Davit pulled them right back into it.

"I can't breathe with this guilt," Davit said.

"You can't breathe because you've been shot in the lung."

Davit huffed a soft smile. "I'm not like you. I can't bury this and hope it will die of neglect."

Orion regarded his young cousin, mulling over his words. The boy was still untouched by bitterness and disappointment.

"I'll teach you to play the violin," he said.

"Is that why you play?"

Orion only stared at him, not willing to answer such a personal question.

"Because it is better than talking," Davit murmured. It was not a question, but a mere statement of fact. In that moment, Davit understood what Orion would not admit – he too was alone and fighting for his next breath.

Chapter 26

Visiting John's grave had understandably deepened Sebastiaan's brooding mood. Danielle noticed it in the way his shoulders sagged, as though an unseen weight was pushing down on them. At times, in unguarded moments his eyes held a depth that hinted at a quiet inner turmoil; troubled thoughts still waiting to find words. This shadowed side of him was foreign to Danielle, leaving her to wonder if it had always been there, hidden beneath layers of youthful exuberance, or if it had developed over the years, forged by the demands of a harsh life.

De Coninck had chosen a beautiful place for Van Leyen's grave. He had prepared them beforehand, explaining only that it was a bit away, but he'd failed to say that 'a bit' equated to roughly half an hour's walk, then a climb down a steep, rocky outcrop to a small glade a few yards below, overlooking the ocean and cradled by jagged rocks with a single large tree rooted at its heart. It was the perfect place for a solitary grave, too small and secluded to invite visitors or future inhabitants.

"I asked him to find a special place," Sebastiaan said, watching his uncle's retreating form as he made his way back to the beach, climbing the ridge with an agility unbefitting for his age.

"I lit a fire in your memory each year," Danielle said. "Had I known this place existed, I would have come here instead. It is perfect."

It was a sheltered place, yet alive with sound. Seagulls screeched as they swooped toward the ocean below, chasing their next meal, while waves crashed against the cliffs in tireless cadence.

"Davit told me that you did that at the beginning of every summer and that you sat by your fire all night." He looked at her with such a wealth of emotion, her heart stuttered.

"They told me your ship went down on the eighth of November." She shrugged as if it was a trifling matter. "After leaving the settlement, I had no means of keeping track of days and dates, only a rough estimation of the year, but I knew the first moon of the summer would fall on or around that date. I picked the darkest night to build a fire large enough for you to see from heaven." He drew her into his arms and pressed his lips to the top of her head. They stood like that for a long while before he let her go. She stepped back, and he sat down beside John's grave to stare at the ocean.

Danielle understood Sebastiaan needed silence, not solitude. Born with an inability to sit still for long, she had not even tried to join him in his observance. Instead, she roamed the area, gathering stones to encircle the grave. With each stone placed, she whispered a prayer of protection. Then she climbed back to the top of the escarpment to pick wildflowers, which she scattered over Van Leyen's resting place until every patch of dirt was hidden beneath a floral blanket. When the breeze blew some away, she didn't bother retrieving them; she simply picked more to pour over the cheerful pile. Through it all, Sebastiaan remained still, at times closing his eyes, his hand resting on the grave. She watched his lips move as he spoke to his friend, saw the single tear roll down his cheek.

By late afternoon, the storm, roiling with swirls of gray and purple, growled overhead, stirring Sebastiaan from his thoughts. When the first fat drops splattered on the ground, he rose to his feet and took in the transformed surroundings, as if seeing them for the first time. A riot of flowers blanketed the mound of earth, spreading softly from its heart to the farthest reaches of the clearing and he slowly turned toward Danielle.

"I'm sorry," she said, and dropped her gaze guiltily. "Everything looked so dreary. And I couldn't let him be that way," she shook her head and cleared her throat, searching for words to excuse what she knew could be interpreted as an overreaction.

"He would have liked it," Sebastiaan smiled. "He would have liked it a lot." Looking up at the dark clouds, he wondered briefly if Van Leyen was stirring this sudden surge of atmospheric violence, urging him and Danielle to get going. He was never one to ponder over things that could not be changed. *Life should be lived forward* – was the banner under which John had lived his life.

Reaching for her hand Sebastiaan guided her up the rocky slope. Danielle smiled and accepted his polite gesture, not pointing out that she'd made the trip countless times earlier. Then, keeping her hand in his, their fingers intertwined as they strolled back to the beach. Their pace was lazy as if there were no rush, no one waiting for their return, and no storm brewing overhead. By the time they reached the narrow beach, two skiffs stood ready to carry them to Sebastiaan's ship. De Coninck had insisted they dine together as a family for the first time that evening. Sebastiaan settled Danielle onto a bench in the middle of the rowboat, where she was shielded by him and the other rowers. Davit joined De Coninck and Orion in the second skiff.

The storm nipped at their heels, more bluster than bite thus far, but the men were rowing at a feverish pace. The air was laden with the scent of rain, every so often a few drops spattered their linen shirts.

When they cleared the mouth of the lagoon Danielle instantly remembered why she despised traveling by skiff. It always left her with the distinct impression of being stuck on a small piece of flotsam while at the mercy of the mighty ocean. They were rowing with the tide and it dramatically increased their speed. As they hit the open sea, a sudden swell hoisted the small boat skyward, then plunged it sharply into the calmer waters beyond. Danielle could see the next wave rolling toward them and squeezed her eyes shut, gripping the bench beneath her, knuckles whitening, fingertips digging into the wood. None of the men, Sebastiaan included, spared her a glance, their focus locked on steering and timing their strokes to keep the skiff from capsizing. She knew they didn't consider the journey perilous in the least, having faced conditions much worse than this, but as she sat there clinging to her seat, she vowed that this was the last time she would ever subject herself to this torture. Another wave lifted them high, and her eyes snapped open of their own accord. As they crested the last wave the heavens opened. Through the curtain of rain, Sebastiaan's ship loomed larger as the men guided the small boat expertly to its side with a gentle bump.

Sebastiaan let out a sharp whistle, and moments later, sailors swung a boatswain's chair over the side of the ship. Dread filled Danielle when she realized they meant for her to sit on that narrow strip of wood as they hoisted her aboard. The worst part of the ordeal would be rising from the seat she was currently sitting on. With the small boat rolling precariously beneath her feet, she feared she'd topple into the water before even reaching the wretched chair. The first words of her refusal were primed and ready to spill with scathing earnestness, when her eyes caught the ship's name blazoned in large letters along its hull: *Danielle.* Her breath caught, and tears flooded her eyes. She blinked hard, fighting the rush of emotion. He'd named his ship for her. All these years, her name had crossed the seas, a silent testament to his unwavering devotion. Her fingers flew to her mouth, and she could not look away from the bold white letters. Sebastiaan's hands slipped under her arms, lifting her effortlessly from the bench and lowering her onto the boatswain's chair.

"Hold on tight," he said, ensuring she gripped the thick ropes by her sides. She meant to argue a poignant case for the rope ladder instead, but as soon as her fists closed around the lines, he flashed a signal to the men above. In her next breath – drawn deeply with the express purpose of shouting at him – she shot up the ship's side, streaking past the white letters that had gripped her moments earlier. It all happened so fast. By the time she had rolled her berating words into a full-bodied scream, the chair had already cleared the railing. A sailor lifted her from it and gently set her down on her feet.

"Thank you," she breathed, as she tried to calm her racing heart and still her shaking knees.

Within moments, she found herself in the midst of a reverse exodus. Men from both skiffs swarmed over the bulwark, shouting orders, catching ropes midair, and hurling them across the deck as they prepared to hoist one of the rowboats aboard. She dodged to the side, but every spot she picked earned her a gruff 'Excuse me, madam.' Then Sebastiaan's hand pressed unexpectedly against the small of her back, guiding her toward a narrow companionway that led to the cabins below decks.

They walked down the confined hallway. Sebastiaan led her to the last of three doors, pushed it open and gestured for her to enter. Danielle stepped over the sill, easing aside as Sebastiaan brushed past to light an oil lamp above a narrow desk against the far wall. She listened to the wick as it sputtered to life. Deep shadows danced as the flame flickered, until he lit a second lamp, bathing the cabin in a warm amber glow that emphasized its sparse dimensions and the few utilitarian pieces of furniture. A cushioned chair flanked the ledger-strewn desk. A washstand blunted one corner, cluttered with an assortment of male accoutrements – a washbowl and pitcher, comb, straight razor, whetstone, strop, shaving brush, and a worn cake of soap. No sleeping bunk softened the room, instead a hammock stretched between two hooks in the low-beamed ceiling. The only indulgence was a trio of wall hooks, bearing a shirt, a coat, and a wilted neckcloth. She stood there taking in the details of his life, folded neatly into this small space.

A knock at the door heralded two burly sailors, each hefting a stout seaman's chest. Danielle pressed herself against the wall at her back as they wrestled the heavy loads through the cramped space, setting them against the opposite side. They nodded to Sebastiaan and slipped out again as quickly as they'd entered. The door clicked shut, leaving them once more alone, tongue-tied in a sudden flush of self-consciousness. Danielle's wet hair was dripping down her back and her leather clothing reeked of damp hide. Sebastiaan was in no better state. His shirt clung to his skin, but he seemed oblivious as he stared at her, locked in a moment they'd both imagined for nearly twenty years. Sebastiaan was the first to break free from the spell. Snatching a cloth from the washstand's side rail, he stepped toward her. With a soft grip, he cupped her chin, tilting her face upward, and dabbed the dampness from her skin before smearing the cloth over her hair in a clumsy attempt to dry it.

"We are not staying here," he reassured her. "There is a cabin perfectly set up for guests, with a proper sleeping bunk, soft rugs, and comfortable furniture. I will ask the cabin boys to prepare it for us."

"I don't mind where we stay," she said, "as long as you don't exile me to a cabin by myself."

Another heavy silence landed between them. His eyes trapped hers, unreadable yet piercing, while a faint twitch at the corner of his mouth betrayed his thoughts. Then he slowly shook his head at her foolish words.

"What is in the chests?" she asked and took the cloth from his hands.

"Your trousseau," he said with a doubtful frown.

"My what?"

"You know," he said, rubbing the back of his neck, "clothes and such." When Danielle only stared, offering no reply, he pressed on. "It is a gift from Orion's carpenter."

That only muddied the matter further, and she nodded along as if it was the most obvious of explanations. She flung open lid of the nearest chest, gaping at its contents before crouching to sift through the items. The chest was filled with garments suited to a wild array of occupations, from a drab brown monk's robe to a dress tailored for a buxom woman of dubious repute.

"Good heavens," she quipped, eyeing a burgundy silk dress with a neckline that plunged like a sinner's prospects. Folding the garment with care, she set it aside, opting instead for the monk's habit, which she snapped taut with a brisk shake. The musty relic released a sigh laced with early onset decay and dust, causing her to expel three rapid-fire sneezes.

"I'm kind of partial to that dress," Sebastiaan said, and pulled his wet shirt over his head. Danielle's mind skipped an entire puddle of thoughts, the habit in her hands forgotten as she stared at his naked chest. Lamplight danced across his frame, glazing the contours of his muscles as they shifted beneath his skin. He had aged with a beauty that was tempered rather than softened. Where youth had lent him a light, effortless charm, time had carved it into a weighted elegance.

She must have made a sound because his attention snapped to her as he reached for the dry shirt on the hook. Heat rose from her neck like mercury on a humid day, climbing rapidly until the tips of her ears glowed. Releasing a tight cough, she looked down at the ugly brown robe strangled in her hands.

"I think the habit will do for dinner," she said, her words spilling out a little too fast as she put the robe down to fumble with the leather ties along her side. The sodden dress clung to her skin, its strings swollen and obstinate, refusing to yield. She tugged at the knot on her shoulder next, but it held firm. Sebastiaan, catching her struggles from the corner of his eyes, reached for his dagger.

"It won't loosen that way," he said. "We'll have to cut the strings."

He approached with the blade in his hand and then paused, waiting for her permission. This was more than just cutting her dress. This was severing her previous life. Once cut, the dress would be ruined, unwearable, a relic of what she'd once been. He understood the significance of this unspoken threshold.

"Cut it," she said.

He did not linger and deftly cut the strings until the dress hung limp around her body.

"Sebastiaan," she said. She did not speak again until he looked up from his task. "I would not presume to know your mind, but the shadows in your eyes run deeper than the loss of our friend." She studied his mouth, once so quick to smile, now drawn into a harsh, stern line. "I've no right to your thoughts, but I hope in time you might share them with me – pleasant or not."

"You have every right." His voice dipped low with the sincerity and he looked away to needlessly fumble with the dagger and its sheath.

Danielle used his moment of inattention to lift the ruined leather covering over her head, wishing feverishly that a strong gust might rush through the small window and snuff out the candles. She was standing before him, completely naked and utterly afraid of his reaction. Years without a looking glass had not made her ignorant of what her fourth decade, having given birth to a child and living a life devoid of any softness, had done to her body. Though they'd spent an intimate afternoon by the river the day before, this time was different. They were half-clothed and rushed then. Now there was time, doubt, and nowhere to hide.

Sebastiaan stilled, every emotion carefully hidden behind a cool façade as he stared at her. The silence in the small cabin stretched to breaking point until all she could hear was the hammering of her heart. She did not dare look into his face, fearing what she might see there. Instead, her eyes settled somewhere on the expanse of his chest.

"Woman," he rasped in a voice that sounded as if it was torn from his throat, "If you don't put that robe on this very instant, we'll miss dinner entirely, and you'll be lucky if lunch even graces your tomorrow."

Danielle released a shaking breath that seemed to rise from the soles of her feet.

"As to your observation," Sebastiaan continued, voice still rough from the earlier heat, "There is not a single facet of my life I wish to keep from you, though I suppose it will take us both some time to grow accustomed to having someone with whom to share our burdens. Still, barring you from my thoughts is not my intention."

There were more questions she wished to ask. He could see them dancing in her eyes and the way she thoughtfully chewed her bottom lip, but she restrained herself and instead continued to wrestle with the robe.

"Danielle," he said, and her movements slowed. "I can't keep lying to Davit. No good will come of it. This charade is burning my guts and eating me alive. I need to tell him the truth."

He shook his head as he watched her getting lost in the folds of the habit, her movements growing gradually more aggressive, and he stepped closer.

"Easy," he said, and with steady hands, he guided her arms into the sleeves, smoothing the coarse fabric over her. The garment was too long and pooled around her feet.

"There is a rope belt in the chest," she said, slightly out of breath, scrunching and rubbing her nose to shake off the musty smell. Sebastiaan scooped it up and cinched it snug around her waist. "We shall tell him together. The lie began with me. I never meant to cause harm, and I never thought in a thousand years that I would face this situation. But be that as it may, I'm the one who placed you in this position."

He began to protest, but she laid her fingers over his mouth. "I don't regret the lie – it gave him you – only the need to have woven it in the first place."

Kissing her fingers, he gently removed her hand. "This matter is between Davit and I. No one could blame you for what you've done, and once he learns the truth, he'll understand it too. But some of the blame lies with me as well. I could have told him from the start – there was nothing holding me back other than my own selfishness. I thought you were gone, and still I let the lie continue. For us to have any hope of a future, we must have this conversation alone. He is no longer a child. I am not willing to lose the man he has become over the one that I am now."

Seeing the anguish on his face and the mixture of shame and guilt in his eyes, knowing it was her doing, gave her heart a nasty stab. "Sitting back while you clean up this tangle makes me feel like a coward, and I loathe it," Danielle said, pinching her bottom lip between her fingers as she searched for another way.

"You're no coward." Sebastiaan's hands closed on her shoulders in a firm grip. "But you are mine now; mine to protect, and mine to defend." He waited for her to yield, but when she met him with that familiar, defiant silence, he pressed on. "This is not about you alone. You gave me a son, and you gave Davit a father. Let us find our own way to keep each other."

"I think I understand," Danielle conceded, her tone soft but edged. "And I promise not to interfere, but I still don't like it."

"Do you trust me?" he asked, letting go of her shoulders.

"Yes."

The darkness drifted from his eyes, and a small smile played on his lips. He stared at her, taking in the delicate lines of her face, and the few sun-freckles scattered across her forehead.

"I believe God looked at the world and gifted it Africa – a place of boundless potential and breathtaking beauty. Then He turned to me

"… and gave me you."

***

A week had passed since the *Sword of Orion* limped into the lagoon. Now fully repaired, freshly painted and her stores replenished, she was ready to set sail on the first high tide. It was amid the bustle of replenishing stores that Danielle had ventured her first and last intercession in the crew's affairs.

Harja had taken a deep liking to Danielle once he learned of her boundless knowledge and skill with healing plants and their uses, yet that fondness had landed arse-first in the water and was sinking to the bottom fast when the matter of culling the cattle arose.

"You *cannot* slaughter the calf," she'd argued. Amongst the *Cochoqua*, cattle were prized as dearly as kin. None would ever butcher a calf so tender, as they believed it carried the future of the herd, also it was utterly impractical since there was not nearly enough meat on its frame to feed the entire tribe.

"Why not?" Harja had bitten back in a tone no one had ever heard him use before. "We'll keep the cow since she is in milk, but there is no need for the calf."

"She is too small to feed all the men, and besides –" Danielle cut her argument short when she noticed that their less than subtle *tête-à-tête* had drawn a crowd.

"Besides what?" Harja had his fists planted on his sides, making him look like an angry posset pot.

"I already gave her a name, and I want to keep her," Danielle said quietly, and stared at her feet when she realized how foolish she sounded.

"Aye, I am aware. Everyone is referring to my future *Blanquette de Veau* as the Daisy-Dish." Harja snapped. His usually genial face had turned an unfortunate shade of red as his blood boiled closer to the surface of his skin.

"That is just cruel," Danielle returned.

"Not cruel," Harja barked. "Addle-pated, that is what it is. You should not have named it!"

Danielle had stubbornly stood her ground. However, she had no more arguments to offer as she knew full well how precious fresh meat would be for the journey ahead.

"Harja," Orion's stern voice had cut through the murmuring crowd. "Stow the calf with its mother in the hull. We can decide its fate later." Thus, the matter was settled promptly and to the appeasement of both parties.

Sebastiaan had tactfully kept himself out of the dispute, as he was not captaining either ship, and had quietly been looking forward to Harja's creamy veal stew. After that, and not because of it, Danielle had remained onboard Sebastiaan's ship. De Coninck had given her access to his small library, and she'd spent her days reading and lounging on the quarterdeck under a faded red and white awning, resizing and adapting Niccolò's generous gift into wearable garments.

For everyone else it had been a week of backbreaking labor with every spare hand and minute poured into repairing Orion's battle-damaged ship. After each long day Sebastiaan and De Coninck returned to the *Danielle*, only to depart again when dawn was still just a silver promise on the horizon. At first, Davit had joined them, mainly at his mother's insistence to keep an eye on his mending wound, but as he grew stronger, he'd opted to stay on the beach with Orion and his new crew.

The tension between Sebastiaan and Davit had eased, and they'd often found themselves working side by side, as they'd done at the *Shack*. Both enjoyed the return to their old rhythm, and though each was keenly aware of the unfinished conversation looming over them, neither was eager to break their fragile truce. Hard work had patched some of the cracks between them, and time had softened the rest.

***

Sebastiaan was leaning against the bow railing, staring at the thieves' moon flickering through scattered clouds. After dinner, Danielle had retired to their cabin. Davit had trailed after to bid her farewell; he had opted to sail with Orion at dawn. De Coninck and Orion had pressed Sebastiaan to join them in the stateroom for after-dinner brandy and talk. Not being in the mood to listen to their bickering over the best route to Batavia, he had politely declined the invitation, retreating instead to the bow, hoping Davit would seek him out.

He did not have to wait long. Davit soon emerged at the top of the narrow ladder from the upper deck below. His gait was marked with hesitation and uncertainty. Sebastiaan had pilfered a bottle of French brandy and two glasses from the stateroom. He held one out to Davit, who took it with a strained smile. Then they turned their backs to the world, standing shoulder to shoulder, shrouded in heavy silence, savoring the smooth, velvety burn of their first sips.

"Did you say goodbye to your mother?" Sebastiaan asked.

"I did," Davit replied and turned to face Sebastiaan. "She is different."

"How so?"

"My mother was never quick to anger, not with me at least, but she regularly locked horns with Kai. I always thought her steady, never truly sad. There were days when her silences stretched longer than usual, but she'd pull herself back from those dark places quick enough. Yet, she was not happy either. I hadn't seen it then, but I see it now. I feel like I know her and I don't all at once – a familiar stranger," he said, with a darting smile that did not reach his eyes.

"But?" Sebastiaan prompted.

Davit studied his face, searching for answers to questions yet to be asked. "Do you love her? Or is all this," he said with a sweep of his hand, "just the thrill of something new, relief at finding each other at last?"

Sebastiaan did not answer immediately. The lad was healing fast but still too frail to weather any type of confrontation, be it physical or verbal, and here he was, shielding his mother with nothing but pure grit.

"Yes, it's new and exciting – joys that grow fewer and further apart the older we get. But I reckon I fell in love with your mother the moment

I scraped her from the hull of your grandfather's ship," Sebastiaan said with a winsome smile. "Over the years, many small things had slipped away. One morning I woke and I couldn't remember the lilt of her voice or the exact slant of her nose, and as time wore on, the image of her had faded until it was nothing but a mere shadow, an idea too vague to even be a memory. Now I get to unearth those lost treasures again, plus some surprising new ones, and that's the thrill."

"You scraped her from the hull?" Davit's forehead wrinkled with his question.

"For heaven's sake, out of all that, the hull is what stuck in your mind?" Sebastiaan chuckled. "Did she never tell you how we met?"

"Aye, she did, but she only mentioned that you met onboard grandfather's ship. It was a conversation that always made her sad. As I got older, I quit asking, and she quit sharing. She told me about the time you took a whipping for her."

"Well, that did not go quite as planned," Sebastiaan said and scratched his jaw. "Truth is, it wasn't supposed to have happened at all." He described how Danielle, in a fit of anger, had struck De Coninck after he accused her of spying for the French. That outburst earned her five lashes, leaving her tied over a barrel on deck to face Arent's wrath, until Sebastiaan intervened and took her place.

Davit's eyes were large with intrigue and amusement. "I can see her do something like that." He shook his head as he thought about his mother's antics. "Why were you whipped so badly then, if it was all just for show?"

"I wasn't," Sebastiaan said. "The lashes barely left a mark."

"Then those scars on your back came not from that?" Davit asked, his voice faltering with hesitation. He'd seen the lash marks on his father's back, raised and silvered with age, and wondered at the brutal story behind them but never dared to ask.

Sebastiaan rested his forearms on the railing, gazing into the night once more. This was not the turn he'd intended for the conversation to take, but the more the lad knew, the better he might deal with the truth of his parentage. Without taking his eyes from the dark water, he unfolded the past. He repeated what he'd told Danielle days before, layering in dates, place names, and the story of meeting Jiya in Muscat. He told him how, on the day he had parted from Danielle all those years ago, he'd traded his dagger for her small knife, and how he'd instantly recognized it when Davit drew it that night at *The Heart*.

Davit drained the last of this brandy, the glass warm as he rolled it between his palms, letting the weight of the story settle in his mind. It was a tale woven with so much unspoken heartache and loss and yet, told with the cold proficiency of a man who sought neither sympathy nor understanding.

He stole a glance at Sebastiaan, his profile etched stark against the night. It was difficult to reconcile this forceful, unbowed man to the wretch he described, once bound in chains and beaten so brutally that scars still corded his back. Images of his father's bleeding body, the chains biting into his wrists and ankles, humiliated, starved and tortured, bloomed in his mind. He tried to snuff them out, but his imagination kept conjuring up the terrible events. Anger ignited in his gut, the heat rising so swiftly that it scorched the back of his tongue, pulling the muscles in his face taut. There was always a steely look in his father's eyes, a lethal warning behind their soft green, and a quiet power in every word he spoke, whether in seriousness or in banter. Now Davit understood why. Beaten to a breath shy of death, Sebastiaan had, instead of letting his past diminish or embitter him, used it to temper him. Davit's chest swelled pride, knowing that he shared this man's blood, that he too carried that iron in his veins.

"Wait," Davit said as he remembered something Sebastiaan had mentioned earlier. "You said you left the Cape in the middle of 1652." He looked to Sebastiaan for confirmation.

"Yes," Sebastiaan said softly, knowing that the boy's sharp mind had found the clue he had left for him amidst his telling.

Davit's eyes darted from side to side as he did a quick calculation, then revised it when it didn't add up. "I was born at the beginning of '54." A heavy silence coagulated between them. "How ..." His voice trailed off as he once more tried to count the months backward from the time of his birth to the time his father had left the settlement, and again he came away with too many months unaccounted for. "I don't understand," he said. "Might you have gotten the dates wrong?" his voice was barely above a whisper. Perhaps his father misspoke and meant that he left in 1653.

Sebastiaan shook his head and pinned Davit with a gentle stare. Waiting. Dreading. Hoping.

A beat passed. Davit inhaled sharply. "When did you get married?" he asked, his confused mind refusing to acknowledge the conclusion that was screaming at him in a fevered voice.

"We didn't," Sebastiaan said. "We were engaged to be married when I left. The plan was for us to marry once we'd settled in Batavia, but that never came to pass."

"Then how …" Davit could not finish his question. It was as if someone had plunged a dagger into his stomach. He struggled to draw breath, the understanding, and compassion in Sebastiaan's eyes only twisting the knife deeper. "Then how can you be my father?" he finally managed, clearing the knot from his throat and waiting for everything he'd always believed about himself to shatter into a million pieces.

"A man named Elias Coopman fathered you," Sebastiaan said in a heavy voice, but it was the cold deathmask sliding over his face that made it impossible for Davit to look away, nor could he have, as he was trapped by the chilling shift in Sebastiaan.

Questions, accusations, rage, and a sense of betrayal burst inside Davit in a lurid explosion of noxious vapors and brilliant sparks. The attack was so sudden and overwhelming that for an intense moment, he had to actively think how to blink and breathe concurrently.

Sebastiaan De Vries was not his father. Davit knew there were supposed to be more thoughts following that one, but they didn't come. His heart was beating into his skull, and he focused on the painful hammering. Somewhere deep inside, there was a spark of light struggling to pierce the dense fog that filled him; he could feel it trying to push to the surface. He reached for it, wanting to grasp it, but it kept slipping from his fingers, disappearing into the muck.

"Did my mother play you false?" Davit asked, wondering why he did, and why it mattered, but like any nitwit, this question was the loudest and first to push to the front.

"No," Sebastiaan said, understanding that the query slipped out in a moment of impulsive confusion. "She received word that I'd died and was eventually forced into a marriage not of her choosing. You were conceived on their wedding night, which was steeped in hatred and violence. She fled the next morning, running for her life. Kai found her and had helped her escape the settlement."

Davit's jaw hung slack, and he quickly snapped his mouth shut. "What had this Coopman done to her?" he bit out. The profusion of emotions rumbling inside him started to come together in a tight ball of anger. His lips turned cold, and the air coming through his nose felt hot and coarse.

Sebastiaan shook his head. "I cannot tell you."

"But you know, don't you?" His voice cracked. "My mother told you. I can see it on your face."

Davit had a tremulous hold on his temper. Sebastiaan watched as he wrestled to keep it under control.

"She did," he said in a calm voice. "However, it is her story to tell, and one day, when she's ready, she will tell you in her own way." Sebastiaan wanted to pull the boy close, showing him that none of it mattered that he was his father in every way but the moment of conception, but he held back, keeping his distance.

Davit's fingers tightened around the delicate crystal glass. In the next instant, he hurled it into the corner where the bulwark met the deck planks. It shattered into a pathetic pile of fine shards. A raw cry rent the air – his own, he realized. A moment of utter silence followed the gust of violence as they stared at the wreckage. Sebastiaan was the first to recover. Tipping his glass, he drained it and then held it out to Davit. "Another?" he asked, his eyes dancing with amused concern. Davit slowly turned his head to the proffered glass, then to Sebastiaan's face, and then to the evidence of his temper.

"No, thank you," he said politely if not still a bit shaky. Swiping the back of his hand across his mouth and then his eyes.

"I am sorry," Davit said, enunciating each word clearly, when he finally felt more or less under control.

"Don't be." Sebastiaan was leaning with his hip against the railing, his ankles lazily crossed, one hand in his pocket, the other dangling over the gunwale. "It was a good kill. I once slew an inkwell in a similar fashion."

"That night in the tavern, I lied when I told you my mother was dead. I don't know how to apologize for it, other than to say I wish I had never said those words," Davit offered the long overdue apology.

"You defended your mother," Sebastiaan reasoned. "I would never hold that against you."

Davit could only stare at the man before him. How had he ever feared that Sebastiaan would turn his back on him? Now, in the light of his acceptance, everything seemed so simple.

Since they were clearing the air, there was a question he needed an answer to. "Why did you not tell me the truth back then? Surely you must have known that I was not your son."

"I don't know why I didn't," Sebastiaan said, at a loss for how to explain what he had felt that night. "At the time, I had a multitude of reasons; none seem valid now."

"Was I a means to an end?" Davit asked. "Something of my mother that you wanted in your life?"

"No and yes," Sebastiaan said in a voice deep with conviction. "No, you were never a means to an end." He looked at Davit, choosing his next words carefully before casting them aside to let the raw truth speak for itself. "You were a gift." Davit stayed silent, waiting for him to go on. "I'm not going to lay my feelings bare to serve as a sop for our consciences, but that night shook me to my core."

Davit's gaze was shuttered, and Sebastiaan knew he owed him the rest of the explanation.

"And yes, there is so much of your mother in you, and I wanted it in my life. I wanted her son to be mine and when the opportunity presented itself, I took it. Given the same chance, I would do it again, every day for the rest of my life. Call it selfish, dishonest, opportunistic; I don't care. I regret nothing, not even the lie, because it brought me you."

Davit snapped his eyes to the deck planks and swallowed thickly.

"I would do anything to keep you and your mother in my life. *Anything.* There is not a line I would not cross, a law I would not break, or a sin a would not commit." Sebastiaan's face was hard with determination and the unspoken covenant that bound them together.

Davit nodded. Once more, that faint spark of light beckoned him, and this time, he seized it, and it flared brighter. The more he focused on it, the more it grew, illuminating everything with stunning clarity. This man was the only father he'd ever known, and now, given the choice, the only one he'd ever wanted. It was a simple truth that needed no argument and no persuasion.

"Father," he breathed.

Sebastiaan closed his eyes. *Thank God.* The prayer thundered through him as he hauled Davit into a bone-crushing embrace. Davit's fingers twisted into his shirt, gripping as though he feared he'd drown if he let go.

They released each other slowly. Sebastiaan watched through misted eyes as Davit struggled to bring his heightened emotions under control. The boy opened his mouth several times to say something but failed. When Davit swiped another agitated hand over his eyes, Sebastiaan took pity on him.

"There is however one more secret," he said in a casual tone, but something in his voice must have finked on his intentions because it sharpened the boy's gaze instantly.

"Elias Coopman was Alain Du Bois' half-brother." At first Davit displayed nothing more than a shaky frown and a fractional pulling back of his head as he tried to understand the significance of the disclosure.

"What?" Davit asked, not understanding why his father would pick this moment for pointless, half-filled statements. "Why would I care about the man's – " He stopped, his eyes frozen like those of a marble statue. "Oh, shit!" he exclaimed and searched for somewhere to sit, finding none, he consigned himself to slide down the railing until his bottom hit the deck. He felt like that last duckling to hatch, siblings already swimming and snaring worms while he was still pecking eggshells from his feathers, confused as all hell at the bright light of day and shocked to find that water was wet.

"Cousin!" Orion bellowed from the upper deck. "When you're done sitting around doing nothing, get your arse in the rowboat. It's time to go." Davit's head slowly lifted at the sound of Orion's voice but he made no effort to move.

Sebastiaan extended his hand and pulled Davit to his feet. Their grip lingered, firm and steady, before he released it to draw the dagger from the small of his back. Flipping it over he offered it to Davit.

"You may have this back," he said, and smiled as Davit's hand closed around the weapon. "Be safe, my boy."

"Thank you, Father." Davit's voice was firm with newfound resolve, clutching the dagger as a talisman of the father he'd chosen.

Epilogue

The *Sword of Orion* lay near the entrance of the lagoon. Never more beautiful, her freshly painted hull nearly invisible in the dark of the night. Her masts stood tall and proud, adorned with tightly furled sails. The *Danielle* was magnificent in size and power, but the *Sword* was Davit's first love. She was precisely what he thought a ship should be – freedom.

At the far end of the lagoon, the thin strip of beach, scarred by footprints over many days, and littered with the cast-off wood from ship repairs and the cold ashes of countless fires, had now returned to its natural state of quiet. Davit inhaled, drawing the scent of Africa deep into his lungs, carving it into his memory, before his eyes drifted to the spot where he'd first met Orion and Jiya nearly a year ago – a year in which life had chiseled him from a boy into a man.

They were set to leave in a few hours, yet something inside him could not look at the scene and think it was the last time he would ever see it. He was as much a child of Africa as her dark-skinned children, born from her womb and raised at her bosom. For now, he would do what was right by his family, but he would return someday, to breathe this air again and feel the soil beneath his bare feet. This was not farewell; it was merely goodbye.

"Up you go lad," one of the rowers, a large brute on loan from De Coninck's crew, said as he readied the small rowboat that had ferried them from the *Danielle.* Orion was already onboard.

"My cabin, cousin," Orion called as he leaned over the railing and then pulled back, disappearing from sight.

The conversation with his father replayed itself in his mind. They had found each other, but as everything had settled, he felt slightly adrift. As he climbed the stairs leading to the quarterdeck, he skimmed his hand over the intricately carved balustrade, freshly sanded and oiled. A quick rap on the stateroom door and a brusque command from Orion brought him inside the captain's lair.

Orion stood near the bank of windows lining the back wall of the cabin, his gaze fixed on the distant beach, much as Davit's had been moments earlier. Several candles flickered against the darkness, lending a warm glow to the walls.

"Do you remember that day?" he asked without turning around.

"I do," Davit answered.

"It feels both longer and shorter than a year, all at once."

"It does." Davit was not in the mood for reminiscing, for it would bring the conversation to Jiya and he was not ready for that yet. Instead, he focused on the opulence of the cabin. Heavy, dark furniture settled atop rugs, rich in color and thick enough to sleep on. The large sleeping bunk was, as usual, meticulously made, draped in crisp white sheets and the deepest of blue blanket. Bookshelves crowded with leather-bound books and ledgers filled every available space on the wall. The scent of linseed oil and beeswax mingled with the musky smell of the tallow candles. Gamora was curled in her usual place at the foot of the bed. Davit frowned at the ill-tempered feline, but she barely acknowledged him. Only a faint flick of her tail suggested she was aware of his existence.

"She's getting fat," he said.

Orion turned around, leaned his back against the window and folded his arms.

"She's not fat, she's with child." Displeasure curled his upper lip as he, too, looked at his beloved pet. "That bloody tomcat Jiya found in a seedy back alley at the settlement and decided to billet in the hold somehow managed to get to her. My poor darling," Orion's voice was deep with soothing commiseration, causing the cat to mewl in return.

"She doesn't look very upset," Davit said, tipping his imaginary hat to Tom. He'd seen the poor thing once when Harja had tried to feed it, skinny and skittish, pelt knotted and patchy, but the cat had already made a name for himself with his supreme hunting skills and reticent temperament. Taming the fierce Gamora would only see his status soar.

Orion pushed away from the windows, his movements slow and graceful as he sauntered to the deep chair behind his desk. He settled into it, sliding down until his head lolled back comfortably against the leather-softened back. With effortless ease, he lifted one ankle to rest atop the other knee, then pointed to the violin lying on the desk before him.

The instrument was a rich golden-brown, turning darker near the sides and neck. The varnish was worn in some places, but that did not detract from its elegance.

"That was my first violin. A gift from our grandfather on my fifth birthday," Orion said, breathing a soft smile. "It was too big, took me years to grow into it. But once mastered, it produces the most soul-soothing sounds. Your mother taught me how to play." Silent seconds ticked by, Orion lost in some childhood memory while Davit wondered why his cousin had summoned him. "Why don't you try it?" Orion said, raising his eyebrows at Davit in invitation.

Confusion and frustration were coming off the lad in noxious waves. He was like a dog with its tail on fire trying to outrun the stench.

"You want me to play the violin?" Davit was dumbstruck. Of all the topics available for discussion, and with only hours before they set sail, playing the violin was not an event that had occurred to him.

"No, cousin," Orion said. "I want you to pick it up and see if you can rid us of that mosquito I hear buzzing about. Yes, I want you to play it."

"I don't know how." Davit could not contain his annoyance, leaving it to drip like syrup from his words.

"Nobody knows how to do anything until they learn. I said I would teach you. So, here we are." Orion pointed a lazy finger at the violin, then flicked it up when Davit did not jump at the generous opportunity.

"Orion, I am not in the mood for– "

"Fine," Orion said dryly. "Let us talk about the conversation you just had with your father."

Davit snatched the violin from the desk and flicked it under his chin, grabbed the bow and slammed it down on the strings, then pushed it upward, producing a screech raw enough to draw a shudder from the devil and a wet hiss from Gamora.

"Aye, well, that's a start. Now, before you launch another assault, move your feet shoulder-width apart." Orion waited as Davit flicked him a dirty look, then shuffled his feet in the proposed position. "You're not standing on parade. Relax your stance, but don't bend your knees."

"I'm not playing the damn thing with my feet. Why does it matter?" Davit protested, but followed Orion's instructions nonetheless.

Orion couldn't smother the smile that crept onto his face.

"Are you having me on?" Davit asked, instantly suspicious.

"In your fragile state?" Orion drawled. "Perish the thought. Posture is important. Now, hold it under the scroll. Yes, that curly bit at the end," he answered Davit's silent question. "Gently bring it about until the flat side rests on your shoulder. No, wait," he cautioned when Davit pressed his chin down on the wooden body to keep it in place. "Bring your elbow inward and don't stab it with your chin. Instead, tilt your head and lay your jaw against it."

They were making progress. The harsh lines around Davit's mouth were softening, as his mind found something other than his troubled thoughts to occupy it.

"Look at the hand holding the violin, straighten your wrist. Good," Orion praised. "Now, on to the bow."

Davit growled, a low rumble that rose from his belly.

"Relax your grip. Place your thumb underneath, bend the tip."

"Is my hand supposed to cramp?"

"No, stop gripping it like a monkey with a stolen banana. Place the rest of your fingertips on top. Spread your pointer finger out and straighten your pinkie." Orion waited until Davit's hand softened around the bow. "Ease the pressure on the string. Word to the wise?" He waited until he had Davit's full attention albeit bottled in one fiery glare. "Don't move it with your elbow. It will scratch. Instead, guide it with your wrist. Bend up and follow, dip down and glide. Try it."

The sound that came from the elegant instrument was cutting enough to clear the sinuses, but less aggressive than earlier.

"Again," Orion demanded.

"I don't see how this is doing anything other than agitating the cat and hurting my ears. Remember, I'm closer to it than you are," Davit protested, but kept his posture, too afraid to change it lest he need to go through the entire ritual of correcting it again.

"Close your eyes," Orion said, pleased when Davit did not fight the suggestion. "Forget about me, forget about your mother, your father, grandfather." He paused, then ventured into the forbidden. "Forget about Elias Coopman."

Davit tensed.

"Breathe. Find that quiet place in your head." Orion's voice became dreamy, vibrating, low and soothing. Gamora purred. "Stay in that empty place. Relax, and drop your shoulders." He waited until Davit's chest was rising and falling as his breathing evened out. "Fill that space with sound."

Orion watched for a moment as the bow moved slowly up and down, like a child's first steps – awkward at first, uncertain – but gradually finding a rhythm that carried it onward. He listened as the discordant scratches softened, slowly giving way to harmony. Then, he closed his eyes and relaxed in his chair, surrendering to the disjointed, clear notes that filled the cabin and letting the night unfold around them – peace, at last.

THE END

Acknowledgments

First, and most importantly, I'd like to thank my readers for their support. We are all writers until someone buys our book, then we become authors. So, thank you for making me an author and allowing me to live my dream. I hope you enjoyed Danielle and Sebastiaan's journey.

Next, I wish to thank my daughter Esti. Without her, I would never have been able to finish this book, nor any other. She is an absolute rock; her patience, support, and creative insights are second to none.

Thank you to my husband for your boundless love and support and for providing honest, constructive, and invaluable feedback.

Thank you, Liam, for being everything good and true that lives in the heart of all boys who grow to become breathtaking men. I don't care how strong or tall you become. You will always be my little boy, and I love you.

Louise Wesson, my editor, you are a gem! Thank you for the hard work and dedication you put into this project. I know you've spent many hours working late into the night and I appreciate it.

Interview with the Author

This is the last book in the series. How do you feel about that?

Relieved. This has been the longest book of the three, and where the other two could live in obscurity, this one came with expectations which added to the pressure.

This is the last time you are going to write these characters. How do you feel about that?

This is the last time I'll write these characters, and it feels bittersweet. I won't hear their thoughts or see them come alive on the page anymore. They've been a huge part of my life. I've lived and breathed their world for nearly four years. I have sprinkled in little hooks; hints for possible future spin-offs if the mood strikes. But, now it is time to dive into something new.

Danielle and Sebastiaan are the heart of the series. She led *Good Hope*, and they shared the stage in *From Lambs to Lions*. Was he always meant to take the spotlight in *Blood of the Covenant*?

Not quite. I had a rough sense of the story's direction and even played with the idea of Sebastiaan not surviving the second book – but thankfully, I came to my senses. I ended up loving the balance their shared focus brought.

Who was your favorite character to write?

Orion, by a country mile. He flowed effortlessly. His actions and thoughts fell quite naturally into place. I didn't have to overthink him and

I poured a lot of myself into him, my faults, traits, and habits. He allowed me to say and do anything without worrying about the consequences. I love the freedom he gave me.

What part was the most enjoyable to write?

The fighting scenes. Once the action kicks in – blades drawn and blood spilled – it is pure fun. Dynamic scenes are, by far, my favorite.

Which part of the book did you find most challenging to write?

The part where Sebastiaan and Danielle reunite stands out. After all the buildup, there was a lot of pressure to get their connection right while keeping it real. Readers crave a happy ending, but life rarely hands those out and, when it does, it comes with a steep price – they are never free.

What is the weirdest thing you researched and did it actually feature in the books?

For *Good Hope*, it was whether hippopotamus steak exists and how you'd cook it – and yes, it featured. *From Lambs to Lions* had me digging into penguin eggs. Are they edible? How do they taste? The answers are: yes, and not good.

For this book, it was what ostrich legs look like up close, and the answer is, again, not good. I have been chased by an ostrich as a child, but I didn't stop to look at its legs. I knew the sound of that particular pursuit, but the look? That took research. I honestly never thought that childhood misadventure would be immortalized in fiction, but here we are.

De Coninck is a constant throughout each book. Why him?

Well, in *Good Hope*, he was based on an actual person in history and I wrote him as closely as I could based on historical accounts. As the series evolved, he took on a more fictional role, and became one of the pillars of the series, which was unexpected. He's just one of those characters you can't get rid of and justify it. He would leave a gap impossible to fill and hard to overlook.

How do you feel about Danielle's character evolution?

I used to have a love-hate relationship with Danielle. In *Good Hope*, I struggled to connect with her. She was trying to find her feet, discover herself, and that clouded my relationship with her. By *From Lambs to Lions*, she found her grit, and writing her felt easier.

In this book, she became a character I could relate to. I love how she settled into her peace, built a life of her own, and stood firm on her own terms. She's comfortable as a mother, yet she carries quiet uncertainties about aging. It's something many of us recognize: looking in the mirror seeing all the subtle changes, feeling pride tinged with doubt, and then we turn away, square our shoulders, and carry on. That's where our true strength lies.

This whole book really hinged on Davit. How do you feel about him as a character?

To me, Davit has the deepest layers of anyone in the story. He's the embodiment of the inner wolves we all wrestle with – the one we choose to nurture and the one we choose to starve. We each carry both light and dark, and our path depends on which we feed. Davit can embrace the darker instincts of his blood father or the virtues of his adopted father. I'm reminded of Solzhenitsyn's words: 'The line dividing good and evil cuts through the heart of every human being.' That's Davit in essence.

Beyond that, he's symbolic. He's a child of Africa, born and raised there, tied to its soil. Though his appearance might not show it, it's his home, and he belongs to it as much as it belongs to him.

What is the meaning behind the title?

It actually links up well to the previous question.

The bonds we choose are often stronger than the bonds we are born into. Blood determines your relation, loyalty to one another determines who we call family.

People often misuse the phrase, 'blood is thicker than water'. The actual quote is, 'the blood of the covenant is thicker than the water of the womb.'

It is Sebastiaan and Davit's choice and the premise of the novel.

What do you hope readers will take away from this series?

I wish to highlight South Africa's rich, layered history and give it the recognition it's due. Too often, its beauty and complexity are swept under the rug to serve a political narrative. The country's past is diverse and intricate and should be met with kindness, compassion and an open mind, not judged through a modern lens. If my books can offer even a small glimpse into that world, I'd consider it a success.

Also by C.M. O'Neill

Good Hope

Book 1 of *The Cape of Storms Trilogy*

1652 – On the run from her father's murderer, Danielle flees into the night, blindly seeking refuge. Desperation leads her to a ship anchored in the harbor. Despite her intentions, circumstances spiral beyond her control, and she finds herself an inadvertent stowaway bound for the untamed southern tip of Africa, unintentionally joining the expedition to establish a settlement under the leadership of Governor Jan van Riebeeck.

From the moment of her discovery, her world collapses into a pit of suspicion and uncertainty. Amidst the hardships of the journey a sinister threat looms—one who sees in her not just a stowaway, but a witness who must be silenced.

Her only chance for survival lies in how quickly she learns to trust herself, find her inner strength, and embrace her tenacity and resilience before confronting the pivotal choice between following her heart or surrendering to the path fate has laid out for her.

From Lambs to Lions

Book 2 of *The Cape of Storms Trilogy*

1653 – In the untamed wilds of Southern Africa, a fledgling colony fights against the unforgiving grip of nature and the specter of starvation. Amidst this crucible of hardship, a spirited, young woman emerges, seeking her place in a world where survival demands more than resilience – it demands rebellion.

Brave, compassionate, and unyieldingly stubborn, she navigates the treacherous landscape, only to find herself ensnared by her own daring. The perilous path woven by her actions intertwines with heartbreak and sacrifice, molding her destiny.

Inspired by true events, *From Lambs to Lions* is a tale of tenacity, impossible choices, and unbreakable spirits determined to defy the odds.